About

New Zealander **Aliso**... eighty romance novel... worked as a primar... research technician a... living her dream of living – and writing – in a gorgeous village in the south of France.

Carol Marinelli recently filled in a form asking for her job title. Thrilled to be able to put down her answer, she put writer. Then it asked what Carol did for relaxation and she put down the truth – writing. The third question asked for her hobbies. Well, not wanting to look obsessed she crossed the fingers on her hand and answered swimming but, given that the chlorine in the pool does terrible things to her highlights – I'm sure you can guess the real answer.

Kate Hardy always loved books and could read before she went to school. She discovered Mills & Boon books when she was twelve and decided this was what she wanted to do. When she isn't writing, Kate enjoys reading, cinema, ballroom dancing and the gym. You can contact her via her website: www.katehardy.com

Midwives on Call

Midwives on Call: From Babies to Bride

ALISON ROBERTS

CAROL MARINELLI

KATE HARDY

MILLS & BOON

First Published in Great Britain 2020
By Mills & Boon, an imprint of HarperCollins*Publishers*
1 London Bridge Street, London, SE1 9GF

MIDWIVES ON CALL: FROM BABIES TO BRIDE © 2020
Harlequin Books S.A.

Always the Midwife © 2015 Harlequin Books S.A.
Just one Night? © 2015 Harlequin Books S.A.
A Promise...to a Proposal? © 2015 Pamela Brooks

Special thanks and acknowledgement are given to Alison Roberts and Carol Marinelli for their contribution to the *Midwives On-Call* series

ISBN: 978-0-263-28081-4

0120

MIX
Paper from
responsible sources
FSC™ C007454

FSC
www.fsc.org

This book is produced from independently certified FSC™ paper to ensure responsible forest management.

For more information visit: www.harpercollins.co.uk/green

Printed and bound in Spain
by CPI, Barcelona

ALWAYS THE MIDWIFE

ALISON ROBERTS

For Annie, Carol and Linda – who will always make Melbourne a very special place to visit for me.
Love you all xxx

CHAPTER ONE

THE BLIP OF the foetal heart monitor had definitely slowed down. Her decision might be a no-brainer but Sophia knew it wasn't going to be popular.

'I'm sorry,' she told her patient, 'but I'm not happy with the way things are going. We need to get you to hospital.'

'No-o-o…' First-time mother Claire Robinson had her heart set on a home birth. 'You said I'm almost fully dilated. It can't be much longer.'

'You're exhausted, sweetheart. Every contraction is harder for you and things are slowing down.' She still had the hand-held Doppler against the distended abdomen of the pregnant woman. 'Can you hear that the baby's heartbeat has slowed down, too? It's a sign that baby is getting distressed.'

'What does that mean?' Claire's husband, Greg, was looking pale and anxious. 'Is the baby in danger? Is *Claire* in danger?'

'No.' Sophia hastened to reassure them both. 'But that's what I want to make sure isn't going to happen. The labour hasn't progressed quite the way we wanted and…' How could she tell these parents-to-be, without scaring them, that it was her instinct that something wasn't right that was making the transfer seem urgent? 'Let me make a call and see how far away an ambulance might be.'

The call was answered instantly.

'My name is Sophia Toulson,' Sophia said. 'I'm a midwife with the Melbourne Maternity Unit at the Victoria. I'm at a planned home birth…' She moved away from the young couple, lowering her voice as she gave the address details and then voiced her concerns.

'An ambulance is probably fifteen minutes away,' the dispatcher told her. 'But we do have a SPRINT guy in your locality.'

'SPRINT?'

'Single Paramedic Response and Intervention. An intensive care paramedic on a motorbike.'

'I think we just need the transport,' Sophia said. 'It's not an emergency…' But she could hear the note of doubt in her own voice. An exhausted first-time mother and a stalled labour. The potential for an emergency was there. Was that why alarm bells had started ringing?

'I'll change the plan,' Claire offered desperately, as Sophia ended the call. 'I'll have more pain relief than the gas. You can rupture the membranes. Whatever it takes…' She was sobbing now. 'We don't want to have our baby in a hospital…'

'I know.' Sophia smoothed damp strands of hair back from Claire's face. 'But you know what the really important thing here is?'

She didn't wait for a response. Greg was perched on

the end of the bed, holding Claire in his arms as she lay back against him. She caught his gaze and then Claire's.

'My job is to keep both you and baby safe. At the end of the day, the only thing that matters is that you get to hold your healthy baby in your arms. I promise that where the delivery happens is not going to take away even the tiniest bit of joy that moment's going to give you.'

A joy that Sophia might never be able to experience herself but that didn't mean she couldn't share it happening for others. It was precisely why she'd chosen this profession. Why she loved it so much. And why she was so passionate about doing whatever it took to ensure a happy outcome.

'That's all I want,' Greg said, his voice cracking. 'For you both to be okay. We always said that we'd go to the hospital the minute we were worried about anything.'

'But I'm not worried. I'm just so tired… Oohhh…' Claire's face scrunched into lines of pain.

'Another contraction?' Sophia reached for the Entonox mouthpiece. 'Here you go. Deep breaths…'

The loud rap on the door made her jump. Surely the ambulance hadn't arrived this quickly?

'Shall I go?' Greg asked.

Claire spat out the mouthpiece. '*No*—don't leave me… It's…. *Ahhh*…'

Sophia wasn't going anywhere either. The contraction had produced a rush of fluid. Claire's membranes had finally broken. It was a sign that her labour was progressing again but Sophia wasn't feeling relieved. Quite the opposite.

The fluid soaking into the pad beneath Claire's hips had the stain of meconium that meant the baby could be in trouble. And…

Oh, dear Lord…yes…that was a loop of umbilical cord showing.

'G'day…' The rich, deep voice came from behind her. 'I let myself in. Hope that's okay.'

Sophia looked up. The man was wearing a high-vis heavy-duty jacket. He had a motorbike helmet on his head with the red, white and blue colours of Melbourne's ambulance service and the title 'Paramedic' emblazoned across the front. The chin-guard and visor were flipped up so that she could see his face but she barely registered what he looked like. There was relief to be felt now— that she had professional help in what had just become an obstetric emergency.

'Claire's waters just broke,' she said quietly. 'We've got a cord prolapse.'

'What's that?' Greg was leaning in, trying to see what was happening. 'What's going on? And who are you?'

The paramedic's helmet was off by the time he'd taken two steps closer. 'I'm Aiden Harrison,' he told Greg. 'Here to help.' He was right beside Sophia now. 'Modified Sims position?'

'Knees to chest, I think. Claire? We're going to get you to turn over, I want you on your knees with your bottom up in the air. Greg, can you help?'

'What? *Why?*' Claire was panting, recovering from the contraction. 'I don't want to move.'

'We've got a small problem, guys.' The paramedic had dropped his helmet and leather gloves, along with a rolled-up kit he'd been carrying. He didn't sound stressed. Rather, he made it sound as if whatever the problem was, it was going to be easily remedied. 'Your baby didn't read the rule book and part of the umbilical cord has come out first. We need to take any pressure off it, which is why we're going to let gravity give us a hand. Here…let me help.'

Somehow he managed to make it seem like nothing out of the ordinary to be getting a woman in labour to get into what seemed a very unnatural position, on her knees with her head lowered. Sophia was ready with the Doppler to check the baby's heart rate again.

Aiden listened, his gaze on his watch. 'Ninety-eight,' he said. 'What was the last recorded rate?'

'One-forty.' Sophia ripped open a packet of sterile gloves. In a blink of time, this had become a potential disaster. The baby's oxygen supply was being cut off. 'I'm going to try and ease the pressure.'

'Oh, my God…' Claire wailed. 'What's happening?'

'You're going to feel me inside,' Sophia warned her. 'I'm going to be pushing on baby's head to take the pressure off the cord.'

Greg's face was as white as a sheet. 'How are you going to take her to hospital if she has to stay in that position?' He glanced sideways to where the paramedic had discarded his bike helmet. 'You're not even driving an ambulance, are you?'

'No, mate. I ride a bike. Gets me where I'm needed faster.' Aiden reached for the radio clipped to his shoulder. 'SPRINT One to Base. How far away is our back-up?'

They could all hear the woman's voice on the other end. 'Should be with you in less than ten minutes.'

'Copy that. Make it a code one.' He nodded at Greg. 'Hang in there, mate. We're under control.'

'I'm getting another contraction,' Claire groaned. 'Ohhh… I want to *push*…'

'Don't push,' Sophia warned. 'Not yet.'

She looked up to find Aiden's gaze on her face. A steady gaze but she could see he knew exactly what she was trying to decide and the almost crushing responsibility for making the right choice here.

'The cord's pulsatile,' she told him. 'And Claire's fully dilated.'

Aiden nodded. If they were in hospital right now, an assisted delivery with forceps would be the fastest and safest way to get this baby out. With Sophia using two fingers to push on the baby's head, the cord was being protected and the blood and oxygen supply was still adequate. She knew what she was doing, this midwife. Intelligent-looking woman, in fact, which probably explained the anxiety he could see in her eyes. She had to know exactly how dangerous this situation was for the baby.

Her hand was probably already aching, although Aiden couldn't detect any signs of discomfort. Could she keep this up until they arrived at the hospital? The other option was not to slow down a natural delivery but to try and speed it up. To get the baby out fast enough to avoid potentially devastating complications from lack of oxygen. She was still looking at him and he got the feeling she was following his train of thought.

'She's also exhausted,' she added. 'Labour's been a bit protracted. That was why I called for an ambulance in the first place. I'm not sure…' Sophia bit her lip as her words trailed to an inaudible whisper. She hated feeling indecisive and it rarely happened, but a baby's life was at stake here and there was another option. But if they encouraged Claire to push and she was too tired to be effective, they would have to wait for another contraction and they could end up in a much worse position, with the baby's head cutting off any oxygen supply. The baby could end up with severe brain damage. Or it could die.

The weighing-up process was lightning fast but agonising. Sophia found she was holding the gaze of the paramedic. Light brown eyes, a part of her brain noted. Unusual. It was a calm gaze but it was intelligent. He knew what the issues were. It was also confident. Crinkles appeared near the corners, like a smile that didn't involve a mouth. There was a good chance they could pull this off.

It was Aiden who broke the eye contact. He crouched beside the bed so that he could look up at Claire who had her forehead resting on clenched fists.

'How tired are you, Claire?' he asked.

'She's stuffed, mate.' It was Greg who responded. 'We never thought it was going to be this hard, you know?'

But Aiden didn't seem to be listening. He was holding Claire's frightened gaze now.

'The best thing for your baby is going to be getting born as fast as possible,' he said. 'And we can help but you're going to have to do most of the work. Do you think you could do that?'

'I want to push,' Claire said with a sob. 'But I'm scared.'

'We're here with you. How 'bout we give it our best shot with the next contraction?'

'O-okay. I'll try.'

'Good girl.' He was smiling at Claire now and the mix of approval and confidence in his voice was compelling. Sophia could have felt defensive about having someone else make that decision for her, but instead she was as ready as Claire to put every effort into making this work. She believed it was the right decision. It *would* work.

Who was this knight in shining armour who'd ridden up on a motorbike instead of a horse just as things were turning to custard? This paramedic with his warm brown eyes and streaked, golden-blond hair that made him look like a surfer.

When the next contraction was due a couple of minutes later, they turned Claire onto her back again and Sophia released the pressure holding the baby's head away from the cervix and the cord. The clock was ticking from that moment on and the three of them, Aiden, Sophia and even Greg—who couldn't help but catch the urgency—coached Claire into giving everything she had. And then a bit more.

'You can do it,' Aiden told her firmly. 'Push, push, push. Keep going. *Push.*'

'Crowning,' Sophia confirmed. 'Keep going, Claire.'

'You're doing great,' Aiden continued. 'But don't

stop. We can't wait for another contraction. This is it. *Push…*'

'*Can't…*' The groan was agonised.

'Yes, you can. You *are* doing it. You're awesome… One more push, that's all we need.'

Good grief, this man had the most amazing voice. Sophia could feel her own abdominal muscles clenching. *She* wanted to push—how ridiculous was that?

'Oh, my God…' Greg's voice was choked. 'I can see him, Claire. Our baby.'

Sophia could see him, too. Could touch and help him into the world, but she'd lost track of how many minutes it had taken since the blood and oxygen supply had been cut off by the pressure of the baby's head and body on the prolapsed umbilical cord.

The baby was limp and blue. It looked lifeless.

Her heart sank like a stone. This had been the wrong decision, then, to let imminent labour progress instead of stalling it and trying to get Claire to hospital before she delivered. This was her patient and her responsibility. How could she have allowed this man she'd never even met before to come in and take charge the way he had? It would be unthinkable to lose a baby like this.

But the motorbike-riding paramedic was by her side, with a kit unrolled and resuscitation gear at the ready and she hadn't yet lost faith in the calm confidence he displayed.

A tiny bag mask to deliver oxygen. Fingers that looked so large against a fragile chest delivering compressions that were gentle but effective.

'Come on, little guy. You can do it. You're gonna be fine...'

The words sounded incongruously casual but Sophia could see the intense concentration in the paramedic's eyes. The fierce determination to save a tiny life.

And there was movement. A gasp as lungs expanded for the first time. A warbling cry. Skin colour that was changing from a deathly blue to a much healthier pink. Arms and legs beginning to stir.

'Hey...welcome back, little guy.' Aiden's hands cupped the baby to gently lift and place the newborn boy against his mother's skin. Both Claire and Greg had tears streaming down their faces. There was an overpowering sense of both relief and joy but fear hadn't been banished yet.

Sophia was watching anxiously. With the level of resuscitation needed, the baby would have still been under intense monitoring in a clinical setting, not being held and touched like this by his parents.

And then Aiden's gaze shifted away from the infant.

'Apgar score nine at five minutes,' he murmured. She could swear there was a ghost of a wink accompanying the report. He knew how anxious she was and he wanted her to know that he was still doing his job—that the baby was being carefully monitored. Sure enough, she could see him resting a finger lightly on the baby's upper arm, taking a brachial pulse. She could stop worrying and focus on Claire. She could deal with the delivery of the placenta and check for any tissue damage.

The emergency was over, almost as quickly as it had appeared.

The ambulance would be arriving within minutes and then they'd have the bustle of preparations to transfer the new family to the maternity unit, where Claire and the baby could both be checked by specialists, but this was a gift of time.

Private time in their own home—the place they had wanted to be in to welcome their first baby.

Aiden stepped back. He stripped off the gloves he'd put on to work on the baby and moved to one side of the room, where he propped an elbow on a tall chest of drawers. He was due to go off duty and he had his usual visit to make as soon as he was done but he wasn't going to leave until the back-up arrived and he didn't want to crowd the young parents as they had their first minutes with their newborn.

Besides, he could watch the midwife as she dealt competently with the delivery of the placenta, transferring it to a bowl where she inspected it for any damage that could suggest part of it had been retained. She was tiny, he noticed. Only a bit over five feet tall. Funny that he hadn't noticed how small she was before. Maybe that was because she'd given off the impression of being confident. Good at her job and in control.

She hadn't felt so in control at one point, though, had she? He remembered that almost telepathic communication between them as they'd weighed up the option of whether to try and stall the labour or push it forward.

Her eyes were a rich brown, weren't they? A nice match for her hair, which had an auburn tinge to its dark colour. It was pinned up to her head to keep it out of the way and Aiden found himself wondering how long it would be if it was unpinned. How soft it might feel.

Good grief… Okay, she was pretty cute but there was no need to get carried away.

But then she looked up from her work and her smile told him there was nothing to worry about.

He could feel that smile as much as he could see it. Gorgeous was the only word for it.

Sophia hadn't noticed the paramedic moving to the other side of the room. Had he apparently read the vibes in the room in the same way he'd seemed to ever since he'd walked in the door?

He'd done the perfect thing, anyway, so she followed his example. Any more cleaning up of either mother or baby could wait until the ambulance arrived. This was a time these new parents could never have again and it was precious. She wasn't about to leave the room and Aiden had chosen the spot that was far away enough to be unobtrusive while still being available so it was a no-brainer to move quietly until she was standing beside him.

He acknowledged her arrival with a grin.

'Good job,' he said softly. 'Thanks for inviting me.'

Her breath came out in a huff of laughter. How could anyone make a life-threatening emergency sound like a party? But paramedics were like that, weren't they? They lived for the adrenaline rush and a 'good' job was one that other medical professionals dreaded having to face. She'd met paramedics who came across as cowboys—galloping from one callout to the next and over-eager to show off their skills.

This one rode a motorbike, for heaven's sake. A mechanical horse. And he'd had no hesitation in taking command and encouraging management that had had the very real potential to have ended in disaster.

Except it hadn't, had it? Another glance at the bed was enough to bring a lump to Sophia's throat. The baby lay in Claire's arms, tiny eyes open and staring up at his parents. Greg's fingers were touching the tiny starfish hand of the baby and his head was touching Claire's. They were both looking down, aware of nothing but their newborn infant. They were talking softly, too, counting fingers and toes and doing what all new parents did in the first minutes of sharing the miracle of new life.

They had probably forgotten the presence of their medical team and wouldn't even hear the murmur of other voices but Sophia looked away, unconsciously allowing them a little more privacy.

It was somewhat startling to find that the paramedic was still looking at her.

'Babies are my favourite thing,' he said softly. 'It was a treat.'

For the first time since he'd let himself into the house, she realised how good looking he was. Oh, she'd noticed the brown eyes and the way they crinkled at the corners and the streaky blond hair. She'd been aware of the intelligence and intense concentration his features could advertise. But he was still grinning at her and she was distracted enough from her patient to appreciate the way everything came together. And not just his face. He had a presence that she'd appreciated on a professional level. Now she was getting the full force of it on a very personal level. Was it so overpowering because he was so much bigger than she was?

No…everyone was pretty much taller than her when she could only boast five feet three inches in bare feet and he probably seemed broader because of the jacket he was still wearing but he gave the impression of a large man. A powerful man, yet she'd seen how skilful those hands had been, positioning the baby's head and fitting the mask to the tiny face. How carefully controlled and gentle his movements had been.

It felt like something was melting deep inside her belly.

He wasn't just incredibly good at his job. He'd done it with humour. With an ability to defuse a terrifying situation. With a confidence that had given them all the belief that they could do it and maybe that had been the reason why they had been able to do it.

Her smile felt odd. As if she was offering him something that she had never offered anyone before on such short acquaintance. Something that came straight from her heart.

'It's me who should be thanking you,' she whispered. 'I can't believe I told Dispatch that we only needed transport, not a SPRINT paramedic.'

'I was eavesdropping on the radio traffic. I'd just ordered a coffee not far away.' He grinned. 'Don't suppose it'll still be hot when I go back.'

'I owe you one, then.'

The crinkles appeared around his eyes again. 'Might just hold you to that.'

Were the butterflies dancing in Sophia's stomach

embarrassment? Did he think she was flirting with him? Suggesting a date, even?

If he did, he didn't seem put off. Or any less relaxed.

Maybe the butterflies were there for an entirely different reason. How long had it been since she'd met such an attractive man? One who had impressed her on so many levels?

Not in the last six months, that was for sure. Changing cities and throwing herself into a new job had left no time at all to think about expanding her social life to include men. She was only beginning to gather a new circle of girlfriends.

Not that this one would be interested, anyway. She could hear an echo of his voice. *Babies are my favourite thing...*

She could feel herself becoming tense. Trying to squeeze something tight enough to suffocate those damned butterflies.

Could he sense that, too? A flicker of something she couldn't identify passed across his face.

'Might be hard to call in the debt,' he said. 'When I don't even know your name.'

'Oh...' She hadn't introduced herself, had she? How rude was that? He'd have paperwork to fill in for this job. He would need more details about Claire as well. 'I'm Sophia,' she said. 'Sophia Toulson. I'm a midwife.'

His grin widened as an eyebrow lifted. 'I should hope so.'

The information about their patient she'd been gathering mentally to help him with his report evaporated as Sophia laughed.

Those cute eye wrinkles deepened and his eyes

danced. 'Come out with me,' he said softly. 'Sophia Toulson, midwife extraordinaire. Come out with me tonight. I'll take a beer instead of a coffee as payment of that debt.'

Sophia's smile died on her lips.

She wanted to say yes.

She really, *really* wanted to say yes, but she could feel her head beginning to roll from side to side.

'No… I can't… I…' The words followed her smile into oblivion. How could she possibly even begin to explain why she had to say no?

Not that Aiden seemed offended by the rejection. His shrug was casual. 'No worries. Maybe another night.'

And then there was a loud knock on a door outside the room. 'Ambulance,' the call came, along with the rattle of a stretcher's wheels.

The snatch of time was gone and Sophia realised that it would have been better spent starting the enormous amount of paperwork she needed to do to record everything that had happened during the emergency birth.

And then she caught Aiden's glance and, if the same thought had occurred to him, he didn't care—he was happy having spent that time doing exactly what they had been doing. And, suddenly, so was she.

Inexplicably happy, in fact, given that she'd denied herself the pleasure of spending more time in this man's company.

But he'd asked. And, for a blink of time, she'd considered saying yes.

That feeling of connection hadn't been one-sided and that, in itself, was something to feel happy about.

Wasn't it?

CHAPTER TWO

IT MUST HAVE been enough because that happiness stayed with her for the rest of her shift.

In fact, this was turning out to be the best day yet since Sophia had made such big changes in her life, leaving her home town of Canberra to shift to Melbourne.

Word had spread quickly through the Melbourne Maternity Unit about her successful management of an obstetrical emergency in the community. With its international reputation for excellence, the MMU attracted the best in the field but this case was earning her congratulations from every quarter.

Alessandro Manos, who headed the neonatal intensive care unit, had been the specialist called to check the baby and he'd been thorough.

'There's no sign of any complications from oxygen deprivation,' he told Sophia. 'He's a lucky little boy that you were there to manage the birth.'

She fastened the disposable nappy and reached for the soft sleep suit Claire had given her to bring up to the unit.

'It wasn't just me. I probably would have chosen to

try and delay the birth and get her in here if I hadn't had some expert paramedic assistance. He was…' Oh, yes…there was a definite extra buzz to be found in the satisfaction of a job well done. 'He was really amazing.'

'Who was?' Isla Delamere—Alessi's fiancée—had popped into the NICU. Her look suggested that the only amazing man around there was her husband-to-be.

'The paramedic who helped me through an acute cord prolapse this afternoon.'

'Oh, I heard about that. How's the baby?'

'Perfect.' Was Alessi referring to the baby he'd just checked? His gaze was resting adoringly on his wife as he spoke.

Sophia's smile had a poignant edge. They might have wanted to keep Isla's pregnancy secret for a bit longer but the news had slipped out and there was no way these two could hide how they felt about each other. They were so happy. And why wouldn't they be? They'd found love and were on the way to being a family.

That had been her own dream once.

People probably assumed it still was. That—like most women her age—she was simply waiting to find the right person to make that dream come true. Only her best friend, Emily, knew that there was no man on earth who could put the pieces of her dream back together.

That it had been permanently shattered.

Maybe it was just as well that the baby scrunched up his face and started crying at that moment.

'I'd better take this little guy back to his mum. She'll be missing him and he's hungry.'

'I'll come with you,' Isla said. 'I want to hear more about this paramedic. Was he hot? Single?'

Sophia shook her head as she wrapped the baby in a cotton blanket and picked him up. An image of those unusual brown eyes, somewhere between hazel and chocolate, flashed into her head. She could even see the crinkles in the corners—the smile that had seemed intimate because it was only intended for the person who had the eye contact.

'Hot enough, I guess,' she said lightly. 'But I doubt very much that he's single.' Liar, her mind whispered. He wouldn't have asked you out if he wasn't single. Her voice rose in pitch as it tightened. 'And even if he was, I wouldn't be interested.'

'Why not?' Loved up herself, Isla was keen for everybody to share her happiness. And maybe she'd picked up on the fact that Sophia was being less than truthful. 'Work is where most people find their partners, you know.'

'I'm not looking for a partner.' With the baby, who'd stopped crying for the moment, in her arms, Sophia led the way out of the ICU and headed towards the room where Claire had been taken for assessment. 'And I do go out. I'm going out tomorrow.' This was a good opportunity to change the subject. 'You're coming, aren't you? To the gardens?'

'For Em and Oliver's vow renewal ceremony?' Isla smiled. 'Of course. I wouldn't miss it. I think everybody from the MMU is going. It's the perfect way for everyone to move forward, isn't it?' she sighed, probably unaware of the way her hand touched her own belly so protectively. 'Em's very brave, isn't she?'

'She certainly is.' Sophia's arms tightened a little around the precious bundle she was carrying, jiggling him as he started grizzling again. They'd all known that Emily's foster-daughter would only have a short life but her death had been gutting. Only last week they'd all gathered in the children's section of Melbourne's botanical gardens to attend the memorial service for little Gretta. So many tears had been shed as the CEO of the Victoria Hospital—Charles Delamere—had spoken so beautifully about how Gretta's short life had touched the lives of so many others.

They'd all been clutching pink balloons that had been released into the sky at the end of the ceremony. The balloons had all held little packets of seeds—Kangaroo paws—all different colours. Apparently they had been Gretta's favourite and Emily had a vision of new plants growing all over Melbourne. It had been a beautiful ending to a very touching ceremony.

'The plan is that later anyone who can will head for the Rooftop for a drink.'

'I heard that. Did I tell you that Darcie's bringing Flick?'

'The midwifery student?'

'Yes. She's due to start shadowing you next week. We thought it would be a good way for her to get to know everyone a bit better. You don't think Emily will mind, do you?'

'It's an open invitation. We all know Em and Oliver and everyone's thrilled that they're back together. The sad bit's been dealt with and this is about the future. It should be a good party.'

'How formal is it?'

'Not at all. You can wear whatever you like. But I did talk Em into buying a new dress and getting her hair done so I don't plan to turn up in jeans myself.'

Emily Evans had been the first real friend that Sophia had made after moving to Melbourne. They'd clicked instantly and it had been Emily who had helped Sophia settle into her new job and home so happily. An evening with a few wines a couple of months into their friendship had sealed the bond when they'd realised how much they had in common. Their journeys may have been very different but the result was the same—they would never know the joy of holding their own newborn infants in their arms.

Had it been stupid to pick this career? Leaving Isla behind, Sophia had a few moments alone, holding Claire's baby boy. This was the part of her job she loved best. The weight of the tiny body that fitted so snugly against her chest. The joy in the mother's face as she handed it over. Watching a tiny mouth latch onto a breast for that first feed…

It was always there, though…that empty feeling in her own arms. The ache in the corner of her own heart.

Emily's journey had been slower. The hope had still been there for all those attempts at IVF and it must have turned to such joy when she'd finally carried a pregnancy almost to term. How devastating would it have been to experience the stillbirth of her son?

More devastating than it had been to wake from an

emergency surgery to be told that you'd not only lost your baby but that your uterus had had to be sacrificed to save your life? There would never be a transition period of chasing an IVF dream to lead to acceptance for Sophia. She'd only been twenty-one but her life had changed for ever that day.

But it hadn't been stupid to choose this career. Yes, she could have shut herself away from the emotional fall-out by choosing a nursing career that had nothing to do with babies or children, but that would have only made the ache worse in the long run and at least, this way, she got to share the joy every day of her life pretty much.

Love always came with some fine print about what you were risking but if you never took that risk, you shut yourself off from what life had to offer. Nobody had ever promised that life was easy and she'd seen more than her fair share of heartbreak in this job, but she'd seen far more people reaping the rewards of taking risks.

Look at Em. She'd chosen to love two children who weren't even hers, both with medical conditions. She'd been brave enough to risk the heartbreak she'd known was coming right from the start. Sophia had thought she was being brave, becoming a midwife and working with other people's babies every day, but, compared to Em, she was still hiding from life, wasn't she?

The next half-hour was happy enough to banish any personal reflections as Sophia spent time with Claire and Greg and the baby who now had a name—Isaac.

The first breastfeed was no drama and she left the happy parents preparing to go back home for their first night as a family.

Weaving through the busy, inner-city streets to get back to her small, terraced cottage when she finally signed off duty wasn't enough of a distraction, however. The ache was a little heavier today. Not just the empty ache of not having a baby to hold. There was the ache of not having a hand to hold. Having someone in her life who was her special person.

It wasn't that she wasn't making new friends here. Good friends. It was because she was essentially alone. She had no family nearby. Her best friend was back with her husband. Sophia had no one who was always available to share the highs and lows of life. And a best friend could never take the place of a life partner, anyway. She had no one to cuddle up to at night.

How stupid had she been, turning down that offer of a date with Aiden Harrison?

Why couldn't she be a bit braver?

If only she could turn the clock back to that moment. She could see those dancing eyes so clearly. A mix of attraction and humour and…confidence that she would say yes?

He hadn't been upset by her stuttering refusal, though, had he?

Maybe, by now, he was feeling relieved.

Oh, for heaven's sake. Sophia gave herself a mental shake. She needed to get over herself or she wouldn't be contributing anything positive at tomorrow's celebration. Maybe she needed to take a leaf out of Emily's book and convince herself that the risk of loving was always worthwhile.

Maybe she could even go down that track herself one day and think about fostering kids.

'It's only me.' Aiden let himself into the big house in Brunswick—his usual stop on his way home. 'Where is everyone? Nate?'

A dark head popped out from behind a nearby door. 'We'll be out in a sec, Aiden. The other boys are in the lounge.'

The lounge was a large room and, like all the other rooms in this converted house, it had polished wooden floors. Unlike most lounges, it had very little furniture, however, because the residents didn't need sofas or armchairs. The four young men who lived here were all quadriplegics who needed a high level of domestic and personal assistance. The youngest lad, Steve, was only eighteen. Nathan, at twenty-four, was the oldest.

Not that his younger brother intended to live here for long. This was a halfway step—a move towards the kind of independence he really wanted. At some point they were going to have to talk about it and maybe tonight would be a good time. While he hadn't said anything yet, Aiden was worried about the idea of Nate living independently. He himself had a demanding job and he wouldn't be able to drop everything and go and help his brother if something happened. At least here there were always carers on hand and it was a lot better than the residential home he'd been in for the last few years.

Or was the anxiety about the future more like a form of guilt? That he hadn't been able to care for his brother himself when the accident had happened because he'd only been a kid himself?

That it was his fault that the accident had happened in the first place?

That, if Nathan was capable of living in a normal house, he'd want it to be with *him* and then he'd have to take full responsibility. Oh, he'd have a carer to come in a couple of times a day to help with the transfers from bed to wheelchair and for the personal type care of showering and toileting, but what about the rest of the day? What would happen if Nate fell out of his chair or something and *he* was in the middle of a job like that obstetric emergency today?

He wanted his brother somewhere he was protected and surely this was as good as it got? This was like a regular blokes' flat, with a sports programme playing on its huge-screen television and guys sitting around, yelling approval at the goal that had just been scored.

And then he saw what they were watching. Murderball. The loud, fast and incredibly aggressive form of wheelchair rugby that Nate was currently passionate about. Two of the other guys in the house were part of a local team and Nate was desperate to make the grade. Physically, he certainly qualified.

Many people thought that quadriplegics—or tetraplegics—were always totally paralysed from the neck down but the repercussions of a cervical injury or illness were as individual as the people who suffered them and they were graded according to whether the impairment was complete or incomplete and by how much sensory and motor function remained.

With the C6 spinal injury Nate had received at the age of ten, he had little movement or sensation in his lower body. Thankfully, the injury had been incomplete so he still had a good range of movement in his upper body and better hand function than many. If he got his strength up, he'd probably be lethal on a Murderball court.

'Hey, Aiden. Wassup?'

'All good, Steve. How 'bout you?'

'This is our game from last week. Wanna watch?'

'Sure. Not for long, though. I promised Nate I'd take him out for a beer tonight.'

The young woman who'd greeted him came into the lounge. With her short, spiky black hair and facial piercings, Samantha was unlike any of the carers he'd come across in the years of Nate's care so far.

'He's out of the bathroom, Aiden. You can help him finish getting dressed if you want.'

Nathan's face lit up as Aiden went into his room.

'Hey, bro…' The hand held up for a fist bump took away any awkwardness of the height difference between the brothers and Nate's lack of hand strength. 'What do you call a quadriplegic on your doorstep?'

Aiden rolled his eyes. 'I thought you'd given up on the quadriplegic jokes.'

'Matt.' Nathan snorted with laughter and then pushed on one wheel of his chair to turn it towards a chest of drawers. 'What do you reckon? Leather jacket or the denim one?'

'Either's good. We're going to a garden bar but it's not cold out. Want a hand?'

'Nah…I'm good.'

Rather than watch Nate's struggle to put the jacket on unaided, Aiden looked around his brother's room. The poster collection was growing. Action shots of Murderball games, with wheelchairs crashing into each other and flipping sideways and the occupants only staying with them because they were strapped in.

He waved a hand at the posters. 'You could get really injured doing that stuff, you know.'

'Nah.' Nathan had one sleeve of his jacket on but it was taking a few attempts to get his other hand into a sleeve hole. 'A cracked rib or a squashed finger, maybe. Wouldn't be calling you out with any lights or sirens. Hey…any good jobs today?'

'Yeah… Last call was the best. This midwife was calling for transport to take a home birth in to the maternity unit in the Victoria because it had been going on too long. I overheard the call and decided to poke my nose in just because it was handy and things were quiet. Thought I'd just be waving the flag but the minute I walk in, the woman has a contraction and, *boof!* Umbilical cord prolapse and it's turned into an emergency.'

'Wow. What did you do?'

Aiden settled himself onto the end of Nathan's bed. This would need a few minutes because Nate always wanted a blow-by-blow account of every interesting job. If he'd been able-bodied, he would have been a paramedic himself, no question about it. You'd think he'd only be reminded of what he'd never be able to do by hearing about it but he never seemed to get enough of hearing about Aiden's professional exploits.

Or anything else about his big brother's life, come to that. He particularly loved to hear about the women he met and those he chose to date. What they looked like, where they'd gone on their dates and whether they'd stayed the night. He'd been careful how much he'd said about the midwife on today's job because Nate would have picked up on that pretty fast and, for some reason, Aiden hadn't wanted to answer the inevitable questions about how cute she was or whether she was single and, if so, why hadn't he asked her out yet?

Nate was so sure that someone was going to come along one day who would make him break his three-dates rule. Aiden was just as sure it would never happen.

If he couldn't take responsibility for his own brother's well-being, why the hell would he make himself responsible for anyone else? He didn't even own a dog, for heaven's sake, and he'd chosen a medical career where he generally never had to see his patients more than once.

Aiden Harrison was only too well aware of his limitations when it came to relationships and he'd found the perfect balance. Life was good. And it would continue to be good as long as Nathan didn't insist on putting himself at risk. Yes…tonight was the night for having a serious talk about the future.

'Let's go.' He matched the invitation with movement, standing up and opening the extra-wide door so that Nathan could manoeuvre his wheelchair into the hallway.

'Is it okay if Sam comes too?'

'Huh?'

'Samantha. You know…my carer? I asked her if she'd

like to come out and have a beer with us and she was keen. There's plenty of staff on tonight so it's no problem.'

'I…ah…' Was he going to be playing gooseberry while his brother was having a *date*?

Surely not.

But *why* not? He knew better than anyone that a disability didn't change who you were and his brother was an awesome guy. Why wouldn't a girl be smart enough to realise that? He had to admit it was a disturbing thought, though. What if Nathan fell in love and got his heart broken? Maybe a man-to-man talk about how well the three-dates rule worked needed to take priority over the talk about how risky independent living could be.

Not that either of those talks was going to happen tonight.

'Sure,' he heard himself saying, as though it was no big deal. 'There's plenty of room in the van. Maybe one of the other guys would like to come too.'

'Nope.' Nathan scooted through the door ahead of him. 'I only invited Sam.'

They were in a very different part of the botanical gardens this time. The guests crowded around the couple who were standing beneath the wrought-iron archway on the steps to the Temple of the Winds. The greenery of overhanging trees shaded them from the hot sun of a stunning autumn afternoon and once again Charles Delamere was in place as the master of ceremonies

'Ten years ago,' he told them, 'Emily and Oliver made their wedding vows. Circumstances, grief, life drove them apart but when the time was right fate brought them together again. They've decided to renew their vows, and they've also decided that here, in the gardens that are—and have been—loved by the whole family, is the place they'd like to do it.'

Emily and Oliver exchanged a look that was tender enough to bring a lump to Sophia's throat. She glanced over at Toby, Em's foster son, who was being held by Em's mother, Adrianna. This was a real family affair.

There had been so many tears at Gretta's farewell in the children's playground and there were probably just as many as the couple exchanged heartfelt vows, declaring their love and promising their commitment, but there was real joy this time. An affirmation that the risk of truly loving was worthwhile.

It was contagious, that hope. Maybe there was someone out there for her, Sophia thought. Someone who could see past the fact that she could never give him children of his own. Maybe she could find what Emily and Oliver had. How good would that be?

Something would have to change, though, if she was going to become as brave as Emily. Not that she knew quite what that something was but she was definitely going to give it some serious thought.

And, in the meantime, she could celebrate her friend's happiness. The Rooftop Bar was a good place to be on a sunny Saturday afternoon. Adrianna took little Toby home after a short time but told Oliver and Emily to stay and celebrate with all their friends. She would sort the final packing that was needed before they all went on their family honeymoon to the Great Barrier Reef the next day.

As often happened, the men gravitated together at one point and Sophia found herself sitting with a group of the women she knew best around a deliciously shaded table. Right beside Emily, she impulsively gave her friend another hug.

'I'm just so happy for you, Em. For you and Oliver. You so deserve every bit of this happiness.'

'It'll be your turn next.' Emily's smile was radiant. 'I'm sure of it.'

Isla overheard the comment. She was smiling as she refilled Sophia's glass with champagne. 'Good timing that she's met that hot paramedic, then, isn't it?'

'What?' Emily's jaw dropped. 'How come I haven't heard about this? Who is he?'

'Nobody,' Sophia muttered. 'Just a guy that turned up for that cord prolapse job yesterday.'

'And he's gorgeous,' Isla added. 'Soph said so.'

'I said he was good at his job, that's all.'

'She couldn't stop talking about him.' Darcie Green had joined them. 'I can vouch for that.'

Emily's sideways glance was significant. 'Just remember what I told you,' she said, raising her glass. 'You don't have to marry the guy. Just get out there and have some fun.'

'Why shouldn't she marry the guy?' Isla asked, between sips of her tall glass of soda water. 'Have you got something against marriage, Soph?'

'Not at all. I'm thrilled for Oliver and Em. And for you and Alessi. And…' Sophia glanced around the table, trying to distract the focus of attention. 'And what's going on with you and Lucas, Darcie? I'm sure I wasn't the only one to notice the sparks flying at the ball.'

Lucas was the super-hot senior midwife at the MMU and, while the husbands of the women about to give birth were less than impressed with his popularity, there was no shortage of expectant mums keen to become his patients. No shortage of women in Melbourne just as keen to fill another potential role in his life either.

Darcie was an English obstetrician, on secondment to the MMR. She was dedicated to her job and professional enough to have made several people sharpen up at work. Lucas didn't seem to be in that number, however, and the antagonism between them had been noted on the grapevine, but the obvious sparks at the ball had not come across as being between two people who didn't like each other. Not at all.

Not that Darcie was about to admit anything. She shrugged. 'We all had a good time at the ball,' she said, carefully avoiding eye contact with any of the other women. 'But if there was anything serious going on, I'd say it was between Flick, here, and Tristan.'

There was a murmur of agreement amongst the women and more than one knowing smile accompanying the nods.

'I'm sure I wasn't the only one to see you two leaving together,' Darcie continued lightly. 'Just what time *did* you get home, young woman?'

Felicia Lawrence, the student midwife, turned bright red. For an awful moment, Sophia was sure she was about to burst into tears.

Whatever had happened that night was really none of their business. Sophia needed to give her an escape route.

'So you two aren't dating or anything interesting like that, then?'

Flick shook her head with more emphasis than was needed. 'I'm not remotely interested in dating,' she claimed. 'My career's the only important thing in my life right now. Like Sophia.'

'I didn't say I wasn't *interested* in dating.' Sophia eyed her glass of champagne suspiciously. Had she had too much? 'I just…haven't met anybody. It takes time, you know—when you move to a new city.'

'But you've met the hot paramedic now.' Darcie was smiling. 'What was his name? Andy?'

'Aiden.' It seemed to be Sophia's turn to blush now. She could feel the warmth in her cheeks as she said his name aloud. 'Aiden Harrison.'

'Is he single? Did he ask for your number?'

'No.' She bit her lip. 'He did ask me for a date, though.'

'And you said *no*? What were you thinking?'

Darcie and Flick seemed very relieved to have the spotlight turned onto someone else's love life and, for Flick's sake, Sophia was happy enough to take centre stage.

'I'm not sure,' she admitted. 'Maybe I thought he was just being nice. I'd said I owed him a coffee because he'd had to abandon one to come to the job. He said he'd take a beer instead. It seemed—I don't know—a bit of a joke, maybe?'

'Nonsense,' the women chorused. She was gorgeous,

they assured her. Intelligent. Fun. Any guy would have to be crazy not to be genuinely interested.

Emily caught her glance in a private moment. She was the only one who might understand that moment of panic. That dip into a whirl of thoughts that had been spinning for so many years now. The issue of meeting someone you really liked and then agonising over when to tell them. On the first date? Did you say something like, 'Yeah, I'd love to go out with you but you should know that if you want to have kids some time in the future then I'm not the woman for you'? Or did you wait until things got serious and then field the repercussions of someone feeling a bit cheated? Deceived, even.

Yes. Emily's glance was sympathetic. But there was something else there, too. Encouragement?

'What does it matter if it did start out as a bit of a joke?' she said. 'Isn't the whole idea to have fun? To let your hair down a bit and enjoy the best of what life has to offer that doesn't have anything to do with work? It doesn't ever have to be anything serious.'

You don't have to marry the guy. Was that code for 'You don't have to even tell him'?

'How many guys do we know who have no intention of getting serious?' she added. 'They're just out to have fun. We could learn something from those guys.'

'Like Alessi.' Darcie nodded. 'Oops…sorry, Isla, but he was a terrible flirt and nobody lasted more than one night. Until you, of course…'

'Not a good example,' Emily chided. 'But you're right. Soph could use a bit of that attitude and just get out there and enjoy herself with some attractive male company.'

Sophia found herself nodding. And hadn't she just made a silent vow that very afternoon that something needed to change in her life? Maybe she wouldn't have to give too much thought to what that something was.

'Maybe I will,' she said aloud. 'Not that there's anyone around who's offering the company.'

'The hot paramedic did. You're probably putting anyone off asking by sending out *I'm not available* vibes. Change your attitude and they'll be around in droves. You might even meet *him* again.'

Sophia laughed. 'I don't think so.' But she reached for her glass of champagne, feeling lighter in spirit than she had for a long time. 'But, hey…I'll give it a go. The next time I get asked out—especially if it's the hot paramedic—I'll say yes.'

'Promise?' Emily raised her glass to clink it against Sophie's. The other women followed her example and the glasses met in a circle over the centre of the table.

'I promise,' Sophie said.

CHAPTER THREE

HE HAD THE best job in the world, no doubt about it.

Aiden was rolling slowly, the red and blue lights on his handlebars flashing as he eased through the crowds on Southbank. The wide, paved area on the south side of the Yarra River offered spectacular views of the river and city from cafés, restaurants and upmarket hotels.

The gorgeous autumn afternoon had tourists and locals enjoying the exercise, food and entertainment. A juggler had attracted a good crowd and so had an old aboriginal man playing a didgeridoo. Aiden could hear the hollow, haunting notes of the music over the bike's engine. He angled his path to avoid smudging the work of a street artist who was working with chalk and then he could see his destination. Another huddle of people, but they weren't there for entertainment. He'd been called to a woman who'd collapsed on one of the riverside benches beneath the trees.

'I've put her in the recovery position,' a man told Aiden as soon as he'd propped the bike up on its stand. 'I did a first-aid course last year.'

'Good work.' He flipped up the chinguard of his helmet. 'Did anyone see what happened?'

'She was walking around, looking weird,' someone else offered. 'Like she was drunk. And then she sat down and just toppled sideways.'

Aiden had reached the unconscious woman. He stripped off his gloves, tilted her head to make sure her airway was open and then felt for a pulse in her neck. It was there. Rapid and faint enough to suggest low blood pressure. Her skin felt cool and clammy. He shook her shoulder.

'Hello? Can you hear me? Open your eyes, love.'

No response. Aiden looked up. 'Does anyone know this woman? Was she with someone?'

There was a general sound of denial and shaking of heads. Aiden checked for a MedicAlert bracelet or necklace as he ran through the possible causes of unconsciousness in his head. He couldn't smell any alcohol and there was no sign of any head trauma. The woman was young, probably in her early thirties. This could be due to epilepsy or drugs or diabetes. At least he could eliminate one of the possible causes easily. Unrolling a kit, he took a small lancet, pricked the woman's finger and eased the drop of blood onto a testing strip for a glucometer. He also reached for his radio to give Dispatch an update. Whatever was going on, here, this young woman would need transport to hospital.

The glucometer beeped and it was a relief to see that the reading was low. Hypoglycaemia certainly fitted with the limited information he'd been given of her appearing drunk and then collapsing. It also fitted the physical signs of the clammy skin, rapid heart rate and a low blood pressure. Back-up was on the way but it would take time to get a stretcher through the crowds from the nearest point an ambulance could park and Aiden had everything he needed to start treatment.

IV access was the first priority and there were plenty of willing hands to hold up the bag with the glucose infusion. He got the small cardiac monitor out of one of the panniers on the back of his bike as well. It had only been a few days ago that he'd read an interesting article suggesting that sudden death in young diabetics could be due to cardiac problems from electrolyte disturbances.

The glucose infusion was working its magic well before he started attaching electrodes. The young woman opened her eyes, blinked a couple of times and then groaned.

'Oh, no…it happened again, didn't it?'

'I'm Aiden, a paramedic. What's your name, love?'

'Hayley. I…' She looked up at the crowd of onlookers. 'Oh…God…this is so embarrassing.'

'You're diabetic?'

'Yeah…I knew I needed to eat. That's why I came along here. I was heading for the food court in Southgate. It came on so suddenly…'

Aiden could see an ambulance crew manoeuvring a stretcher through the crowd. More people were stopping to stare, wondering what was going on. No wonder the poor girl was embarrassed. The sooner they got her into the privacy of the back of an ambulance, the better.

Checking her blood-glucose levels again could wait until then as well. Aiden kick-started his bike and followed the crew, until he could park beside the ambulance. He needed to fill in his paperwork and he had a feeling that Hayley was not going to be keen to be taken to hospital.

'I don't need to go,' she insisted a few minutes later. 'I feel fine now.'

'When was the last time you had a hypo?'

'A couple of weeks ago,' she admitted reluctantly. 'But before that, it hadn't happened for ages. Over a year.'

'That means your control is becoming more challenging. You need a reassessment.'

'I'll go to my doctor. Soon.'

'It could happen again today.'

'I'll eat. I'll go and get a sandwich right now.'

It took time to persuade Hayley that it would be a good idea to go the emergency department at the Victoria but none of the paramedics were happy to let her go when she didn't have someone with her to monitor her condition. And Aiden had something else that was bothering him.

'Have you thought of wearing a MedicAlert bracelet?'

Hayley made a face. 'It's bad enough having to live with something like this, without advertising it. And have you any idea how much harder it makes it to find a job? People look at you like you've got a disability or something.'

Her words stayed with Aiden as he watched the ambulance take his patient away. He stayed where he was, astride his bike, watching the mill of the people he could still see on Southbank. This wasn't a bad place to park up until he got another call. Central city and covering a patch well away from the nearest ambulance station. A young man in a wheelchair went past amongst the crowd.

There was a disability that couldn't be disguised. And he knew what it was like to attract the intrusive attention of people who felt they had the right to ask personal questions. They'd often been directed at him over the years—as if Nathan's brain didn't work any better than his legs did.

'Why's he in a wheelchair, then?'

'Oh, the poor boy. Can he feed himself?'

'How does he go to the toilet?'

The guilt was always there, welded onto his soul, and the curiosity of strangers turned the screws painfully for Aiden, but Nathan had developed a resilience in his teenage years that had astounded him. He could deal with any situation now with a humour that often shocked the nosy people. Like those awful jokes he kept adding to.

'What do you call a quadriplegic under your car? Jack.'

Despite himself, Aiden found his lips quirking. What did it matter what other people thought? Nathan had it sorted. He was happy. In fact, he was happier than he'd ever been right now. The way he'd been looking at Sam the other night... Was something going on already and, if so, how badly could that end? He needed to have a serious talk with his younger brother. Try and get him prepared for something that would hurt more than public scrutiny or pity.

His radio crackled into life.

'Code One,' Dispatch told him, giving him an address

not far away. 'Twenty-four-year-old female with severe abdominal pain.'

'Copy that.' Aiden tilted the bike off its stand and kicked it into life. He activated the lights and then the siren. Traffic was building up but he'd be able to weave through it fast. He loved a code one response and the freedom it allowed. With a bike, he got way more freedom than an ambulance to break a speed limit or use the tramlines. He just had to be a bit more careful. Hitting tram lines at the wrong angle and the ambulance would have to stop for him instead of getting to the job.

It took less than four minutes to arrive on scene. Another thirty seconds and he was in the room with the young woman who was bent over a chair and groaning loudly.

'It's the fish I had last night. Ohhh…. It *really* hurts and I've been sick.'

Aiden blinked. Dispatch hadn't bothered mentioning that his patient was pregnant.

'How far along are you?'

'Thirty-seven weeks.'

'And how far apart are the pains you're getting?'

'I dunno. It's happening every five or ten minutes, I guess. But I'm not in labour. It's that fish… I knew I shouldn't be eating prawns.'

It took very little time to convince his patient that this was, indeed, labour.

'I'm not going to hospital. I'm having a home birth. Can you call my midwife?'

'Sure. What's her name?'

'Sophia Toulson. Her card's on the fridge.'

The phone in his hand seconds later, Aiden found himself smiling again. It was surprising how strong the hope was that Sophia would be available and able to get here fast.

For his patient's benefit, of course…

Flick was excited. This was the first home birth she had been to since starting to shadow Sophia.

'But what if something goes wrong? Like a post-partum haemorrhage or something?'

'We call for back-up. The Melbourne ambulance service is fabulous. And we're not far from the hospital. In most cases, if there's going to be trouble, we get enough warning.'

'You didn't the other day, with that cord prolapse, did you?'

'No.'

And her pager hadn't warned her that the paramedic on scene had been riding a motorbike. She could see it parked outside Gemma's house.

'Nice bike,' Flick murmured.

'Mmm.'

Those butterflies were dancing in her stomach again. How many SPRINT paramedics rode bikes in the city? It didn't mean that she was about to have another encounter with the man her friends were all now referring to as 'the hot paramedic'.

Except it appeared that she was.

'Hey…' Aiden Harrison was grinning. 'We've got to stop meeting like this. Rumours will start.'

Flick gave a huff of laughter and Sophia gave her

a warning glance before letting her gaze shift back to Aiden, her lips curling into a smile.

'You did say that babies were your favourite thing but you don't have to take over my job, you know.' She moved past him. 'Why didn't you call me when the pains started, Gemma?'

'I didn't think it was labour. I thought I had some dodgy prawns last night because I started getting cramps just after I'd eaten. They went away for a while this morning and then one was so painful I screamed and my neighbour called the ambulance.'

'Contractions are four to five minutes apart,' Aiden told her. 'Lasting about ninety seconds. Vital signs all good. Gemma's been happy to keep walking around.'

'Let's get you on your bed for a minute,' Sophia said. 'I want to check how baby's doing and what stage of dilatation you're at. This is Flick, by the way. Our student midwife. Are you happy to have her assisting? It's very valuable experience for her if she can be hands-on.'

Gemma nodded as she let Sophia guide her towards the bedroom.

'I can stay until I get another call,' Aiden said. 'Unless I'm in the way.'

It was entirely unprofessional to get distracted by noticing how much she didn't want him to disappear. Even worse to take another look at him and find it so hard to look away. Those eyes were just as warm and interesting as she'd remembered, and that smile made it impossible not to smile back.

Oh...help. How long had they been staring at each

other? Long enough for Flick and Gemma to exchange a surprised glance and then a complicit grin.

'It's fine by me if you stay,' Gemma said. *You know you want to*, her tone suggested. 'My mum's on her way but I told her not to hurry. This is going to take ages, isn't it?'

'Let's find out. Flick, get some gloves on and you can examine Gemma and find out what her stage of dilatation is.'

Keeping her voice low, it was possible to use this opportunity as a teaching and practical experience session for Flick.

'Tell me how you'll make the assessment.'

'At two centimetres I'll be able to fit one finger loosely through the cervix but not two fingers. Two fingers will be loose at four centimetres. There's two centimetres of cervix palpable on both sides at six centimetres, one at eight and there's only an anterior lip or a bit left laterally at nine centimetres.'

'And what are you feeling?'

'Nothing.' Flick's eyes widened. 'I can't feel any cervix at all. Am I doing something wrong?'

Sophia smiled as she double-checked Flick's findings, shaking her head at her student, who had been correct in her evaluation. 'You're fully dilated, Gemma,' she told their patient. 'Let's check the baby's position and then get set up. What do you need to do now, Flick?'

'The four Leopold's manoeuvres. First one checks the upper abdomen to make sure it's the baby's buttocks and not the head and then the umbilical area to locate the baby's back and—'

'Can I go to the bathroom first?' Gemma pleaded. 'I really need to go.'

Aiden helped Flick set up for the birth while Sophia stayed close to Gemma. They spread waterproof sheets over the bed and one of the armchairs in the living room and gathered some clean towels. Flick opened a kit and checked the resuscitation gear they carried in case it would be needed.

Aiden found himself glancing frequently at the door, waiting for the reappearance of Sophia and Gemma.

The attraction he'd felt the first time he'd met the cute little midwife had come back with a vengeance. Those lovely brown eyes were so warm and that smile made him feel like he'd just done something outstanding. Something that deserved approval because he'd somehow made the world a better place.

Heck…all he'd done was crack a fairly weak joke. Imagine how Sophia would look at him if he really did something to be proud of.

He wasn't going to let his opportunity slip past. He might have made a note of the number he'd used to call her but that was just her pager service. He was going to ask for her personal number as soon as he got the chance—as long as he didn't get called away first. Who knew how long this labour might take? Gemma was taking long enough just to go to the loo.

And she was being noisy about it, too. They heard a cry of pain. And then another.

And then Sophia's calm voice. 'Could you bring a couple of towels, please, Flick? Lean on me, Gemma…

Yes, that's your baby's head you can feel. Deep breath and give me one good push...'

The wail of a healthy newborn could be heard a moment later and Aiden moved to peer in the bathroom door at the crowded scene. Gemma was still sitting on the toilet and Sophia was guiding her hands to help her hold the slippery baby against her skin. Gemma was sobbing and Sophia looked...as if she was blinking back tears?

'She's gorgeous, Gemma. A dear wee girl... Flick, have you got the clamps and scissors? Gemma, would you like to cut the cord?'

'No...' Gemma shook her head.

Somehow, Aiden had moved further into the small space without noticing and he was now blocking Flick's access to the toilet. Some signal passed between Sophia and her student and Aiden found himself holding the clamps in his gloved hands. He attached one a few inches away from the baby and then another to leave an isolated area to cut. He'd done this before and knew to expect how tough it was to cut through the umbilical cord.

He already felt involved in this birthing scene but then Sophia smiled at him again.

'Can we give baby to Aiden for just a minute, Gemma? I'd like to get you cleaned up and comfortable in bed to wait for the placenta.'

Flick gave him a clean towel and Aiden carefully took charge of the tiny infant, with Sophia's assistance. This was the closest he'd been to her and he could smell the fragrance of her hair. Almost feel the warmth of her skin through the gloves as their hands brushed. And then he looked at the tiny scrunched-up face of the baby and got completely distracted.

The miracle of birth never failed to amaze him but he never wanted the responsibility of one of these himself. The enormity of bringing a new person into the world and trying to keep them safe for ever was overwhelming. As he backed away, carrying the precious burden in his arms, he looked up to find Sophia watching him.

He couldn't read the expression in her face but it struck him as poignant and something inside his chest squeezed hard. But then it was gone. She smiled and turned back to her patient.

'Put your arm around my shoulders and we'll take this slowly. You might find your legs are pretty shaky.'

The five-minute Apgar score was a perfect ten and Aiden returned the pink, vigorously crying infant to his mother. There was no reason for him to stay on the job any longer and watch as Sophia guided Flick to help the baby latch onto Gemma's nipple and begin its first breastfeed.

And then Sophia supervised Flick in attending to the delivery of the placenta and checking it for any damage, and it really was time for him to leave. He stripped off his gloves and picked up his helmet and kit.

Flick was giving Gemma a wash with a hot, soapy cloth and Sophia was putting the placenta into a bag. This was it—the best opportunity he was going to get. He stepped closer.

'I know you were busy last time I asked,' he said

casually. 'But are you doing anything special after work today?'

Wide, surprised brown eyes met his gaze. 'Not really,' she said, 'but I won't finish for a while. We usually spend a few hours with a new mother and make sure she's happy before we go.'

'Maybe we could meet up later, then?'

Gemma looked up from watching her baby suckle. 'Are you asking Sophia for a date?' She grinned.

Flick was staring at Sophia and seemed to be stifling laughter. What was going on here?

Sophia tied the bag and stripped off her gloves. Her cheeks had a rosy glow and she seemed to be carefully avoiding meeting his gaze. 'It's not about a date,' she said. 'I happen to owe Aiden a coffee, that's all.'

She made it sound like that was the only reason he might be interested in taking her out. Aiden couldn't let that pass.

'Yeah…' he said slowly. 'I'm asking for a date. Would you like to come out with me this evening, Sophia?'

'Um… I…' Sophia bit her lip. 'Maybe you can call me later. We're both at work and this isn't, you know, very professional.'

'I don't mind,' Gemma said.

'And I'm not going to tell anybody,' Flick added. She looked as if she was trying not to smile. 'Was that a *yes* I heard there, Soph?'

There was definitely an undercurrent here that Aiden had no way of interpreting but right then Sophia met his gaze again and he didn't care about anything other than hearing her say that word.

'Okay. Yes.' He could see her chest rise as she took a deep breath. 'I'd love to go on a date with you, Aiden.'

'Cool. I'll pick you up about seven? Where do you live?'

'How 'bout I meet you somewhere? A nice bar, maybe?'

So she didn't want him to know where she lived? No problem. When you had a three-dates rule, it was probably better not to intrude too far on anyone's personal space. Aiden named a trendy bar that he knew wasn't too far from the Victoria, guessing that Sophia probably lived reasonably close to where she worked.

'I know it.' She nodded. 'I'll meet you there at seven.'

At six-thirty p.m. Sophia was staring at the pile of clothes on her bed.

It might be a cliché but she really *didn't* have anything to wear. Nothing that would project the image she wanted anyway, which was one of a confident young woman who wasn't the least bit desperate. Who was happy to go out and have a bit of fun but wasn't looking for anything remotely serious.

Something frilly? She didn't possess frills. Something low-cut that would show a bit of cleavage? No. That might send entirely the wrong message about the kind of fun she was after.

What *was* she after? And why was she feeling so ridiculously nervous?

'Oh, for heaven's sake.' Wearing only her jeans and bra, Sophia went to rummage in her handbag for her phone. She would text Aiden and tell him she couldn't make it after all. One of her patients had gone into early labour? Yeah…perfect excuse.

And she wasn't really breaking her promise, was she? She had said yes. She just wasn't going to follow through and actually *go* on the date.

A small problem became apparent the moment she picked up her phone. She didn't have Aiden's phone number, did she?

She had absolutely no way of contacting him unless she fronted up at the bar in…oh, help…twenty minutes.

But there was a message on *her* phone. For a hopeful heartbeat Sophia thought that Aiden might have sent her a message to cancel the date.

No such luck. He didn't have her number either, did he?

The message was from Emily. 'I hear you said yes,' it said. 'You go, girl. And have fun.'

So Flick had spread the word. Her friends would demand details and she was a hopeless liar. Her voice always got sort of tight and high. She'd never be able to make something up and sound convincing.

Gritting her teeth, Sophia marched back into her bedroom. She jammed her feet into knee-high boots, threw on a camisole top and covered it with a velvet jacket. Pulling the band from her hair, she raked her fingers through the shoulder-length waves and spent no more than thirty seconds in front of the mirror, putting on a slick of lipstick.

Then she grabbed her bag and slammed the door of the cottage behind her. She had less than ten minutes to get to the bar but having to rush was probably a good thing. It would give her less time for her stupid nerves to grow wings.

There was no sign of Sophia.

Aiden ordered a beer and stayed at the bar, an elbow propped and his posture relaxed enough to suggest he was thoroughly enjoying his view of the women coming in through the doors. Enjoying the appreciative looks he got in return even more.

Normally, he would be doing exactly that.

So why did he feel…good grief…*nervous*?

A little out of control even?

Maybe it was because he was meeting Sophia here, instead of having picked her up first. What if she didn't show up?

Hey…no problem. There were plenty of very attractive women who seemed to be here unaccompanied by any male friends.

But he hadn't come here to randomly score. He'd come here because he really wanted to spend some time with Sophia.

And maybe the strength of that want was why he was feeling a bit weird. Why this was assuming an importance that it wasn't allowed to have.

No problem. Aiden took another fortifying swallow of his beer. This was only a number-one date. No big deal. If it continued to feel weird, he could just pull the plug and there wouldn't be a number two.

Suddenly, he saw her. Looking small and a little bit lost as she stood near the door and scanned the crowded bar. And then she spotted him and smiled.

The noise of the people around him and the background music seemed to fade away.

The people themselves seemed to fade away. Until there was only himself.

And Sophia.

How weird was *that*?

CHAPTER FOUR

HE WAS THERE.

He must have spotted her the moment she walked through the door because he was already looking straight at her when Sophia turned her head. She'd been worried she might not even recognise him out of uniform but even in a crowd of people there was no mistaking Aiden Harrison.

Her relieved smile faded as she threaded her way to the bar, however. He hadn't smiled back. He'd looked a bit stunned even... Had he been surprised that she'd actually turned up? Or maybe he was disappointed that she had. There was no shortage of opportunities in a place like this. She could feel the gaze of other girls on her as she made her way towards the gorgeous guy standing alone at the bar. Envious glances.

'Hi...' He was smiling now. 'Can I get you something to drink?'

'A white wine would be lovely, thank you.'

'Do you want to have it here or find a table out in the garden? They have live music here tonight so there won't be any room to move in here soon.'

So she'd end up dancing or squashed against him at the bar? Sophia sucked in a breath. 'The garden sounds great.'

There were rustic tables and wrought-iron chairs, flickering candles and the greenery of a rampant grapevine on an overhead pergola. The last unoccupied table they found in a corner with only two chairs was romantic enough to make Sophia hesitate. This was supposed to be fun. Nothing serious.

Aiden put their drinks down on the table. 'Don't know about you,' he said, 'but I'm *starving*. Fancy some nachos or a big bowl of fries?'

That was the right note to hit. They were here for a drink and something to eat and it just happened to be with company. They'd be able to hear the music out here without being deafened. A fun night out.

'Sure. Nachos are my absolute favourite.'

'Mine, too.'

They grinned at each other. They were on the same page and suddenly everything seemed easy. Over the cheese and bean-laden tortilla chips, the conversation was just as relaxed.

'It must be a great job, being a SPRINT paramedic.'

'Best job in the world. I love having no idea of what's coming next or where I'm going.'

'I love being out of the hospital environment most of the time, too. You get to connect a lot more with patients when you're in their own home. Even more when they've had a home delivery. I feel like part of the family sometimes.'

But Aiden shook his head at that. 'It's the opposite

that appeals to me. I get to ride in, do the exciting stuff and then hand the responsibility on to someone else.'

'Don't you ever follow your patients up and see what happened?'

'I'll talk to the crew that transports them. Or, if I've travelled in with them, I might hang around in the emergency department and see how it's handled from there. Some of the docs are great. If I'm ending a shift, they let me go into Theatre or talk over the results of a CT scan or something. If I can learn something that's going to help me manage better next time, I'm in.'

'You should poke your nose into the MMU some time. You're a bit of a hero up there after that cord prolapse job the other day.'

Aiden shook off the compliment. 'We were lucky.' He raised his eyebrows. 'How's that baby doing? Do you know?'

Sophia laughed. 'Of course I know. I'm still doing daily visits. His name is Isaac and he's doing extremely well. Claire and Greg are over the moon.'

'Good to know. Did he get a thorough neurological check?'

It was Sophia's turn to raise her eyebrows. 'Are you kidding? We've got the best doctors there are. He passed every test with flying colours. He might turn out to be a brain surgeon himself one day. Or the prime minister or something. You'll see him on television and think about what might have happened if you hadn't been there the day he was born.'

'I might have a bit of trouble recognising him.' But Aiden was smiling and Sophia felt…relieved? He did have a connection with his patients that wasn't purely technical. Maybe he didn't want to revel in that connection like she did but it was there—whether he wanted it to be or not.

And the idea of him being a maverick medic who rode around the city saving lives and touching those lives only briefly added to his attraction, didn't it? Gave him a kind of superhero edge?

Oh, yeah…the attraction was growing for sure and it didn't seem to be one-sided. Eye contact was becoming more frequent and held for a heartbeat longer. Their fingers brushed as they shared the platter of food. The butterflies in Sophia's gut danced up a storm as she wondered if he would kiss her at the end of this date.

But then what?

She could hear an echo of Em's voice in the back of her mind. *You don't have to marry the guy. You don't even have to tell him anything. Just have fun…*

Maybe the connection was even stronger than it felt. She could see a flicker in Aiden's eyes that had nothing to do with the candles around them.

'I should warn you,' he said, 'that I'm not looking for anything serious.'

Good grief…was that shaft of sensation disappointment? Or shame even? Was there something about her that wasn't attractive enough to warrant any kind of emotional investment?

His smile suggested otherwise. So did the way his hand covered hers, touching her skin with the lightness of a feather—the fingers moving just enough to sound a deliciously seductive note.

'It's not that you're not absolutely gorgeous,' he murmured. 'But I have rules. One rule, anyway.'

'Oh?' This was confusing. His words were warning her off but his eyes and his touch were inviting her closer. Much closer.

'A three-dates rule.'

'A...*what*?'

'Three dates. I've discovered that's the perfect number.'

'Perfect for what?'

'To get to know someone. To have fun but not to let anything get out of hand. You know...to get...*serious*.'

He made the word sound like some kind of notifiable disease. Sophia's head was spinning. Wasn't this exactly what she was looking for? Fun with a gorgeous guy but within limits. Limits that would mean there was no need to tell him anything about herself that could impinge on the fun. She could pretend there was nothing wrong with her. That she was as desirable as any other young woman who was out there dating. That it was only because of 'the rule' that it wouldn't go any further.

'I love it,' she whispered with a smile.

'Really?' Aiden's eyebrows shot up. His fingers tightened over her hand.

'Really.' Sophia nodded. 'I'm not looking for anything serious either. Three dates sounds like exactly the rule that's been missing from *my* life.'

'Wow...' Aiden's gaze was frankly admiring. 'You're even more amazing than I thought.' He stood up, still holding Sophia's hand, so that she was drawn to her feet as well. 'You do realise that means we'll have to make the most of each and every date, don't you?'

The butterflies had congregated into a cluster that throbbed somewhere deep in Sophia's belly like a drumbeat. She couldn't look away from Aiden's gaze, even when he dropped her hand and raised his to touch her face. A finger on her temple that traced a gentle line around her eye, across her cheek and down to the corner of her mouth. Her lips parted in astonishment at the wave of sensation the touch was creating and it was then that Aiden dipped his head and kissed her.

Right there—in a noisy, crowded garden of a trendy bar. Their corner was secluded enough but it was a long way from being private. Not that the kiss got out of hand or anything. The control of those soft, questioning lips on hers suggested that Aiden was a very experienced kisser. The teasing touch of his tongue hinted at where this kiss could go at any moment. Oh, yeah…it ended far sooner than Sophia would have chosen.

What now?

Would Aiden take her home to his place? Should she suggest that he came to hers?

On a *first* date?

The idea was shocking. Okay, she was doing this to have fun but jumping into bed with someone this fast made it feel wrong. But they only had three dates to play with, didn't they? Did 'making the most of them' imply that they shouldn't waste any time?

But Aiden was smiling again and Sophia had the feeling that he knew the argument she was having with herself.

'Let's plan date number two,' he said. 'And give ourselves something to look forward to.'

'So...how was it, then?'

'What?'

'Date *numero uno* with the cute midwife?'

Aiden shrugged as he looked away from his brother to stare over the veranda railings into the garden of the old house. He upended his bottle to catch a mouthful of his beer. 'Not bad.'

'Score?'

Aiden frowned. Nate loved to hear about his love life as much as his job and he'd always been happy to share the details. He couldn't remember who had come up with the scoring system but it had become a tradition. This was the first time it had occurred to Aiden how degrading it would seem if the women he dated ever knew about it.

Not that he would ever tell them, of course.

But he'd never told any women about the three-dates rule until now, had he? It was a secret, known only to himself and Nate. The astonishment factor of actually sharing the secret with a woman he was on a date with was only surpassed by the totally unexpected way Sophia had embraced the idea.

What was with that? Was there something about him that didn't make him attractive longer term?

The thought shouldn't be disturbing but it was. So was the niggle of doubt that he'd come right out and put a limit on how much time he was going to have with the gorgeous Sophia. How the stupidity of that move had been plaguing him ever since he'd left her at the end of their date with no more than another kiss.

She was…

'That good, huh?' He could hear the grin in Nate's voice. 'Off the scale, was she?'

Aiden merely grunted.

She was perfect, that's what she was. Absolutely gorgeous. Smart. So easy to talk to. And that all too brief taste of her lips…

Man… The way she'd felt in his arms. The way she'd responded to his kisses. He had a fair idea of exactly where their second date was going to end up and he couldn't wait. How, in fact, would he be able to enjoy the day on the beach they now had planned for when their next days off coincided? He would be hanging out to get her somewhere a lot more private. Somewhere they could *really* get to know each other.

But that would mean there was only one date left. And then what?

This had never bothered him before. He'd never even thought ahead like this before.

'Could be the one, then.' Nate was nodding. 'A four-dates woman.'

'No way.'

'Why not?'

'Because I'm not getting into anything serious, that's why.'

'Why not?'

This was getting annoying. Aiden had stopped by after work for his usual visit. He just wanted a quiet beer with his brother, not some kind of interrogation.

'You know why. I'm not interested in getting married or having kids.'

'Doesn't mean you can't have a long-term relationship. Not every woman out there is hanging out to walk down the aisle in a meringue dress or stockpile nappies.'

'They all get to that point at some stage. I know that from painful experience. And the longer it goes on for, the harder it is when you break it off. I'm not going to be responsible for someone else's happiness.'

'Why not?' There was an edge to Nate's voice he hadn't heard before. 'Because you feel you have to be responsible for mine?'

'Whoa…where did that come from?' Aiden glanced over his shoulder as he broke the moment of startled silence. Wasn't it about time for the boys to all roll their chairs into the dining room for their evening meal? Where was everybody else, anyway? In the lounge, watching reruns of Murderball games? If he stepped away from the corner he could probably see through the window and, if there was a game on, he could distract Nate. He had a feeling that he wasn't going to like whatever Nathan was about to unbottle.

'You do, though, don't you?' Nathan swivelled his wheelchair with practised ease and trapped Aiden so that it would look like a deliberate evasion if he tried to step past him. 'You feel responsible for what happened to me and so you think you have to *be* responsible for me for the rest of your life.'

Of course he felt responsible for what had happened. It had been his fault.

Nate was staring at him. He shook his head. 'It wasn't your fault.'

Aiden stared back at him. 'You were too young to remember what it was like. If I hadn't lost my rag and yelled back at Dad, he'd never have come after me. He'd never have knocked you down the stairs and broken your neck.'

The horror of that day as a sixteen-year-old whose life had changed for ever in a heartbeat had never gone. Crouched over the crumpled form of his ten-year-old brother at the bottom of the stairs, his hands had been shaking as he'd tried to hold his phone still enough to call for an ambulance. To stop Nathan moving, even as they'd both heard the dreadful sound of the gunshot that had come from an upstairs room.

Maybe the worst horror had been the relief of knowing that he didn't have to protect Nathan from their father's tyranny any more—the twisted bitterness that had come from blaming an innocent baby for his wife's death.

He'd held Nathan's head still, knowing that moving him could make it worse. And he'd talked to him as he'd crouched there, waiting for help to arrive.

'*I'm here,*' he'd said, over and over again. '*I'll look after you. I'll always look after you.*'

'I remember a lot more than you give me credit for. And you know what? I've had enough of this.'

Nate sounded angry. His clever, brave, determined kid brother was letting his irrepressible good humour go for once. He was angry with him.

Finally. There was a relief to be found in that. He

deserved the anger. He could handle it. He was the one who could still walk. The one who had a job he loved. Who could get out there and kiss gorgeous women. Nate was allowed to be angry about what had happened in his life. The opportunities he would never have.

'It was Dad who pushed me down the stairs. Not you. It's ancient history. Get over it, Aiden. *I* have.'

'How can you say that?' Aiden was shocked. 'You have to live with that accident for the rest of your life. It should never have happened.'

'Oh, get off the guilt train,' Nate snapped. 'Yeah…I have to live with it for the rest of my life. *Me*. And you don't get to feel so guilty about it that you stuff up your own life. I'm not having that put on me, thanks.'

'I'm not—'

'Yeah, you are. You baby me. You're always here, checking up on me. Trying to make life better for me, but guess what? I like my life. I don't need this.'

Aiden stared at his brother. He'd thought he could handle the anger but that was when he'd thought it was going to be about the accident that had wrecked a young life—not about him honouring a vow to look after the only person who'd ever been so important to him.

This hurt, dammit. Enough to make him feel angry right back at Nate.

'I've only ever done what I could to help. You were ten years old.'

'And you're still treating me like I'm ten years old. I'm twenty-four, man. I'm grown up. I've got a *girlfriend*.'

How on earth had this all come out after sharing the news that he'd gone on a date with the cute midwife?

'And there's no way I'm going to play by your stupid three-dates rule.'

So that was it.

'You do know it's stupid, don't you?'

'Works for me.' Aiden's voice was tight. At least, it had.

'I'm going to live by myself one of these days,' Nate continued fiercely. 'I'm going to try out for the Murderball team and if I get in I'll give it everything I've got. I'm going to make the best of my life. I don't want to end up like you.'

'What's that supposed to mean?'

'Shut off. Scared of losing control.'

'People get hurt if you lose control.' Surely Nate knew that better than anyone after what had happened.

'So? That's life.' Nate shook his head. 'Get over it and start having some fun. Like me.' The crooked smile was a plea for understanding. Forgiveness, too, maybe, for saying some hard stuff?

The lump in his throat made it hard to suck in a breath. Okay, he was hurt but, man, his little brother had courage, didn't he? He was so proud of him.

A window got pushed up along the veranda and a dark, spiky head emerged. 'You coming in for dinner, Nate?'

'Sure.'

'You want to stay, Aiden? There's plenty.'

'Nah…I'm good.' He needed some time to think about what had just happened. That his brother had grown up and just let him know in no uncertain terms? Or that he thought he had, anyway. He still needed his big brother, even if he didn't think he did. More than ever, in fact, as he strived for independence. Did he think he could do that without a lot of help? Even if he wasn't welcome, there was no way Aiden could back away from his responsibilities here. He might just have to be a bit cleverer in how he looked after Nate.

'Hey…' Nathan stopped the movement of his chair. He looked back at his brother. He looked a lot younger all of a sudden. Worried. Aiden could see him swallow hard. 'We okay?'

If he'd needed any evidence that his brother still needed him, it was right there in how vulnerable Nate looked right now. Aiden didn't hesitate. 'Sure.'

But it was an awkward moment that could go either way.

Aiden did his best to smile. 'You were right, man. She was off the scale.'

Nate's grin tugged at his heart. 'So she gets a second date, at least?'

'Already sorted. We're going to the beach.'

'Maybe me and Sam can come, too.'

Aiden snorted. 'No way. I only invited Sophia.'

CHAPTER FIVE

MELBOURNE IS FAMED for the ability to produce four seasons in one day with its fickle weather. It was also capable of pulling something astonishing out of its meteorological hat—like a blazingly hot day in April when it could just as easily have been more like winter than summer.

How lucky was it that it was like this for date number two when they had agreed that the beach was a good place to go? Sophia stood on the pavement outside the picket fence of her cottage at the appointed time. She was wearing her bikini as underwear beneath her jeans and shirt and she carried a beach towel in her bag—just in case it was warm enough to swim. The thick jacket she had on over her shirt earned her a few curious looks from passers-by but she was just following the instructions that had come with the plan.

Had her choice regarding the mode of transport been a mistake?

'The van's old and clunky,' Aiden had told her as he walked her home from the bar and they'd planned this date. 'But it does have walls. If you're brave, you can come on the back of my bike.'

'You get to use your work bike at home?'

'No. I've got one of my own. A Ducati. A red one.'

'Red, huh? What colour is the van?'

'White. Boring, boring white.' He wanted her to choose the bike. She wanted to see the approval in his eyes when she made the right choice.

'Then it's no contest, is it? I pick red.'

But her stomach did an odd little flip as she saw the sun glinting on the red metal of the huge bike as it rolled to a halt in front of her.

Or was it Aiden's grin as he lifted the visor of his helmet that was doing it?

He unclipped a second helmet and held it out to her. 'Are you ready?'

Sophia had to suck in a big breath. *Was* she ready? This was about way more than a long bike ride, wasn't it?

Those unusual light brown eyes were doing that dancing thing again. A look that implied mischief. *Fun...*

She reached for the helmet as she nodded and returned the grin. 'I'm ready.'

It was a long ride. Leaving the outskirts of Melbourne behind, they took to the open road, heading south. They bypassed the large town of Geelong and sped towards the point where the harbour met the open sea—the quaint seaside village of Queenscliff.

'It's gorgeous,' Sophia exclaimed as they parked the bike and took off on foot to explore. 'Look at the turrets on that house!'

'We're lucky it's not a weekend. With weather like this, it gets really crowded.'

'You've been here before?'

'It's a great destination when I want to get out on the road and blow a few cobwebs away.'

'It certainly does that.' Sophia made a face as she threaded her fingers into the end of her hair where the waves brushed her shoulders. 'I should have tied this up. I might never get the knots out. I didn't even think to bring a brush. It probably looks like a rat's nest.'

Aiden stopped walking. They were outside the door of a bakery and a woman came out, laden with paper bags. She had to walk around them but Aiden didn't seem to notice because he was only looking at Sophia. He caught her hand and pulled her fingers out of her hair. Then he flattened her hand gently against her head with his still on top of it.

'Forget about it,' he told her. 'You look gorgeous.'

And then he bent his head and kissed her. Right there on the footpath, half blocking the door to the bakery.

Sophia had relived the softness of that first kiss in a bar a hundred times by now. Had conjured up the tingle of anticipation and the curl of desire so many times that she'd been sure she had magnified it out of all connection with reality.

Turned out she hadn't.

This was even better. It still had the restraint that being in a public place required but there was a new depth to it. A familiarity. The knowledge that they both wanted this and it was going to go somewhere else. Very soon.

'*Excuse* me.' The voice sounded annoyed. Breaking apart, they could see why. A young woman with a twin pushchair had no chance of getting past them to the door.

Aiden smiled at the mother as he murmured an apology. He held the door open for her but it was obvious she had already forgiven him.

'No worries,' she said, smiling up at him. 'You have a great day.'

'Oh…' Aiden's glance went over the top of her head, straight to Sophia's. 'I already am.'

The woman turned her head and her smile widened. Her gaze told Sophia exactly how lucky she was. Then she winked and disappeared into the shop. The smell of something hot and delicious wafted out as the door swung shut.

'Hungry?'

'Starving.' Sophia took a step towards the door but Aiden shook his head.

'Bit crowded in there. I've got a better idea.'

He took her across the road to the fish-and-chip shop. A short time later, they were walking down the hill and away from the shops. Aiden held the big white paper parcel in one hand and Sophia's hand in the other. He led her across the railway lines and onto a track that took them to a grassy spot with a view through the trees to the water. The meal was still hot and absolutely delicious. A woman walked past on the track with a dog and then a whole family with a toddler in a pushchair and a small child on a bike, but nobody came to share their patch of grass or even looked their way. It felt as if they were almost invisible.

'This is perfect.' Sophia licked salt off her fingers as she looked away from the pelicans and swans gliding peacefully on water still enough to mimic glass.

'Mmm. I find it pays to put some effort into planning date number two.' Aiden turned away from the view with a smile.

'One of the rules? I'll—um—have to remember that.'

Not that she was likely to remember anything other than the look in Aiden's eyes that she could already recognise as the intention to kiss her. She barely even noticed the colourful cloud of parakeets landing on the fig tree that was shading them as Aiden leaned towards her.

The cloak of invisibility was still around them but Sophia would have forgotten about the rest of the world anyway as soon as Aiden's lips touched hers. Or maybe it was the moment she felt things change as the intensity kicked up several notches. Aiden's hand cradled her head as he pushed her back to lie on the grass. Their tongues danced, the pang of lingering salt a delicious foil to the sweetness of escalating desire. She felt the touch of Aiden's fingers beneath the hem of her shirt, a trail of fire on the delicate skin of her belly, and the heat when it reached her breast was enough to make her gasp into his mouth.

He pulled away with a groan.

'You make me forget where I am,' he murmured.

'You're on date number two,' Sophia whispered back. 'I think it's okay to get distracted. Isn't it?' she added, feeling her eyes widen.

'Yes, but there's a time and place for everything. And

this probably isn't the place for what I'm thinking about right now.'

Sophia's inward breath was audibly ragged as she sat up. She'd been thinking along similar lines and she certainly hadn't wanted him to stop. Anybody could have seen them. Like that woman with her dog, who was coming down the track towards them again, presumably on the homeward stretch of their walk. The dog—a very cute miniature schnauzer—ran towards them and the woman called it back with an apologetic smile.

'I doubt there's enough time anyway.' There was a wicked edge to Aiden's smile as the woman disappeared along the track. 'It'll get cold around here when the sun goes down.'

He wanted a whole night with her? The thought made Sophia's toes curl. But this was a daytime date.

Oh, help... What if there was a rule about not going any further until date number three? What if this three-dates business was just a build-up for a one-night stand?

Hard not to believe that it would be worth waiting for, if that was the case.

'We have options,' Aiden added. 'You get to choose.'

'Oh?' Maybe one of those options included going somewhere really private. Sophia grinned. 'Fire away. I like choosing.'

'Option one: we could take the ferry over to Sorrento to get dessert. There's a shop there that has the best vanilla slices in the world and we might get to see some dolphins on the way.'

Sophia nodded thoughtfully. He really had planned

this date carefully. Or—the thought sent a chill down her spine—was this a standard number-two date?

'Option two is a swim. The water is probably arctic but it's warm enough to dry off on the beach and, by then, it'll be about time to head home.'

Home? To his place? After getting almost naked and lying in the sun for a while? It wasn't hard to make a choice.

'It would be a shame to come to the seaside and not have a swim.'

'I knew you were brave.' The kiss was swift but sweet. 'Let's go.'

The walk made the day seem even warmer and by the time they went down the sandy stairs to the endless white beach with a misty lighthouse far away, they were more than ready to pull off their clothes and brave the curl of the surf. The beach was a popular place to be but most people were sunbathing. Some sat in beach chairs, reading, and others were having picnics or playing ball games. There were children paddling and building sand-castles but there were very few people swimming.

And no wonder. The first splash of water was cold enough to make Sophia shriek but Aiden simply laughed and dived through the next wave. She jumped up and down as she went further out, getting more of her body wet each time, and suddenly it wasn't so bad. And then Aiden surfaced right beside her and his smile made her aware of the silky caress of the sea water over her entire body.

'This is gorgeous,' she called over the sound of the waves. 'I love it.'

'I knew you would,' he called back. 'You're my kind of girl.'

They couldn't stay in the water for long and they were both shivering as they towelled themselves dry but then they lay on their towels on the soft sand and there was enough warmth in the sun for the chill to ebb slowly away.

For the longest time, they lay there, absorbing the warmth. Side by side on their backs, saying nothing. And then Sophia felt the brush of Aiden's fingers and his hand curl itself around hers.

'I really like you, Sophia.'

'I really like you, too, Aiden.' Sophia's eyes were still closed and her smile grew slowly. She couldn't remember the last time she'd felt this happy. Even the noises around them—the roll of the waves and the shouting of children enjoying themselves—only added to this feeling of contentment. 'I think this has been the best second date I've ever been on.'

Aiden tightened his grip on Sophia's hand. This was by far the best second date he'd ever been on as well. The only thing wrong with it was that it would have to end soon. They were almost dry and they needed to get dressed again because the heat of the day would start dropping rapidly before long. They had a long ride to get back to the city as well and by then it would be evening. They both had an early start for work tomorrow but did that really mean that it had to be over? Sophia believed that he'd planned this whole date after they'd agreed to go to a beach. She didn't need to know that he'd kept his options open and hadn't planned it to continue on into the evening, did she?

'It's not over yet.'

He heard the words come out of his mouth and they felt…right. Of course it couldn't be over yet.

'Oh? What else is in the plan?'

He could hear the smile in Sophia's voice. And something more. A willingness to go along with whatever he wanted?

He wanted to take Sophia home. To his bed. Okay, they both needed to get to work early but there were a lot of hours between now and then. Why shouldn't they make the most of every single one of them?

'Well, I was thinking…' Aiden propped himself up on one elbow. Maybe he didn't need to say anything here. He could just kiss her again. And then he could look into her eyes and he'd know whether she was happy with the new plan.

He let his mouth hover over hers for a deliciously long moment. Feeling the tingle of their lips not quite touching. Knowing just how much better it was going to get in a nanosecond.

And then he heard it. Faintly at first but getting steadily louder.

Sophia's lips moved under his. Tickling. 'What *is* that?'

'My phone.' He didn't want to answer it. Dammit… all he wanted to do was kiss Sophia but her lips were moving again. Smiling?

'It's a *siren*?'

'Yeah, I know. Cheesy. My kid brother chose it for me.'

And it could be that kid brother who was calling right now. Highly likely to be, seeing as they hadn't spoken yet today. In fact, they hadn't spoken very often for a few days now. Ever since that tense conversation about Aiden smothering Nate because of his misplaced guilt.

He still wanted to kiss Sophia more than answer it but something else was making his skin prickle and he recognised that sensation.

Guilt. He barely knew this woman and suddenly she was more important than his brother? What was he thinking?

'I'd better get that. Sorry.'

'No problem.'

A soft breeze had sprung up, making it colder. Or maybe he just had more skin exposed as he sat up and rummaged in his coat pocket for his phone. Sure enough, the caller ID said 'Nate'. Aiden swiped the screen.

'Hey… What's up?'

'Guess.'

'I can't. You'll have to tell me.'

'I went for the team trials today.'

'Yeah? How'd that go?'

'I got in, man. I'm in the team.'

'That's…fantastic.' The smile that pulled at his lips was genuine. 'Great news. I reckon it calls for a cele-bration.'

'Too right. We're having a few beers back at our place. Thought you might want to drop by.'

He was listening to Nate but he was looking at Sophia. She still lay on her back, shading her eyes from the sun with her arm. Her hair was still damp and looked almost

black where it lay against the pale skin of her shoulders.
He couldn't help his gaze travelling further. Over the
rest of that gorgeous, soft-looking skin and the perfect
proportions of her small, slim body.

He'd never wanted anybody this much.

He'd have to take a rain-check on that celebratory
beer with Nate because otherwise he wouldn't get to take
Sophia home and make love to her properly.

Slowly…

Or maybe not so slowly the first time…

His throat suddenly felt dry.

'You still there, man? Where *are* you, anyway?'

Impressions flashed through Aiden's brain with the
speed of light. That note in Nate's voice when he'd made
that suggestion so casually that he 'might' want to drop
by.

Things hadn't been quite right between them since
that conversation the other day. And if he didn't join in
the celebration of Nate making the Murderball team,
it could be interpreted as not being supportive of his
brother as he achieved one of his long-held ambitions and
that could push them further apart. What then? Would
Nate choose not to even tell him when he was moving
out of the house to try living independently?

His brother was trying out his wings and surely that
meant that now—more than ever—he needed support.
Aiden had to be there for him one hundred per cent.

How could he even entertain the idea of letting a
woman get between them? It wasn't as if she'd still be in
his life in a week or two from now but Nate would be. He
would always be in his life and he'd always take priority.

'I'm still here,' he said. 'Bad line. I'm out of the city but I'll be back soon.'

'No worries. You went for a ride? You on a date or something?'

'Yeah…Queenscliff.'

'Oh…of course. This is your number two with Sophia. Hey…hope I'm not interrupting anything.' His laugh made a lie of his words but didn't quite ring true for some reason.

'Not at all. Just went for swim, would you believe?'

'Well, don't hurry back, man. Enjoy yourself. Catch you soon.'

The beeping signalled that Nate had hung up. The note of disappointment in his words was still there, though. And the odd edge to the laughter as he'd tried to make light of things.

Aiden dragged his eyes away from Sophia. Closed them, in fact.

'Not a problem,' he heard himself saying into the silence of a dead line. At least he could sound reluctant now. As though there was something he really had to do even though he didn't want to. 'I'll get there as soon as I can.'

Sophia was already pulling her clothes on by the time he shoved his phone back into his pocket.

'Sorry about that.'

'It's not a problem.' He could hear the note of determined cheerfulness in her voice as she echoed his own words. 'We've had a lovely day. If there's somewhere else you need to be now, it's okay. I understand.'

She might understand but he could see the disappointment in her eyes and he felt like a jerk. He could say it wasn't that important and the only place he needed to be for now was with her.

But Nate was disappointed too. He'd have that in the back of his mind all evening if he stayed with Sophia.

The feeling of being torn was unpleasant. The desire to tell Sophia he only wanted to be with her was strong enough to ring warning bells.

It wasn't supposed to feel like this. It was supposed to be fun.

For both of them.

And it wasn't any more, was it? How could being between a rock and a hard place ever be considered fun?

He pulled his clothes on, feeling the added unpleasantness of the sand in his shoes. He watched Sophia roll up her damp towel and shove it in her beach bag.

'You dry enough? It'll be cold on the bike, otherwise.'

'I'm fine. I've got my coat.'

The coat wasn't enough to make her feel fine.

Not at all.

Maybe it would have helped if they'd been able to talk but there was no way they could do that on a bike. Sophia held onto Aiden's waist and kept her face hidden against his back. Damp tendrils of hair still flicked her face and her skin was cold enough to make them sting.

How had that happened?

One minute she'd been feeling more blissful than she could remember ever feeling and then it had all gone wrong, the atmosphere lost thanks to the intrusion of a phone call. He'd just been about to kiss her. To tell her the plans that meant the date wasn't over yet.

Why hadn't he just ignored the call? Why did he have a stupid siren call tone that made it impossible for anyone to ignore? Just as impossible as it was not to think it was probably another woman who'd been calling him. Was he already lining up the next contender in his three-dates game?

What was so fantastic about the news he'd received? Was whoever she was available? *Tonight?*

It wasn't fair. Their first date hadn't really counted and date number two had just been sabotaged.

So much for getting out there and having some fun.

This wasn't fun at all any more.

Did she even want a third—and last—date?

There was plenty of time on that long, cold ride to turn that question over in her head. As she made her stiff limbs co-operate in climbing off the big, red bike in front of her house and her fingers work well enough to undo her helmet and hand it back, Sophia was sure that this was goodbye and she had decided that she was quite happy about that.

She was, in fact, more angry than disappointed now.

But then Aiden caught her gaze and held it.

'I'm really sorry about this,' he said. 'If I could get out of it, I would.'

There was something in his gaze that told her he was being absolutely sincere. That he wanted to be with her—maybe even more than she'd wanted him to be. And that it *was* something really important that was dragging him away.

She wanted to tell him that it didn't matter. That they still had one date left so everything would be okay. That it was no big deal.

But the words wouldn't come out. She managed half a smile. A shrug that said, Yeah, it sucks but that's life, isn't it?

And then she turned away and went into her house without a backward glance, leaning her forehead against the closed door until she heard the sound of a motorbike's engine being gunned and then fading into silence.

'What are you doing here?'

Aiden held up the six-pack of beer. 'I heard there was a bit of a celebration going on.'

Nate had been the one who'd come to open the door when Aiden had rung the bell. The wide hallway of the old house was empty behind him.

'You ditched your date to come *here*?'

Aiden's shrug said that it was no big deal but Nate shook his head and his huff of sound was disgusted. 'Man, you're an idiot. How d'you think that made Sophia feel?'

The cardboard handle of the beer pack was cutting into Aiden's hand. He had been an idiot. He'd made Sophia feel bad only to find he wasn't welcome here.

Something was going wrong in his life right now. The wheels were still turning but it felt like they weren't quite on the tracks and he couldn't, for the life of him, figure out why. He looked away from Nate.

'I thought this was more important.' He cleared his throat. 'And…I wanted to…I dunno…put things right,

I guess. Wouldn't want you to think I don't support you in whatever you want to do.'

Nate gave an audible snort this time. 'It's only selection. Miss my first game next week and you'll definitely be in trouble.'

The lightness in his tone didn't match the expression on his face when Aiden turned back. Nate understood what he'd been too clumsy to articulate well and held up his hand, the fingers curled into a fist. 'There's nothing to put right, man. We're brothers. Family.'

Aiden bumped the fist with his own. Nate shook his head but he was grinning as he swivelled the chair on the polished floor. 'Seeing as you're here, you might as well come in for a beer. Hey, what do you call a quadriplegic in a pile of leaves?'

There was relief to be found as he followed Nate towards the lounge. Enough to stop the automatic protest at a joke that would seem so distasteful to people outside this community.

'I dunno. What?'

'Russell.'

There was even more relief in the shared laughter but it still wasn't quite enough to put the wheels completely back on track. Nate had said there was nothing to put right but that wasn't entirely true, was it?

Things had gone unexpectedly wrong with someone else as well. A woman he'd had no desire at all to hurt. Quite the opposite, in fact.

How on earth was he going to put that right?

CHAPTER SIX

'YOU OKAY?'

'A bit nervous, I think. I watched a Caesarean before but I've never been actually involved.'

'I won't ask you to do anything you're not ready to cope with, don't worry.'

Flick nodded, pulling her theatre cap over her dark blonde hair. She looked a bit pale, Sophia thought, which was probably nerves on top of the weariness of a long day.

She was feeling weary herself. It didn't help that she'd been feeling as flat as a pancake ever since that date with Aiden had ended on such an unsatisfactory note.

She hadn't heard from him since and the mix of disappointment and—it had to be admitted—frustration had made her wonder if the downside of dating outweighed any of the potential benefits.

She'd brushed off Flick's friendly query about how the date had gone and she'd tried really hard to focus on her work and let the satisfaction her job always gave her chase the blues away, but that hadn't worked very well today either. Not when they were now in a situation none of them had expected—or wanted—to be in.

They should be heading home by now, after the home birth of their patient Kim's second baby, but things hadn't gone according to plan and, after transferring Kim to the MMU hours ago, a Caesarean section had been deemed the best option for an exhausted mother and a now distressed baby.

Kim and her husband, Peter, were in the theatre's anteroom under the care of an anaesthetist as she received an epidural.

'Put some theatre booties on over your shoes.' Sophia pulled the disposable covers from the dispenser on the wall of the changing room. 'And here's a mask.'

'Do we have to scrub in as well?'

'No. We don't go anywhere near the operating site. Our role is to support Kim in getting the best birth experience she can under the circumstances.'

'Like making sure she gets the skin-to-skin contact?'

'Exactly. But only if the baby's well enough, of course. We have to be prepared, though. What's the most important thing to make sure we've sorted?'

'That her gown can be moved without disturbing the theatre drapes?'

'Good.' Sophia smiled at her student. 'Now, let's get moving. We've got a few things to organise. I'm going to liaise with the ward and check that a midwife is available to take transfer of care in the recovery room and I want you to ring the lab and order a bucket of iced water.'

'For the cord blood gas samples?'

'You're onto it. We've also got to check that both the

transport cot and the resuscitation cot are turned on and I want to make sure you know where all the equipment is. Follow me.'

There was a hum of activity in Theatre as the staff prepared for the surgery.

'We'll move the resuscitation cot over to here,' Sophia decided.

'Why?'

'Hopefully, it's not going to be needed, but if it is, we want a line of direct vision for both the parents so they can maintain visual contact with their baby at all times.'

Kim was wheeled in moments later. Lights were shifted and positioned and monitoring equipment attached. An ECG trace blipped into action on an overhead screen and numbers flashed and changed as they displayed heart rate, blood pressure and blood oxygen levels. Sophia showed Peter where he was allowed to stand, checked the function of the foetal monitor and then smiled at Kim.

'All good?'

'I'm scared.'

'I know.' Sophia squeezed her patient's hand, careful not to dislodge the IV line. 'You've got a fantastic team who are here to look after you and you'll be amazed how fast it goes.'

'I'm not sure any more…about…you know…'

'Watching baby come out?' Sophia glanced at the drape screen the theatre nurses were putting up at chest level. The plan had been to lower the screen after the incision to the uterus had been made but another glance showed how pale Peter was looking. A definite contender for fainting.

'You don't have to see that bit,' she told Kim. 'We can still put baby straight onto your chest.' Her gaze caught Flick's. 'Let's put a chair in for Peter. That way he can hold Kim's hand and he doesn't have to see anything he doesn't want to either.'

The surgeon and her registrar came into Theatre and, for a while at least, Sophia could totally forget about her personal life as she got caught up in one of the more dramatic ways to bring a new life into the world.

She made sure Flick could stand close enough to see what was happening as the surgeon and her registrar stood on either side of Kim's swollen abdomen. The only sounds were the beeping of the monitors and the calm requests for instruments as the initial incision was made and then the tissues quickly dissected with gloved fingers in use more often than a scalpel or scissors.

Sophia was sure that Flick was holding her breath—as she always did—when the careful incision into the uterus was made and they could see the dark whorls of wet hair on the baby's head. Forceps were fitted to lift the head far enough for the surgeon to be able to hold it with her hands and then the baby was eased out, pausing long enough for the registrar to suction the infant's airways.

The baby's eyes were open and an arm waving slowly. Sophia breathed a sigh of relief. It started crying as its legs were lifted clear of the uterus and she heard a gasp that was more like a strangled sob of relief from both Peter and Kim. Flick was focused on the registrar clamping and cutting the cord but then her gaze caught Sophia's and she gave a quick nod. She took the baby from the registrar as Flick helped a nurse to move the screen and she could place the newborn on her mother's chest.

The longest part of the surgery came now, with the precise task of repairing all the layers of tissue, but, with the screen back in place, Kim was unaware of what was happening and time ceased to matter as she and Peter touched and marvelled at their new baby.

'Did you note the time and sex of the baby?'

Flick nodded. 'I've got the labels ready for the cord blood gas samples.'

'Good. Now, double-check this with me. We have to make sure that the details on the maternal and neonatal wrist labels match.'

Thirty minutes later, Kim was ready to be transferred to a ward bed and taken into Recovery. The paediatrician had checked their daughter and she was wrapped and warm. Sophia put the small bundle into Peter's arms to be carried into Recovery. The transfer of care to the ward midwife would happen there but Sophia wasn't ready to leave yet. This was her favourite time after the tension of a Caesarean, to help with the first breastfeed and watch the bonding happening between the baby and her parents. Kim's mother was waiting nearby, too, with their three-year-old son, who would be able to come and meet his new sister before they got transferred to the ward.

'That was amazing,' Flick said quietly, when they were finally heading home. 'But I am *so* tired.' She stepped into the lift and leaned against the wall.

'Me too. This is when you really feel it, when the excitement's all over.' Sophia pushed the button to take them to the ground floor. It wasn't just physical weariness either. With the prospect of heading home alone as soon as she stepped out of the Victoria's front doors, she knew that she would end up feeling flatter than ever. 'The café will still be open. Let's go and get a coffee.'

Flick groaned. 'Oh, no…not coffee. Even the thought of it makes me feel ill.'

'Really?' Sophia's head swivelled to take a closer look at her student. 'That's not like you.' She noted the pale skin and dark circles under Flick's eyes. Something clicked into place. 'Wait…you're not pregnant, are you?'

'I think it's just something I ate.'

The lift stopped with a jerk as she spoke and then the doors slid open but was that enough to explain the way Flick was avoiding her gaze?

'I've got to go. See you tomorrow, Soph.'

'Hang on…' She'd put her foot in it, even making the suggestion, hadn't she? It certainly hadn't been her intention to upset her student. 'Hey…I'm sorry, Flick. I didn't—'

Flick raised her hand, without turning. 'It's okay. I'm fine. Really.'

'Sophia?'

The voice from behind made her spin round without thinking. It was so unexpected. So…welcome?

'Aiden… What are you doing here?'

No. It wasn't welcome. She didn't want to talk to him right now. She needed to talk to Flick. Or maybe Flick needed to talk to *her*. Turning her head again, just as quickly, she could see Flick disappearing towards the front doors. She could hardly run away from Aiden.

She didn't want to talk to him. He'd interrupted a conversation she'd been having with her student and she was on the brink of excusing herself and running away.

He didn't want that to happen. Catching sight of her as she'd stepped out of the lift had been like a slap in the face. Enough to bring back the guilt he'd been wrestling with ever since he'd cut their date short to go and see Nathan.

He'd picked up the phone half a dozen times since then, with the intention of trying to contact Sophia, but something had always got in the way. A call to a job made it easy to hang up but it was never enough of an excuse. He'd been...scared? Well, nervous anyway. He hadn't been able to come up with any plausible plan to put things right so he'd known he could well make things worse. And he hadn't wanted to face the potential rejection.

But actually seeing her instead of a faceless phone call brought back all the reasons why he wanted to put things right.

She looked tired. The way she stared after her student had a worried edge to it. And he could sense that her mood was different. More serious. Sad, even? Oh, help...was he flattering himself or could that have something to do with him?

Despite all of that—or maybe because of it—she was still the most gorgeous woman he'd ever met. He wanted to put his arms around her and hold her close. Kiss whatever it was better. But he could only say something and hope that she might choose to stay in his company for just a little longer. Long enough for him to think of something. Some way to put things right.

'I came in to check up on a patient from today,' he heard himself saying. 'Cyclist that got clipped by a tram. I was worried about her.'

'Oh…' A rush of mixed emotions washed through Sophia. The attraction that came from imagining him on the job, weaving through heavy traffic with the lights and siren going on that huge bike. Admiration that came from knowing how calmly he would have taken charge of the emergency. Warmth that came from knowing that he did care about his patients.

And there was more threaded through those feelings. She couldn't pretend that the personal attraction had been quashed by the disappointment of that last date. Maybe the strongest memory right now was the sincerity she'd seen in his eyes when he'd left her on the footpath. She'd been too angry to believe that he wouldn't have been abandoning her unless it had been for something too important to ignore, but that anger had faded into the flatness of the last few days.

She wanted to believe it now.

She wanted…

'Would you like to grab a coffee or something?' Aiden seemed to be watching her carefully, as though he was aware of the struggle she was having, trying to capture a thought that would determine her response to this unexpected meeting.

'I…um…' There was no point looking towards the

main entrance but she turned her head again anyway, despite knowing that Flick was long gone.

'Do you need to catch up with her?'

'No.' Sophia pushed her concern about her student to one side. She would see her soon enough and, if that startling suspicion had any grounds, it would only become more apparent with the passing of time. She sucked in a breath and looked back at Aiden.

'I was planning to get a coffee,' she admitted. 'It's been a long day. We had a case that got complicated and we had to bring her in for a Caesarean. And...' Something she couldn't identify was melting away deep inside her. 'I believe I still owe you a coffee?'

Aiden's smile lit up his face and she saw a flash of what looked like relief in his eyes.

'I believe you do.'

The tension eased as they began walking towards the cafeteria together but now Sophia was aware of how she must look. Her hair had been squashed beneath a cap for too long and she had crumpled scrubs on under her jacket. Any make-up she'd started the day with must have worn off long ago and she was probably tired enough to look years older.

Except that—oddly—she didn't feel that tired any more. And a sideways glance showed that Aiden's uniform was pretty crumpled as well. His boots looked scuffed and he had a big scratch on one hand.

For both of them, their appearance was nothing more than evidence of what they did for a living. A badge of honour even?

Aiden held the door of the cafeteria open for Sophia.

The relief he'd felt when she'd agreed to have a coffee with him should have been a warning but he was going to ignore it. So what if it felt like a major victory? That the wheels were back on exactly the right tracks? It shouldn't feel this good, of course. Not when all he might be winning was the chance for a third—and final—date.

But he was feeling better than he had for days so why shouldn't he make the most of it? Sophia looked happier too. She was smiling as they headed for the machine that provided coffee that was dreadful but free. She put a polystyrene cup under the dispenser.

'What can I get you?' she asked. 'Cappuccino? A latte?'

'I think a long black might be the safest choice.'

'Done.' With the button pushed the machine whirred into life. 'And I think I might push the boat out and have a hot chocolate.'

There would be a rush before too long, when staff on an early dinner break came in, but, for now, the cafeteria was almost completely deserted. They found a table in the corner and sat down. Sophia was at right angles to Aiden. Their knees bumped under the table and the eye contact they made was instantaneous. And intense enough to make her heart skip a beat.

'This doesn't count as a date,' she murmured.

'Of course not.' Aiden nodded, his face serious. 'It wasn't planned so how could it be?'

'Mmm.'

'And besides…we never got to finish date number two, did we?'

'Ah…' The tension was back again. They had to both

be thinking of that moment. Not that any words had been spoken but Sophia could actually feel the impression of that half-smile she'd summoned. The dismissive way she'd shrugged and turned away. 'No...' She had to drop her gaze. 'It didn't feel finished.'

'We should do something about that, then.'

It took courage to meet his gaze. 'Yes. I think maybe we should.'

The intensity humming between them bore no relation to the casual words from Aiden.

'I've got a thing I have to go to tomorrow night. Would you like to come with me?'

'What sort of a thing?'

Not that it mattered. She would have agreed to go anywhere with him.

Or maybe it did matter. A flicker of something in Aiden's face made Sophia realise that, whatever it was, it was important to him. That he was inviting her into a part of his life that might not be something he shared with just anyone. That he was taking a risk?

'A surprise,' he said, after that tiny hesitation. 'If I tell you what it is, that would make it more like a new date and it's not. It's—'

'A half-date?' Sophia suggested.

'Just a thing. Let's not try and define it.'

'Okay.'

'So you'll come?'

'Sure. How could I resist? I've never been to a "thing" before. I'm intrigued.'

'Don't get too excited. It's a bit...different.'

'I'm even more intrigued now. Give me a clue?'

'Uh-uh.' Aiden shook his head but he was smiling. 'I'll pick you up at seven-thirty.'

'Dress code?'

'Definitely casual. And warm.' Aiden took a sip of his coffee and made a face. 'This is awful. I don't even think it deserves to be called coffee.'

A bubble of happiness made Sophia giggle. 'Guess I still owe you one, then.'

Aiden's nod was thoughtful. 'I'll put this in the category of medication. Something to wake me up after a tough day.'

'So what happened? How badly injured was your cyclist?'

'Multi-trauma. She's up in Intensive Care now but I wanted to see what had been found. The head injury made her combative so it was hard to assess her.'

Sophia nodded. She had plenty of questions and was genuinely interested in the responses as Aiden told her more about the case, but there was an undercurrent that made it all so much more enjoyable.

She was going to see him again tomorrow night.

They were going to a *thing*…

Parking outside a suburban gymnasium was a surprise. So the 'thing' was a sporting event of some kind? This was weird but Sophia was prepared to keep an open mind, especially when Aiden took her hand to lead her inside.

And there was another surprise. The seats were crowded and the atmosphere loud and vibrant but the last thing she'd expected to see were the teams on the basketball-style court. They were all young men and they were all in wheelchairs.

'What is this?'

'Murderball.' Aiden waved to a girl with spiky black hair and facial piercings who was in the first row of seats. 'Wheelchair rugby.' He led her towards some empty seats in the third row. 'It's my brother's first game.'

Wow. No wonder she'd got the impression that this was a private part of Aiden's life.

'Your brother is paraplegic?'

'Tetraplegic. You have to have disability in all four limbs to qualify to play.'

'But…' Sophia stared at the activity below as she took her seat. The team members were rolling across the floor with some doing fast spins, looking like they were warming up. They were definitely using their hands and arms.

'There's a scale,' Aiden told her. 'The level of disability is graded from zero point five, which is the greatest restriction, to three point five. If you were able-bodied you'd score five and if you were totally paralysed you'd be a zero. There are four on the court at any one time and they have to have a total score between them of no more than eight points.'

The teams were lining up, face to face in the centre of the court, and then they peeled off, high-fiving each other.

'Which one is your brother?'

'Number three for the Melbourne Mobsters. The red and black team. He's not going to be on in the first quarter. He may not get on at all but I hope he does. This is his first game.'

'Oh…' That made it even more of a big deal to be here. No wonder Aiden was looking tense, with his jaw knotted and his focus intently on the court. Sophia slipped her hand over his to give it a squeeze and found it caught and gripped hard.

'What's his name?' Sophia grinned. 'Just so I can yell when he scores a goal.'

'Nathan. Nate.'

A whistle blew and the referee threw a ball high in the air and then it was all on. A player for the Canberra Cowboys put the ball on his lap and sped away from the others to cross the goal line between cones. A cheer erupted from the crowd but it was nothing on the noise level when one of the local boys scored less than a minute later.

The game was fast and furious and Sophia was hooked well before the first quarter ended. She gasped at the first collision she saw between three players going for the ball that made the chairs tip and her jaw dropped when one player fell backwards with a crash, but the game carried on with a supporter rushing onto the court to right the upturned chair, and within seconds the fall was forgotten.

A hooter sounded to signal the rolling rotation of the players but Nathan wasn't one of the new team members. Sophia tried to figure out the rules but the game was so fast, she was having trouble. This was like a mix of basketball, rugby and bumper cars.

'Why do they bounce the ball sometimes?'

'You have to either bounce it or pass it to someone else within ten seconds.'

'What happened there?'

'Penalty awarded for a foul. That cowboy hit a mobster's chair behind the main axle, which makes it spin out of control.'

Scores jumped quickly but stayed close. The noise level steadily increased until Sophia had to shout to be heard as the final quarter began.

'That's Nathan. He's *on*.'

She'd barely known this game existed before coming here tonight, but suddenly it felt personal. Nathan looked a lot younger than Aiden and he looked a bit nervous. Sophia felt nervous herself. The chairs were clearly designed to cope with the impacts with their metal bumpers and spoke guards. And the players wore gloves and elbow protection but surely there was a huge potential for injury down there?

Aiden obviously thought so too, given the way he winced visibly the first time Nathan's chair got hit. But, moments later, a wide overhead pass from the other side of the court saw Nathan catch the ball and dump it on his lap. He spun his chair on the spot and took off, his arms almost a blur as he powered towards the goal line. Three other chairs converged on his path but he saw them as he looked up to bounce the ball off to one side. With another lightning-fast spin, he changed direction and had a clear line to speed towards the cones.

The cheer was the loudest yet. Maybe because she and Aiden were both on their feet, yelling at the tops of their voices. She saw the girl in the front row, who'd waved at Aiden when they arrived, leaping about and waving two huge pompoms in the red and black team colours.

The Melbourne Mobsters lost by two points but it didn't seem to matter. The crowd was happy to cheer any of the players who came close enough to the spectators to receive a high five or a kiss from a girlfriend. Still holding Sophia's hand, Aiden pulled her towards the front row as a chair rolled directly towards them. Nathan got a kiss from the girl with the spiky black hair and then a fist bump and a one-armed hug from his brother.

'You made it. Didn't see you up there, bro.'

'Wouldn't have missed it for the world. You rocked it, man.'

Sophia nodded her agreement, unable to wipe the grin off her face. 'Most exciting game I've ever watched,' she said. 'Of anything.'

Nathan Harrison's eyes were the same unusual shade of brown as Aiden's and they had the same ability to focus with instant intensity. The slow grin was eerily familiar as well.

'You have to be Sophia,' he said.

She nodded again but didn't miss the glance that flicked between the brothers. Or the disconcerting way Nathan was shaking his head as he looked back, still grinning.

He must have seen her confusion. 'Sorry. It's just that it's the first time I've met one of Aiden's girlfriends. He doesn't usually give me the honour.'

Because a three-dates rule didn't allow for inclusion in a private part of his life? She hadn't imagined that hesitation in inviting her, had she? Or underplayed the

significance? But she had no idea whether it meant anything. Or whether she even wanted it to mean anything.

The moment could have been incredibly awkward but
it was the girl beside Nathan who saved it.

'There's a first time for everything,' she declared.
'Otherwise nothing would ever change.' She grinned at
Sophia. 'I'm Sam,' she said. 'And I'm delighted to meet
you—which is what Nate's really trying to say.'

'I knew that.' It was impossible to miss the significance in the glance Sam shared with Nathan. Their love
for each other was blindingly obvious.

So was the bond between the brothers. Aiden declined the invitation to join the team and supporters at
a local bar, saying he had a horribly early start the next
day, but she could hear the fierce pride in his voice when
they took their leave.

'You did good, man. Can't wait for the next game.'

Aiden could feel the remnants of a ridiculously proud
smile he'd been suppressing as he started up the old van
he'd used to collect Sophia that evening. He could also
feel the way she was looking at him. The intensity was
almost palpable.

'Aiden?'

'Yeah?'

'That call you got at the beach the other day.'

'Yeah?' Oh, help. He'd hoped that had been forgotten
by now. That he'd put things right. It had needed something special and inviting her into a part of his life he'd
never shared with a woman had seemed like the way to
go, but maybe he'd been wrong.

Maybe he was still in the dog box.

'Was it a call from Nathan?'

'Um…yeah…' He turned his head, the query of why she was asking on the tip of his tongue but the word never escaped.

He didn't need to ask why.

She understood.

She might not have any idea why the bond was so strong between him and Nathan but she knew it was there and how important it was.

Weirdly, he could feel something inside his chest crack and something warm seeped out.

Something really nice.

He did have a really early start tomorrow but that hadn't been the real reason for declining the after-game social occasion with the team. He'd known he wanted to take Sophia home and be alone with her.

And the desire to do that had just leapt right off the scale.

CHAPTER SEVEN

THIS WAS THE way the last date should have ended.

Once again, Sophia was pressed against her front door the moment it shut behind her but she wasn't standing there with her head bowed, listening to the sound of a fading engine.

This time, it was her back against the door. And her arms, as she lifted them in a helpless gesture, unable to think of anything else to do with them as she met the intensity of the kiss she was receiving.

Who knew that you could actually *taste* desire? Was it her own or Aiden's or the chemical reaction of mixing them that made this so incredibly delicious?

For the longest time, that was enough. The silky glide of tongue against tongue. The endless variations of pressure in lips that was a conversation all by itself. But then Aiden's hands left her neck, where they'd been cradling her head, and they trailed down to cup her breasts. His lips left hers to touch the soft skin below her ear where she could feel her own pulse pounding and suddenly it wasn't enough.

Not nearly enough.

And she knew what to do with her arms, now, too. She could wrap them around his neck and run her fingers through the softness of that closely cropped hair. Press her lips against that vulnerable spot on his temple.

She couldn't say who started moving first. If it hadn't been her, Aiden didn't seem to have any problem finding her bedroom, but it was a tiny house. The interruption of removing clothes felt like a nuisance and Sophia hastily stripped off her sweater at the same time Aiden peeled off his leather jacket. They both kicked off their shoes but then they looked at each other and abandoned undressing to kiss again.

And time seemed to stop. Taking their clothes off was no longer a nuisance. It was a game to be savoured. A slow reveal of buttons coming undone and zips being separated. Exposed skin that needed exploring. Touching and kissing with murmurs of appreciation and the odd whimper of escalating desire.

Too soon—and not nearly soon enough—they were in her bed and now there were no limits on the touching. No stopping the roller-coaster of sensation that was pushing them towards ecstasy. The interruption of Aiden leaning over the side of the bed to find his discarded jeans and fish in the pocket for a foil packet was unbearable.

There's no need, Sophia wanted to say. *Don't stop.*

But, of course, she didn't say it. And it wasn't entirely true, anyway. Okay, there was no way she could get pregnant but there were other reasons to use protection…

And maybe that was why she found the interruption unbearable. She didn't want to have to think about anything like that—even for the few seconds it took.

Easy to forget about it again, though. To cry out with the pleasure of feeling him inside her and then to simply surrender to the mounting tension that was taking them both to that place like no other. Where the world could stop turning for as long as it took.

It took quite a while for either of them to get their breath back as they lay there, their limbs entangled and the only sound their rapid panting.

'Oh, my God,' Sophia whispered, when words were finally available. 'How did you *do* that?'

'I was going to ask you the same thing.' There was a smile in Aiden's voice as he eased himself free. He didn't let go of Sophia, though, and she found herself rolling onto to her side, with her head cradled against his chest. 'You're amazing. You do know that, don't you?'

She could feel the edge of his nipple against her lips as she smiled. 'I do now. You're pretty amazing yourself.'

He pressed his lips to the top of her head. 'Maybe it was the combination.'

'Mmm.' Post-coital drowsiness was enveloping Sophia. She could feel herself relaxing into sleep and the thought that she would wake in Aiden's arms was blissful.

But he moved, just a little. 'I should go,' he murmured. 'I wasn't kidding about the early start.'

'You don't have to.'

The soft sound was regretful. 'But I know exactly what would happen if I stayed and I only had one condom in my pocket.'

The temptation to say something was even stronger this time. 'You don't need to worry about me getting pregnant.'

He moved enough to break the contact between their bodies. 'Don't take it personally but I've never relied on anyone else for contraception and I'm not about to break that rule.'

'Oh...' Sophia could feel the chill of exposed skin. And then she felt the dip of her mattress as Aiden sat up and swung his legs over the side of the bed.

He turned then but it was too dark to read his expression. 'I'm never going to have kids,' he said quietly. 'I had to be a father to Nate when he was growing up and that was enough. More than enough.'

There was a world of pain behind those words. But there was also a warning note. He'd shared more than his body with her tonight. He'd shared a lot of his personal life but there were limits. This wasn't something he was ready to talk about.

He leaned towards her and gave her a swift kiss. 'I do have to go.'

'Okay.'

Sophia listened to the sounds of him getting dressed again. She sat up, pulling the duvet around her like a shawl.

'It was the best half-date I've ever been on,' she told him. 'Thank you.'

The glimmer of his smile gave her the impression she'd said exactly the right thing. Not pushing him to talk any more about his 'rules' or the reason they were so iron-clad.

He came close and this time the kiss lingered.

'Just as well it was a half-date,' he said. 'That means we still have one left.'

One.

Sophia's heart sank.

'Would it count as a date if we didn't go anywhere? Like—if you came round for dinner one night or something?'

Something like a chuckle rumbled in Aiden's chest. 'I don't reckon it would. Do you?'

'No.' Sophia injected complete authority into her voice. 'I'm quite sure it wouldn't. Give me your phone number and I'll text you when I've had time to go shopping.'

Finding time to go grocery shopping wasn't so hard because there were supermarkets that regularly stayed open until at least midnight.

Finding time to cook something as amazing as Sophia wanted it to be was another matter. With what felt like a blinding flash of inspiration, a couple of days later she remembered the slow cooker tucked away at the back of one of her kitchen cupboards. Perfect. Getting up a little earlier to get ready for work, she had time to sear meat and brown the vegetables and then all she had to do was push the button and let the cooker work its magic while she worked with Flick for another busy day of home visits.

The concern about her student was still there but had been pushed into the background. Flick had dismissed her reaction to coffee after that Caesarean case as being due to a bit of a tummy bug and Sophia had been embarrassed that she'd blurted out the first suspicion that had sprung to mind—that Flick might be pregnant. The fact that she'd been pale and quiet for a few days after that fitted with her having been off colour and if she still seemed on the quiet side now, that could well be due to the extra studying she was doing. Flick seemed determined to learn everything about her chosen career and today was a great one for introducing her to things she hadn't done before.

It was good for her to have her teaching to distract her, as well. If she hadn't had Flick in the car with her as she negotiated the heavy traffic in places, she might have been tempted to wonder about how that meal was progressing as it simmered gently.

Or notice the desire that was simmering a little less gently deep in her belly. Would they go to bed again? Or maybe the real question was when and not if. Before or after dinner?

The car jerked a little with the firm pressure of her foot on the accelerator. 'What do you think is the most important thing about the postnatal care we give for up to six weeks after birth?'

'Support,' Flick answered promptly. 'Help with things like breastfeeding and bathing baby and how to cope with fatigue.'

'And?'

'Monitoring the health of both the baby and the mother. Especially after a Caesarean in case of infection. And making sure they don't think that breastfeeding is a reliable form of contraception.'

Hmm. Expanding on that topic was not going to help her stay focused. 'Good. What else do we do?'

'Watch out for signs of postnatal depression?'

They discussed the kind of signs that could be important as Sophia drove them to their first visit of the day but their first mother—Judith—seemed to be coping extremely well, having had a home birth two days ago.

'I'm lucky I've got Mum staying. I'm getting plenty of sleep between feeds.'

'Looks like baby's getting plenty of sleep, too.' Sophia smiled at the tiny, perfect face peeping from the folds of blanket in Judith's arms.

'I've been a bit worried about today's visit, though. I'm not sure I want her to have the test.' Judith's voice wobbled. 'It's going to hurt her, isn't it?'

'They usually cry,' Sophia said gently. 'But I think it's more about having their foot held still than any pain. It's a tiny prick. And the crying helps. It makes the blood come out faster so the test is over quickly.'

'It's important, Jude.' Their patient's mother was sitting nearby. She looked over at Sophia. 'There's all sorts of diseases it can test for, aren't there? Treatable things?'

'Absolutely. More than twenty different disorders, in fact.'

'Like what?'

'Maybe Flick can tell you about some of them.' Sophia smiled encouragingly at her student.

'There's hypothyroidism,' Flick said. 'And cystic fibrosis. And the enzyme disorders that prevent the normal use of milk.'

'And amino acid disorders,' Sophia added. 'Things

that can lead to something like brain damage if they're not picked up but which can be easily treated by following a special diet.'

'But she's not going to need a special diet for ages. I'm breastfeeding. Can't we put the test off until then?'

'It needs to be done as soon as possible after baby is forty-eight hours old.' Sophia checked her watch. 'And that's right about now.'

'I'll hold her, if you like,' Judith's mother offered. 'Why don't you go and have a quick shower or something?'

'No.' Judith closed her eyes. 'If it has to be done, I want to be the one holding her. Let's just get it over with.'

Flick stored the card with its four blood spots in Judith's file. 'I'd better remember to take that to the lab later,' she told Sophia as they drove to their next appointment. She shook her head. 'Poor Judith. I think she cried more than the baby did. Imagine how hard the six-week vaccinations are going to be for her.'

'Remind me to give her some pamphlets about that on our next visit. And we'll talk to her about how important it is.'

They had a hearing screening test to do on a final visit to a six-week-old baby later that morning and a lesson in hand-expressing breast milk for a young mother in the afternoon.

'I want my partner to share the night feeds,' she told them. 'And he really wants to, don't you, John?'

The young father nodded. The look and smile he gave his partner was exactly what Sophia would want for herself. Overflowing with love and a determination to

provide support—even if it meant sacrificing sleep. Un-
accountably, an image of Aiden filled her mind. How
ridiculous was that? He was so against the idea of ever
having a baby that he wouldn't trust anyone else to deal
with contraception.

'But I really hate the thought of using one of those
breast pumps,' the mother continued. 'It's so…mechani-
cal.'

'Hand expression isn't hard. We'll show you how to
do it.'

Flick took notes as Sophia provided the instruction.
By the end of the day she'd also had plenty of practice
taking blood pressures and temperatures on mothers,
weighing babies and filling in report forms.

'You're getting very competent,' Sophia told her.
'You'll be doing all this on your own in no time.'

'Thanks. I'm loving it.' Flick opened her mouth as
though about to say something else but then she merely
smiled. 'See you tomorrow, Soph. Have a good night.'

Sophia smiled back. 'I intend to. You have one too.'

'Oh, man…that has to be the most amazing thing I've
ever smelt.'

As an icebreaker, on opening the door to her dinner
guest, this was enough to make Sophia smile and stop
wondering about what was going to happen before or
after they ate.

'Let's hope it tastes as good as it smells.' At least
that was something she was pretty sure she didn't need
to worry about. She'd been pretty impressed herself to
come home to the aroma of those slow-cooked lamb

shanks with red wine and mushrooms. The potatoes were cooking now and all she needed to do was mash them and dinner would be ready.

They had time to relax and, seeing as Aiden was holding out a bottle of very nice wine, it would have been rude not to taste it.

'Come in. I've got the fire going. It's pretty cold out there tonight, isn't it?'

'Sure is.' Aiden went straight to the flames of the small gas fire and stood with his back to it, his hand fanned out to catch the heat. He looked around. 'This is really nice.' His grin grew. 'Can't say I really noticed the other night.'

That grin—along with a ghost of a wink—chased away any lingering awkwardness over this date that wasn't a date. Suddenly, Sophia felt completely comfortable in his company. No, it was more than that. Being with him in this small, book-filled room with the smell of hot food and the sound of rain on the roof felt…well, it felt like *home*.

'It is nice, isn't it? Most of this stuff isn't mine, though. I'm house-sitting for a nurse at the Victoria who's gone overseas for a year. Sad to say, the year's half-over now. I'll have to start thinking about finding a place of my own before too long.'

'Where were you before this?' Aiden took the corkscrew Sophia handed him and dealt expertly with opening the wine while she took a couple of steps back into the kitchen to fetch glasses.

'Canberra. It's where I grew up.'

'You've got family there?' Aiden poured the wine.

'Just my parents. Dad's a pharmacist and Mum's a teacher.' Sophia sat down on the sofa and it felt good when Aiden came to sit beside her. 'How 'bout you?'

'No folks. There's just me and Nate. Mum died due to complications with his birth.'

'Oh…that's awful. Do you remember her?'

'Yeah…' For a second, Sophia could see the pain of that loss in his eyes but then his gaze slid sideways, as though he knew he might be revealing too much. 'Not as well as I'd like to, though. I was only six when she died.' He took a huge swallow of his wine.

Sophia's heart ached for the little boy who'd lost his mother. She'd never lost one of her maternity patients but she knew it still happened in rare cases and she could imagine how terrible it would be for the whole family.

'That smell is driving me mad.' Aiden's tone had a forced cheerfulness to it. An attempt to dispel any negative vibe? 'I didn't get time for lunch today.'

'Oh…' Maybe she couldn't do anything to comfort that little boy of years gone by but she could certainly fix this. 'Let's eat. Why don't you choose some music to put on while I mash the potatoes?'

His choice was surprising. 'You went for vinyl?'

'Retro, huh? The girl who owns this place is really into the old stuff.'

Sophia laughed. 'It's more like she's never thrown anything out. Dot's in her early sixties. At least you chose one of my favourites. I adore Cat Stevens.'

'Me, too.' Aiden took the plate from her hands but held her gaze. 'And how did you know that lamb shanks are my all-time favourite food?'

The warmth in that gaze made the pleasure of approval all the more intense and Sophia had to break the eye contact. 'Lucky guess. Or maybe we just have a lot in common.'

The food tasted just as good as it had smelled. The flames on the fake logs of the gas fire danced merrily and the music was the perfect background. All that was missing, Sophia decided, was candlelight.

Except wouldn't that make it too romantic to be a non-date? And what could she talk about that wouldn't take them into ground that might be deemed too personal and put it into the same category?

'You must have had a busy day, if you didn't get time for lunch.'

'Sure did. Two cardiac arrests, one straight after the other, would you believe?'

'Did you get them back?'

'Transported the first one with a viable rhythm but I think the downtime had been too long. The second guy woke up after the third shock and wanted to know what all the fuss was about.'

'No, really?'

'Yeah...' Aiden refilled their glasses and then raised his in a toast. 'Doesn't happen very often but when it does, it makes it all worthwhile. Even missing lunch.' He picked up his fork again. 'Did I tell you how amazing this is? I can't even mash potatoes without leaving lumps in.'

Sophia smiled. 'Tell me about the save. How old was he? Was there bystander CPR happening when you got there?'

Aiden told her about the successful case in so much detail she felt like she'd been standing there, watching the drama.

'You're really good at that.'

'What?'

'Telling a story. You could write a book about your job and people would want to read it.'

Aiden shook his head. 'I've just had practice, that's all. Nathan is a frustrated paramedic, I think. He always wants every gory detail about everything and doesn't let me get away with leaving stuff out. It's become a habit.'

Sophia forgot about any boundaries she might have been watching so that they could keep this time light. And fun. There was such a strong undercurrent to Aiden's words. It had the strength of showing the bond between the brothers in that Aiden was so used to sharing every detail of his life with Nathan, but it had rocks and rapids in it, too. Did Nathan resent that Aiden was out in the world, doing such an exciting and physical job, while he was trapped in a wheelchair? Did Aiden feel guilty about it?

'How did it happen?' she heard herself asking quietly. 'How did Nate become a quadriplegic?'

Aiden stopped chewing his mouthful of food and swallowed. Carefully. He reached for his glass of wine but didn't look at Sophia.

'He got pushed down a set of stairs.' His voice was flat.

'Oh, my God…' If she'd still had any appetite, it evaporated at that moment. 'How old was he?'

'Ten.'

A ten-year-old boy who'd probably loved to ride his bike and play soccer or rugby. A boy who'd already had it tough by having to grow up without his mother.

An echo of those sombre words Aiden had spoken the other night slipped into her head.

I had to be a father to Nate when he was growing up and that was enough. More than enough.

Had he been referring to the growing up before that dreadful accident or the trauma of readjustment that would have come afterwards?

She had so many questions she wanted to ask but didn't dare push further into such personal territory. The silence grew. Aiden was staring at his wineglass.

'Must have been drinking on such an empty stomach that did it,' he mused. 'I never talk about this.'

Then he looked up and caught Sophia's gaze. 'Or maybe it's because I'm with you.'

Something inside her melted into a liquid warmth. Some of it reached her eyes and she knew she'd have to blink a lot to make sure it didn't escape and roll down her cheeks. Her voice came out as a whisper.

'You can tell me anything. Or not. You're safe, either way.' She tried to smile but it didn't quite work.

Aiden wasn't smiling either. He felt like he was drowning in that moisture he could see collecting in Sophia's eyes. The *caring* behind them hit him like an emotional brick and tugged at something long forgotten. Poignant.

Did it remind him of the way his mother had looked at him, maybe?

'It was my father who pushed him down the stairs,' he found himself telling her. 'And it was my fault.'

The shock on her face was all too easy to read and Aiden cringed inwardly. He shouldn't have told her. She would think less of him. As little as he thought of himself?

But then her face changed. She looked like she was backing away even though she didn't move a single muscle.

'I don't believe that,' she said. 'Not one bit.'

How could she say that with such conviction? She barely knew him and she knew nothing of what had happened. A flash of anger made it easy to unchain words.

'My father was an alcoholic. He resented having to raise kids on his own and he blamed Nathan for causing Mum's death. He was a bully and he got really nasty when he was drinking, which was pretty much every day.'

The horror of that childhood was written all over Sophia's face. He could see it that way himself now, with the benefit of hindsight but, at the time, it had just been how things were.

'I knew how to handle him. I learned how to keep Nate safe. But that day? I was sixteen and I'd had enough. Instead of trying to defuse him, I flipped the coin. I started yelling at him and telling him just what a miserable bastard he was. I knew I had to get out of the house before I attacked him physically and I'd almost made it to the front door.' He had to stop for a second. To swallow past the constriction in his throat. 'He came after me but Nate was trying to follow me, too, and he was at the top of the stairs. Dad pushed him to get past and he fell.'

'You *saw* it happen?' Sophia's words were raw. Had she even thought before she reached out and covered his hand with her own? The warmth and pressure of that human contact almost undid Aiden but he couldn't pull his hand away. Instead, he turned it over and threaded his fingers through hers to lock them together.

'That wasn't the worst of it. I didn't know how badly hurt Nate was but I knew not to let him move before the ambulance could get there. So I held his head and kept him still and told him that everything would be okay. And then…and then…'

He could feel the tension in her hand. The terrible anticipation.

'And then we heard it. I didn't even know he had a gun in the house. Just as well, maybe, given how much I hated him that day. But I never had to think about killing him again. He did it himself.'

He choked on those last words. He'd never told anybody this story. Ever. Something was breaking inside his chest. Making him shake. Forcing a kind of horrible, dry sobbing sound to come out of his throat. He had his eyes screwed tightly shut so he didn't see Sophia standing up but he felt the tug on his hand and it was easy to comply with the silent instruction because he had no idea of what to do. How to deal with this awful emotional tidal wave.

How did Sophia know what to do?

She was tiny but he could feel an enormous strength

in the way she wrapped her arms around him and held him so tightly. He had no idea how long they stood there like that but it was long enough for the wave to recede. And now it felt like a huge expanse of sand that had been washed clean.

Deserted. And amazingly peaceful.

He loosened the grip of his arms around Sophia. How had she managed to keep breathing for so long?

'Sorry. I shouldn't have dumped all that on you.'

'I'm glad you did.' She moved a little in his arms so that she could look up at him. 'And, Aiden?'

'Yeah?'

'I was right.'

'What about?'

'It wasn't your fault. Not one bit of it.'

The anger was gone but he could still feel disappointed. Sophia was taking Nathan's side. Was there nobody out there who could understand? See the truth the way he saw it? He stepped back. Could he make some excuse and simply leave?

No. One look at Sophia and he was caught.

'I know why you think that,' she said. 'And when you love someone, it's easy to find a way to take the blame when something bad happens to them, but this wasn't your fault. It was your father's fault.'

'I *provoked* him.'

'And how many times did you *not* provoke him? You'd been living with that for ten years. You'd found every way under the sun to keep your little brother safe. Confronting your father and escaping would have been the only way to make sure of that in the long run and I think you'd finally got old enough to know that, even if it was subconscious. Okay, it went horribly wrong but it was a brave thing to do. How old were you?'

'Sixteen.' Aiden could barely get the word out. He was trying to process what she was saying. Was there any truth in it?

He'd been *brave*?

No way…

'There you go.' Sophia's smile was heartbreakingly tender. 'Just a kid yourself.' She raised her eyebrows. 'Was that when you decided you wanted to be a paramedic?'

'Yeah… They were amazing. I think they looked after me just as much as they looked after Nate. It's something I have in the back of my mind with every job I go to. It's not just the person who's sick or hurt that's your patient. The people who love them are too.'

'And that's part of what makes you so good at your job. No wonder Nate wants to hear your stories.'

That was how this had all started, wasn't it. Aiden jerked his gaze to the table. To the half-eaten meals of that delicious food Sophia had prepared.

'I'm sorry,' he said again. 'I kind of ruined dinner, didn't I?'

'It was my fault,' Sophia said. 'I asked the questions that got you started.'

'I didn't have to tell you. I chose to. Because I wanted to.'

The look he was receiving could only have come from a woman.

'Mmm…okay. I accept that it wasn't my fault.'

In the heartbeat of silence that followed, Aiden made the connection. And found himself smiling, albeit reluctantly.

'How 'bout I zap those plates in the microwave? You still hungry?'

He couldn't look away from her eyes. He was drowning again but this time it came with a lick of fire that would evaporate any moisture.

'Oh, yeah…I'm hungry.'

He caught her hand as she turned towards the table.

'But not for food.'

She gave a tiny gasp as he pulled her into his arms and bent his head to taste her lips. And then she melted against him and he knew, with absolute certainty, that things were going to be all right. He didn't have to leave. Didn't want to.

Things were going to be better than all right, in fact.

Life itself seemed to have just become that much better.

CHAPTER EIGHT

This was nothing like last time.

Oh, the desire was the same. That being carried away on a wave of physical sensation that led to ultimate satisfaction, but there was something very different about the way Sophia could feel herself responding.

This physical nakedness had come in the wake of emotional nakedness on Aiden's part. He'd opened his heart to her and made himself vulnerable and it made her want to protect him, even as her own heart broke to think of what his childhood had been like. Weird how it could break but swell at the same time as she saw the depth of the love he had for his brother.

No wonder he shied away from any other responsibilities in his life—like a relationship that lasted more than three dates. Or having a child of his own.

And the guilt he'd carried with him ever since that accident. Was it more than not wanting extra responsibilities? Was he preventing anyone else getting too close as a kind of penance?

She'd told him he was safe to tell her anything and he had. Way more than she'd expected.

He deserved the same kind of honesty from her. To know that he was safe from more than any emotional repercussions of being close, but something stopped her saying anything when he tore open the foil packet of the condom.

It would spoil the moment, she told herself. Bring the rush of escalating desire to a grinding halt and maybe it was more than simply desire for Aiden at the moment. Maybe he needed the intimacy as a kind of reassurance. A reminder that he deserved the good things in life because of who he was.

The good things in life.

Like being loved…

No. Sophia had to shut down the realisation because it was blinding. And terrifying. Far easier to stop thinking and simply feel. To give herself up to the touch of Aiden's hands and mouth. To give in to her own need to feel the closest physical touch possible from another being.

It came back, though, in those quiet minutes of lying there entangled in each other's arms, as heart and breathing rates gradually settled back to normal.

No. This was nothing like last time. Because this had been more than sex. More than having fun. On her part, it had been making love.

Aiden had opened his heart to her and she had fallen into it. Fallen in love with him.

This wasn't supposed to have happened. How could it, when you knew right from the start that it was only going to last for three dates?

* * *

He'd fallen asleep.

He hadn't meant to. He never stayed a whole night because it was one of the rules. He'd learned long ago that it added a depth that made things more difficult when it was time to move on because it gave the impression that he might be happy to stay longer. That it was about more than a bit of fun.

He'd taken the fun element out of the evening himself, though, hadn't he? Spilling his guts like that about Nate. About his father.

Good grief…he'd never told a woman any of that stuff.

But she'd told him it was safe and nobody had ever said that to him before.

And he'd *felt* safe.

He'd even felt…absolved from the guilt for just a heartbeat. The way she'd twisted the idea of being at fault and tipped it towards being someone else's choice.

There was a truth in that. Maybe he'd be able to catch that feeling of absolution again one day. It had been too huge not to push away at the time, though. To shut off everything except the need to take Sophia to bed. To try and thank her for what she'd given him? It wasn't surprising he'd fallen asleep after the roller-coaster of emotions that had been stirred up and then released. Physical release had been the last push into a totally new feeling of being at peace.

Safe.

Such a roller-coaster. Like that extraordinary sensation he'd had when she'd told him he'd been brave.

Brave?

She admired him? Remembering it now gave him that same weird feeling of being…what…special? But she didn't know the truth of it, did she? How scared he'd been so often. The way he'd taken Nathan under his bed sometimes and held the toddler close until he'd known that his father had been drunk enough to be no threat for the rest of the night. How he'd stolen money from their dad's wallet so he could buy a toy for Nate's birthday. How often he'd wagged school or lied about being sick so that he could make sure the housekeeper was taking proper care of his brother.

She wouldn't think he was brave if she'd known the awful relief he'd felt when it had become clear after the accident that Nathan would have to be cared for by people far more qualified than he was. That all he needed to do was visit him every day. That he was free to follow the dream that had been born on that dreadful night and become a paramedic so he could help others.

He'd created exactly the life he'd dreamed of but he had hurt other people along the way, he knew that. Some women in the past had been angry. Had accused him of using them. Others had been upset and the tears had been harder to handle than angry words.

How would Sophia react when they'd had their third—and last—date?

The last thing he wanted was to make her cry.

Even thinking about it made him hold her a little tighter as she lay in his arms, with her head tucked against his chest. The movement made her stir and make a tiny sound, almost like a cat purring.

He loved that sound.

'Mmm.' This was more like a word and it was followed by a slow, deep indrawn breath that was painted into sensation by the small hand that moved across his chest.

'You're still here,' Sophia whispered. 'That's nice.'

'Mmm.' He had to agree. It *was* nice.

'What time is it?'

'I don't know. Close to dawn, I think. The birds are getting noisy.'

'We don't have to get up yet, though.' Her hand was moving again. The soft touch reached his abdomen and Aiden could feel his body coming a lot more awake.

'We don't.' Okay, maybe this wasn't the best idea but how could he resist? 'Just as well I came prepared this time.' His jeans weren't far away. There was another foil packet in the back pocket.

He couldn't miss the way Sophia stilled in his arms, though. The way the fuzzy sense of sleepy peacefulness took on a spiky edge.

'What?' The word was no more than a puzzled murmur. Had he done the wrong thing in being prepared for more than once?

'I…' The hesitation lasted long enough for Sophia to take another deep breath. He could feel the press of her breast against his hand swell and then recede. 'I meant what I said the other night. You don't need it.'

Whoa… This was a step into totally forbidden territory. He didn't care what precautions any woman took. He had to know he was taking responsibility for contraception himself.

The desire for sex was ebbing fast. He needed to escape. Carefully, he started pulling his arm away from where it encircled Sophia but he had no idea what he could say. How he could stop this becoming an unpleasant conversation for both of them.

But he didn't have to find anything to say because Sophia spoke first.

'I can't get pregnant, Aiden. I had a hysterectomy nearly ten years ago.'

'What? *Why?*' Oh, God...had she had cancer? The idea that she'd had to face something so terrible at such a young age was unbearable. Instead of taking his arm away, Aiden found himself pushing it further around her. Pulling her closer, as if he could protect her from something.

'It was an accidental pregnancy.' Her voice was quiet. Matter-of-fact. 'It was ectopic but I ignored the early warning signs. It went on too long and then ruptured really badly. They had to perform a hysterectomy to control the bleeding.'

Aiden swore softly, his eyes tightly shut. He could imagine all too easily the emergency that rupture would have caused. The urgent, major surgery that would have been necessary to save her life. But...

'But why did you ignore the signs?'

It seemed a long time before she spoke again and when she did, her voice was so quiet he barely heard it.

'I wanted the baby,' she said.

That took a few moments to process. 'How old were you?'

'Twenty-one. I was a student midwife. I'd always

loved babies. Maybe because I was an only child and I was so envious when my best friend got a baby sister. My parents both worked full time and it felt like we were…I don't know…less of a family, I guess.'

'But you said the pregnancy was accidental.'

'Of course it was. I wasn't stupid. I was only twenty-one and it wasn't as if the relationship was going any-where. We were both young. Just out to have a bit of fun.'

Like he was with the women in his life? Aiden had to swallow a nasty pang of guilt. Those women had had every right to be angry or upset, hadn't they? He *had* been using them.

'So he wasn't keen on the idea of being a father?'

'He did his best to be supportive but we both knew it couldn't have worked. I actually went down the track of having a termination but when I went to ring up to make an appointment, I couldn't do it. I realised then that I wanted that baby. I…I already loved it.' There was a wobble in her voice. 'So I ignored the abdominal pain that came and went. I told myself that a bit of bleeding could be perfectly normal in the early stages of some pregnancies. That things would settle down once I got to the end of the first trimester and I'd go and get checked out and have a scan after that. When it was less likely that anyone would try and talk me into getting rid of it.'

'And then it ruptured.'

'I was about fourteen weeks by then. I guess it was lucky it happened while I was at work. I might have bled out pretty fast if I'd been anywhere else.'

'I'm glad you were at work, then. Lucky for me, too.'

A tiny sound that could have been an embryonic sob

came from Sophia but then they were both silent for a long time.

'I'm sorry,' Aiden said, finally, into the light of a new day that was filtering through the gap in the curtains. 'You lost something huge and it must have been devastating.' Not only had she lost the baby she'd already loved but she'd lost the chance of ever having another one.

'Yeah…it was tough but that's just the way it is. I'm not going to let it define me. I'm going to make the best of my life. This isn't a practice run, you know? It's the only life we get.'

She reminded him of Nathan. Totally different things to deal with, of course. Or were they so different? Nathan lived with the loss of mobility. He'd had to come to terms with a different perception of his body and where he was going in life.

Sophia lived with the loss of a dream. Wouldn't being unable to ever be a mother involve the same sort of process in coming to terms with that different perception and direction?

The similarity was there. Perhaps the greatest similarity was in the positive attitude to making the best of his life.

He was so proud of his brother's attitude. He loved him to the point where it made his chest ache.

And right now he was feeling a very similar pride in Sophia.

A similar kind of love?

Oh, man…that was a scary thought. He'd never actually fallen in love with a woman. He'd known to get out as soon as there were any warning signs. Had he ignored them for some reason this time?

He tried to search his memory.

Had it been the first time he'd seen her smile? Or when he'd heard her laugh—way back, when they'd first met and she'd introduced herself as being a midwife and he'd joked that he hoped *she* was, given the emergency cord prolapse she'd just dealt with.

No. That had simply been attraction. No danger signs that could have been spotted there.

What about that first date, though? When he'd seen her at the door of that crowded bar? The way the noise of the people and music had just faded away until it had felt like he and Sophia were the only people on the planet?

Yeah…maybe that should have rung an alarm bell, given that it had never happened before.

And she'd loved his three-dates rule. Maybe that was the problem. She'd made him feel safe.

Or maybe it was the way she'd made him feel safe last night. Safe enough to tell her anything.

He couldn't tell her what he was feeling right now. No way.

She'd said that a three-dates rule was exactly what was missing from *her* life. She didn't want the complications of a long-term relationship. She couldn't have a family so maybe it simply wasn't a part of her life plan now.

She wouldn't want to know how he was feeling. It might make her feel bad when she walked away from him to get on with the life that wasn't a practice run.

He didn't want her to feel bad.

He'd make her feel good instead.

Her lips were easy to find. Soft and deliciously responsive. They still had time, didn't they?

This would be a first for him. Sex without protection, but Sophia had shown him something that made her vulnerable and she deserved at least the reassurance of trust.

And…man, it made things feel different.

Nothing like the last time.

Nothing like any time. Ever.

The text message on Aiden's phone came when he was on the point of leaving her house to go to work.

The atmosphere was a little odd. Sophia thought it was because they'd come out to find the remnants of last night's dinner still on the table and it had been a shock. So much had happened since they'd been sitting there.

So much had changed between them?

Yes. The atmosphere was strange. As if they both realised how huge that change had been and it was making them both nervous.

So much for having fun. A limited amount of time to enjoy each other's company. Some 'no-strings' sex.

'I could help clean up,' Aiden offered.

'No. I've got more time than you. I don't start till eight. You've only got ten minutes if you want to get to the station in time to start at seven.'

'Okay. But next time I'm doing the dishes.'

Next time?

Was that going to be date number three or would it still be a non-date if they didn't go out anywhere? Sophia found herself smiling. On the point of clarifying the 'rules' again when the text message bleeped.

That was even more of a shock than the messy table had been. Not that there was someone else who wanted to make contact so early in the day but the way it made Sophia feel.

Jealous?

'It's only Nate,' Aiden said after a glance at his phone. 'I'll call him when I get to work.'

He kissed her goodbye and once again Sophia found herself listening to the sound of his bike roaring away.

No. That feeling hadn't been jealousy. It was deeper than that. She'd known it was probably his brother rather than another woman who was texting him and that made her remember that he had another part of his life that was more important than any woman could ever be to him.

Another part of his life that would swallow him without a ripple when she was no longer a consideration.

Oh, help… If she could feel this bleak before it had even ended, how bad was it going to be when they said goodbye at the end of date number three?

But did it have to end?

Aiden didn't want to have kids.

She *couldn't* have any.

She'd avoided serious relationships because she had less to offer than most women but Aiden didn't want what she didn't have to offer anyway.

Didn't that make them perfect for each other?

The thought came with a leap of something that felt like hope and Sophia found herself holding it as she took plates to the kitchen sink, scraped off the abandoned food and rinsed them clean.

Who would have thought that she might find a man who could not only accept that she couldn't have a baby but would welcome it?

Except that something didn't feel right about this picture. The pieces didn't quite fit. Or maybe there were some missing that were leaving a hole she couldn't identify.

A wipe down of the table obliterated any reminder of last night's meal and Sophia collected her bag and coat to set off on her walk to the Victoria.

She couldn't shake the feeling that something was wrong, however.

That she was too far along a track for turning around to be possible. That she might be heading for some kind of crash and there was nothing at all she could do to prevent it.

CHAPTER NINE

WHAT WAS A girl to do when she couldn't figure out what it was that was bothering her?

Talk about it, of course. To someone she knew she could trust. Someone who knew more about her than anyone and loved her enough to want to help her figure it out.

Her mum?

Sadly, for Sophia, that couldn't be her first port of call. The love was there but the depth of understanding wasn't. Even after all these years, the relief her mother hadn't been able to hide when she'd lost her baby was hurtful.

'It would have ruined your life, being a single mother,' she'd said. 'Your career would have gone out the window and there aren't many men who really want to take on raising someone else's child.'

But she'd loved that baby. That potential little person to love and be loved by. Her career had seemed far less important in comparison.

'There are worse things than not having children.' Had her mother really thought she was offering comfort? 'You're about to be qualified to do the job you've always wanted to do. Focus on that. It'll make you happy.'

Had it been her mother's job that had made *her* happy? Had it been a mistake to have a child at all? One that would have ruined her life if she'd become pregnant accidentally before she had established her career or found a husband?

If it had been a mistake, her parents hid it well and had done the best job they could in raising their child, but that childhood had been a lonely one. There had clearly never been the possibility of siblings and with both her parents working full time, even a family dog had been ruled out as company.

Which was why it had been such a joy to spend time at home with her best friend, Emily, ever since she'd first arrived in Melbourne. To soak in the chaos of an extended family that included an adorably woolly, brown dog by the name of Fuzzy.

With her next day off coinciding with one of Em's, it was a no-brainer to invite herself for a visit and a chance to talk to the person most likely to be able to identify what it was that was bothering her so much.

They were in the garden of Emily and Oliver's house. Well, the house actually belonged to Em's mother, Adrianna, but it was the family home for them all now. And the family was growing, despite the sadness of losing Emily's foster-daughter, Gretta, a few weeks ago.

'How's it working out, having Ruby here with you?'

'Couldn't be better.' Emily lifted two-year-old Toby from his tricycle and took him to sit under the tree. 'I wish she'd rest a bit more, though. Look—she's over there, pruning roses. It's not that long since the in utero surgery on her baby.'

As if sensing she was being discussed, the waif-like teenager looked across the garden and waved at the two women.

'Am I doing it right?' she called. 'I've never tried this before.'

'You're doing a great job,' Emily called back. 'But you don't have to.'

The shy grin in response came with a shrug that was pure teenager.

'She feels like she has to help out,' Emily told Sophia, 'because we're not charging her any rent for the bungalow. And Mum wouldn't let her help with any housework this afternoon. Said it could wait till tomorrow because she felt like putting her feet up and reading her book. I'd rather Ruby was reading a book, too. She could be doing a bit of study or something so that she feels ready to go back to school after the baby comes.'

'I'm sure she will, when she gets used to being here. It must be a big thing, feeling like she's part of a family.'

Emily's smile was that of a contented woman as she nodded, watching Toby doing his stiff-legged crawl towards Sophia.

'Huge,' she agreed quietly.

Toby stopped and held up his arms. Sophia gladly gathered him onto her lap and let the toddler bury his head against her shoulder as he settled in for a cuddle. The faded blue kangaroo toy in his other hand felt a bit damp against the back of her neck.

'That's Kanga, isn't it? Gretta's toy?'

'Mmm.' Emily's smile grew misty. 'He's barely let it go since we lost her. I don't think he understands that she died but he's missing her.'

Toby's curls were springy and too irresistible not to stroke. An African child, Toby had been brought to Australia so that he could receive treatment for his spinal deformity and the scarring on his face from infection.

'How's it going with the adoption process?'

Emily groaned. 'The paperwork is endless. Ollie's confident that we'll get there, though. He says not getting there simply isn't an option.'

Her smile was proud now. Full of love for the man she 'remarried' so recently.

For a long moment, Sophia focused on the gorgeous cuddle she was receiving. Then her gaze drifted over Toby's head to where Ruby was eyeing up another rose bush, rubbing her back as she straightened.

'Do you remember when Ruby was waking up after the operation on the baby?'

'Of course.'

'What we were talking about?'

'Josh?'

'Mmm.' Josh. The baby Emily had lost at twenty-eight weeks—about the stage that Ruby was in her pregnancy now. The one successful round of all the IVF Emily and Oliver had gone through. 'After that. About why you and Oliver had split up.'

'Because he couldn't face adopting a baby?'

'He'd been adopted himself, hadn't he? And it hadn't been happy?'

'Mmm.'

'But he really wants to adopt Toby now, doesn't he?'

'Even more than I do, I think. Although that's not really possible. Hey, Toby…it's about my turn for a cuddle, isn't it?'

Obligingly, Toby crawled off Sophia's lap and threw himself at Emily with a joyful crow.

'Mumma!'

Even more obligingly, Fuzzy slithered closer and put his head on Sophia's lap so that she still had a head to stroke.

'You wanted kids so much,' she said quietly. 'You weren't going to let infertility stop you. And look what you've got now. A whole family, including a husband who adores you.'

'I'm the luckiest woman in the world,' Emily agreed.

'But you did it anyway, even without Oliver, and you were still happy, weren't you?'

'Ye-es…' Emily peered around Toby's head to give her friend a searching look. 'Where's this coming from, Soph? Is something bothering you?'

Sophia nodded. 'I'm not sure what it is. But I remember being at your vow renewal ceremony and thinking how brave you were. And that I needed to get braver too. Make changes in my life so that I could find something as good as what you've found. I even thought I could maybe try fostering or adopting kids one day, too.'

'You have made changes.' Emily's smile was encouraging. 'It's going well with that gorgeous boyfriend of yours, isn't it?'

'It's almost over,' Sophia told her. 'He has a three-dates rule.'

'A *what*?'

'He only ever goes out on three dates with a woman. That way you can have fun but it doesn't get heavy, you know?'

'No.' Emily shook her head. 'You've been out on more than three dates, haven't you?'

'Hmm. The rules got bent a bit. One of them was finishing off a date that got interrupted. And one wasn't really a date because he came to my place and we didn't go out anywhere.'

Emily laughed. 'Sounds like the rule isn't a real rule at all. I wouldn't worry about it.' She frowned. 'In fact, I don't like it. Sounds like an easy escape route for a commitment-phobe to me.'

'Yeah…well, I told him I liked the rule a lot, the first time we went out. That I was only after a bit of fun, too. Nothing serious.'

'Ohh…' Emily gave her another searching look. 'You've fallen for him, haven't you?'

'Yeah…' The word was a sigh. 'The weird thing is that, on paper, we're perfect for each other. I can't have kids and he doesn't want any.'

'Really? Why not?'

Sophia closed her eyes for a long moment, drawn back instantly to that night when Aiden had bared his soul to her and told her things he'd never told anyone. He'd trusted her.

And, yes, Emily knew all about her own story but that was hers to tell. She couldn't share Aiden's. Couldn't break that trust. But there were parts that weren't as private as an abusive childhood with an alcoholic father. Or the guilt of feeling responsible for a dreadful accident.

'He's got a brother. Nathan. He's a quadriplegic. Aiden's more than a big brother to him. He's like a parent, too, I guess. A whole family. I think he's got an unwritten rule about not letting anything interfere with that responsibility.'

'Wow…' Emily was silent for a minute. 'Does he feel the same way about you?'

'I don't know. I think he's let me into his life more than he ever has with any other woman. I've met Nathan. We went to a Murderball game.'

'Is that the wheelchair rugby?'

'Yes. It's really exciting to watch. And Nathan's cool. I really like him. He lives in sheltered accommodation but he seems to have his life pretty well sorted. He's got a girlfriend who has more facial piercings than I've ever seen and they clearly adore each other.'

Sophia was rubbing Fuzzy's head and pulling gently on his ears. She bent her own head, horrified that she could feel tears gathering. It was great to be talking to Emily but she didn't want to spoil a lovely afternoon by falling to pieces. What was wrong with her?

'Oh, hon…' Emily's voice was full of sympathy. 'You've got it bad, haven't you?'

The nod dislodged a tear. She swiped it away.

'I don't know what I'm so upset about. I knew it was never supposed to last more than three dates and the next one has got to count for number three. We can't keep bending his silly rule for ever.'

'That's not the real problem, though, is it?'

Sophia swallowed. 'Isn't it?'

Emily shook her head. She tickled Toby, making him chortle, and then pulled him closer for another hug. 'I think it goes deeper than that.'

'In what way?'

'You're not really perfect for each other. Paper doesn't count.' Emily's gaze was serious now. 'Aiden doesn't want kids. And maybe he has good reason for that. But you do want them, even if you've tried to convince yourself you didn't for all these years. You probably want that as much as I did. You want a real family and you know it's quite possible to have that, even if you can't give birth to your own babies. Look at me.'

'I know.' Sophia drew in a long, slow breath as she found herself nodding slowly.

Yes. That was it, in a nutshell. What had been niggling away in the back of her mind. Aiden didn't want children. And she did. It could never work.

End of story?

Maybe not.

'But Oliver didn't want to adopt children either and look at him, now—leading the crusade to let you keep Toby in the country.'

'He didn't want to adopt,' Emily agreed, 'but he always wanted to be a father. It's a bit different.' It was her turn to sigh. 'Life's an unfair business sometimes, isn't it?'

Toby had crawled off Emily's lap now and was heading towards Ruby. Fuzzy abandoned Sophia and went after Toby like a sheepdog looking after his charge. Ruby grinned as she saw them coming. She bent to pick Toby up but then froze. Something about her posture made both Emily and Sophia share an alarmed glance.

'Ruby?' Emily was on her feet in a flash. 'What's wrong?'

It was too quiet today.

So much easier to silence an annoyingly persistent voice in the back of your head if you could keep busy. Even better if you had a real challenge to rise to.

What Aiden needed was something dramatic. A cardiac arrest, maybe—one that led to a successful outcome, of course. Or some trauma. A crush injury perhaps, that would need careful management, especially if whatever was doing the crushing was still in place. A prang would do. A mess of two or three vehicles with an unknown number of potential injuries and the chaos of disrupted traffic and impatient onlookers creating difficulty for any emergency personnel to get to the scene. He'd get there first and get to do the scene management and triage, which was always a challenge of unknown quantity.

But no. What he had was an elderly homeless guy in central Melbourne suffering from double pneumonia. He was sitting just under a bridge beside the popular walking track that led to Southbank. Apparently, he'd been sitting there for the last three days so people had eventually noticed that he had barely moved. Finally, a concerned pedestrian had called the police. The police had called the ambulance service for a medical assessment. They knew this man and knew he didn't talk much. Asking questions wasn't going to solve anything.

'His name's Bruce,' they told Aiden. 'But that's all we know about him, other than that he's been living on the streets for years. Him and his dog.'

The dog looked as old and thin and unkempt as his owner and seemed happy to sit just as immobile, with his head on Bruce's lap. It seemed to know that Aiden was trying to help but growled ominously if any of the police came too close.

After an initial assessment, Aiden had called for transport so now he was just keeping Bruce company. He had his patient on oxygen and a foil survival blanket was wrapped around his shoulders. He'd taken a baseline set of vital signs. Blood pressure was too low, temperature too high. The respiration rate was way too high and blood-oxygen level way too low. Even with the mask on and oxygen coming from the small cylinder he carried on the bike, there had been little improvement over the last ten minutes. Bruce's lips were still blue and he could almost hear the crackle in his lungs without using a stethoscope.

Where on earth was the back-up for transport? Had they been diverted to exactly the kind of drama he was desperate for himself? Something that would stop the argument in his head that was gaining momentum—on both sides.

He couldn't even talk to the two police officers who had moved a safe distance away from the dog and seemed to see something on the river that was interesting enough to keep them chatting.

He only had Bruce, who didn't talk. And a sad-looking dog who was going to look even sadder when they had to take his master away in the ambulance. The police had called a pet shelter that was sending a rescue crew to help. Aiden doubted that these two would ever be reunited and that sucked.

'I'm sorry about this,' he told Bruce quietly, crouching beside him and checking that the oxygen saturation probe was still covering a finger. 'But we have to take you somewhere you can be warm and comfortable so the antibiotics have a chance to work.'

He took Bruce's heart and respiration rate again, just for something to do, but it felt wrong to be so silent. The noise of the city was a distant hum. The sound of voices and laughter came occasionally as a pair of joggers or cyclists went past on the track but the snippets of normality vanished as quickly as they came. He had to talk to Bruce even if the old man couldn't respond or possibly didn't even understand. But what could he talk about? He'd only had one thing on his mind for the last couple of days.

'I'd like to go out tonight,' he found himself telling Bruce. Still quietly enough for nobody but the dog to overhear. 'But, at the same time, I don't want to because if I do, it's going to be the last date I have with this girl and that would be a real shame because she's…well… she's perfect, that's what she is.'

The perfect woman for him, at any rate.

He never wanted to have children.

Sophia couldn't ever have children.

And hadn't that vow to never take on the responsibility of a family of his own been the whole basis of the three-dates rule? To get out before he fell in love? Before she fell in love with him and wanted more—like living together or getting married? Before her biological clock started ticking more and more loudly and the desire to have a baby became the priority?

But he'd never been on this side of the equation. Never been the one who didn't want things to end.

Sophia had welcomed the rule. She didn't want anything long term either. And why would she? She wasn't planning on having a family any more than he was so she wouldn't see herself in the role of a mother. Or a wife.

Someone was going to get hurt and Aiden had the horrible feeling it was going to be him.

Could they stay friends, perhaps, after their official dating period was over?

Friends with benefits even?

No. As if that could work.

As if it could ever be enough.

'I didn't get out in time.' The words came out like a sigh of defeat and triggered a move to check his watch. Where on earth was that back-up? He could hear a siren in the distance but that wouldn't be the crew coming to transport his patient because the job wouldn't have been assigned the urgency of needing lights and sirens. It would be well down the list and probably getting bumped repeatedly as calls came in for more serious incidents.

A glance towards the police officers showed them to be in deep conversation now. Maybe they were enjoying the enforced break from their duties. Life still flowed along the track beside them. A young mother was jogging as she pushed a twin stroller that had a toddler on one side and a baby cocoon strapped on the other. Behind her, an older couple walked hand in hand, and as Aiden watched they turned to each other and shared a smile. In his peripheral vision he saw Bruce move, too. A tiny movement of just his hand as it rested on the dog's head. One finger moving to gently rub a floppy ear.

Something inside Aiden twisted painfully. That dog was probably the only living thing that Bruce had a relationship with. Responsibility for. And, any moment now, someone was going to turn up with a van to take the dog away.

'They'll take good care of him,' Aiden said. 'There are families out there who love to foster dogs.'

Was it his imagination or was Bruce's level of consciousness slipping further? He put his hand on the old man's wrist to feel for a pulse. The dog nudged his hand with a cold nose and that twisting sensation in his gut intensified.

It wasn't just about whether or not you could have kids, was it? Responsibility came with any relationship if you wanted to do the best you could and Aiden had never taken anything on without making sure he did his absolute best.

He was the best paramedic he could be.

The best brother.

When you loved somebody enough, their happiness became as important as your own. More important, maybe. Nathan's happiness had always been more important than his own. Right now, it felt like Sophia's happiness was important, too.

He wanted her to be happy.

He wanted to be the one to *make* her happy.

But if he was really honest, he wanted to be happy himself and that was why this was so damned hard.

Sophia didn't want more than three dates so he couldn't throw the rule book away. And that meant that if he wanted to see her again, it would be for the last time.

And *that* meant he would never see her again.

Did that mean he *didn't* want the date even more than he did want it?

Two men were coming along the track now, carrying a wire crate between them. They wore overalls with the logo of the animal rescue service. Not far behind them, an ambulance crew was wheeling a stretcher. The police officers noted the arrival of assistance and started to move closer in case they were needed.

The wait was over.

The speed with which things were sorted seemed almost indecent after the long wait. Surprisingly, the dog didn't protest at being bundled into the crate and Bruce seemed equally defeated—barely conscious as he was lifted to the stretcher and covered with warm blankets. After handing over his paperwork to the ambulance crew, the last thing Aiden needed to do was change the oxygen supply and take his own small cylinder back to the bike.

'All the best, Bruce,' he said. 'I'll keep an eye out for you next time I'm down this way.'

The old man's eyes opened slowly. His lips moved. Aiden lifted the mask.

'Ask her,' Bruce mumbled. 'Tell her…'

Oh, man… It was a cringe-worthy moment to realise

that he'd been heard and understood when he'd been sharing something so decidedly unprofessional. Aiden didn't want to have to think about it and, lucky for him, he didn't have to. He'd barely got his helmet back on his head when a priority call came through to an address in Brunswick.

'Premature labour,' he was told. 'Approximately twenty-eight weeks gestation. Mother seventeen years old. Nearest ambulance is at least ten minutes away.'

Aiden kicked his bike into life and flicked on the beacons. Anticipation was tinged with relief. This was exactly what he needed.

Drama. A life—other than his own—that was hanging in the balance.

'The ambulance is on its way.'

'How long?' Sophia was kneeling behind Ruby, holding the girl in her arms to support her.

'I don't *want* an ambulance,' Ruby sobbed. 'I just want this to *stop*. It *hurts*…'

'I know, sweetheart.' Sophia tightened her hug. 'But sometimes it's baby who decides when things are going to happen.' She turned to catch Emily's gaze and mouthed her question again silently.

Emily held up the fingers of both hands and her look said it all. Ten minutes could well be too long. She tilted her head towards the house with her eyebrows raised but Sophia had to shake her head. They'd already tried to get Ruby inside but she'd been almost hysterical as the first pain had hit and her waters had broken. She'd frozen and then collapsed onto the ground when Emily and Sophia had taken her arms to help her walk.

Emily's mother, Adrianna, came rushing out of the house with an armload of blankets. 'I'll keep Toby in with me,' she said. 'Where on earth is that ambulance? We called them ages ago.'

'It was only a few minutes, Mum,' Emily said. 'And I can hear a siren.'

'Oh…thank goodness.' Adrianna tucked a blanket around Ruby's shoulders. 'You'll be okay now, love. You'll be safely in hospital in no time.'

'I won't,' Ruby sobbed. 'It's too early. I didn't think I wanted this baby but I do…I want it *so* much…'

'I know.' Sophia kept hugging her. She knew how it felt to be faced with the fear of losing an unborn baby you'd already fallen in love with. She also knew that Ruby's fears were justified. This was far too early—especially if this baby was going to arrive before they had the benefit of all the resuscitation gear that the MMU would have on hand. Emily was looking desperately worried and that was enough to pull Sophia even further from the calm, professional space she was trying to hang onto.

And that siren sounded…different?

It wasn't really a surprise to see the big bike pulling in to the side of the road and a helmeted figure opening panniers to grab equipment.

What was surprising was the way her fear seemed to evaporate the moment she saw that it was Aiden who had responded to the call.

'The ambulance isn't far away,' he told Ruby, as he crouched beside her. 'I'm just the advance party.' He looked up to include all of them. 'Tell me what's happening. How far apart are the contractions?'

Emily filled him in on the sudden start of Ruby's labour. She also told him that the baby had had in utero surgery a few weeks ago to correct spina bifida and that Ruby had been kept on complete bed rest until they had been confident she wouldn't go into labour. By the time she finished speaking, the ambulance had arrived.

'We'll get you into the ambulance,' Aiden said. 'But we'll need to check where we're at before we roll.'

'I'm coming too,' Emily said.

There would be no room in the ambulance for Sophia to go as well but she went as far as the ambulance and waited while Aiden and Emily examined Ruby. Everything seemed under control but suddenly Ruby cried out as another contraction hit and then nothing was under control. Within seconds Aiden was holding a tiny scrap of a baby in his hands.

'Soph? Open that kit for me and get the ziplock bag.'

Her hands were shaking as she complied. She knew to wrap preterm infants in bubble wrap but a plastic bag? The baby wasn't making any sound and this was not looking good.

But Aiden seemed to know exactly what he was doing. He cut and clamped the cord and then put the baby into the bag leaving the head outside.

'Dry the head for me,' he told Emily. 'And cover it with a corner of the blanket. Soph—can you bring that airway kit a bit closer, please?'

One of the ambulance crew got there first and Sophia edged further away. The back of the ambulance was crowded now and all Emily could do was hold Ruby's hand and try to reassure her as she watched what was happening with the baby.

Sophia stood pressed against the open back door of the ambulance. She couldn't look away from that fierce concentration on Aiden's face. He was invested in this job a thousand per cent, determined to succeed, and she loved him for that.

And she felt so proud of him. That he knew exactly what to do and that he was doing it with such confidence and skill.

His hands moved so fast. They looked huge against the tiny pieces of equipment, like the smallest ever size of a laryngoscope blade and breathing tube. The ventilation bag was also tiny and he was squeezing it so gently to deliver such small puffs of oxygen.

'Hook up the monitor,' he told one of the crew. 'I need continuous monitoring of end tidal CO_2.'

The baby still wasn't moving but Aiden wasn't starting any chest compressions. His gaze was flicking between the baby and the monitor.

'Heart rate's over sixty,' he said. 'Let's roll. I want to get this little girl into NICU asap.'

Sophia had to step back so that the doors could be slammed shut. Within seconds, the ambulance took off, with its beacons flashing and the siren on. It looked like any other ambulance by the time it got to the end of the street but Sophia knew what was happening inside and she shut her eyes for a moment, sending out a fervent wish that they were going to be successful in saving that tiny life.

Then she opened her eyes and found herself staring at Aiden's bike.

He'd have to come back for that, wouldn't he?

Adrianna would be only too happy if Sophia hung around until Emily got back so that she could hear a first-hand account of how things had gone during transport and what was happening with the baby. It was quite reasonable to also assume that Aiden would come back with her so that he could collect his bike and get back on the road. Sophia picked up his helmet.

For a moment she held it in her arms, close to her chest. It felt like a connection to the man who'd been wearing it a short time ago. It also felt like an insurance policy. He'd have to come in to find it before he could go anywhere else. Like the way her fear had receded when Aiden had arrived at a potentially tragic scene, the knowledge that she would be able to see him again before long made everything feel a bit different.

Better?

Oh, yes… A great deal better.

But would he ask her out on another date when they actually had a chance to talk?

Their last ever date?

Her breath came out in a long, heartfelt sigh.

Maybe she didn't feel better after all.

CHAPTER TEN

MINUTES TURNED INTO hours but still Aiden hadn't come back for his bike.

Sophia helped Adrianna peel a mountain of vegetables that went into the oven to roast, along with a huge leg of lamb.

'Oliver won't be far behind Em and I'm sure they're both starving. Maybe that nice young paramedic will be able to stay and have some dinner as well.'

This household was like that. A real family home where all comers were made to feel welcome.

'Wasn't he marvellous?' Adrianna added. 'It was such a relief when he arrived and even from here I could see how good he was with Ruby. A very impressive young man.'

'Mmm.' Sophia hadn't dared meet the gaze of the older woman. 'He is.'

When the front door finally opened, it was Emily's voice that could be heard.

'We're home. Sorry we were so long.'

Her tone was upbeat enough to suggest that the news was going to be good.

Adrianna came rushing from the kitchen and Sophia dropped the book she'd been reading to Toby as they cuddled on the couch.

It wasn't just Emily. Aiden was right behind her and Oliver was only a step behind them.

'Ollie gave us both a ride back,' Emily said. 'Aiden was going to get an ambulance to drop him back but when he heard that Ollie had a sixty-four Morgan sports car, he couldn't resist the invitation.'

'How did you all fit in?' Adrianna was wiping her hands on her apron.

'Bit of a squeeze,' Emily admitted, 'but we coped.' Her grin in Sophia's direction was accompanied by a ghost of a wink that suggested she hadn't minded the squeeze at all.

'I'm glad.' Adrianna smiled at Aiden. 'I hope you won't resist an invitation to stay for dinner either. I've made enough to feed an army and I want to thank you for helping our Ruby.'

'How *is* Ruby?' Sophia steadied Toby as he tried to stand up on the couch beside her, holding his arms out to his parents.

'Mumma,' he demanded.

Emily scooped him into her arms. 'Ruby's fine. No complications. She's in NICU. We couldn't persuade her to come home and get some sleep. She won't take her eyes off her daughter.'

Sophia couldn't let her breath out. She'd been too scared to ask. Her gaze shifted to Oliver. As the surgeon who'd been in charge of the in utero surgery on Ruby's baby he would be well up to date on what was happening now and he would be able to tell her. But her gaze kept travelling and only stopped when it caught Aiden's. He was smiling.

'She's doing amazingly well,' he said quietly. 'I had the privilege of being allowed to get involved while they got her settled and stable.'

'Of course you did,' Emily said. 'It was you who saved the baby in the first place.' She stepped closer to Sophia. 'You should have heard what they said about Aiden's management. He's brilliant.'

'I knew that.' It felt like her heart was in danger of bursting with pride and an odd lump in her throat made her words a little hoarse. Sophia looked back at Aiden but he seemed to be avoiding her gaze now.

'I learned a lot,' he said. 'It's not often we get to follow on with our patient's treatment like that. Luckily I've got a boss who knows how valuable it is, so I got covered for the rest of my shift.'

'You're off duty?' Adrianna beamed. 'So you can stay for dinner?'

'Well…'

'How 'bout a beer?' Oliver had taken Toby from Emily's arms to get a cuddle but now he put the small boy onto the floor. 'I think we all deserve a bit of wind-down time.'

Toby was doing his stiff-legged crawl towards his new, favourite toy.

'So that's where my helmet got to.'

'I was just looking after it,' Sophia said. 'I knew you'd come back.'

'Of course.' His gaze caught hers. And held. Sophia

could feel Emily and Oliver watching them. She knew they were both smiling and she could feel the colour creeping into her cheeks.

'For the bike,' she added.

A soft chuckle came from Adrianna, who disappeared back into the kitchen.

Aiden cleared his throat. 'I'd better ring HQ and let them know I'll be a bit late dropping it back.'

'And I'll find us a beer. A wine for you, Soph?'

'Thanks, Oliver. I'd love one.'

'Me, too,' Emily said. 'Toby, what are you doing?'

It was Aiden's turn to chuckle. 'I think he fancies riding a bike. Do you want to try that on, Toby?'

The helmet was far too big but Toby whooped with happiness when Aiden held it over his head.

'Where's my phone? I've got to get a picture of this.' Emily was laughing as she went to find it. 'Ollie, come and see. This is priceless.'

It *was* priceless. Aiden sat on the floor with Toby on his lap, wearing the helmet. All you could see was the white grin on the small, dark face. And the smile on the face of the man protecting the toddler's head from too much weight from the enormous helmet.

Something huge caught in Sophia's chest and squeezed so tightly it was hard to breathe.

Maybe it was the way Aiden was holding Toby so protectively. Or that look on his face that revealed that he was enjoying this as much as anybody else.

Or maybe it was just part of the puzzle. Another piece was that expression she'd seen when he'd been working with such determination to save Ruby's baby. How gently he'd done what had needed to be done.

And what about the first time she'd ever met this man? When he'd been holding Claire's baby boy after that emergency delivery. What had he said? Oh, yes...

'Babies are my favourite thing. It was a treat.'

Right now, toddlers seemed to be his favourite thing.

There was no question that he was more than capable of caring for and loving children. Look at the love he had for his younger brother and the way he still took responsibility for Nathan. So much so that he wasn't going to allow anything—or anyone—else to interfere with continuing to make Nathan his priority.

That was why he'd come up with that stupid three dates rule in the first place, wasn't it?

But he'd make such an amazing father.

Did he have any idea how good he would be? Was it really that he never wanted to have his own child or was he denying himself the opportunity to experience the kind of joy it could bring? Did he realise that he was shutting himself away from the chance of having a real family for himself? From having people who could support him instead of it always being the other way around?

It was actually painful to swallow the lump in her throat but Sophia managed. She even kept her tone light.

'I'll go and see if Adrianna needs some help in the kitchen.'

The kid was adorable.

The fun of the helmet wore off but Aiden apparently

had plenty of other attractions. Like the penlight torch clipped to his pocket. He showed Toby how to turn it on and it was dark enough now for the beam to show up and dance along the wall. The dog, Fuzzy, seemed to find this as good a game as Toby did. He bounced from one spot to the next, wagging his tail and barking to announce that he'd found where the light had escaped to, and this never failed to make Toby giggle with delight.

The beer hit the spot and he got the chance to talk about the in utero surgery that that tiny baby had had prior to her birth, while Emily and Sophia took Toby away for his bath. Fascinating stuff and yet his interest seemed to evaporate when the women returned. It was Sophia who was carrying Toby in his fluffy sleep suit, a bedraggled-looking toy kangaroo dangling from one hand. Sophia's cheeks were pink and her hair was a tousled mop of damp curls. And there was something about her expression that made Aiden catch his breath.

Something so tender it actually gave him a lump in his throat. When he saw the way she pressed a kiss onto Toby's head before she handed him to Oliver for a goodnight cuddle, he had to turn away.

How sad was it that she would never be able to have children of her own?

To be a mother?

She'd be…amazing.

It was easy to push that disturbing sense of regret on Sophia's behalf away during the course of the delicious dinner Adrianna served up in the kitchen. There was great conversation and plenty of laughter, a dog sitting under the table in the hope of something falling his way, and an atmosphere of…what was it?

Something Aiden had never really experienced before.

Family, he realised as he reluctantly made his farewells immediately after the meal. He had to get the bike back to HQ and he'd promised Nate he'd drop in this evening so he couldn't stay any longer.

He wanted to, though.

He'd grown up in a house devoid of the kind of warmth this house was full of, and he'd pretty much lived alone ever since then. Nathan's sheltered accommodation had something of this warmth but it was very different. This was a real home—with parents and a child and a dog and even a grandma thrown in for good measure.

A real home. A real family.

Sophia looked different here. She came with him when he went to find his helmet and torch in the lounge and then saw him to the front door. Her hair was still extra-curly and there was a sparkle in her eyes that made her look extra-happy. Totally irresistible. There was nobody to witness their kiss and it was so good it would have been rude not to have another one.

She didn't just look different here. She *felt* different. Softer. More confident?

As if she was in a place where she felt completely at home?

He was even more reluctant to leave now.

'I have to go,' he murmured against her ear as he held her close. 'Nate asked me to drop in on my way home and he'll be wondering why I'm so late.'

Sophia melted out of his arms like a deflating balloon. 'Of course.'

'See you soon?'

She nodded but some of that sparkle had gone. It looked like she was holding herself very still. Holding her breath even?

'This wasn't a date.' Oh, help...why had he said that? Why bring up the fact that they only had one official date left?

Sophia didn't say anything. She smiled but she was turning away at the same time and Aiden was left with the feeling that he'd killed the sparkle completely. Pretty much like he had when he'd ruined their second date by cutting it short to go and visit his brother.

But that was precisely why he *had* to go, wasn't it?

And why he couldn't let how he felt about Sophia go any further.

It was his problem to deal with. His heart that was going to bleed when this was over.

Gunning the powerful engine of his bike gave him a momentary reprieve from the downward spiral of his mood.

He'd survive.

He'd always survived. He'd learned that long ago. Just like he'd learned how to hide how he felt so that nobody knew.

Nate knew.

He took one look at Aiden's face and his eyes narrowed. 'Man—what's up with you? Bad day?'

'No. Great day. Delivered a premmie baby. Twenty-eight-weeker. Not only that, she'd had in-utero surgery to correct spina bifida a few weeks ago, which is probably why the labour came on so early. I got to hang around in NICU while they stabilised her. You wouldn't believe some of the high-tech gear they've got in there.'

But, for once, Nathan didn't want to hear every detail of the interesting job.

'I've got something to tell you,' he said.

His tone suggested that he didn't think it would be something Aiden wanted to hear. Sudden fear made Aiden sink onto the edge of his brother's bed. What had happened? Was there something wrong that he hadn't been told about? Had Nathan's condition worsened in some way? Had he injured himself playing that fierce wheelchair rugby? Was he *sick*?

'What's the matter?' The query came out more tersely than he'd intended. 'You're not sick, are you? I hope it's not another UTI. Have you been—?'

'For God's sake,' Nathan interrupted. 'Will you stop fussing like some mother hen? No. I'm not sick. It's Sam.'

'Sam's sick?'

'No.' Nathan gave an exasperated huff of sound. 'She's not sick. She's pregnant.'

The silence fell like a brick.

Nathan shook his head. 'Don't even think about asking that one. Yeah…it's mine.'

Aiden was still too stunned to say anything. This was the last thing he'd expected to hear. Astonishment warred with something else that was even less pleasant. Fear for the challenges Nate was going to have to face? Or was it more than that? Jealousy, maybe, that there were going to be people in his brother's life who would be more important than he was? Sam. A *baby*…

'You're going to be an uncle,' Nathan told him. 'How cool is that?'

It was Aiden's turn to shake his head. 'How did that happen?'

Nathan laughed. 'You mean you don't know?' He tipped his chair, balancing on the back of the wheels. 'And you with all that medical training. Bro…'

A flash of anger surfaced. 'Cut it out, Nate. This is serious. It's not your physical capabilities I'm questioning. It's your level of intelligence in not using any kind of protection. Have you even thought about what happens next?'

The chair came down with a thump. 'What happens next is that I'm going to marry Sam. We've already applied to get a house of our own. We're going to make this work and we're very, very happy about it.' He had an odd expression on his face. 'It'd be nice if you could manage to be happy about it, too.'

'I…' Again, words failed Aiden. It felt like he was being pushed out of Nathan's life. As if the whole foundation of his own life was crumbling.

'It'll work,' Nathan said fiercely. 'I'm going to make sure it works. I can be a good dad, I know I can. And a good husband. I'm going to have a real family, Aiden, and…and I can't wait.'

You've got a family, Aiden wanted to say. *You've got me.*

But he couldn't utter the words. He knew exactly what Nathan was talking about. He'd just spent the evening with a real family, hadn't he? Did he not want that for his brother if it was possible? That kind of security?

That kind of love?

Nathan was watching him.

'It doesn't mean that I don't still need you in my life, you know.'

'I know.' The words were strangled.

But he wasn't enough. He got that but it still hurt.

'You can't make me feel guilty about this.' Nathan's words were raw. 'I know how much you've given up for me. You've felt responsible ever since the accident happened. You decided then and there you were going to be a paramedic, didn't you?'

'I guess…'

'Because you felt guilty about what happened. How many times do you have to be told, bro?' Nathan's glare was fierce. 'It. Was. Not. Your. Fault.'

'Okay…' Aiden held up his hands in a gesture of surrender. Or maybe a signal to stop. He knew that. Sophia had told him the same thing and he had—on some level—accepted it. Now Nathan was making it crystal clear that he had no choice but to let it go. To believe what everybody told him.

Sophia had done more than try to absolve his guilt. She'd thought he'd been *brave…*

'You don't get to feel guilty about me any more,'

Nathan continued. 'And that means I don't get to feel guilty about you either. Is it a deal?'

'Of course you don't get to feel guilty about me. Why would you?'

'Ooh, let me think…' Nathan shook his head. 'Maybe because you also decided you weren't going to let anything get in the way of looking after me. Anything like a pet. Or a partner. Or—heaven forbid—*kids*…'

Surely it hadn't been that obvious? It wasn't as if Aiden had even articulated what lay beneath the decisions about how he lived his life. The boundaries had simply evolved. And strengthened.

Okay, maybe he had articulated the three-dates rule. It had become a joke that was part of the bond between the brothers. He just hadn't expected Nathan to see through it with such clarity. To come to *disapprove* of it with such vehemence…

Was it because he'd fallen in love himself and was determined to make it the best relationship possible? Hurtful words spoken weeks ago drifted into his mind.

Being told that Nathan didn't want to end up like him. Shut off. Scared of losing control.

As if he was reading Aiden's mind, Nathan spoke again. The anger had gone from his voice. It was quiet now. Serious.

'We only get one life, mate, and if we don't make the best of it, we've only got ourselves to blame. You can't keep me safe because I don't want to *be* that kind of safe any more. I want to live. *Really* live. And that's what you should be doing, too.'

He reminded Aiden of Sophia saying that life wasn't

a practice run. Had he missed something along the way? Had he done the wrong thing in trying to be the best brother he could be?

'I wouldn't be where I am if it hadn't been for you,' Nathan said quietly. 'I'll love you for ever for that.'

Aiden tried to swallow the lump in his throat but it wasn't budging.

'You could have that too, you know. You and Sophia. You're perfect for each other.'

'She doesn't want that. She…she can't have kids. Doesn't want a family.'

Except that didn't really ring true, did it? Not after the way she'd looked when she'd been holding a sleepy Toby. How happy she'd been in that family kitchen.

'And you don't want kids. You've always said that being a dad to me was more than enough.'

Aiden swallowed. He had said that. He'd meant it, too. Hadn't he?

'So it's my turn to find out what it's like. You get to be the favourite uncle. Maybe Sophia would like to be an auntie. Hey, can I tell Sam it's okay to come in now? That you're not going to rain on our parade?'

'Sure.'

But Nathan hesitated at the door. 'You've got one date left with Sophia, haven't you?'

Aiden shrugged. What difference did it make?

'Make it count,' Nathan said. 'Tell her that you love her, man. It might change your life.' He grinned and his face lit up with joy. 'It changed mine.'

There were congratulations to be given after that. And plans. Not that Aiden got to say much. Nathan and

Sam seemed to have everything going just the way they wanted it to and they had the support of everybody in the house.

It was impossible not to get captured by the love these two young people had for each other. The hope that shone in their eyes as they looked at each other and shared the plans for their future.

Impossible not to come away without the realisation that he wanted that for himself, too.

That it was something worth fighting for.

It was late but maybe it wasn't *too* late.

The phone rang and rang. Any second now, and it would go to voice-mail and Aiden had no idea what he would say. Somehow he had to tell Sophia how he felt about her but you couldn't do that in a voice-mail, could you?

But then the ringing stopped and he heard Sophia's soft voice.

'Hey, Aiden…what's up?'

'Ah…' He couldn't do it over the phone either. He couldn't tell Sophia how much he loved her when he couldn't see her face. Couldn't touch her. He cleared his throat. 'I just wanted to…to…ask you out.'

'On a date?'

Oh, God…was that reluctance he could hear in her voice? A hint of fear even?

'Yeah…'

He heard what sounded like a slow, indrawn breath. 'Okay. When?'

'Um…I'm not sure. I'll text you.'

'Needs planning, huh?'

'Yeah…' He found a smile. 'The best dates always do.'

'Especially number three?' There was a catch in Sophia's voice. 'Saving the best for last?'

'Something like that. I'll text you as soon as I've got it sorted.'

It wasn't until after he'd put the phone down and started browsing his computer for ideas worthy of the perfect date that it clicked.

That reluctance.

Making it clear that this was date number three and therefore the final one.

Maybe Sophia didn't *want* it to be the final date any more than he did.

He turned back to his browsing with renewed enthusiasm.

Hope even?

The trill of her phone announcing a text came at a truly ungodly hour but Sophia woke instantly and completely as she reached to grab her mobile.

Not that she was expecting any of her women to be going into labour, but a phone call at this time of night could only signal an emergency.

Except it wasn't one of her mums-to-be.

It was an invitation for a date. If she was up for it, a taxi would be arriving to collect her in twenty minutes.

What kind of date started at four a.m.?

Certainly not a kind that Sophia had ever experienced. But, then, she'd never gone on a date knowing that it would be the last either. And she'd certainly never gone on a date with a man she was so totally and hopelessly in love with.

Her fingers were shaking as she entered her response.

Bring it on.

CHAPTER ELEVEN

WITHOUT THE LIGHTS of the city, the night became an inky blackness surrounding the car.

Where on earth was she being taken?

Sophia had rugged up, knowing there could well be a hint of frost with the approaching dawn, but in the heat of the taxi, being wrapped in her puffer jacket and woolly accessories had her feeling drowsy.

Maybe this was all a dream?

Pulling off one woollen glove, she checked her phone. Yes. There were the text messages sent and received so recently. The last one had sent her digging through a drawer to find items of clothing that wouldn't normally make an appearance for a month or two yet.

Dress for something cold! Aiden had instructed.

Real doubt might have surfaced surrounding this date at that point but Aiden had sent another message.

Trust me.

So here she was. Speeding off in the night to an unknown destination. In a car being driven by a total stranger.

Her mother would be horrified. Sophia could almost hear an echo of her voice.

'How could you be so *reckless*, Sophia?'

A smile tilted her lips as she silently answered that voice.

Because it was Aiden who asked me, Mum. That's how.

Maybe she dozed for a while, lulled by the warmth and the rumble of the car's engine, overlaid with some easy listening music on the radio. Any minute now and she'd be hearing a track from Cat Stevens. Not that she needed the cue to think back to that evening with Aiden. To the shock of hearing about his appalling childhood. To the way his vulnerability had stolen her heart. To the understanding she had gained about why he had chosen the career he had and why he felt he had to shut anything out of his life that could get in the way of his devotion to his younger brother.

She loved him enough to know that she would never do that.

Enough to have this final date and let him go?

Yes.

But she was going to make the most of every minute of it. Especially when it had obviously been planned with great care. Like date number two. He'd taken her a long way out of the city that time, too. Was she being taken back there, perhaps? Were they going to watch the sunrise from a lighthouse overlooking one of those gorgeous beaches?

'Where *are* we going?'

'We're here, love.' The taxi driver was slowing his

vehicle, as if he was looking for a signpost. 'In the heart of the Yarra Valley.'

Nowhere near Queenscliff, then. This was pretty much the opposite direction out of Melbourne. Sophia hadn't been in this area yet but she knew it was famous for food and wine and stunning scenery.

A long way to go for a date for breakfast, though.

And the driver wasn't heading for the winery the sign had advertised. He was turning onto a side road that appeared to lead to nothing more than a big paddock beside a small lake.

Well…there was something more. A couple of trucks parked near a group of people. And a motorbike.

And someone breaking away from the group to come and meet her taxi.

Aiden had a big, puffy jacket on, too. And woolly gloves. And a beanie that covered his head and ears, but Sophia would have recognised that smile anywhere.

Her heart recognised it as well. She could feel its joyous squeeze.

'Have you guessed?' His smile widened. 'Have you ever done this before?'

Shaking her head, Sophia took hold of his hand. They were both wearing gloves but she could still feel the warmth and strength of his grip. He led her towards the huddle of people. What looked like a small house made of wicker turned out to be the bottom of a huge basket. On the other side, an enormous puddle of fabric lay on the ground.

A balloon.

This was date number three? A ride in a hot-air

balloon? How scary was this? Sophia's grip on Aiden's hand tightened. In response, he put his arm around her shoulders and pulled her firmly against his side.

You're safe, the gesture told her. *I won't let anything bad happen to you.*

Torchlight showed that the balloon had a background colour of deep gold. Big fans were positioned on either side of the basket and, as Sophia and Aiden watched, people held up the base of the fabric and air began to fill the balloon. And then, with a roar that made Sophia gasp in alarm, a huge flame emerged from the burner as someone turned it on and the air began to heat. Slowly, majestically, the balloon began to rise, tipping the basket into an upright position.

There were openings in the side of the basket and the pilot showed Aiden how to use them as footholds to climb in. Standing inside, he waited only until Sophia had her foot in the first rung and then his hands came under her arms and he lifted her as easily as if she weighed no more than a child.

And there they were, standing inside this huge basket with only the pilot for company.

'This is Jim,' Aiden told her. 'You're in safe hands.'

Sophia shook the pilot's hand. Then she looked at the ground crew, who seemed to be packing up. This was puzzling. She'd seen pictures of balloon rides like this and people were usually crammed into these baskets like human sardines.

'Haven't you got any more passengers?' she asked.

'Not today.' Jim grinned at Aiden. 'This man saved my kid's life a while back. I owed him a favour.'

Another blast of the burner punctuated his sentence and they were lifting off the ground. Aiden led her to the opposite side of the basket and pointed. Far in the distance, over the top of the Dandenong Ranges, the sun was starting to appear—a blindingly brilliant sliver of light that painted the bottoms of nearby clouds deep shades of orange and pink.

Despite the layers of clothing, it was freezing. Sophia was more than happy to be tucked against Aiden's side and each blast of the burner surrounded them with a welcome wave of warmth. It illuminated the balloon, too, and Sophia gasped with delight the first time she looked up. The dark gold of the fabric she'd seen on the ground was now a glowing, rich hue and there were patterns on it. Aboriginal designs of lizards and kangaroos and birds, and there were hand- and footprints and chains of coloured shapes filling other gaps.

'It's gorgeous.' She raised her voice to be heard over the roar of the burner but then it stopped and Aiden's response fell into complete silence.

'So are you,' he said. 'I love you, Sophia.'

Hearing Aiden say those words was like an emotional version of a burner being turned on inside her heart, lighting it up and making it glow.

The silence around them was astonishing. Somewhere down below a rooster was crowing to announce the approaching dawn but Sophia only had to whisper to be heard.

'I love you, too.'

Saying the words out loud was like a seal. The truth was out there now and it would never change. Dawn might be breaking around them to reveal stunning scenery but there was nothing she wanted to see more than what she was seeing in Aiden's eyes right now.

But it was heart-breaking, too. They loved each other but this was the last time they would be together like this. On a date.

The prickle of imminent tears made her wrench her gaze free of Aiden's. She was not going to cry in front of him. Or ruin this spectacular date he had organised. She blinked hard. Gulped in a breath of the icy air. Tried to find something to focus on. There were ponds of ground fog on the patchwork of fields and vineyards below and away in the distance she could see other balloons rising over the misty landscape. One was coloured like a rainbow. She concentrated on that, waiting for its burner to make it glow again, but it wasn't enough. She could feel a tear escape and trickle down the side of her nose.

'Oh, hon…'

Her view of the rainbow balloon vanished as Aiden gathered her into his arms. And when she raised her head all she could see was that look of love in his face. That vanished, too, as his face lowered and he kissed her.

Slowly. So tenderly her heart broke all over again.

A long blast of the burner made them finally break that kiss. Maybe the reminder that they weren't quite alone made them both look out to take in the magic of where they were, floating in the clear air of what was going to be a perfect day. There seemed to Sophia to be nothing more to say but Aiden obviously didn't think so.

'Do you remember our first date?'

'Of course. You kissed me in that garden bar.'

'Do you remember me telling you about my three-dates rule?'

Sophia nodded. How could she have forgotten? She had embraced the idea so enthusiastically. Had she really said that it was exactly the rule that was missing from her own life?

'There's something else you should know about that rule,' Aiden said softly.

'Oh?'

'Mmm.'

Aiden was staring intently at something on the ground. That flock of sheep perhaps?

'It's a load of bull.'

Sophia's jaw dropped. A loud bleating sound came from one of the sheep far below and it sounded like laughter.

'Is it…?' she managed.

Aiden straightened and met her gaze. 'It is if you find the person you want to spend the rest of your life with.' He caught her hands and gripped them tightly. 'I don't want to go on any more dates with you, Soph. I want…I want us just to be together. For ever. I want to marry you.'

'Oh…'

This was the last thing Sophia had expected to happen on this—the final—date. Had she really thought her heart had been breaking earlier? It had only been a crack. This was what it felt like to really break. To shatter into a million little pieces.

'I love you,' she whispered. 'Please, know that.' She had to close her eyes. 'But I could never marry you.'

* * *

Oh…*God*…

How devastating was this?

Aiden had planned this date knowing that his future was on the line here. That the stupid three-dates rule he'd not only invented but had given to Sophia meant that this was his last chance.

And he'd blown it.

The silence around them was deafening. Excruciating. Had Jim heard him putting his heart on the line and being turned down?

His dating rule wasn't the only stupid idea he'd ever had either. He'd chosen what seemed to be the most romantic place in the world to propose but he hadn't given any thought to failure. To being trapped in a floating box in the sky with nowhere to go. Nowhere to hide.

He would just have to grit his teeth and ride it out. To look as if he wasn't dying inside. Surely there was something out there he could focus on. Those other balloons, maybe, dotted in the sky at various levels. Yeah…there was one that had rainbow stripes. Pretty.

'It's not about the three-dates rule,' Sophia said quietly. 'It's about why you made it. About the responsibility you feel for Nate and…and how you feel about having a family.'

'I—' He had to tell her that his brother's world had changed. That his level of responsibility had been downgraded, but she didn't let him continue.

'I understand,' she told him. 'Honestly, I do. And I know that me not being able to have my own babies should make us perfect for each other but…'

He could see the way she took a deep breath. Could see the soft light that came into her eyes. 'But I *want* a family,' she said. 'And there are lots of ways of doing that without giving birth yourself.'

Aiden hadn't expected that. How arrogant had he been, assuming that Sophia had embraced the idea of limited relationships because she had no reason to want something long term when she couldn't have her own children? He had no idea what he could say to that but he didn't need to say anything yet.

Sophia's smile was poignant. 'You should know,' she said. 'Nathan is your brother, not your son, but you pretty much raised him. I love that you love him so much and it says a lot about what an amazing person you are that you've kept up that caring for him.' She scrubbed at her face with her glove as if she was wiping away a tear. Sure enough, her next words sounded choked. 'And I know it was tough. I understand why you wouldn't want to do it again.'

'I've just never considered it as an option,' Aiden put in. He needed a minute to get his head around this. Was this why Sophia couldn't marry him? Because he'd said he never wanted kids?

'I look at Emily,' Sophia said, 'and I know that that's what I want. A family. And I know it can be easier to adopt kids that aren't quite perfect and I'd be okay with that. But you've already spent your life caring for someone who needed extra help.'

'So doesn't that make me an expert?'

That surprised her into silence and it gave Aiden a moment to clear his head. To let the pieces fall into place.

Maybe it was the mention of Emily that did it. The memory of what it had been like in the Evanses' house that night. The way Sophia had looked when she'd been cuddling Toby in his fluffy sleepsuit. The laughter and warmth in that kitchen. The dog under the table.

Family.

He wanted that too, dammit.

The burst of the burner was the longest yet and it ignited something inside Aiden. Determination?

Jim's voice added a sense of urgency.

'Sorry, guys, but we're on the way down now. You'll see our chase vehicles parked up near that lake.'

Aiden didn't even look.

'The "not wanting kids" was just another stupid rule,' he told Sophia. 'Like the three-dates one. I convinced myself that's what worked because I didn't think I had the option of anything else. I felt guilty about Nate and I stuck to the promise I'd made when the accident happened. That I would look after him for ever.'

'Of course you did. Your loyalty is up there with all the other amazing things I love about you.'

'I was wrong,' Aiden insisted. 'Not about being loyal. About believing it was my fault. Nate told me but it wasn't until *you* told me that I started believing it. And now I really do. Nate and I made a deal. I'd stop feeling guilty about him and he wouldn't have to feel guilty about me.'

'He feels guilty about you?'

'He thinks I'm throwing away my own life because I think I need to look after him. He's made it very clear he's going to live his own life. He's getting married. Sam's going to have his baby.'

'Really?' Sophia sounded delighted. 'You're going to be an uncle? That's perfect for you.'

'No it's not,' Aiden growled. 'It's not enough.' He shook his head to emphasise his words. 'Yeah, I convinced myself that I didn't want anything that got in the way of putting Nate first but I did that for too long and it's a good thing that I'm not allowed to do it any more. And it means that for the first time in my life I'm going to be able to choose what *I* want. Just for myself.'

They were getting close to landing now. He could see the shadow of their balloon and its basket clearly outlined on the ground below. There was a truck parked that would carry the balloon back to its base. A car with support crew to help pack up.

Sophia wasn't looking at their shadow getting larger as the land rose to meet them. She was staring at him.

'What *do* you want?' she asked softly.

There was no hesitation on his part. 'You. Us. A family. A dog even.'

There were tears in Sophia's eyes but she was smiling. Laughing, in fact.

The bump of the basket touching the ground knocked them both off balance. A perfect excuse to take the woman he loved in his arms. To kiss her with all the joy of knowing there was hope that nothing was left to get in the way of them being together.

'That's it, folks.' Jim's voice came over what sounded like applause from the ground crew surrounding them. 'The ride's over.'

But it wasn't. Aiden couldn't keep a grin off his face as he helped Sophia from the basket and then pulled her close for another kiss.

The real ride was only just beginning.

'What happens now?' Sophia asked when he finally let her go.

The basket was on the back of the truck now and people were squashing air out of the balloon so it could be rolled up and put in its bag.

'A champagne breakfast,' he told her.

Her smile lit up the world. 'Is that a date?'

He grinned. 'Only if we have a new rule.'

'What's that? A thirty-dates rule?'

'I'm thinking more like a three-hundred-dates rule. And if that runs out, we'll make a new rule.'

Laughing, with their arms around each other, they made their way to the car that would take them to the vineyard restaurant.

'Or maybe we should make a rule about never having another date,' Aiden suggested.

'No.' Sophia tugged him to a halt and peered up at him, her bottom lip caught between her teeth as if she was trying not to smile. 'It's good that you've had so much practice because there's one date that's going to need quite a bit of planning.'

'What's that?'

'Our wedding?' Yes. The smile escaped.

Aiden's smile was coming but not quite yet. After a kiss, maybe. When that tight feeling in his chest of too much joy to handle had had a chance to subside a little.

It might need to be a long kiss, he realised as his lips captured hers.

Just as well Sophia didn't seem to mind.

* * * * *

JUST ONE NIGHT?

CAROL MARINELLI

PROLOGUE

'ISLA...' THE PANIC and fear was evident in Cathy's voice. 'What are all those alarms?'

'They're truly nothing to worry about,' Isla said, glancing over to the anaesthetist and pleased to see that he was changing the alarm settings so as to cause minimal distress to Cathy.

'Was it about the baby?'

Isla shook her head. 'It was just letting the anaesthetist know that your blood pressure is a little bit low but we expect that when you've been given an epidural.'

Isla sat on a stool at the head of the theatre table and did her best to reassure a very anxious Cathy as her husband, Dan, got changed to come into Theatre and be there for his wife.

'It's not the baby that's making all the alarms go off?' Cathy checked again.

'No, everything looks fine with the baby.'

'I'm so scared, Isla.'

'I know that you are,' Isla said as she stroked Cathy's cheek. 'But everything is going perfectly.'

This Caesarean section *had* to go perfectly.

Isla, head nurse at the Melbourne Maternity Unit at

the Victoria Hospital, or MMU, as it was more regularly known, had been there for Dan and Cathy during some particularly difficult times. There was little more emotional or more difficult in Isla's work than delivering a stillborn baby and she had been there twice for Cathy and Dan at such a time. As hard as it was, there was a certain privilege to being there, too—making a gut-wrenching time somehow beautiful, making the birth and the limited time with their baby poignant in a way that the family might only appreciate later.

Cathy and Dan's journey to parenthood had been hellish. They had undergone several rounds of IVF, had suffered through four miscarriages and there had been two stillbirths which Isla had delivered.

Now, late afternoon on Valentine's Day, their desperately wanted baby was about to be born.

Cathy had initially been booked in next Thursday for a planned Caesarean section at thirty-seven weeks gestation. However, she had rung the MMU two hours ago to say that she thought she was going into labour and had been told to come straight in.

Cathy had delivered her other babies naturally. Even though the labours had often been long and difficult with a stillborn, it was considered better for the mother to deliver that way.

As head of midwifery, Isla's job was supposedly nine to five, only she had long since found out that babies ran to their own schedules.

This evening she'd had a budget meeting scheduled which, on the news of Cathy's arrival, Isla had excused herself from. As well as that, she'd had drinks scheduled at the Rooftop Garden Bar to welcome Alessandro Manos, a neonatologist who was due to start at the Victoria on Monday.

For now it could all simply wait.

There was no way that Isla would miss this birth.

At twenty-eight years of age Isla was young for such a senior position and a lot of people had at first assumed that Isla had got the job simply because her father, Charles Delamere, was the CEO of the Victoria.

They'd soon found out otherwise.

Yes, outside the hospital Isla and her sister Isabel, the obstetrician who was operating on Cathy this evening, were very well known thanks to their prominent family. Glamorous, gorgeous and blonde, the press followed the sisters' busy lives with interest. There were many functions they were expected to attend and the two women shared a luxurious penthouse and dressed in the latest designer clothes and regularly stepped onto the red carpet.

That was all work to Isla.

The MMU was her passion, though—here she was herself.

She sat now dressed in scrubs, her long blonde hair tucked beneath a pink theatre cap, her full lips hidden behind a mask, and no one cared in the theatre that she was Isla Delamere, Melbourne socialite, apparently dating Rupert, whom she had gone to school with and who was now a famous Hollywood actor.

To everyone here she was simply Isla—strict, fair and loyal. She expected the same focus and attention from her staff that she gave to the patients, and she generally got it. Some thought her cool and aloof but the mothers generally seemed to appreciate her calm professionalism.

'Here's Dan.' Isla smiled as Dan nervously made his way over. He really was an amazing man and had been an incredible support to his wife through the dark times. His tears had been shed in private, he had told Isla, well away from his shocked wife. Many had said he should share the depths of his grief with Cathy but Isla understood why he chose not to.

Sometimes staying strong meant holding back.

'Dan, I'm sure that something is wrong...' Cathy said.

Dan glanced over at Isla, who gave him a small, reassuring shake of the head as her eyes told him that everything was fine.

'Everything is going well, Cathy,' Dan said. 'You're doing an amazing job, so just try and relax...'

'I can feel something,' Cathy said in a panicked voice, and Isla stepped in.

'Do you remember that I said you would feel some tugging?' Isla reminded her.

'Cathy!' Isabel's voice alerted Isla. 'Your baby is nearly out—look up at the screen...'

Isla looked up to the green sheets that had been placed so that Cathy could not see the surgery going on on the other side. 'Your baby is out,' Isabel said, 'and looks amazing...'

'There's no crying,' Cathy said.

'Just wait, Cathy,' Dan said, his voice reassuring his wife, though the poor man must be terrified.

Even Isla, who was very used to the frequent delay between birth and tears, found that she was holding her breath, though Cathy could never have guessed her midwife's nerves—Isla hid her emotions extremely well.

And not just from the staff and patients.

'Cathy!' Isla said. 'Look!'

There he was.

Isabel was holding up a beautiful baby boy with a mass of dark, spiky hair. His mouth opened wide and he let out the most ear-piercing scream, absolutely furious to be woken from a lovely sleep, to be born, of all things!

'He's beautiful,' Dan said. 'Cathy, look how beautiful he is. You did so well, I'm so proud of you.'

The baby was whisked away for a brief check and Isla made her way over as Isabel continued with the surgery.

He really was perfect.

Four weeks early, he was still a nice size and very alert. The paediatrician was happy with him and the theatre midwife wrapped him in a pale cream blanket and popped on a small hat. He would be more thoroughly checked later but that visit to the parents, if well enough, came first.

Isla took the little baby, all warm and crying, into her arms and she felt a huge gush of emotion. She had known that this birth would be emotional, but the feeling of finally being able to hand this gorgeous couple a healthy baby was a special moment indeed.

She held the baby so that Cathy could turn her head and give him a kiss and then Isla placed him on Cathy's chest as Dan put his arms around his little family.

Isla said nothing. They deserved this time to themselves and she did all she could to make this time as private as a theatre could allow it to be. She stood watching as they met their son. Dan properly broke down and cried in front of his wife for the first time.

'I can't believe I'm finally a mum…' Cathy said, and then her eyes lifted and met Isla's. 'I mean…'

When Isla spoke, she was well aware of the conflicting feelings that Cathy might have.

'You've been a mum for a very long time,' Isla said, gently referring to their difficult journey. 'Now you get the reward.'

Isla's time with Cathy and Dan didn't finish there, though. After Cathy had been sutured and Recovery was happy with her status, Isla saw them back to the ward. Cathy simply could not stop looking at her baby and Dan was immensely proud of both his wife and son.

They had made it to parenthood.

Before Cathy was discharged Isla would have a long talk with her. Often with long-awaited babies depression followed. It was a very confusing time for the new mother—often she felt guilty as everyone around her was telling her how happy she must be, how perfect things were. In fact, exhaustion, grief over previous pregnancies, failure to live up to the standards they had set themselves could cause a crushing depression in the postnatal period. Isla would speak with both Dan and Cathy about it before the family went home.

But not tonight.

For now it really was about celebrating this wonderful new life.

'I'm going to have a glass of champagne for you tonight,' Isla said as she left them to enjoy this special time.

She said goodbye to the staff on the ward then headed around to the changing room.

She'd forgotten her dress, Isla realised as soon as she opened her locker. She could picture it hanging on her bedroom door and hadn't remembered to grab it when she'd dashed for work that morning.

She glanced at the time and realised she would be horribly late if she went home to change. She knew that she really ought to go straight there as there weren't many people able to make it, given that it was Valentine's Day. Alessandro had apparently been doing a run of nights in his previous job and had booked to go away for the weekend with his girlfriend before he started his new role.

Isla rummaged through her locker to see if there was an outfit that she could somehow cobble together. She didn't have much luck! There was a pair of denim shorts that she had intended to wear with runners. Isla had actually meant to start walking during her lunch break but, of course, it had never happened. She could hardly turn up at the Rooftop Bar in shorts and the skimpy T-shirt and runners that she had in her locker, but then she saw a pair of cream wedged espadrilles that she had lent to a colleague and which had been returned.

Isla tried it all on but the sandals pushed her outfit from far too casual to far too tarty.

Oh, well, it would have to do. She was more than used to turning heads. She didn't even question if there was a dress code that needed to be adhered to. Isla didn't have to worry about such things—it was one of the perks of being a Delamere girl. You were welcome everywhere and dress codes simply didn't apply.

She ran a comb through her long blonde hair and added a quick dash of lip gloss and some blusher before racing out of the maternity unit and hailing a taxi. As she sat in the back seat she realised that she was slightly out of breath—she hadn't yet come down from the wonderful birth she had just witnessed.

Elated.

That was how she felt as she climbed the stairs and then stepped into the Rooftop Bar.

And that was how she looked when Alessi first saw her. Tall, blonde and with endless brown legs, she walked into the bar with absolute confidence. She looked vaguely familiar, he thought, though he couldn't place her. At first he didn't even know if she was a part of the small party that was gathered.

He knew, though, that, whoever she was, he would be making an effort to speak with her tonight. He watched as she gave a small wave and made her way over and he found out her name as the group greeted her.

'Isla!'

So *this* was Isla.

Alessi knew who she was then. Not just that she was head midwife at The Victoria. Not just that she must be Charles Delamere's younger daughter, which would explain why she was in such a high-up role at such a young age. No, it was more than that. Though he could not remember her from all those years ago, he knew the name—they had attended the same school.

'I'm sorry that I'm so late.' Isla smiled.

'How did it go?' Emily, one of the midwives, asked, referring to Cathy's delivery.

'It was completely amazing,' Isla said. 'I'm so lucky to have been there.'

'And I'm so jealous that you were!' Emily teased, and then made the introductions. 'Isla, this is Alessandro Manos, the new neonatologist.'

Isla only properly saw him then and as she turned her slight breathlessness increased.

He was seriously gorgeous with black, tousled curly hair and he was very unshaven. The moment she first met his black eyes all Isla could think was that she wished Rupert were here tonight.

Isla and Rupert were seemingly the golden couple. They had been together since school, where Isla had been head girl and Rupert had been head of the debating team. One night they had gone to a party and it had been there, after a very awkward kiss, that Rupert had confessed to her that he was gay.

Rupert had no idea how his parents would take the news and he was also upset at some of the rumours that were going around the school.

Isla had covered for him then and she still did to this very day.

Rupert's career had progressed over the years and his agent had strongly advised him that the roles that were being offered would be far harder to come by if the world knew the truth. He was nothing more than a wonderful friend who, in recent years, had questioned why Isla chose to keep up the ruse that they were going out.

It suited Isla, too.

Despite her apparent confidence, despite her ease in social situations, despite the questions raised by magazines about her morals, because she put up with

Rupert's supposed unfaithfulness after all, no one had ever come close to the truth—Isla was a virgin.

Her entire sexual history could be written on the back of a postage stamp. She'd had one schoolgirl kiss with Rupert that hadn't gone well at all. Now she'd had several more practised kisses with Rupert but they had been for appearances' sake only.

Often Isla felt a complete fraud when she spoke with women about birth control and pelvic floor exercises, or offered advice about lovemaking during and after pregnancy, when she had never even come close to making love with anyone herself.

Yes, how she would have loved Rupert to be here tonight, to hold her friend's hand and to lean just a little on him as the introductions were made and she stared into the black eyes of a man who actually had the usually very cool Isla feeling just a little bit dizzy.

'Call me Alessi,' he said.

'Sorry, Alessi, I keep forgetting,' Emily said. 'Isla is Head of Midwifery at MMU.'

'It is very nice to meet you,' Alessi said. He held out his hand and Isla offered hers and gave him a smile. His hand was warm as it briefly closed around the ends of her fingers and so, too, were Isla's cheeks. 'Can I get you a drink?' he offered.

'No, thanks.' Isla was about to say that she would get this round but for some reason, even as she shook her head, she changed her mind. 'Actually, yes, please, I'd love a drink. I just promised Cathy, my patient, that I was going to have a glass of champagne for her tonight.'

Alessi headed off to the bar and Emily took the opportunity to have a quick word. 'Isla, thank you for getting here, I know you were held back, but I'm really going to have to get home.'

'Of course,' Isla said. 'I know how hard it is for you to get away and I really appreciate you coming out tonight. The numbers were just so low I didn't want Alessandro, I mean Alessi, to think that nobody could be bothered to greet him. Go home to your babies.'

As Emily said her goodbyes, another colleague nudged Isla. 'Gorgeous, isn't he?'

'I guess.' Isla shrugged her shoulders. She could get away with such a dismissive comment purely because she had Rupert standing in the wings of her carefully stage-managed social life. Isla glanced over to the bar and looked at Alessi, whose back was to her as he ordered her drink. He was wearing black trousers and had a white fitted shirt on that showed off his olive skin. Isla felt a flutter in her stomach as it dawned on her that she was actually checking him out. She took in the toned torso and the long length of his legs but as he turned around she flicked her gaze away and spoke with her colleagues.

'Thank you for that,' Isla said when he handed her her drink. She was a little taken aback when he came and sat on the low sofa beside her, and she took a sip.

Oh!

With all the functions that Isla attended she knew her wines and this was French champagne at its best! 'When I said champagne…' Isla winced because here in Melbourne champagne usually meant sparkling wine. 'You must think me terribly rude.'

'Far from it,' Alessi said. 'It's nice to see someone celebrating.'

Isla nodded. 'I've just been at the most amazing

birth,' she admitted, and then, to her complete surprise, she was off—telling Alessi all about Cathy and Dan's long journey and just how wonderful the birth had been. 'I'm sorry,' she said when she realised that they had been talking about it for a good ten minutes. 'I'm going on a bit.'

'I don't blame you,' Alessi said. 'I think there is no greater reward than seeing a family make it against the odds. It is those moments that we treasure and hold onto, to get us through the dark times in our jobs.'

Isla nodded, glad that he seemed to understand just how priceless this evening's birth had been.

They chatted incredibly easily, having to tear themselves away from their conversation to say goodbye to colleagues who were starting to drift off.

'I can't believe that we went to the same school!' Isla said when Alessi brought it to her attention. 'How old are you?'

'Thirty.'

'So you would have been two years above me...' Isla tried to place him but couldn't—they would, given their age difference, for the most part, have been on separate campuses. 'You might know my older sister Isabel,' Isla said. 'She would have been a couple of years ahead of you.'

'I vaguely remember her. She was head girl when I went to the senior campus. Though I didn't really get involved in the social side—I was there on scholarship so if I wanted to stay there I really had to concentrate on making the grades. Were you head girl, too?'

Isla nodded and laughed, but Alessi didn't.

Alessi was actually having a small private battle

with himself as he recalled his private-school days. Alessi and his sister Allegra had been there, as he had just told Isla, on scholarship. Both had endured the taunts of the elite—the glossy, beautiful rich kids who'd felt that he and his sister hadn't belonged at their school. Alessi had for the most part ignored the gibes but when it had got too much for Allegra he would step in. They had both worked in the family café and put up with the smirks from their peers when they'd come in for a coffee on their way to school and found the twins serving. Now Allegra was the one who smirked when her old school friends came into Geo's, an exclusive Greek restaurant in Melbourne, and they realised how well the Manos family had done.

Still, just because they had been on the end of snobby bitchiness it didn't mean that Isla had been like that, Alessi told himself.

They got on really well.

Isla even texted him an image she had on her phone of a school reunion she had gone to a couple of years ago.

'I remember him!' Alessi said, and gave a dry laugh. 'And he would remember me!'

'Meaning?'

'We had a scuffle. He stole my sister's blazer and she was too worried to tell my parents that she'd lost another one.'

'Did you get it back?'

'Oh, yes.' Alessi grinned and then his smile faded as Isla pointed to a woman in the photo who he hadn't seen in a very long time.

'Do you remember Talia?' Isla asked. 'She's a doctor now, though she's moved to Singapore. She actually came all the way back just for the reunion.'

Alessi didn't really comment but, yes, he knew Talia. Her name was still brought up by his parents at times—how wrong he had been to shame her by ending things a couple of days before their engagement. How he could be married now and settled down instead of the casual dates that incensed his family so.

Not a soul, apart from Talia, knew the real reason why they had broken up.

It was strange that there on Isla's phone could be such a big part of his past and Isla now dragged him back to it.

'She's got four children,' Isla said. 'Four!'

Make that five, Alessi wanted to add, his heart black with recall. He could still vividly remember dropping by to check in on Talia—he'd been concerned that she hadn't been in lectures and that concern had tipped to panic as he'd seen her pale features and her discomfort. Alessi had thought his soon-to-be fiancé might be losing their baby and had insisted that Talia go to hospital. He had just been about to bring the car around when she had told him there was no longer a baby. Since the morning's theatre list at a local clinic he had, without input, no longer been a father-to-be.

Of course, he chose not to say anything to Isla and swiftly moved on, asking about Isla's Debutante Ball, anything other than revisiting the painful past. She showed him another photo and though he still could not place a teenage Isla he asked who an elderly woman in the photo was.

'Our housekeeper, Evie.' Isla gave a fond smile. 'My parents couldn't make it that night but she came.

Evie came to all the things that they couldn't get to. She was very sick then, and died a couple of months later. Evie was going to go into a hospice but Isabel and I ended up looking after her at home.'

Isla stared at the image on her phone. She hadn't looked at those photos for a very long time and seeing Evie's loving smile had her remembering a time that she tried not to.

'Would you like another drink?' Alessi offered as Isla put away her phone, both happy to end a difficult trip down memory lane.

'Not for me.'

'Something to eat?'

She was both hungry enough and relaxed with him enough to say yes.

Potato wedges and sour cream had never tasted so good!

In fact, they got on so well that close to midnight both realised it was just the two of them left.

'I'd better go,' Isla said.

'Are you on in the morning?'

'No.' Isla shook her head. 'I'm off for the weekend. I'm pretty much nine to five these days, though I do try to mix it up a bit and do some regular stints on nights.' They walked down the steps and out into the street. 'So you start on Monday?' she checked.

'I do,' Alessi said. 'I'm really looking forward to it. At the last hospital I worked at there was always a struggle for NICU cots and equipment. It is going to be really nice working somewhere that's so cutting-edge.' He looked at Isla—she was seriously stunning and was looking right into his eyes. The attraction between them had been instant and was completely undeniable. Alessi dated, flirted and enjoyed women with absolute ease. 'I'm looking forward to the weekend, too, though.'

'That's right, you're going away with your girlfriend…'

'No,' Alessi said. 'We broke up.'

'I'm sorry,' Isla said, which was the right response.

'I'm not,' Alessi said, which was the wrong response for Isla.

She was terribly aware how unguarded she had been tonight. Perhaps safe in the knowledge that he was seeing someone.

She looked into his black eyes and then her gaze flicked down and she watched as his lips stretched into a slow, lazy smile.

His mouth was seductive and he hadn't yet kissed her but she knew that soon he would.

As his lips first grazed hers Isla's nerves actually started to dissolve like a cube of sugar being dipped into warm coffee—it was sweet, it was pleasurable, it was actually sublime. Such a gentle, skilled kiss, so different from the forced ones with Rupert. It felt like soft butterflies were tickling her lips and Isla realised that her mouth was moving naturally with his.

Alessi's hands were on her hips, she could feel his warm hands through her denim shorts and she wanted more pressure, wanted more of something that she didn't know how to define, she simply didn't want it to end. But as the kiss naturally deepened, her eyes snapped open and she pulled back. Her first taste of tongue was shocking enough, but that she was kissing a man in the street was for Isla more terrifying.

He thought her easy, Isla was sure, panic building within her about where this might lead. She almost *was* easy with him because for the first time in her life she now knew how a kiss could lead straight to bed.

She had many weapons of self-defence in her armoury but she leapt straight for the big one and shot Alessi a look of absolute distaste.

'What the hell do you think you're doing?' she snapped, even if she had been a very willing participant. 'I was just trying to be friendly…'

Alessi quickly realised that he *had* been right to be cautious about her.

He knew the looks she was giving him well.

Very well!

She didn't actually say the words—*do you know who I am?* Though Isla's expression most certainly did. It was a snobby, derisive look, it was a get-your-hands-off-me-you-poor-Greek-boy look.

'My mistake,' Alessi shrugged. 'Goodnight, Isla.'

He promptly walked off—he wasn't going to hang around to be trampled on.

Her loss.

Alessi knew she'd enjoyed the kiss as much as he had and that her mouth, her body had invited more. He simply knew.

Isla *had* enjoyed their kiss.

As she climbed into a taxi she was scalding with embarrassment but there was another feeling, too—despite the appalling ending to tonight her lips were still warm from Alessi's and her body felt a little bit alive for the very first time, a touch awoken to what had seemed impossible before.

As she let herself into her flat, a gorgeous penthouse with a view of Melbourne that rivalled that of the Rooftop Bar, she smiled at Isabel.

'Sorry I didn't get there,' Isabel said. 'Did you have a good night?'

Isla, still flushed from his kiss, still a little shaken inside, nodded.

It had, in fact, been the best Valentine's night of her life.

Not that Alessi could ever know.

CHAPTER ONE

NEW YEAR'S DAY.

Isla saw the sign for the turn-off to Melbourne International Airport and carried on with her conversation as if she and Isabel were popping out for breakfast.

They were both trying to ignore the fact that Isabel was heading to live in England for a year and so, instead of talking about that, they chatted about Rupert. He was back in Melbourne for a week and the *supposed* news had broken that he'd had a fling with one of the actresses in his latest film. Not even Isabel knew that Isla's relationship with Rupert was a ruse.

'You're truly not upset?' Isabel checked, and Isla, who wore her mask well, just laughed as she turned off the freeway.

'What, I'm supposed to be upset because reports say that he got off with some actress in America a few weeks ago?' Isla shook her head. 'It doesn't bother me. I couldn't care less what they say in some magazine.'

'You're so much tougher than I am,' Isabel sighed. 'I simply can't imagine how I would feel if...' Her voice trailed off.

The conversation they had perhaps been trying to

avoid was getting closer and closer and neither wanted to face it.

Isla knew what Isabel had been about to say.

She couldn't stand to hear about Sean if he was with someone else.

Sean Anderson, an obstetrician, had been working at the Victoria since November and was the reason they were at the airport now. Sean was the reason that Isabel had accepted a professional exchange with Darcie Green and was heading for Cambridge, just to escape the re-emergence of her childhood sweetheart into her life.

The large multistorey car park at the airport had never made Isla feel sick before but it did today.

They unloaded Isabel's cases from the boot, found a trolley and then headed to the elevator. Once inside Isla pressed the button for the departure floor and forced a smile at her sister as they stood in the lift.

'If Darcie's flight gets in on time you might have time to see her,' Isla said, and Isabel nodded.

'She sounds really nice from her emails. Well, I hope she is, for your sake, given that she's going to be sharing the flat with you.'

Isla had never lived alone and so, with her older sister heading overseas and as their flat was so huge, it had seemed the perfect idea at the time. Now, though, Isla wasn't so sure. Isabel was going away to sort her heart out and Isla was going to do the same. She really wanted things to be different this year, she wanted to finally start getting on with her life, and that meant dating. That meant letting her guard down and dropping Rupert and, despite being terrified, Isla was also determined to bring on a necessary change.

Not tonight, though!

Tonight there were drinks to greet Darcie at the Rooftop Bar and Alessi would be there.

It was almost a year since that Valentine's night and since then the atmosphere between them had been strained at best. He was a playboy and made no excuse about it and Isla loathed his flirting and casual dating of her staff, though he barely glanced in her direction, let alone flirted with her. Alessi, it was clear, considered Isla to be a stuck-up cow who had somehow wormed her way into her senior position thanks to her father. They rarely worked together and that suited them both.

The early morning sun was very low and bright as Isla and Isabel crossed the tunnel that would take them from the car park to the departure lounge. A few heads turned as the sisters walked by. It wasn't just that they were both blonde and good-looking but that, thanks to their frequent appearances in the celebrity pages of newspapers and magazines, people recognised them.

Isabel and Isla were more than used to it but it felt especially invasive this morning.

Today they weren't minor celebrities but were sisters who were saying goodbye for a whole year, for a reason even *they* could not discuss—an event that had happened twelve years ago. Something that both women had fought to put behind them, though, for both, it had proved impossible.

What had happened that night had scarred them both in different ways, Isla thought as she watched Isabel check her baggage in.

She didn't really know Isabel's scars, she just knew that they were there.

They had to be.

Isla forced a smile as Isabel came back from the check-in desk.

'I'm not going to wait to meet Darcie,' Isabel said, and Isla nodded. Yes, they could stand around and talk, or perhaps go and get a coffee and extend the goodbye, but it was all just too painful. 'I think I'll just go through customs now.'

'Look out, England!' Isla attempted a little joke but then her voice cracked as they both realised that this was it. 'I'm going to miss you so much!' Isla said. She would. They not only worked and lived together but shared in the exhausting round of charity events and social engagements that took place when you were a Delamere girl.

They shared everything except a rehash of that awful night but here, on this early summer morning, for the first time it was tentatively broached. 'You understand I have to go, don't you?' Isabel asked.

Isla nodded, not trusting herself to speak.

'I don't know how to be around him,' Isabel admitted. 'Now that Sean is back, I just don't know how to deal with it. I know that he doesn't understand why I ended our relationship so abruptly. We both knew it was more than a teenage crush, he was the love of my life...' Tears were pouring down Isabel's cheeks and even though she was younger than Isabel, again, it was Isla who knew she had to be strong. She pushed aside her own hurts and fears and cuddled her big sister and told her that she was making the right choice, that she would be okay and that she could get through this.

'I know how hard it's been for you since he came to MMU,' Isla said.

'You won't say anything to Sean…'

'Oh, please,' Isla said. 'I'd never tell anyone, ever. I promised you that a long time ago. You've got this year to sort yourself out and I'm going to do the same.'

'You?' Isabel said in surprise. 'What could you possibly have to sort out? I've never known anyone more together than you.'

Isla, though, knew that she wasn't together. 'I love you,' she said, instead of answering the question.

'I love you, too.'

They had another hug and then Isla stood and watched as her sister headed towards customs and showed her passport and boarding pass. Just as she went past the point of no return Isabel paused and turned briefly and waved at a smiling Isla.

Only when Isabel had gone did Isla's smile disappear and Isla, who never cried, felt the dam breaking then. She was so grateful that she had an hour before Darcie arrived because she would need every minute of it to compose herself. As she walked back through the tunnel towards the car Isla could hardly see where she was going because her eyes were swimming in tears, but somehow she made it back to the car and climbed in and sat there and cried like she never had in her life.

Yes, she fully understood why Isabel had to get away now that Sean had returned. The memories of that time were so painful that they could still awake Isla in the middle of the night. She fully understood, with Sean reappearing, how hard it must be for Isabel to see him every day on the maternity unit.

It was agony for Isla, too.

She sat there in her car, remembering the excitement of being twelve years old and listening to a sixteen-year-old Isabel telling her about her boyfriend and dating and kissing. Isla had listened intently, hanging onto every word, but then Isabel had suddenly stopped telling her things.

A plane roared overhead and the sob that came from Isla was so deep and so primal it was as if she were back there—waking to the sound of her sister's tears and the aftermath, except this time she was able to cry about it.

Their parents had been away for a weekend. Evie, their housekeeper, had lived in a small apartment attached to the house and so, effectively, they had been alone. Isla, on waking to the sounds of her sister crying, had got out of bed and padded to the bathroom and stood outside, listening for a moment.

'Isabel?' Isla knocked on the bathroom door.

'Go away, Isla,' Isabel said, then let out very low groan and Isla realised that her sister was in pain.

'Isabel,' Isla called. 'Unlock the door and let me in.'

Silence.

But then came another low moan that had Isla gripped with fear.

'Isabel, please.' She knocked on the door again, only this time with urgency. 'If you don't let me in then I'm going to go and get Evie.'

Evie was so much more than a housekeeper. She looked after the two girls as if they were her own. She worried about them, was there for them while their parents attended their endless parties.

They both loved her.

Isla was just about to run and get Evie when the door was unlocked and Isla let herself in. She stepped inside the bathroom and couldn't believe what she saw. Isabel was drenched in sweat and there was blood on the tiles, but as she watched her sister fold over it dawned on Isla what was happening.

Isabel was giving birth.

'Please don't tell Evie,' Isabel begged. 'No one must know, Isla, you have to promise me that you will never tell anyone…'

Somehow, despite the blood, despite the terror and the moans from her sister, Isla stayed calm.

She knew what she had to do.

Isla dropped down to her knees on instinct rather than fear as Isabel lay back on the floor, lifting herself up on her elbows. 'It's okay, Isabel,' Isla said reassuringly. 'It's going to be okay.'

'There's something between my legs…' Isabel groaned. 'It's coming.'

Isla had been born a midwife, she knew that then. It was strange but even at that tender age, somehow Isla dealt with the unfolding events. She looked down at the tiny scrap that had been born to her hands and managed to stay calm as an exhausted Isabel wept.

He was dead, that much Isla knew, yet he was perfect. His little eyes were fused closed and he was so very still.

Tomorrow she would start to doubt herself. Tomorrow she would wonder if there was something more that she could have done for him. In the months and years ahead Isla would terrorise herself with those very questions and would go over and over holding her little nephew in her hands instead of doing more.

But there, in that moment, in the still of the bathroom, Isla knew.

She wrapped her tiny nephew in a small hand towel. There was the placenta and the cord still attached and she continued to hold him as Isabel lay on the floor, sobbing.

'He's beautiful,' Isla said. He was. She gazed upon his features as her fingers held his tiny, tiny hands and she looked at his spindly arms and cuddled him and then, when Isabel was ready, Isla handed the tiny baby to her.

'Did you know you were pregnant?' Isla asked, but Isabel said nothing, just stared at her tiny baby and stroked his little cheek.

'Does Sean know?' Isla asked.

'No one knows,' Isabel said. 'No one is ever to know about this.' She looked at Isla, her eyes urgent. 'You have to promise me that you will never, ever tell anyone.'

Some promises were too big to make, though.

'I have to tell Evie,' Isla said.

'Isla, please, no one must know.'

'And so what are we supposed to do with him?' Isla demanded.

'I don't know.'

'You know what you *don't* want me to do, though. You know that he needs to be properly taken care of,' Isla said, and Isabel nodded tearfully.

'You won't tell anyone else,' Isabel sobbed. 'Promise me, Isla.'

'I promise.'

Isla sped through the house and to Evie. The elderly housekeeper was terribly distressed at first, but then she calmed down and dealt with things. She understood, better than most, the scandal this might cause and the terrible impact it would have on Isabel if it ever got out. She had a sister who worked in a hospital in the outer suburbs and Evie called her and asked what to do.

Isla sat, her tears still flowing as she recalled the drive out of the city to the suburbs. Isabel was holding the tiny baby and crying beside her till the lights of the hospital came into view. Evie's sister met them and Isabel was put in a wheelchair and taken to Maternity, with Isla following behind. The midwife who had greeted them had been so lovely to Isabel, just so calm, wise and efficient.

'What happens now?' Isla asked. It was as if only then had they noticed that Isabel's young sister was there and she was shown to a small waiting room.

It had been the last time Isla had seen her nephew.

She didn't really know what had gone on.

Evie had come in at one point and said that the baby was too small to be registered. Isla hadn't known what that meant other than that no one would have to find out.

Her parents would later question Isla's decision to become a midwife. They had deemed that it wasn't good enough for a Delamere girl but Isla had stood by her calling.

She'd wanted to be as kind and as calm as the staff had been with Isabel that night.

With one modification.

Though her sister had been gently dealt with by midwives who had been used to terrified sixteen-year-old girls who did not want their parents to find out, one person had been forgotten.

Isla had sat alone and unnoticed in the waiting room.

Now she knew things should have been handled differently—the midwives, the obstetrician, at least one of them should have recognised Isla's terror and spoken at length with her about what had happened. They should have come in and taken care of the twelve-year-old girl who had just delivered her dead nephew. They should have carefully explained that the baby had been born at around eighteen weeks gestation, which had meant that there was nothing Isla could have possibly done to save him.

It would be many years before Isla got those answers and she'd had to find them out for herself.

Yes, that night had left scars.

Despite appearances, despite her immaculate clothes and long glossy hair and seemingly spectacular social life, Isla had equated sex with disaster. Not logically, of course, but throughout her teenage years she had avoided dating boys and in her final year at school Rupert had seemed the perfect solution. Still she'd kept the secret of that night to herself.

She had promised her sister after all.

CHAPTER TWO

ISLA DID WHAT she could to repair the damage to her face—her eyelids were puffy, her nose was red and her lips swollen. Isla never cried. Even at the most difficult births she was very aware that even a single tear might lead back to that memory and so she kept her emotions in check.

Always.

She put on some sunglasses and made her way to Arrivals, where she stood, her eyes moving between the three exit doors and wondering if she would even recognise Darcie when she came out.

As it turned out, it was Darcie who recognised her.

'Isla!' Her name was called from behind the rail and the second she turned Isla's face broke into a smile.

'I was watching the wrong door.' Isla greeted Darcie with a hug. 'Happy New Year,' she said.

'Happy New Year, to you, too.' Darcie smiled.

'I was starting to worry that I wouldn't recognise you when you came out,' Isla admitted.

'Well, I certainly recognised you. You're as gorgeous as you are in the magazine I was just…' Darcie's voice trailed off and she went a bit pink, perhaps guessing that the article she had read on the plane might not be Isla's favourite topic, given that it had revealed Rupert's infidelity.

Isla let that comment go and they stepped out into the morning sun. Melbourne was famous for its fickle weather but this morning the sky was silver blue and the sun had been firmly turned on to welcome Darcie.

'It shouldn't take too long to get home,' Isla said as they hit the morning rush-hour traffic. 'Did you get much sleep on the plane?'

'Not really.' Darcie shook her head. 'I shan't be much company today.'

'That's fine.' Isla smiled. 'I'm dropping you home and then I'll be going into work so you'll have the place to yourself.'

'You should have told me that you were working this morning!' Darcie said. 'I could have taken a taxi. You didn't have to come out to the airport to meet me.'

'It was no problem and I was there anyway to see Isabel off.'

'Oh, of course you were.' Darcie glanced at Isla. Despite the repair job that Isla had done with make-up and dark glasses, it was quite clear to Darcie that she had been crying. Now, though, Darcie thought she knew why. 'It must have been hard to say good-bye to your sister.'

'It was,' Isla admitted. 'I'm going to miss her a lot, though I bet she's going to have an amazing year in England.'

They chatted easily as they drove into Melbourne. Isla pointed out a few landmarks—Federation Square and the Arts Centre—and Darcie said she couldn't wait to get on a tram.

'We'll be catching one tonight,' Isla told her. 'I've

organised for some colleagues to get together and have drinks tonight. It's a bit of a tradition on the maternity unit that we all try to get together before a new staff member starts, just so we can get most of the introductions out of the way and everything. If it's too much for you, given how far you've flown, everyone will understand.'

'No, it won't be too much, that sounds lovely. I'm looking forward to meeting everyone.'

'Have you left a boyfriend behind?' Isla asked, and Darcie shook her head.

'No, I'm recently single and staying that way. I'm here to focus on my career. I've heard so much about the MMU at the Victoria—I just can't wait to get started.'

'There it is.' Isla drove slowly past the hospital where Darcie would commence work the next day. It was a gorgeous old building that, contrary to outer appearances, was equipped with the best staff and equipment that modern medicine had to offer.

They soon pulled into the underground car park of the apartment block and took the lift to the penthouse.

'Wow,' Darcie said as they stepped inside. 'When you said that we'd be sharing a flat…' She was clearly a bit taken aback by the rather luxurious surroundings and looked out of the floor-to-ceiling windows to the busy city below. 'It's stunning.'

'It will soon feel like home,' Isla assured her. 'I'll give you a quick tour but then I really need to get to work.'

'There's no need for a tour,' Darcie said. 'I'll just be having a very quick shower and then bed. I'll probably still be in it when you get home.'

Isla showed Darcie to her room. It had its own en suite and Isla briefly went through how to use the remote control for the blinds and a few other things and then she quickly got changed to head into work. 'I'll try and get back about six o'clock,' Isla said. 'I've told people to get there about seven, but if I do get stuck at work I'll send a colleague to pick you up.'

'There's no need for that.' Darcie was clearly very independent, Isla realised. 'Just tell me the name of the bar and if you can't make it home in time, I'll find my own way there.'

Isla smiled, though she shook her head. 'I'm not leaving you to make your own way there on your first day in Melbourne.'

Darcie was nice, Isla decided as she drove to work. She still felt a little bit unsettled from her breakdown earlier. She had never cried like that. In fact, she did everything she could not to think about that terrible morning. The trouble was, though, since Sean had arrived, that long-ago time seemed to be catching up with both Isabel and her. As if to prove her point, the first person she saw when she walked into MMU was Sean. With no dark glasses to hide behind now, Isla's heart sank a little when he called her over.

'I was wondering if you could have a word with Christine Adams for me,' Sean said. 'I know how good you are with teenagers and, in all honesty, nothing I say about contraception seems to be getting through to her. At this rate, Christine is going to be back here in nine months' time. I inserted an IUD after delivery but, as you know, she had a small haemorrhage and it's been expelled so I can't put another one in for six weeks. She's also got a history of deep vein thrombosis so she's not able to go on the Pill. Can you just re-iterate to her and her boyfriend that they need to use condoms every time? She's told me that she doesn't want another baby for a couple of years, and I think she's right—her body needs a rest.'

'She's very anaemic, isn't she?' Isla checked.

'She is. I was considering a transfusion when she bled but she's going to try and get her iron up herself.'

'I'll have a chat,' Isla agreed. She was very used to dealing with young mums and last year had started a group called Teenage Mums-To-Be, or TMTB, as it was known. Even though she couldn't always be there to take the group, one of the other midwives would run it for her if necessary and they often had an obstetri-cian come along to talk to the young women, too. It was proving to be a huge success.

Christine had attended TMTB for two babies in one year. Robbie, who had been born a couple of days ago, was her second baby. This morning Christine was going home to look after a newborn *and* a ten-month-old with her iron level in her boots. Isla knew that Sean was right, she could be back again at the MMU very soon.

'One other thing, Isla,' Sean started as Isla went to head off, but whatever he'd been about to say was put on hold as he looked over Isla's shoulder. 'Good morning, Alessi, thanks for coming down—you're looking very smart.'

Especially smart, Isla thought! Alessi's good looks and easy smile she did not need this morning, espe-cially as he was looking particularly divine. He was dressed in an extremely impressive suit, his tie was immaculately knotted and he was, for once, freshly

shaven. He might as well be on his way to a wedding
rather than dropping into the unit to check a newborn
that Sean was worried about.

'Good morning, all,' Alessi said.

'Morning, Alessi,' one of Isla's midwives called.

'Looking good,' someone else commented, and Isla
bristled as she heard a wolf whistle come from the
treatment room.

They were like bees to honey around him and
Alessi took it all in his stride and just smiled, though
it did not fall in Isla's direction. They didn't get on.
Of course they were professional when they worked
together. Their paths often crossed but they both tried
to make sure that there was as little contact as possible. His flirting with her staff annoyed the hell out
of Isla, however, and she was very tempted to have a
word with him about it. She had recently found out
that he was dating one of her students, Amber.

That made it sound worse than it was, Isla knew—
Amber was a mature-age student and older than she
herself was, but even so, Isla wasn't impressed.

What she couldn't dispute, though, was that Alessi
was one of the hardest-working doctors she had ever
known. As hard as he dated, he worked. He was there
in the mornings when she arrived and often long after
she went home.

'What do you have for me?' Alessi asked Sean, but
before he could answer Isla made to go.

'I'll leave you both to it,' Isla said.

'Could you hold on a second, Isla? I still want to
speak with you,' Sean said, thwarting her attempt to
make a swift getaway. He turned to Alessi. 'I've got
a baby I delivered in the early hours. He seemed to be

fine when delivered but there's no audible cry now. All observations are normal and he seems well other than he isn't making much noise when he cries.'

'I'll take a look.' Alessi nodded.

'So why are you all dressed up?' Sean asked, given that Alessi usually dressed in scrubs and looked as if he had just rolled out of bed.

'I'm having lunch today with the bigwigs...' Alessi rolled his eyes and then they did meet Isla's and he gave her a tight smile. 'I'm actually having lunch with Isla's father.'

She couldn't quite put her finger on it but Isla knew that he was having a little dig at her.

'Enjoy,' Isla said.

'I shan't,' Alessi tartly replied. 'Sometimes you have to just suffer through these things.'

The lunch that Alessi was speaking about was due to the fact that he was soon to be receiving an award in recognition of his contributions to the neonatal unit over the past year. There was a huge fundraising ball being held in a couple of weeks' time and Charles Delamere was attempting to push Alessi towards the charitable side of things—hence the lunch today, where it would be strongly suggested that Alessi, with his good looks and easy smile, might be a more visible presence. While Alessi knew how essential fundraising was and felt proud to have his achievements acknowledged, a part of him resented having to walk the talk. He'd far rather be getting on with the job than appearing on breakfast television to speak about the neonatal unit, as Charles had recently suggested.

Alessi chatted for a moment more with Sean but, during that brief exchange with Isla, he had noted the puffiness around her eyes and had guessed, rightly, that she had been crying. He was wrong about the reason, though. Alessi assumed Isla's tears were because of the weekend reports about her boyfriend's philandering. Even if she was upset there was still plenty of the ice-cold Isla, Alessi thought as she stood there. Her stance was bored and dismissive and she didn't even deign to give him a glance as he headed off to examine the infant.

Isla was anything but bored, though. Seemingly together, she was shaking inside as Alessi walked off because she knew that Sean was going to ask her about Isabel.

'How was this morning?' Sean asked.

'Fine.'

'Isabel got off okay?'

'She just texted to say that she's boarding.' Isla nodded and then did her best to change the subject. 'What did you want to speak with me about?'

'Just that,' Sean answered. 'Isla, my working here didn't have any part in her decision—'

'Sean, Isabel was offered a year's secondment in England. Who wouldn't give their right arm for that?'

'It just—'

'I'm too busy to stand here, chatting,' Isla said, and walked off.

Yes, she could be aloof at times but it was surely better to be thought of as that than to stand discussing Isabel's leaving with Sean.

Isla went to the store cupboard and got some samples of condoms. She put them in a bag and then headed in to speak with Christine, who was there with

Blake, her boyfriend, who was also eighteen. Little Joel, their older baby, was also there.

Isla was usually incredibly comfortable approaching such subjects with her patients. She discussed contraception many times a day both on the ward and in the postnatal clinic but when she walked behind the curtains, where Christine was nursing her baby, she also saw Alessi's shoes gleaming beneath the other side of the curtains. That he was examining the baby in the next bed to Christine made Isla feel just a little bit self-conscious.

'Hi, there, Christine.' Isla smiled. 'Hi, Blake. I hear that you're all going home this morning?'

'I can't wait to get him home,' Christine said, and gazed down at Robbie. He was latched onto Christine's breast, beautifully and happily feeding away.

'You're doing so well,' Isla commented. 'You're still feeding Joel, aren't you?'

'Just at night,' Christine replied, 'though he's jealous and wants me all the time now, too.'

Isla glanced over at Joel, who was staring at his new brother with a very put-out look on his face. Christine really was an amazing mum, but Isla could well understand Sean's concern and why he was asking her to reiterate what he had said. Christine was incredibly pale and breastfeeding a newborn and a ten-month-old would certainly take its toll. 'I wanted to have a word with you about contraception—'

'Oh, we've already been spoken to about that,' Christine interrupted. 'The midwife said something this morning and Dr Sean has been in, so you really don't need to explain things again.'

'I do.'

'I'll leave you to it, then.' Blake went to stand but Isla shook her head.

'Oh, no.' Isla smiled as Blake reluctantly sat down. 'I want to speak with both of you. As you know, the IUD insertion didn't work. That happens sometimes, but now it's better that the doctor waits for your six-week checkup to put another in.'

'Dr Sean has explained that,' Christine sighed.

'You do know that you can't rely on breastfeeding as a form of contraception,' Isla gently reminded them, and Christine started to laugh as she looked down at Robbie.

'I know that now—given that I'm holding the proof.'

'And you understand that you can't take the Pill because of your history of blood clots,' Isla continued as Christine vaguely smiled and nodded. She really wasn't taking any of this in. 'You need to use condoms every time, or not have intercourse…'

'There's always the morning-after pill,' Christine said, and Isla shook her head. Privately she didn't like the morning-after pill, unless it was after an episode of abuse, not that she would ever push her own beliefs onto her patients. It was the fact that Christine had a history of blood clots that ruled it out for her and Isla told her so. 'You need to be careful—' Isla started, but Christine interrupted again.

'I'm not waiting six weeks and he…' she nodded her head in Blake's direction '…certainly can't wait that long.'

'I'm not asking you both to wait till then,' Isla said patiently. 'Though you don't *have* to have penetrative sex, there are other things you can do.' Christine just rolled her eyes and Isla ploughed on. 'If you are going to have sex before the IUD is put in then you are to use condoms each and every time.' She looked at Blake. 'That's why I asked to speak to you, too.'

'Oh, leave him alone.' Christine grinned.

'Christine, you're very anaemic and the last thing your body needs now is another pregnancy. I'm just asking Blake to make sure that he's careful.'

'It's not his fault, he tries to be careful,' Christine said, happy to leap to Blake's defence. 'Haven't you ever got so carried away that you just don't care, Isla?'

Isla glanced at the shoes on the other side of the curtain and just knew that Alessi could hear every word and was no doubt having a little laugh.

Rarely, her cheeks were pink as she looked back at Christine.

'Well?' Christine demanded. 'I think you know what I'm talking about, Isla.'

'But this isn't about me,' Isla answered calmly. 'I've raided the store cupboard.' She handed Blake what would hopefully be adequate supplies. 'One each time!' Isla said. 'Or I'll be seeing see you very soon. Perhaps with twins this time, wouldn't that be nice? Four under two, what fun!'

She saw Blake blink and he glanced at Christine and then back at Isla, and hopefully the message had sunk in. 'Got it?' Isla said.

'Got it,' Blake agreed.

As she left them to go through their goody bag she walked straight into Alessi, who was wearing a smile, and there was an extremely rare truce because all Isla could do was let out a little laugh.

'You didn't answer the question, Isla,' Alessi teased.

'No, I didn't.'

'A case of do as I say, not as I do?' Alessi nudged and Isla gave a non-committal smile. He'd die on the spot if he knew the truth but thankfully the small armistice was soon over and Alessi got back to talking about work, which Isla knew better how to handle. 'I'm very happy with the baby that Sean just asked me to see. There's no sign of infection—I think he has a floppy larynx, which is causing the husky cry. Still, I'm going to do a blood test and can his temperature be checked every two hours? Any deterioration at all then I'm to be called straight away.' He watched as Isla nodded and he again took in her puffy eyes and was tempted to say something.

But what could he say?

I'm sorry to hear that your boyfriend's been screwing around on you again?

Alessi wasn't sorry.

Well, perhaps he was sorry for the hurt that had been dished out to Isla but he wasn't sorry that her relationship with Rupert was over.

Close to a year on, despite not particularly *liking* her, Alessi still found himself thinking about that night.

Still, despite her cool disdain, despite having been born with a silver spoon in her mouth, as opposed to the plastic café one that he had been born to, he could not quite get her out of his head.

'What time is everybody meeting tonight?' he asked.

'About seven.'

'Good. Shall I see you there?'

'You shall.'

This was as close to a personal conversation they'd had since that night.

And that was how it would remain, he decided as he walked off.

He didn't like his attraction to her, didn't like that eleven months on, the scent of her was a familiar one whenever they were close, and he didn't like that, despite trying not to, today he had found himself with no choice but to smile into her eyes.

Stay back, Alessi, he told himself.

He liked to keep things light with women. Since Talia he hadn't liked to get too involved. But all that aside, Alessi was determined that Isla Delamere would not be changing her mind on him twice.

CHAPTER THREE

ISLA GOT CAUGHT up in a delivery and didn't make it home until well after six, but Darcie was up and it was actually nice not to come back to an empty flat but share in a glass of wine as they got ready.

'Can I borrow your hair dryer?' Darcie asked. 'The adapter that I brought isn't working.'

'Sure,' Isla said, and went and got it. 'I'll just text Rupert and let him know that I'm running a bit late and to meet us there.'

'Oh, so you're still seeing each—' Darcie abruptly halted whatever it was she'd been about to say. 'I'm so sorry, Isla. That is absolutely none of my business. I think I must have left my manners in England!'

'It's fine.' Isla shrugged. 'My sister said pretty much the same thing this morning. Look, it really isn't awkward. I don't get upset by what's said in the magazines, they're full of rubbish and lies…'

'Of course they are. It's nice that you can trust him.' Darcie smiled but Isla could see a small flicker of pity in her eyes and knew that Darcie, like everybody else, assumed that Isla was being taken for a fool.

Isla went to have a very quick shower, though perhaps it wasn't quite as quick as the one she had intended to have.

New Year, new start, Isla decided as she soaped up.

She *was* going to break up with Rupert.

Isla already knew that she had to stop hiding behind him and certainly she didn't like it that people thought she was somehow standing by her man as Rupert seemingly made a fool of her.

Rupert had rung and explained what had happened before the news had hit. The actress had the same agent as Rupert and the supposed tell-all had been at the agent's direction. Only when the exposé had happened had Rupert found out it had been planned.

'Not good enough,' Isla had said. Still, she found it hard to be cross with him—after all, she knew that what had been said in the article was all lies.

Isla was determined to end it, though she was tempted to put off the break-up. She had asked Rupert to stick close to her tonight and she was nervous about the charity ball coming up in a couple of weeks. Alessi's award meant that he would be sitting at the same table as her father—the same table as her!

Yet things had seemed better when they'd spoken today, Isla thought, recalling the smile he had given as she'd come out from behind Christine's curtain. She closed her eyes for a moment and remembered their kiss that night and just how nice it had been to briefly be in his arms. She stood in the shower, the water cascading over her, as she returned to the blissful memory. Her hands moved over her hips as she remembered his there, and then her eyes snapped open as one hand started to move down of its own accord as she ached, honestly ached to return to the memory and bring it to a more fitting conclusion. She wanted to know what might have happened had she not said no. She wanted to explore the possibilities, her body was almost begging her to.

Isla stood, stunned by her own arousal.

She had buried her sexuality completely.

Since the night she'd delivered Isabel's baby she'd just quashed that side of herself.

Now, though, her breasts felt so heavy she was fighting herself not to touch them and the intense ache between her legs refused to recede. For the first time she wanted to explore her own body.

Shocked, Isla turned off the shower taps and stepped out. She quickly dried herself and pulled on some underwear and dressed. She wore a very pale green summer dress that did nothing to reduce the flush on her cheeks. She simply couldn't stop thinking about Alessi and that he'd be there tonight and so, too, that smile.

And the memory of that kiss.

He'd use you, Isla reminded herself as she put on lip gloss. The same way he'd worked his way through half of MMU.

Not that any of the staff seemed to regret their flings with Alessi.

Would she regret one?

Isla snapped herself out of it.

There was no way she was going to do anything about the reluctant torch she carried for Alessi. She could actually picture his incredulous smile if she told him her truth. Scrap that, incredulous laughter, she amended, and then headed out to the lounge.

'You look great.' Darcie smiled. 'I'm actually nervous about meeting everyone.'

'Well, don't be,' Isla said. 'They're a friendly bunch.'

It was a warm, sultry night and they took a tram for a couple of stops and then arrived at the bar and, as promised, everybody was incredibly friendly and pleased to meet the new obstetrician.

'This is Lucas,' Isla introduced them. 'He's a senior midwife on the MMU…'

'It's nice to meet you,' Darcie said with a smile, and Isla continued the introductions.

'And this is Sophia, a community midwife…' Thankfully, for Isla, Alessi wasn't there, and she allowed herself to relax. She went and bought some drinks and ordered a couple of bottles for the table but as she walked back she saw Alessi had just arrived. What gnawed at Isla was that he was there with Amber.

'This is Alessi.' Isla pushed out a smile. 'He's a neonatologist. Alessi, this is Darcie…' She watched as he smiled his killer smile at Darcie and then Isla continued. 'And this Amber, a *student* midwife…' Isla almost winced as she heard the tart note to her voice and she caught Alessi's eye. She wasn't jealous that he was dating her student; she wanted to tell him instead that she was cross.

'Hi, there.' Isla jumped as she heard Rupert's voice and felt his arm come around her waist. 'Sorry if I'm a bit late.'

'It's fine.' Isla had never been more pleased to see him and gave him a kiss—the practised kiss that they were both used to. What she wasn't so used to was turning back to the table and the black look Alessi was throwing in Rupert's direction.

He looked then at Isla and gave the smallest shake of his head.

All evening she found herself aware of his disapproval.

Well, she very much disapproved of who Alessi was dating, too.

Her skin prickled when he spoke with Amber. Her usually cool edge seemed to be melting and though the conversation flowed at the table, for once Isla wasn't the perfect hostess. Thankfully everybody was keen to hear about how things worked in Cambridge, where Darcie was from and where Isabel would now be working. No one, apart from Rupert and Alessi, seemed to notice her tension.

'Take it easy,' Rupert said, because Isla was again topping up her glass. Isla rarely drank more than one glass of champagne but tonight she was rather grateful for the wine, and Rupert, who could sense her volatility, was right to warn her.

Not that Alessi approved of Rupert telling her what to do—Isla saw the sharp rise of his eyebrows at Rupert's words.

Alessi didn't like it that Rupert, given what he was putting her through, had just warned Isla to slow down. He didn't like it that Rupert was here in the least. Alessi was, in fact, having an extremely uncomfortable evening, though it wasn't Isla that he felt bad for, but Amber. Alessi, even if his relationships didn't last very long, would never cheat or flirt with another woman, except his mind was fighting not to do just that.

It felt wrong to be sitting with Amber while Isla was there.

He was very aware that he was sitting next to the wrong woman.

'I'm just going to go to the loo,' Isla said, and as she got up to leave, Alessi made himself sit there, though the temptation was to follow her.

The restrooms were located right on the other side of the bar and Isla headed off. She knew she had maybe had a little bit too much to drink and was glad of the chance to just take a breath.

No one had said a word about Rupert. They were all used to Isla bringing him along but she was aware of slight pity in her colleagues' eyes and Isla loathed it.

Tonight she *was* ending it, which left her without a safety net, and as she walked out of the loos and straight into Alessi the Rupert-free tightrope got its first wobble, the first inkling of what was to come.

'Everything okay?' Alessi asked, because the look that she gave him was less than pleasant.

'Actually, no,' Isla said. 'What are you doing, dating one of my students?'

'Excuse me?'

'You heard.'

'She isn't *my* student,' Alessi pointed out. 'You're talking as if Amber's eighteen when, in fact, she's a thirty-two-year-old single mother of two. I'm hardly leading her astray—'

'I don't like the way you flirt with my midwives,' Isla interrupted, and Alessi gave her a slow smile, though his eyes told her he was less than impressed with what she was saying.

'Have there been any complaints?'

'Of course not.'

'Any hint as to inappropriateness on my part?' Alessi checked, and watched Isla's cheeks turn to fire as she shook her head. 'Then I'd tread very carefully here if I were you, Isla,' he said. 'The staff don't have an issue?' He raised an eyebrow and Isla gave a terse shake of her head. 'And I don't have an issue,' he drawled. 'So, in fact, the only person who has a problem with my dating Amber is you. I wonder why that is?'

Isla stood, her face flaming. She knew that she shouldn't have said anything, especially not tonight, but now that she had it was impossible to take it back. 'I'm just letting you know how I feel about the issue.'

'What issue?'

Isla licked her tense lips as he backed her to the wall but her lack of response didn't end the conversation.

'I flirt, Isla. I date. I enjoy women but only women who get that it's only ever going to be short-term...'

'Why?'

The question was out before she considered it but it was pertinent enough to halt Alessi in his tracks.

Why?

It was a question few, outside the family, asked him. A question he had never truthfully answered and he had no intention of doing so now.

'Because that is how I choose to live my life. I don't need your approval, or you to rubber-stamp who I date from MMU, but I can tell you now I have never once cheated on anyone. I don't have to make up lies or excuses about what's been said or where I've been...'

'I need to get back,' Isla said, not liking where this

conversation was leading, but Alessi wouldn't let her off the hook.

'We've only just started talking,' he said. 'And given you're so inclined to discuss my sex life, I'm sure you won't mind if I share my feelings about yours. Have some respect for yourself...' He met her eyes and Isla took a sharp breath as he now voiced what nobody else had had the guts to. 'What are you with him for, Isla? It's all over the internet and plastered across every magazine that he's screwing around and yet you're carrying on as if nothing's happened.'

'It's none of your business.'

'Well, I'm making it mine,' Alessi said. 'Why would you let him treat you like that?' He looked over as Rupert came around the corner and stood for a moment as he witnessed the angry confrontation.

'There you are,' Rupert said, and, having been instructed by Isla to stay close, he came and put an arm around her waist, dropping a kiss on her head. 'Darcie is starting to droop. I think she might need to go home.'

'Sure,' Isla said as Alessi just stood there, staring at Rupert with a challenge in his eyes. 'If you can tell Darcie that I'll be there in a few minutes, that would be great. I just need to discuss something with Alessi.'

As Rupert walked off Alessi's angry eyes met Isla's. 'He's got a nerve,' Alessi said, 'telling you that you've had too much wine and coming to check up on you, yet he gets to carry on exactly as he chooses...'

'Our relationship is not your concern,' Isla said, her voice shaking. There was no doubt about the sudden flare of possessiveness in Alessi's voice. 'Anyway, you flirt, you...' She tripped over her words, not quite sure of the point she was trying to make. 'You're such a chauvinist.'

'It's the Greek in me.'

They stood angry and frustrated. A kiss was there but not happening. They were back to where they had been a year ago, only the stakes were much higher now. Alessi looked at her full mouth and noticed that she ran a very pink tongue over her lips as if to tempt him.

And tempt him it did.

Isla was looking at his mouth. She was back to how she'd felt in the shower, only now Alessi was less than a step away. Her body was on fire, there was sex in the air, and when walking away might be safer, because it was Alessi, he forced the issue, voiced the truth, stated what was. 'I could kiss you now.'

Isla lifted her eyes to his and saw that the lust and the want in his matched hers. 'You could,' she invited.

She wanted his kiss. The world had disappeared and she had no thought about anything other than now and a kiss that was nearing, but she blinked at his caustic response to her provocative words.

'But I won't,' Alessi said, distaste evident in his voice. 'I happen to have respect for the person I'm with. I have no intention of getting mixed up in whatever twisted game it is that you're playing.'

Isla stepped back, felt the wall behind her and wished it would swallow her up. Alessi was right. It was twisted. The wall would not give, though, and she had to stand there and take it as Alessi continued venting, eleven months of frustration contorting his lips savagely. 'And there's another reason that I shan't kiss you—I won't give you the chance to blow me off again, Isla. You'll be the one to kiss me,' he warned. 'After you've suitably apologised.'

And with that he walked off, leaving Isla standing there, trying to think of an appropriate response to that most delicious threat.

'Never,' she called to his departing back.

'We'll see,' Alessi called, without turning around.

He was furious. He flashed a look at Rupert as he left but what angered Alessi most was that to not kiss Isla had taken all the self-control he could muster. To not press her to the wall and angrily claim her mouth had taken every ounce of his resistance.

He wasn't like that.

Yes, he might have dated an awful lot of women but he was always faithful.

This was why he ended things with Amber that night.

He wanted Isla.

He wanted her in a way he never had.

He wanted to see that snobby, derisive woman begging.

Yes, for the best part of a year he'd convinced himself otherwise but the truth remained—he wanted her.

CHAPTER FOUR

DARCIE REALLY WAS DROOPING. Once home she thanked Isla and Rupert for the night out and went straight to bed. Thankfully Isla didn't have to work out what to say—Rupert said it for her.

'I'm guessing we're breaking up?'

'We are.' Isla forced a brave smile. 'You can say that I'm sick and tired of all your other women.'

'How are you going to go at the ball with your Greek friend there? I assume he's a big part of the reason for us finishing tonight.'

'He hates me,' Isla said. 'And I don't particularly like him, either.'

'Well, that sounds like a good start to me.' Rupert smiled. He knew Isla very well and there were very few people that she allowed to get under her skin. He had felt the undeniable tension all night and had seen Alessi's eyes all too often turn to look towards Isla. 'It's more than time you got out there.'

'Well, I shan't be *getting out there* with Alessi. His relationships seem to last as long as a tube of tooth-paste.'

'Ah, but you have to brush your teeth, Isla.' To Rupert, it was that simple. 'Go for it. It's as clear as anything that you fancy each other. Why not just give the two of you a try? If it doesn't work out, it's no big deal.'

It was to Isla, though.

They said goodbye at the door—it was possibly the nicest break-up in the world.

'This is way overdue, Isla,' Rupert said as he gave her a cuddle. Even he didn't know about Isabel and just how deep Isla's fears ran, and saying goodbye to her rock of ten years was hard.

'I know.' She gave him a smile. 'Will you be okay?'

'I shall, but, Isla, can I ask that you don't—'

Isla knew what he was about to say and said it for him. 'I shan't tell anyone about you.'

'Promise me.' His voice was urgent. 'I'm auditioning soon for a really big role. If I do get it then I'm going to be even more in the spotlight…' She could hear his fear and she understood it. She, too, would be terrified to have her sex life, or lack of it, put under the scrutiny of anyone, let alone having it discussed the world over. 'I haven't even told my parents, Isla…'

'It's okay,' Isla soothed, remembering the promise she had made all those years ago. 'I gave you my word.'

When Isla awoke the next morning and headed into work with Darcie, the world felt very different without her safety net.

Not that anyone could know just how exposed and vulnerable she felt. She was her usual cool self while secretly hoping that the world might treat her gently.

The world, though, had other plans for Isla—around eleven, she answered a page from the antenatal clinic.

It was Sophia, one of the community midwives, who, because of low staff numbers, was doing an extra shift on-site today and running the antenatal clinic.

'Thanks for answering so quickly,' Sophia said. 'I wasn't sure whether or not to page you. I'm probably—'

'Always page me,' Isla interrupted. 'It doesn't matter how small your concern is, I hope you know that.'

'I do,' Sophia said. 'It's not a patient I'm concerned about, more a situation that I'm not sure how to handle. Alessi dropped by this morning and said that when his sister arrived for her antenatal visit I was to page him so that he could come down. Allegra is actually his twin sister.'

'Okay,' Isla replied, wondering where this was leading as Sophia continued.

'She's thirty-two weeks gestation and Darcie has asked her to go onto a CTG monitor now for a checkup—all is well but Darcie just wanted to be thorough as she's taking over her care and Allegra has quite a complicated history. The trouble is, when I said that I would let Alessi know that she was here, Allegra asked me not to. She wants me to just say that I forgot to page him...'

'And no doubt you're worried about what Alessi will say when you tell him that you *forgot* to let him know?' Isla said, and then thought for a moment. 'It is a bit awkward,' she admitted as she pondered the issue while doing her level best to think this through as she would for any patient who was related to one of the staff here. She had to somehow forget that the staff member happened to be Alessi who, after last night, she was doing her level best to avoid.

Ignore that fact, she told herself.

'I'll come over to Antenatal now and speak with Allegra,' Isla offered. 'And I'll also deal with Alessi. Thank you for letting me know, Sophia.'

Isla made her way down to the antenatal clinic and Sophia told her where Allegra was. Isla knocked on the door and went in and smiled when she saw Allegra. She was the female version of Alessi with black eyes and black hair and, while strapped to the CTG monitor, she was also doing her level best to keep a wriggling little boy of around three years old amused.

'Hi, Allegra,' Isla greeted her. 'I'm Isla, the head of midwifery.'

'Hello, Isla.' Allegra smiled. 'Is this about Alessi? I realised as soon as I said it that the midwife was feeling a bit awkward when I asked her to pretend she'd forgotten I was here. I'm so sorry about that. I should have discussed this with Alessi myself, instead of landing my problems on Sophia.'

'It's fine,' Isla said, and looked over at the little boy. 'You've got your hands full, I see.'

'Very,' Allegra agreed. 'Sophia gave him a colouring book and some pencils but he's just climbing all over me at the moment. I think Niko's starting to fathom that he's not going to have me all to himself for much longer.'

'Probably,' Isla said, and sat down in a chair near Allegra. 'They're very intuitive and they often sense that change is about to come. Hey, Niko, do you want to come and sit with me?' Isla suggested to the little black-eyed boy who had the same curls as his uncle. 'Look what I've got...'

Niko looked at Isla, who had taken out her pen torch

and was flicking it on and off. It worked as a diversion tactic almost every time with three-year-olds and thankfully it worked today. Niko climbed down from his mum's lap and made his way over to Isla. She noted that he had a slightly abnormal gait as he walked over and climbed up onto her lap.

'Look,' Isla said, flicking the pen torch on and off and then giving it to Niko, who tried to do the same. Only he soon found out that it wasn't as easy as Isla had made it look and he would hopefully take several moments to work it out and give Allegra a small break while they chatted and Allegra explained her reasons for not wanting Alessi there.

'I had a very difficult labour with Niko,' Allegra said. 'We were living in Sydney at the time. He was a breech birth and I ended up having an emergency Caesarean section after a very long labour.' Allegra paused for a moment before continuing—clearly the memory of it still distressed her. 'Niko wasn't breathing when he was born and had to be resuscitated. As a consequence he was without oxygen and has now got mild cerebral palsy.'

'That must have been a very scary time for you,' Isla offered.

'It was,' Allegra agreed. 'I wasn't at all well after the birth, either. The thing is, there were a couple of mistakes made and possibly what happened could have been prevented. I chose not to pursue it. I just wanted to put it all behind me. Alessi, though, was pretty devastated as well as furious. I know he thinks if he'd been there, or at least around, then I'd have been taken to Theatre more quickly and Niko's birth injury could have been avoided. My parents said pretty much the same to him, too.'

Isla said nothing but her heart went out to them both.

'I don't want Alessi to be involved in this birth, not because I don't think he's brilliant, it's more that if something does go wrong this time around then I don't want him blaming himself for it.'

'I completely understand that you'd feel that way.' Isla nodded but because she'd had a brief look at Allegra's notes before she'd come in, she knew that there was more. 'And?'

'And?' Allegra smiled at Isla's question.

'Is there another reason that you don't want Alessi's input?'

'There is.' Allegra rolled her eyes in the very same way that her brother did. 'I want to try and have a natural birth this time. Given what happened in my previous labour, Alessi is against the idea of trial of labour and thinks I should have a planned Caesarean section.'

'So, not only do you have to convince your obstetrician, you have to convince your brother, as well?'

'Ah, not just those two,' Allegra sighed. 'I've had to convince my husband and also my mother.' She gave a tired shake of the head. 'Usually I'm the golden one and Alessi's the black sheep but in this she thinks I should listen to him, because he's a doctor.'

Isla fought her own curiosity about that statement—while she wanted to know more about Alessi, this wasn't the place, and she could see Allegra was close to tears. 'What happened with Niko has brought up a lot of stuff for my parents. Maybe I should just have a planned Caesarean. I really am sorry for trying to involve your staff in this.'

'It's our job to be involved,' Isla said, and she truly did her best to pretend this wasn't Alessi's twin pouring her heart out to her. Which meant, if this hadn't been Alessi's twin then Isla knew exactly what she would do in this case. 'It's your pregnancy and your labour. You shouldn't go through an operation just to please your family. I can explain all that to him.'

Allegra looked dubious. 'I don't know how well he'd take it.'

'I would imagine that when I explain what's going on to Alessi, he's going to feel bad for causing you so much stress…'

'I know that he shall,' Allegra agreed. 'We're very close. The thing is Alessi has always looked out for me at school and things…' She looked at Isla. 'I remember you from school.'

Isla felt a little guilty that she didn't remember Allegra clearly.

'I got picked on a lot at school,' Allegra said. 'Well, we both did.'

'Really?' Isla couldn't imagine for a moment Alessi being picked on by anyone, he was so confident and assured, but then Allegra continued speaking.

'We were scholarship kids,' she explained. 'Which meant from the day that we started we didn't belong. At every opportunity it would be rammed down our throats that we couldn't afford to go skiing or that we didn't have the right uniform. It was very cruel. Alessi looked out for me then and is just trying to do the same now. The thing is…' Allegra hesitated and Isla stepped in.

'You don't need him to any more?'

'No, I don't.' Allegra sighed. 'I'm not going to take any risks with this baby but I really do want to try and have a natural delivery.' She thought for a long moment. 'It would be great if you could speak to him for me. I really have tried and I seem to get nowhere.'

Isla nodded. 'You're not the first patient to have this sort of problem. I've dealt with this on several occasions. No doubt I'll be the same if my sister ever gets pregnant. It's very hard to step back when you love someone, though Alessi needs to in this.'

'Thanks, Isla.'

Niko had actually fallen asleep while they'd been talking. Isla carried him over to one of the empty reclining chairs next to Allegra and laid him down, then went and looked at the CTG monitor. 'Everything looks very good,' Isla said. 'Right, I'm going to have a word with that brother of yours and don't worry. If you have any concerns, any at all, ring through to MMU and ask to be put through to me.'

'Thanks so much.'

As she walked out of the room there was Alessi, speaking with Sophia and frowning.

'I asked you to page me as soon as Allegra arrived—'

'Alessi,' Isla said, and gave a small smile to Sophia, excusing her from the conversation. 'Sophia paged me. I need to speak with you about your sister.' She saw concern flash across his features and immediately put him at ease. 'There's nothing wrong with the baby, but before you go in and see Allegra there is something that I need to discuss with you.'

Alessi's eyebrows rose and she had a feeling he was about to walk off but he gave a small nod.

'What is it that you want to discuss?'

'Perhaps not here.' Isla gestured to one of the consulting rooms and they both walked over to it.

It was awkward to be in there with him, given all that had, or rather hadn't, taken place between them, but Isla pushed all that aside and dealt with what was important—the patient. She took a seat at the desk and Alessi did the same. With the door closed she could smell his cologne and she really wished this conversation didn't have to take place on the tail end of last night, but she had no choice in the timing of things and so she pushed on.

'I've just been speaking with Allegra. We've had quite a long conversation, in fact,' she ventured. 'The thing is, while Allegra really appreciates your concern about the pregnancy—'

'I don't need you interfering in my family, Isla,' Alessi interrupted, and it was clear that he knew what the discussion would be about and wanted no part of it.

'I'd prefer not to have to but it's not about what I'd prefer and it's not about what you need—this is about Allegra.'

Alessi took a breath. 'Isla, I'm not going to discuss this with you.'

'You don't have to discuss anything with me, Alessi,' Isla answered calmly. 'I'm just asking that you take a few minutes to listen.' He went to stand but Isla halted him. 'Alessi, Allegra isn't your patient, she's *my* patient in *my* unit.'

'I'll discuss this directly with Allegra,' Alessi said, and headed for the door.

'And cause her more stress?' Isla responded, and watched as his shoulders stiffened. It really was a difficult subject to approach. She hadn't been lying when she'd said to Allegra that she'd handled this sort of situation several times and she would be blunt if she had to be. 'Allegra knows that you're just trying to look out for her and while she does appreciate it she wants you to be the baby's uncle rather than some hovering neonatologist. Everything is going well this pregnancy.'

'Everything was going well the last one,' Alessi said, though at least he sat back down.

'Do you think that Allegra doesn't already know all that?' Isla asked, and watched as Alessi closed his eyes and breathed out. 'Do you think she hasn't wrestled for a long time with her decisions before making them?'

'I'm really causing stress for her?' he asked. When she didn't say anything his black eyes met hers and he gave a wry smile as he answered his own question. 'Clearly I am. God, I never meant to, Isla. The thing is, what happened during Niko's labour was preventable. I just want to...' His voice trailed off.

'You want to ensure that nothing goes wrong with this one,' Isla finished for him, and Alessi nodded. 'I get that but if something *does* go wrong, if an emergency does arise, do you really want to be a part of it?'

'I want to be there to ensure nothing untoward happens in the first place.'

'Look, I do get that...' Isla started but Alessi didn't let her finish.

'Allegra going for a natural delivery is a crazy idea, given what happened last time.'

'It's not a crazy idea to Allegra, and it's not a crazy idea to her obstetrician—'

'Darcie's been here all of five minutes.'

Isla chose to ignore that. She knew it was hard when another doctor took over a patient's care but it wasn't for Alessi to air his concerns to his sister so she continued with what she was saying. 'And it isn't a crazy idea to me. A lot of women want to experience a natural delivery. She'd have a closely monitored trial of labour and if things didn't progress well then, perhaps more quickly, given her history, things would move towards a Caesarean. Even if Darcie is new, our recruitment policy is vigorous and she's joined an amazing team, which means that your sister *shall* be well looked after here, Alessi, you know that.'

Alessi thought for a long moment. Really, he could only admire Isla for confronting him on this difficult subject but her help didn't end there.

'If it makes it any easier for you,' she continued, 'I'm happy to oversee Allegra's care.'

Alessi's eyes jerked up and met hers.

'Whatever you think about me personally, Alessi, however you think I landed the role, the truth is I think that we both know that I do a very good job. I will, if you would like, keep an eye on Allegra during her antenatal visits and, as far as possible, I will be there for the birth.'

'You'd do that?'

'Of course.'

Alessi was surprised by her offer but, then again, was he? For nearly a year he had chosen to believe she had got the job because of who her father was. He had been wrong about that. Alessi had known it deep down and it was confirmed right now. The patients all raved about her, there was no doubt that she ran a very good midwifery unit and now she was offering to take care of Allegra when both knew how tense things were between them. Even the fact that Allegra had discussed so much with Isla told Alessi something—she didn't open up easily to anyone, yet she had with Isla. 'I would like that and I'll back off, too,' Alessi said, and then stood. 'Thank you.'

'No problem.'

He went to go but then turned around. 'I was going to come and see you later,' Alessi said. 'But now that we're here, I might as well just say it now—I would like to apologise for the things that I said last night.' Isla found she was holding her breath as he continued, 'I had no right to lecture you about your partner and the choices you make. It was out of character for me and I really would like to apologise.'

'It's fine.'

'Also, I broke up with Amber last night, so you don't have to worry that I'm dating one of your students.'

'Because of what I said?'

Alessi let out a very mirthless laugh. 'No.'

'But…'

'As I said, I don't cheat and, given that last night the only person I wanted was you, it seemed appropriate to end things.'

And with that he was gone and only when the door closed behind him did Isla let out the air trapped in her throat—her lungs were still closed tight.

Had he just said what he had?

Yes.

Did that mean…?

It did.

Oh, God.

It was like being tossed three flaming torches and having to learn to juggle with absolutely no clue how.

She walked out of the consulting room into a world that felt very different—Alessi liked her, in that way, and had made it clear that he was single. There was no Rupert to hide behind any more, not that she'd told Alessi that.

She was on the edge of something—scared to step off yet somehow compelled to.

Allegra was holding Niko and speaking with Sophia, but Isla watched her turn and smile widely at her brother as he came over, and as Isla approached she heard their conversation.

'You should have said.' Alessi gave her a cuddle.

'I tried,' Allegra gently scolded. 'Several times.'

'I'll back off and I'll make sure Mum and Dad do, too,' Alessi promised. 'I just…'

'I know,' Allegra said. 'I know you were just trying to do your best for us.' She looked at Isla as she joined them. 'Thank you so much, Isla.'

'It's no problem. I've spoken with Alessi and, if you're happy for me to do so, I can oversee things and come down and check all your antenatal visits, rather than your brother, and then, if you'd like, I'd be delighted to be there for your birth of your second child.'

'I'd really like that, Isla.'

'Good.'

She nodded goodbye and as Isla walked off Allegra smiled. 'I feel so much better. You really will speak to Mum and Dad?'

'Yep.'

'They'll give you a hard time,' Allegra pointed out.

'So, what's new?'

''Lessi!' Niko, fed up with all the adults, held out his arms to his uncle and, from a slight distance Isla watched as Alessi took his little nephew in his arms and gave him a kiss and then he must have said something funny because Niko laughed and laughed and Alessi grinned, too.

Then he turned and caught her staring at him and the smile remained as she blushed and returned it then quickly walked away, to return to the ward.

Yes, she was on the edge of something.

Something temporary, though. She knew that much about Alessi and she had almost reconciled herself to that.

Yes, this year was going to be very different. Alessi was going to be her first.

Even if he mustn't know it.

Somehow she had to hold onto her glamorous, sophisticated reputation while releasing a little of her heart.

CHAPTER FIVE

DARCIE SETTLED INTO the flat and hospital amazingly well.

With one exception.

Her first week at the Victoria passed smoothly but at the start of Darcie's second week Isla heard an angry exchange coming from the treatment room and then Darcie marched out. Frowning, Isla stepped into the treatment room to find Lucas standing there, the tension still in the air and a wry smile on his face.

'Issue?' Isla checked, trying to hide her surprise because Darcie got on with everyone, and no one, no one *ever* had an issue with Lucas—he was down-to-earth and seriously gorgeous and for him to have had upset Darcie or vice versa was a surprise indeed.

'You tell me.' Lucas shrugged.

'Lucas?' Isla frowned. He was a part of the glue that tied the MMU together. He got on with everyone, was intuitive, funny and so damn good-looking that his smile could melt anyone. It would seem it simply didn't melt Darcie.

'I don't need the new obstetrician telling me I'm late and to get my act together.'

Isla let out a breath. No, that much Lucas didn't need.

'And,' Lucas drawled, 'I also don't need you to have a word for me, Isla. Whatever her issue with me is, I'll deal with it myself.'

'Fine,' Isla said, 'but whatever the hell your issues are with each other, keep them well away from the patients.'

'You know that I will.'

'I do,' Isla said. 'Let me know if you need anything…' She turned to go but Lucas halted her.

'Isla, I hate to say this, I know I was late in this morning but I really need to go home…' He blew out a breath and then went to explain but Lucas didn't need to explain things to Isla. She knew that his home life was complicated at best and if Lucas said that he needed to go home then he was telling the truth.

'Go, then,' Isla said. 'I'll take over your patients.'

'I've only got one,' Lucas said. 'I'm expecting her to arrive any minute, I'm just setting up for her. Donna Reece, she's pretty complex.'

'You think I can't handle complex?' Isla teased.

'No, I just feel like I'm landing an awful lot on you.'

'Return the favour someday.' Isla smiled. 'Hand over the patient to me and go home.'

As Isla wheeled through the drip Lucas had set up, there was Darcie, checking drugs for the imminent arrival of Donna Reece. She was forty years old, at twenty-four weeks gestation with twins and a direct admission from the antenatal ward as she had been found to be in premature labour.

'Where's Lucas?' Darcie frowned. 'He was supposed to—'

'I've got your orders,' Isla said. 'I'm taking over this patient.'

'Oh, so he doesn't want to work with me?'

'Lucas has gone home,' Isla said. She was about to tell Darcie why and to tell her to back off Lucas, but then she remembered that Lucas had asked her not to step in. Anyway, there was no time for that. Donna was about to arrive.

'Did he page Alessi?'

'Yes,' Isla said, and as Donna was wheeled in, just the look on her face had Isla reaching for the phone to page for an anaesthetist to come directly to the delivery ward, too.

'Hi, Donna, I'm Isla…'

Isla kept her voice calm as she attached Donna to all the equipment. Things didn't look good at all and it was made worse that Donna's thirteen-year-old daughter was present and clearly distressed.

As Alessi arrived Isla was taking the young girl down to the waiting room and she gave him a grim smile, in way of small preparation for what he was about to face.

'Have a seat in here,' Isla said to Jessica. 'I know that you've had a horrible morning…'

'I thought that Mum was just coming here for a checkup,' Jessica said. She was holding a large backpack and Isla could see a towel sticking out of it. It was the summer holidays and clearly they had intended to head out to the beach for the day after the routine appointment that had suddenly taken a different turn. 'Mum said she didn't feel well this morning and I said she'd promised we'd go out. I should have listened…'

'Jessica, I'm going to come and talk to you later.

You've done nothing wrong and your mum is going to be okay.'

'But what about the babies?' Jessica asked.

'Right now the doctors are in with your mum and we'll know a lot more soon. Is there anyone I can call for you? Your dad's overseas?' Isla checked, because Lucas had told her that he was.

'He is but Mum's going to ring him and tell him to come home.'

'I'll speak to your mum and we'll see about getting someone to come and sit with you. Right now, do your best to take it easy and I'll go and see how Mum is doing.'

She went back into the delivery ward. Alessi was doing an ultrasound and his face was grim and he wasn't trying to hide it. He was clearly concerned.

'How's Jessica?' Donna asked.

'She's just worried about you and the babies,' Isla said. 'Is there anybody that you'd like me to call who can come and be with her?'

'Could you call my sister?' Donna asked. 'Tom, my husband, is in Dubai. I'm going to see what Darcie has to say and then call him and ask him to come home.' Donna closed her eyes. 'Jessica and I had an argument last night. I told her that I needed more help around the house, especially with the twins coming. Then we had another row this morning because I'd promised to take her to the beach but I told her I was too tired, when really my back was hurting and I was starting to worry that something was going wrong with the twins.' Donna started to cry. 'She said in the ambulance that she thinks this is all her fault.'

'We both know that none of this is her fault,' Isla

said. 'These things happen all the time, whether there's an argument involved or not. I'll speak with your daughter at length about this,' Isla promised, and Alessi glanced up at the determined note in her voice. 'Right now, though,' Isla continued, 'we need to take care of you and your babies.'

'Darcie's said that the medicine might postpone the labour.'

'That's right,' Isla nodded, and then glanced up as Alessi came over.

'Hi, Donna.' He gave a pale smile. 'As I said, I'm going to be overseeing the twins' care.'

'Hopefully not for a while,' Donna said, but Alessi glanced at Isla and her heart sank as Alessi continued to speak.

'I'm not sure. I have to tell you that I am very concerned about one of the twins on the ultrasound. Do you know what you're having?'

Donna nodded. 'Two boys.'

'That's right, and you know that they're not identical?'

Again Donna nodded.

'The twins are in two separate amniotic sacs and they each have their own placenta,' Alessi explained. 'The trouble is that one of the twins is smaller than the other, and the fluid around this twin…' he placed a hand high on Donna's stomach '…is significantly reduced. Most of the time our aim is to prolong the pregnancy for as long as possible but in some cases it is better that the baby is born.'

'Even at twenty-four weeks?' Donna asked, and there was a very long silence before Alessi answered.

'No,' he said gently. 'It is far too soon but this is

where it becomes a very delicate balancing game. Darcie has given you steroids that will mean that if the twins come after forty-eight hours then their lungs will be more mature than they would otherwise be. However, I'm not sure that I want the delivery to be held off for much longer. This little one needs to born soon. The placenta isn't doing its job and that twin stands a better chance out of the womb than inside.'

'But what about the other one?'

'That is why it is such a delicate balance,' Alessi said. There were no easy answers—twin A needed as long as possible inside the womb; twin B, to have a chance of survival, desperately needed to be born. The diagnosis was indeed grim. Twenty-four weeks was, in the best of cases, extremely premature but for an already small undernourished baby it didn't look good at all. Isla listened as Alessi gently led Donna down the difficult path of realisation that the babies' chances of survival were poor and that their outlook, if they did live, might not be bright.

It really was a horrible conversation to have, and he did it kindly and with compassion, but he was also clear in that he didn't offer false hope. By the end of the consultation Donna had said that she wanted everything, *everything* possible done for both twins when they were born.

'We shall,' Alessi assured her. 'Donna, I can say that you are in the very best place for this to happen. I am going to be there for your boys and I shall do all that I can for them.' He stood and looked at Isla, asking if he could have a word outside.

'Any changes, particularly to twin B, I want to be urgently paged. I've spoken to the anaesthetist and he's going to set up an epidural so that we can do an urgent section if required.'

'How long do you think twin B has got if he isn't delivered?'

'I'm hoping to buy a few days,' Alessi said. 'Though I doubt we can wait much longer than that, though that would be to the detriment of twin A, who looks very well.'

'It's a tough choice.'

'I don't think I'll have to make it.' Alessi sighed. 'She has marked funnelling,' he said, and Isla nodded. The cervix was dilated at the top end and that meant that Donna could deliver at any time.

'I'm going to go and speak with Jessica now,' Isla said, 'and then ring her aunt and ask her to come in.'

'Do you want me to speak with her?' Alessi offered, but Isla shook her head.

'I'm sure you'll be having a lot of contact with the family in the coming days and weeks. If you could just bear in mind that she's feeling guilty, when really, whether Donna was in labour or not when she presented in Antenatal, the outcome was always going to be that she was admitted today...'

'I'll keep it in mind,' Alessi said. 'Oh, and I just had a call from Allegra. She's very grateful to you. Things are much better.'

'That's good.'

'I spoke with my parents, as well, and they are doing their best now not to interfere.'

'How did that go?' Isla asked.

'Ha.' Alessi smiled. 'They do listen to me when it's about work.'

'Only then?' Isla asked, her curiosity permanently

piqued when it came to Alessi, but he simply gave a small nod.

'Pretty much. I'd better get back.'

'Sure.'

'Isla?'

'Yes?'

Alessi changed his mind. 'It will keep.'

He left her smiling.

When Alessi had gone back to NICU and things were settling down with Donna, Isla had a very long chat with Jessica. Rather than speaking in her office, Isla took the young girl to the canteen and they had a drink as Isla did her best to reassure her that none of the situation was her fault.

'None of this happened because of your argument with your mum,' Isla said, when Jessica revealed her guilt. 'I promise you that. One of the twins is very small and we'd have picked up on that today at her appointment and she would have been admitted.'

'It's too soon for them to be born, isn't it?' Jessica asked.

'They're very premature,' Isla explained. 'But as I said, there's a problem with one of the twins and your mum was always going to have to deliver the twins early. Do you understand that you didn't cause this?'

'I think so,' Jessica said. 'I'm scared for my brothers.'

'I know that you are, but we're going to do all we can for them and for your mum. I've spoken with your aunt and she's on her way in and you're going to be staying with her tonight. Your mum's rung your dad and he's on his way back from Dubai.'

'It's serious, then.'

'It is,' Isla said. There was no point telling Jessica that everything was going to be fine. It would be a lie and even with the best possible outcome, her mum and brothers were going to be at the Victoria for a very long time. 'But your mum is in the best place. Darcie, the doctor who is looking after her, is very used to dealing with difficult pregnancies. In fact, she's just come over from England and we're thrilled to have her expertise, and Alessi, the doctor who will be in charge of your brothers' care, is one of the best in his field. He'll give them every chance.'

She let the news sink in for a moment. It was a hard conversation, but Isla knew that it might be easier on Donna if she prepared Jessica and ultimately easier on Jessica to be carefully told the truth. 'Why don't we get Mum a drink and take it up to her now?'

Jessica nodded and they headed back up to the ward. Isla was pleased to see Jessica and Donna have a cuddle and Donna reiterate to Jessica that none of this was her fault.

It was a long day and it didn't end there because just as Isla was about to head for her home she got an alert on her computer that it was her fortnightly TMTB group tonight.

'I completely forgot,' Isla groaned to Emily. 'I honestly thought it was next week.'

'Do you want me to take it?' Emily offered. 'I can go home for an hour and then come back.'

'That's lovely of you but, no, it's fine.' Isla smiled. She knew how stretched Emily was and it was incredibly generous of her to offer to stay back.

Isla did some paperwork to fill in the time and then

headed over to the room they used for TMTB. She turned on the urn and put out a couple of plates of biscuits and set up. Usually there were five to ten young mums, all at various stages of pregnancy.

As Isla was setting up a young girl put her head around the door. She was clearly nervous and Isla gave her a warm smile.

'Are you looking for Teenage Mums-To-Be?' Isla asked, and the girl gave a tentative nod.

'Then you're in the right place. I'm Isla.'

'Ruby.'

'I'm just setting up but come in and help yourself to a drink. The rest of the group should start arriving any time now.'

Isla watched as the young girl came in. She was incredibly slim and, Isla guessed, around sixteen years old. She was wearing shorts and a large T-shirt and if she hadn't been here, Isla wouldn't have guessed that she was pregnant. It was good that she was here so early in her pregnancy, Isla thought, but when she looked over to where Ruby was making a drink her heart sank as she saw the young girl slipping a few biscuits into her pocket and then a few more.

She was hungry, Isla realised.

Pregnant and hungry.

'I'll be back in a moment, Ruby,' Isla said, and headed back to the ward. In her office Isla rang down to Catering and asked for sandwiches and a fruit platter and some jugs of juice to be sent up. There were some perks to being a manager because her request went through unquestioned and Isla only wished that she had thought of this long ago. Still, TMTB was a relatively new project and they were all still feeling their way.

Gradually the other girls started to arrive and at seven the group started and introductions were made. Harriet was nineteen and this was her first pregnancy. She had already been told that her baby was going to have significant issues.

'He's going to have to have an operation as soon as he's born,' Harriet said. 'I don't really understand what is happening, but Mum said that she'll come to my next appointment with me.'

'That's good,' Isla said. 'It's really helpful to have someone with you at these appointments because sometimes you can forget to ask a question or later not remember what was said.'

Then it was Alison's turn. She was about four weeks away from her delivery date and very excited. 'I didn't even want to be pregnant,' Alison admitted, 'and now I can't wait.'

Isla smiled. This was one of the reasons that she loved this group so much. It was very helpful for others to realise that the conflicting emotions they might be feeling weren't reserved for them. Here the girls got to share in each other's journeys and Isla had seen that Ruby was listening intently, though she was guarded when it was her turn to speak.

'I'm Ruby,' she said. 'I'm fourteen weeks pregnant.'

'How old are you, Ruby?' Isla asked, and suspicious eyes looked back at her before she answered the question.

'Seventeen.' She was immediately defensive. 'My mum wanted me to have an abortion but I'm not getting rid of it.'

'How are things with you and Mum at the moment?' Isla gently pushed, and Ruby shrugged.

'I haven't really seen much of her. I'm staying with friends at the moment.' Isla made a mental note to look at Ruby's file and see if there was anything more that she could do to support her during this difficult time. She would talk to her away from the group, Isla decided, but for now she moved on.

Alison had some questions about delivery and pain control and said that she didn't want to stay in bed.

'You don't have to,' Isla said. 'We usually encourage mothers to move around during labour—walking around is wonderful.'

There were always a lot of questions. Isla loved the enthusiasm of the teenage mums and more often than not both the questions and answers were interspersed with a lot of laughter.

It was that sound of laughter that alerted Alessi as he walked out of Maternity, having just checked in again on Donna.

He hadn't stopped all day and seeing a huge trolley laden with food being delivered to the room, he assumed that there was an administration meeting going on.

He was starving and, completely shameless, he followed the trolley into the room, to be greeted by a sight that he wasn't expecting!

Isla felt awkward around Alessi and possibly she had every reason to now as he put his head around the door just in time to capture her in a deep squat on the floor as she showed the girls how that position opened up the pelvis nicely!

Here, though, was not the place to be awkward and

so, instead of hurriedly standing, as was her instinct, she remained in a rather embarrassing position and gave him a very bright smile as the girls turned round to see who had interrupted the group.

'Did you smell the food, Alessi?' Isla asked.

'I did.' Alessi grinned. 'Sorry to disturb you. I thought it might be a work meeting and I could steal a few sandwiches. I'll let you guys get on.'

'Shall we feed him?' Isla said to the girls, and they all agreed that they should. Well, of course they did— Alessi was seriously gorgeous. He went over to the trolley and as he selected some sandwiches and fruit Isla introduced him.

'Alessi is one of our neonatologists. Some of you may have quite a bit to do with him once your baby is here.'

He gave a small wave but instead of taking his food and walking off he turned to the group. 'For feeding me you can ask any questions that you want.'

Isla was more than pleasantly surprised and, yes, the girls, especially Harriet, did have questions that they wanted to ask, and Isla knew she had lost her audience.

'Why don't we all get something to eat?' Isla suggested, and before she'd even finished the sentence chairs were scraping as the girls headed over for supper and to talk to the gorgeous doctor who had joined them.

She was going to provide food each time, Isla decided, watching as Ruby and another young mum really did fill up their plates. They were hungry, seriously hungry, Isla realised, kicking herself that she hadn't thought to do this before.

Well, that would change now.

'We'll have pizza next time,' Isla said, and she saw Ruby's ears prick up. Anything that brought these young mums back to the group was more than worth it. Not only did their questions get answered but through meeting regularly friendships were forged, and it also meant that Isla could keep an extra eye on these vulnerable young girls.

Alessi was really fantastic with them, answering Harriet's questions easily. 'Do you want me to come again?' Alessi asked Isla. 'I could prepare a talk if you like.'

'That would be great,' Isla said. 'We meet each fortnight.'

Alessi pulled out his phone and checked his calendar. 'I already have a meeting scheduled for the next one and the fortnight after that is my parents' wedding anniversary...' He thought for a moment. 'What time does it finish?'

'About eight thirty or nine,' Isla said.

'That's fine, then,' Alessi said, then turned to the group. 'Think up some questions for me.' He smiled at Harriet and then said goodbye to them and left. There were a few wolf whistles as he went and Isla laughed, glad to see the lift to the group that Alessi had given.

And also terribly aware of the lift in her.

After she finished up, instead of heading straight for home Isla went up to the ward.

She guessed he'd be there and she was right.

'Aren't you finished?' Isla asked.

'I'm staying tonight,' Alessi said.

'You're not on call.'

'Tell that to the twins.'

'Thanks for offering to come and speak. It will be good.'

'No problem,' Alessi said. 'They seem a nice group. Truth be told, I admire them.'

'I do, too,' Isla said, and turned to go.

'Isla?'

'Yes?'

This time he didn't tell her that whatever he had to say would keep. 'Are you ready for Saturday?' Alessi asked.

'Saturday?' Isla frowned. 'Oh, yes, the ball. I'd forgotten.'

'You attend so many things, I'm not surprised that it slipped your mind.'

It hadn't slipped her mind. It was just that she had been so focused on Donna that for a little while she had managed to push aside the fact it was the ball on Saturday.

She had seen the seating plans and would be sitting between her father and Alessi. Both were there to represent the maternity and neonatal units. She was excited, nervous and never more so than when she looked into his eyes, and Alessi touched on a necessary topic if things were going to proceed.

'I promise I'll behave this time if Rupert is there.' Even saying his name, even thinking of being there with Isla and him made Alessi's skin crawl, but he did his best not to show it as he broached the sensitive subject.

'Rupert's not going.'

'Oh,' Alessi said. 'Is he back in the States?'

'I think so.'

'Think so?'

Jump, Isla told herself, but her legs were shaking and she wanted to turn and run, not that Alessi could tell. As coolly as she would face the guests on Saturday, as easily as she delivered a speech, even if she was shaking inside, Isla somehow met his gaze as she took that dangerous leap.

'We broke up.'

'Oh.' Alessi had to concentrate on not letting out a sigh of relief. 'I'm sorry,' he said, just as Isla had said to him on the night they had met.

'I'm not,' Isla said, just as Alessi had once said to her.

She watched as his lips stretched into a smile, and either every baby on the delivery ward simultaneously stopped crying and every conversation had suddenly halted, or the world simply stopped for a moment. Whichever it was, it was irrelevant to them as silence invaded and realisation dawned on them both—Saturday night was theirs to look forward to.

CHAPTER SIX

ISLA HAD TRIED to speak with Ruby at the end of the TMTB meeting but she hadn't been able to get very far. Ruby had merely shrugged in answer to Isla's questions and given her a look that only teenagers could, a look that said, *what would you know?*

After the group there had been loads of sandwiches left over and a couple of the girls, Ruby included, had taken up Isla's suggestion to help themselves as it would only be thrown out, but when Isla had tried to speak with her Ruby had said that she had to go.

Isla didn't mind being snubbed. She was just very glad that Ruby had turned up and hoped that the promise of pizza might lure her back, if nothing else, and she dropped in on handover the following morning to tell her team the same.

'If I'm not there and one of you is taking the TMTB group, either ring down to Catering or get some pizza delivered,' Isla said.

'Can we bring in a cake?' Emily asked, and Isla smiled. Trust Emily to want to do more.

'No, Emily, you've already got more than enough on your plate without feeding hungry teenagers.' Isla shook her head. 'There's room in the TMTB budget to ring for pizza or to order from Catering. I do want to have a think about it, though. I can't stand the idea that these girls might be hungry…'

A bell buzzed and Isla gave her staff a smile. 'I'll get it. You carry on with handover.' But as she walked out of the staffroom the bell buzzed again and Isla quickly crossed the ward, her heart galloping when she saw that it was coming from Donna and that it must be urgent because she wasn't taking her finger off the bell.

Flick, one of the midwifery students, was, in fact, the one who was pressing the bell.

'Well done,' Isla said, because as soon as Isla appeared Flick moved to open a delivery pack.

'They're coming…' Donna sobbed.

'It's okay,' Isla said, pulling on gloves and giving instructions to Emily, who on hearing the urgency of the buzzer had followed Isla in. 'Fast-page Darcie and the neonatal crash team.'

'I wanted Tom to be here…' Donna sobbed.

'His flight gets in this morning, doesn't it?' Isla asked, and Donna went to answer but nature got in first.

'Something's coming…' Donna said, and Isla recognised the fear in Donna's voice, not just professionally but personally, too, and, just as she had that night with Isabel, she stayed calm.

At least now she knew what to do professionally.

'It's okay,' Isla said. 'We're ready for them.'

They were ready, almost. Staff were busy plugging in two Resuscitaires in the side room that Donna had been allocated. Isla could hear footsteps running along

the corridor and was grateful for the sound for indeed
a baby was coming.

'Don't push, Donna,' Isla said as she felt the baby's
little head. 'I know that you want to, but let's just try
and slow this down a little.'

Isla wanted to slow things down, not just to mini-
mise any trauma to the tiny baby's brain but also to
ensure there were plenty of staff and equipment ready
when this baby made its rapid entrance into the world.
Isla met Donna's gaze. 'Just breathe,' Isla said, and a
petrified Donna nodded, using all her power to give
her baby a few more vital seconds inside her.

Alessi came in then. He was a bit out of breath from
running and his hair was soaking and his scrubs were
damp—clearly he had been in the shower when his
pager had gone off. He stood, watching, but even with
Donna doing her best not to push, the next contraction
saw the baby delivered into Isla's hands.

He was tiny but vigorous and very red. He let out
a small cry as Alessi quickly cut the cord, took the
tiny bundle from Isla and carried him over to the resuscitation table.

'Twin A,' Isla said to Darcie, who was running in.
'Born at seven forty-eight.'

'So we're waiting on twin B,' Darcie said to Donna,
who lay back on her pillow and started to cry. Isla
glanced over to the Resuscitaire where Alessi was concentrating hard, and so, too, were the rest of the team.

'What's happening?' Donna asked. There was a
huge crowd around the cot but it was all very calm
and controlled.

'Looking beautiful!' came Alessi's strong voice.
'He is moving and fighting me, Donna, but I have

put down a tube to give him some medicine to his lungs, that's why you can't hear him crying. Do you have a name?'

'Elijah.'

There was a flurry of activity and Isla looked over as the staff started to prepare to move the baby over to NICU. Then Alessi came over and spoke with Donna. 'He's doing as well as can be expected,' Alessi said. 'We are going to get Elijah over to NICU now, where they are ready for him.'

'Can I see him?'

'Briefly,' Alessi said. 'Later you will have more time with Elijah but we want him over there now.'

The incubator was wheeled over but Donna's brief time with her son was soon thwarted as she first folded over and then lay back on the bed. The second twin was coming and Alessi nodded to his team to take the baby up to NICU as Darcie took over the second delivery.

'Cord's around the neck,' Darcie said. 'Very friable...' The umbilical cord was so thin and weak that it tore as Darcie tried to loop it over the baby's head but already the tiny baby was slipping out.

When Isla saw him delivered she was holding her breath, even as she clamped the severed cord. She never made comparisons—in fact Isla did everything she could not to think of that awful night with Isabel whenever a baby was born.

She couldn't help but compare this morning, though.

He was so tiny and his arms and legs were spindly and his little eyes were fused closed. The difference was that this little one started to put up a fight.

Even as Darcie lifted him and handed him straight to a neonatal nurse his arms were flailing and he let out a tiny mewing cry as the nurse took him over to Alessi.

'Let me hold him,' Donna called out. 'Alessi, I want to hold him.'

Alessi didn't say anything at that point, at least not to Donna. Instead, he spoke to the little boy.

'Hello, beautiful baby,' he said, and Isla felt tears prick at the backs of her eyes as Alessi did his best to shut out Donna's pleas to hold her baby and instead did everything he could to give this little life a chance. 'Do you have a name for your son?' Alessi asked.

'Archie,' Donna said, and then lay back on the pillow, exhausted and defeated, aching to hold her son but knowing he needed the skill of the medical team now.

Isla did her best to comfort Donna as the team worked on. There was no way to see what was happening. Alessi, the anaesthetist and two neonatal nurses were around the resuscitation cot. They could hear the baby's fast heart rate on the monitor and Alessi issuing instructions. The mood was markedly more urgent than it had been for Elijah, and Donna started to cry.

'I just want to hold him,' Donna said to Isla.

'I know you do,' Isla said. 'But right now he needs to be with the medical team—they're doing everything they can for him.'

It was an interminable wait, made all the more difficult because Donna's husband called to say that he had landed. When Donna couldn't speak Isla took over the call and Alessi glanced up at the calmness in her voice as she introduced herself to the distraught husband.

'Tom, Donna is exhausted and upset but we're

taking care of her. Elijah was born first and has been taken up to the neonatal intensive care unit, and Archie...' she glanced over and met Alessi's sombre gaze '...is being worked on by the team now. We hope to get him up to the intensive care unit soon.' She took a breath. 'Have you cleared customs? Good, go over to the information desk and explain what's happening and hopefully they can see you to the front of the taxi queue.' There was another pause. 'They're very premature, Tom. Right now the team are doing their best for your sons.'

It wasn't an easy call but somehow she did her best not to scare Tom while still conveying the need for him to get there urgently because it was clear that Archie especially was struggling. That was confirmed when Alessi came over and spoke to Donna, his expression grim. 'Donna, I am very concerned for Archie. I want to move him up to NICU where we can do some more tests on him and where there is more equipment...'

'I want to hold him.'

'I know you do,' Alessi said, 'but we are not at that stage—Archie is fighting and I will do everything I can to assist him in that. For now we'll bring him over so you can have a little look at him. He's very beautiful...'

The incubator was wheeled over. Archie looked like a little washed-up frog, but Alessi was right—he was a very beautiful baby. 'Put your hand in,' Alessi said, and Donna did, stroking his little cheek and then holding his fingers. 'I'm going to take him up. I also want to see how his brother is doing. As soon as I can I'll come and speak with you or I'll send someone else if I am busy with them.'

'Thank you. If something happens…' Donna couldn't say it but Alessi did.

'If either of the twins takes a turn for the worse you will be told, Donna, and the staff here will do everything they can to get you to your babies. Right now, though, I need to get him to NICU.'

'Mummy loves you,' Donna said, and Isla felt her heart twist, and for once she was struggling to keep up her cool mask. She wanted to go over to Alessi, to tell him to just give Donna her baby, to accept the inevitable and give them this precious time.

It wasn't her place to, though. Donna had made it clear before the twins' birth that she wanted everything possible done for her sons. It was for Isla to support that decision now.

It was a long and difficult day. Isla went through the birth with Flick and all that had happened. Donna's husband arrived and he went up to NICU. Though Donna ached to go and see her twins she had a small bleed after delivery and wasn't well enough to go up till much later in the day.

Isla went with her.

First they saw Elijah, the tiny, though relatively bigger, twin. 'It seems impossible…' Donna said, and Isla just stood back and let her have the time with her son. She looked over to the next cot and Alessi was there and caught her eyes, his expression still grim.

When Isla took Donna over she knew why.

Donna completely broke down when she saw her little man hooked up to so many machines.

'He's not well enough to be held,' Alessi said. 'Just talk to him, he'll know your voice.'

Alessi, Isla noted, looked exhausted. He was also

incredibly patient and kind. For close to a year she had dismissed him as some sort of killer flirt and had avoided him at all costs.

Now there was no avoiding him.

On Friday, at the end of a long shift, at the end of a very long week, she walked into her office to find Alessi sitting there with Jessica, the twins' older sister.

'Excuse me.' Alessi glanced up as she came in. 'I was just speaking with Donna, and Jessica asked if she could have a word. I just came to the nearest room.'

'That's fine.' Isla smiled. 'I'll leave you to it.'

'No, don't go,' Alessi said. 'Jessica was just telling me that she's too nervous to see the twins but that her mother thinks that she should.'

'Do you want to see them?' Isla asked.

'I don't know,' Jessica admitted. 'I've seen their photos and there are so many machines.' ·

'NICU can be a scary place,' Isla said. 'Alessi is actually coming to speak to my Teenage Mums-To-Be group, in a few weeks' time, to prepare them in case their babies have to go there. It can be a bit over-whelming but once you get past the machines you'll see your brothers.'

'That is what I was just telling Jessica,' Alessi agreed. 'They are very cute. Elijah is very much the big brother. Stoic and very strong, he doesn't like to cry or make a fuss...'

'And Archie?' Jessica asked, and Isla heard the twist in the young girl's voice.

'He's way too cute,' Alessi said, and Isla smiled at the genuine warmth in his voice as he went on to tell Jessica about her youngest brother. 'His eyes have just opened and he loves the sound of voices, he really does calm down when he hears someone say his name.'

'I used to talk to him when Mum was pregnant,' Jessica said.

'Then he would know your voice.' Alessi smiled but then looked over when Isla's cool voice broke in.

'Are you scared to love them, Jessica?' she asked, and Alessi could only blink in surprise. Isla asked the tough questions and had clearly got straight to the difficult point because Jessica nodded and started crying. 'I'm guessing you already do love them,' Isla said.

'They might die, though.'

'I know,' Isla said. 'And I know that is so hard to even begin to deal with, but whatever is going to happen you can still have some time with them and let yourself be their big sister. Would you like me to come and spend some time with them with you?'

Clearly it was what Jessica did want because half an hour later, instead of collapsing on the sofa and being grateful that it was the start of Friday night and the end of a long week, Isla was up on NICU with Jessica.

There was no place she would rather be, though. Watching as Jessica's fear was replaced by smiles, seeing little Archie's eyes flicker and possibly, possibly a hint of a smile on his lips was time well spent indeed. They took photos and Jessica let her friends know all about her two brothers via social media.

'I'm off.' Alessi stood by the incubator. He had changed out of scrubs and was wearing black jeans and a gunmetal-grey top and he looked like the man who had made her heart flip over on sight all those months ago. 'I'll see you tomorrow,' he said to Isla.

'There's a big ball tomorrow night,' Isla explained to Jessica. 'Alessi's getting an award.'

'And I'll see you on Monday,' he said to little Archie. 'In the meantime, behave.' He nodded his head in the direction of the corridor and Isla excused herself from Jessica, who was holding her brother's tiny hand. 'It's good she's had some time with them.'

'I know.' Isla smiled. 'It's going to be tough on her. How do you think Archie—'

'It's minute by minute,' Alessi interrupted, the inevitable answer because there were no guarantees in NICU and especially not with a baby who was so fragile and small. 'Just take the good times, that's all you can do sometimes. Are you off now?'

Isla paused before answering; she had a feeling, more than a feeling that they were on the edge of something. That if she said yes, then she'd be joining him for dinner tonight, or for drinks, or for…

Isla looked into his black eyes and there was an absence of fear. Yes, she knew, given his reputation, it could only ever be fleeting. She knew, too, that she couldn't tell him her truth—he would surely run a mile—yet she knew she was ready.

For him.

Yet, while she wanted to say yes, some things came first. 'I think I'm going to be here for as long as Jessica wants me to be.'

'Fair enough.' Alessi smiled. 'I'll see you tomorrow, then.'

'You shall.'

'Funny, but I'm actually looking forward to it now.'

She knew what he meant and her answer told him the same. 'So am I.'

CHAPTER SEVEN

ISLA WASN'T FEELING quite so brave the next morning, though there was still a flutter of anticipation in her stomach for the coming night as she downed a grapefruit juice before heading into work for a couple of hours.

'Haven't you got a ball that you're supposed to be getting ready for?' Darcie teased as they headed out the door.

'I'm getting my hair done at two,' Isla said.

'I guess you've got this type of thing down to an art. Still, if I were going to a ball instead of working this weekend, I'd need more than a hair appointment to get me ball-ready! What are you wearing?'

'Black,' Isla said. 'Or red, I haven't decided. All I know is that I've got a mountain in my inbox that needs to be scaled. The weekends when I'm not officially there are the only times I can get anything done on the paperwork front.'

Instead of taking the tram, they walked. Darcie wasn't on until nine and Isla wasn't officially working anyway, so they took their time, enjoying the morning and stopping at Isla's favourite café. She picked up a coffee and a pastry to have at her desk and Darcie did the same.

'I love the food here,' Darcie groaned. She'd really taken to the café culture of Melbourne and Isla was only too happy to show her her favourite haunts. Once on the MMU, Darcie took her breakfast to the staffroom to get handover from Sean, and instead of saying hi to the staff Isla headed straight for the quiet of her office. She was just unlocking the door when she saw Alessi walking down the corridor.

'I thought you were off this weekend?' Isla frowned.

'Not any more—I got called in at four,' Alessi said. 'I've just been speaking with Donna and her husband.'

He followed her into the office. 'Archie had a large cerebral haemorrhage overnight. We're taking down all the equipment and letting nature take its course. Emily is about to take them up to NICU to have some time with him.'

'Oh, poor Donna...'

'Poor Archie,' Alessi said. 'He's such a fighter...' And then, to Isla's surprise, Alessi cried. Not a lot, but he'd been tired already and being called in at four to find hope had gone and sharing the news with Archie's loving family all caught up with him and Alessi did let out a couple of tears.

Isla just stood there, more than a touch frozen. She wasn't very good with her own emotions, let alone dealing with Alessi's, and her lack of response didn't go unnoticed.

'You're much kinder to your patients when they're upset,' Alessi pointed out, and gave a wry smile as he gathered himself back together as Isla still stood there.

She could cope when it was a patient; she could

survive only by staying a step back. Alessi made her want to take that step forward but she just didn't know how.

'I just hate it that he had everything stacked against him. Had he been a girl he'd have been stronger,' Alessi said. 'Or had it been a single pregnancy at twenty-four weeks...even if he'd been the first to be born, he'd have had more of a chance, but everything that could go wrong went wrong for him.'

'Maybe he's getting to you because he's a twin, too...' Isla offered.

'They all get to me,' Alessi said. 'Though Archie has more than most—he really did want to live.' He looked at Isla. Was it exhaustion that made him be honest, or was it simply that it was her? 'I'm not actually a twin. I was the second born of triplets, with Allegra the last. My brother was the firstborn and died when he was five days old.'

The same age as Archie.

'Is that why you're so driven?' Isla asked.

'Oh, I'm driven now, am I?' Alessi teased. 'Last week you were warning me away from your staff.'

'It would seem you're both.'

Alessi shrugged. 'I guess. You feel you have to make up for all the opportunities that they never had.'

She remembered the black-sheep comment that Allegra had made about Alessi, and curiosity got the better of her now for she wanted to know more about him. 'Did your parents push you?'

Alessi nodded. 'You know, apparently, Geo, my brother, would never have spoken back to them. In fact, he'd be married by now and would have given them grandchildren.'

Isla smiled.

'And he wouldn't have given up piano at fifteen or...' Alessi shook his head. Things were moving closer to a painful part of his past than he would like, so he wrapped it up there. 'The list goes on. I really feel for Elijah, too. If he makes it.'

She watched as Alessi yawned. She could see he was exhausted and if it were any of her staff Isla would have told them to go home.

'Shouldn't you let Jed take over Archie's care?' Isla ventured, referring to the neonatologist on this weekend. 'You've been here all week and you've got a big night tonight. Surely you need—'

'What I *need*,' Alessi interrupted, 'are three things from you.'

'Three things?'

'Your coffee and whatever smells good in that bag...'

'What's the third?' Isla said, handing them over.

'If I don't get there tonight, can you give my speech for me?'

'Alessi, you're up for an award, I think it's taken as a given that you'll be there. My father—'

'Archie is having seizures,' Alessi interrupted. 'Violent ones, and they aren't nice for his family to see. Jessica wants to be there also and I want his death to be as gentle and as pain-free as possible. I want to be there for him. I'm sorry if it upsets your father that I might not make it but right now Archie is my priority.'

Alessi waited. He knew she was about to protest and he actually wanted her to. *That* was his tipping point. When anyone tried to come between him and his work Alessi walked away very easily. He wanted not to get in too deep; he wanted her to insist that he be there tonight.

Instead, she nodded her assent.

'Fine,' she said, though her father would think it anything but fine if Alessi didn't show up. 'What do you want me to say on your behalf?'

'Whatever is said at such things. I'm sure you'll give an excellent speech,' Alessi said.

'That sounds like an insult.'

It was, actually. He looked at her, so completely calm and unruffled, even as he had broken down, and knew she'd be the same tonight. 'Do any of them get to you?'

'Sorry?'

'I remember the night we met. You were all animated, completely enthralled about a baby that had just been delivered.' He watched her cheeks redden and rather than leave things there he chose to pursue them. 'I've seen you elated but I've never seen you upset and, though avoiding each other, we've still found ourselves working together at times.'

'When have I avoided you?'

'Come off it, Isla,' Alessi said. 'And don't avoid the question. Do any of them get to you?'

'I don't let them get to me,' Isla said, hopefully slamming the door closed on that observation, but Alessi wrenched it straight back open.

'That would take an awful lot of self-control.'

'Not really.' She tried to keep her voice even.

'Yes, really. Otherwise it would mean that you're completely burnt out and I don't believe that you are.'

'You don't know me,' Isla said.

'I know that I don't, because a year ago I could have

sworn that we were getting on, that we were enjoying each other's company, that you wanted me as much as I wanted you,' he said. 'Yet it would seem I was wrong.'

Isla wanted to tear her eyes from his but somehow she made herself hold his gaze.

'I may be wrong now,' Alessi said, and Isla knew that she could turn and head to her desk and he would go, but she didn't. Instead, she stood there as he continued speaking, the air between them crackling with tension. 'The thing is, I won't put myself in that position again. You'll never give me that look again, Isla…'

She wanted to point out that she wasn't giving him *that* look now; she wanted to point out that she wasn't turning and walking off. The air seemed too thick for her lungs and Isla's eyes flicked to his mouth, to his soft, full lips, and she wanted to place hers there, or for his mouth to move to hers, but Alessi just stood his ground.

'When you're ready to apologise for that night…'

'Apologise?' Isla gave an incredulous smile.

Alessi didn't return the smile. 'Yes, apologise,' he confirmed. 'The next move is yours.'

'I'm not with you.'

'You'll kiss me, Isla.'

'And if I don't?'

'Then we both die wondering.'

She would, Isla realised.

No matter what the future held, if a part of it did not contain a night with Alessi, then she would die wondering because he was possibly the most beautiful, sensual man to cross her path and, yes, she wanted her time with him, for however long they had.

'I need to go,' Alessi said. 'Thank you for the coffee.'

'I hope today goes better than expected for you,' Isla croaked.

'It won't,' Alessi said, 'but some things have to be faced and dealt with.' He turned and opened the office door.

Her face was on fire, his words playing over and over.

Some things had to be dealt with and faced, but not this.

Alessi's invitation turned fears into pleasure.

CHAPTER EIGHT

DARCIE HAD PROVED to be a brilliant flatmate but as Isla got ready for the ball she was actually relieved to have the place to herself.

Nothing was going to happen between her and Alessi tonight, she told herself, except Isla knew where their kiss could lead.

She'd fought it once after all.

Isla got back from the hairdresser's at four, where she'd had her thick blonde hair curled and pinned up and had also had her nails done in a neutral shade as she still hadn't decided what to wear tonight.

Red, Isla thought, taking out her dress and holding it up, yet it was everything she wasn't—it was bold, confident and sexy, and Alessi could possibly sue her under the Trade Descriptions Act once he got the dress off!

Black.

Safe.

Only it felt far from safe when she put it on. It showed her cleavage, it showed the paleness of her skin and the flush in her cheeks whenever his name came to mind, which it did at regular fifteen-second intervals.

He might not even be there, Isla reminded herself.
Except that thought didn't come as a relief.

She could still feel the heat between them from
that morning. Her body, as she dressed for the night,
acutely recalled the burn of his gaze and the delicious
warning that the next move was hers. There had been
no physical contact that morning yet it felt as if there
had been.

Isla was shaking as she put on her make-up, shaking
with want, with nerves, with the absolute shock of
the availability of Alessi should she choose to make
a move.

Should she choose?

Isla looked at herself in the mirror and realised she
already had.

She wanted Alessi.

A car had been arranged—Charles Delamere didn't
want his daughter arriving in a taxi—and Isla sat in
the back, staring ahead. The sights of Melbourne were
familiar; the feeling inside wasn't. There was no Isabel to chat with, no Rupert to deflect male attention.

She stepped into the venue alone.

Her eyes scanned the reception room as she drank
champagne and sparkled as she was expected to.

There was no sign of him.

Relief and disappointment mingled as they were
called to take their seats.

'Where's Manos?' Charles frowned at the empty
seat at the table.

'I think that he may be stuck at the hospital,' Isla
said. 'He's asked me to make a speech on his behalf
if he can't get here.'

'You are joking?' Charles snapped. 'The whole point of this award is to raise NICU's profile. How are we going to get people signing cheques if the star of the show can't even be bothered to turn up?'

'Dad.' Isla looked at him. 'He's with a family—'

'Isla,' her father broke in. 'To be able to take care of the *families*, sometimes you have to look at the bigger picture. I told him the same when I had lunch with him the other day. Not that he wanted to hear it. He's an arrogant...' Charles's voice trailed off as Alessi approached the table but then he stood and shook Alessi's hand.

'Good to see that you *finally* made it,' Charles said. 'I thought I'd clearly outlined how important tonight was.'

'You did.' Alessi pushed out a smile but didn't elaborate or explain the reason for his lateness. He looked like heaven in a tux, but he'd clearly rushed. His hair was damp and he hadn't shaved, which somehow he got away with. There was a teeny stand-off between the two men and Isla found herself holding her breath, though why she didn't know.

Alessi took a seat beside her and the fragrance of him, the scent of him, the warmth of him was the reason Isla turned. Greeting the guest, manners, polite conversation had nothing to do with the turn of her head.

'How was today?'

'I've had better,' Alessi responded. 'I'm pretty wrecked. I don't want to talk about it here.' He wasn't in the mood for conversation. It had been a hell of a day and it had depleted him, and he didn't need Isla's coolness, neither did he need Charles's sniping.

'I'm sorry,' Isla said, and he glanced over and those two words and their gentle delivery helped.

'It was peaceful.' Alessi conceded more information. 'I'm glad that I stayed.' He couldn't think about it right now so he looked more closely at Isla, who was a very nice distraction from dark thoughts, and the night seemed a little brighter.

'You look amazing.'

'Thanks.' Isla smiled. 'So do you.'

They shared a look for a moment too long. She could have, had there been no one else present, simply reached over and kissed him. It was there, it just was, and Alessi knew it, too, and he confirmed it with words.

'You have to say sorry first.'

Isla just laughed. There was a thrill in her spine and all the nerves of today, of yesteryear just blew away. It should be just them but the entrée was being placed in front of her.

'I'm going to have to disappear,' Alessi said, 'and write my speech. I didn't get a chance today.'

'I've already written it,' Isla said, and handed him a piece of paper. 'Just lose the first part.'

'The first part?'

'"Dr Manos regrets that he's unable to be here tonight."'

'Dr Manos is suddenly very glad that he is.' Alessi smiled. It was a genuine smile and one that had seemed a long way off when he had left the hospital. Had it not been for this commitment, tonight would have been spent alone. Alessi took each death very personally and had long since found out that a night on the town or casual sex did nothing to fill up the black hole he climbed into when a little life was lost.

His grief was still there yet her smile did not dismiss it and neither did his.

Isla could hear her father asking a question, breaking the spell, dragging them back to the table, to the ball, to the world.

Dinner was long, the speeches even longer, and Alessi noted that Isla chatted easily with the guests at the table during dinner and listened attentively to the speeches.

She really was enjoying herself. Alessi shared her humour. His foot pressed into her calf on one occasion, not suggestively, more to share an unseen smile when one of the recipient's speeches went on and on and on.

Then it was Alessi's turn to take to the stage. Charles gave a rather long-winded introduction about the work he had done in the year that Alessi had been at the Victoria and how pleased they were to have such talent on board.

Isla watched as Alessi went up to the stage, the speech she had written in his hand, and he took a moment to arrange the microphone. Absolutely she could see why it was her father wanted a more visible profile for Alessi because, even before he had spoken, he held the room.

She watched him glance down at his speech and, yes, he omitted the first part where Isla had explained that, regretfully, he couldn't be there.

He thanked everyone present and then Isla froze as Alessi hesitated and she realised she had omitted to mention a small joke she had written—*I'd especially like to thank the extraordinary Isla Delamere for her amazing work on the MMU.* It would have been funny had *she* read it out. Instead, Alessi's face broke into a smile and he met her gaze.

She could feel her father's impatience at the small lull in proceedings, she could feel her own lips stretching into a smile as Alessi omitted her joke and then moved on.

"'I am very proud to receive this award,'" Alessi said, reading from Isla's notes. "'But more than that, I am incredibly grateful to work alongside skilled colleagues at such a well-equipped hospital. It helps when you can say, in all honesty, to parents that everything possible is being done or was done. It makes impossible decisions and difficult days somewhat easier to be reconciled to.'"

It was the truth, Alessi thought.

That Archie had been given every chance had been a huge source of comfort to Donna. That the facilities were top class, that there had been a private area for the family to take their necessary time with empathetic staff discreetly present had made his passing more bearable.

He wrapped up the speech and then added a line of his own, or rather he didn't completely omit Isla's.

'I would especially like to thank Isla Delamere for being here tonight and for her amazing work on the MMU.'

Ouch!

Isla was blushing as Alessi returned to his seat.

'Thank you,' Alessi said. Her words had hit home. Yes, he might loathe this side of things but he was starting to accept that it might be necessary. No, he wouldn't be appearing on morning television, as

Charles had in mind for him, but he would make more effort, Alessi decided. That was the reason he stood around talking, being polite and accepting congratulations, while others headed off to dance. That was the reason he didn't make his excuses and head home.

Isla watched in mild surprise as her student Flick danced with Tristan, a cardiac surgeon. She could almost feel the sparks coming from them, or was it just that Alessi was standing close?

'Well done,' Isla said, when finally the crowd gathered around him had dispersed enough for them to have a conversation.

'Thanks,' Alessi said.

'Not too painful?' Isla checked.

'No. Your speech was perfect. I really am very grateful for such a well-run hospital. I just don't like the fact that your father seems to want me to be the poster boy for the NICU.'

'What was that?' Charles came over and Alessi didn't even flinch.

'I was just telling Isla how well run and well equipped the hospital is.'

'Because of nights such as this one,' Charles said. 'You cut it very fine getting here.'

'I already explained that, Dad,' Isla said, but Alessi didn't need Isla to speak for him and told Charles exactly how difficult it had been to get there, albeit a little late.

'I certified a patient dead at eight minutes past six,' Alessi responded coolly, and Isla frowned at the tension between the two men. 'As I said to you at lunch, please don't rely on me to be your front person. I'll do what I can on the social side of things but my job is to keep up the stats while yours is to bring in the funds.'

Isla swallowed. There were few people who spoke to Charles Delamere like that and got away with it, but it was what her father said next that truly confused her.

'You could have at least shaved before you got here.'

'Dad!' Isla was shocked that her father would be so personal but Alessi didn't seem remotely bothered.

'It's fine,' Alessi briefly addressed Isla, then turned his attention back to Charles, who was looking at Alessi with thinly disguised murder in his eyes. 'I stayed with the parents of the baby that died until seven and then I spoke at length with their daughter. Shaving really wasn't my priority.' He looked at Isla. 'Would you like to dance?'

She said yes just to get the two of them apart.

'Alessi, I'm so sorry about that!' Isla said as they hit the dance floor. She was honestly confused by the way her father was acting. 'I don't know what's wrong with him. He had no right to say anything about you not having shaved.' Privately she was glad that Alessi hadn't shaved—he looked wonderful and she actually ached to feel his jaw against her skin, but she held back from dancing with him the way she wanted to.

'Don't worry about it.' Alessi shrugged.

'Even so, I don't know what's got into him.'

'I do.' Alessi smiled. 'He knows tonight I am going to be sleeping with his daughter.'

'You assume a lot,' Isla croaked as he pulled her in closer.

'I never assume,' Alessi said. 'I just aim high.'

His fingers were stroking her arms and now his

cheek was near hers as he spoke, his jaw was all scratchy against her cheek, even more delicious than Isla had predicted, and she found she could barely breathe.

'I thought you were exhausted.'

'Do I feel tired to you?' Alessi said, and Isla guessed he was referring to the hard heat that was nudging at her stomach.

'No.' A single word was all Isla could manage.

'I'm never too tired for you, Isla.'

She was beyond turned on. She wanted to move her face so their mouths could meet, she wanted the wetness of his tongue and the heat of his skin on hers.

Did she tell him how scared she was?

Did she tell him that he would be her first?

Isla would possibly die if he found out she was a virgin.

She'd had an internal when she'd had appendicitis and the doctors had thought it might be an ovarian cyst.

There was going to be no bloodshed, no 'Oh, my God, is that your hymen?' Just utter inexperience in very experienced arms.

Yet she wanted him and she had never till now wanted a man.

She wanted to be made love to and kill this demon for ever, choke it at the neck and get on with her life.

She knew his reputation, knew his relationships were fleeting at best. This might be just a one-night stand but it would be one that would help her step into her future.

Isla pulled her head back and looked into black, smiling eyes and, no, a heavy heart was not what was needed tonight. A long confessional could not help things here.

It was lust looking back at her, not love, she reminded herself.

Yet it was the beginning of the end of the prison she had trapped herself in and, however unwittingly, Alessi could set her free.

'What are you thinking?' he asked.

'I'm not going to tell you.'

It was the truth and it was also *the* truth.

Isla's decision was made.

Alessi would never know that he was her first.

'I'm going to go soon,' he said in a low voice that made her shiver on the inside. 'I don't want to offend your father by leaving with you. I'll text you my address.'

'You don't know my number.'

'I do,' Alessi said. 'Don't you remember sending me that school reunion photo on the night we met, the night you blew me off?' She was on fire in his arms as he scolded her for her actions that night. 'You're going to apologise *properly* for that tonight.'

'Meaning?'

'Meaning I am going to go and say my goodbyes,' Alessi said. His fingers were at the tie of her halter neck and she had an urge for him to unknot it, to be naked against him, to give in to the kiss that they both craved.

As the song ended, so, too, did their dance and Alessi gave her a brief smile of thanks before walking off.

To the world it might have looked like a duty dance, but for Isla it had been pure pleasure. She joined her father and tried to carry on a conversation with a prominent couple as her heart hammered and her mind whirred as to what to do. She saw Flick leaving with Tristan but this time Isla could only smile with the realisation that she had reprimanded Alessi just a few weeks ago for the very same thing—a doctor seeing one of her students.

She had been jealous, Isla could see it so clearly now.

Her phone buzzed and she glanced at it.

There was no message from Alessi, just his address.

'Heading off already?' Charles frowned. 'It's a bit soon.'

Isla looked at her father. She always did the right thing by her parents, by her sister, by Rupert, by her staff, her patients, by everyone but herself.

It was far from too soon.

Putting herself first was way overdue, in fact.

Isla left without another word.

CHAPTER NINE

ALESSI STEPPED INTO his apartment and swapped the crystal of his award for the crystal of a brandy glass.

He sent a text and wondered.

Would she come?

And if she did, then what would tomorrow bring?

He had spent close to a year wondering about Isla. Disliking her, yet wanting her. A whole year of trying to fathom what went on behind that cool facade.

No one had ever got into his head-space more and yet, rarely for Alessi, he did wonder about the consequences of tonight. He didn't want to be shut down by Isla again, yet a part of him knew it was inevitable. Rare were the glimpses of the true Isla and he found himself craving them. From the first unguarded night to the smile when she had walked out from speaking with Blake and Christine, or sitting on a birthing ball with her teenage mums-to-be.

It was a case of one step forward and a hundred steps back with Isla and, despite the promise of their dance, despite the passion he had felt, Alessi actually doubted now that she'd even turn up at his door.

He checked his phone and, no, she hadn't responded

and Alessi found himself scrolling back and looking at their brief communication.

There was an eighteen-year-old Isla, as blonde and as glossy as she was now and smiling for the camera, but there was still that keep-out sign in her eyes. Alessi stared at the image for a long time, zooming in to avoid seeing Talia, for she had no place here tonight. Instead, he looked into Isla's cool gaze and wondered about the secrets she kept, especially when he heard a knock at the door.

'I was wrong,' Alessi said as he opened the door to her. 'I was starting to think you wouldn't come.'

'Why would you think that?' Her voice lied—it was clear, it was confident, it was from the actress she had learnt to be.

'Because you're impossible to read.'

'Better than boring,' she said as he poured her a drink and handed it to her. She didn't like brandy but it was a necessary medicine tonight. She was on the edge of both terror and elation and she wanted her demons gone.

To him.

He really was impossibly beautiful. His tie and jacket were off. If she ignored their surroundings, if she could pretend that they weren't in his apartment, it could almost be the night they'd met for he had been wearing black pants and a white shirt then. He was just as toned, just as sensual, just as confident as he had been that night as he walked over to her, removed her now empty glass from her hand and placed it on a small table. His hands returned to her hips as they had that night, only his mouth did not take hers.

'So...' Alessi looked at her. 'Here we are again.'

He was going to keep to his word, Isla realised as his lips did nothing to meet hers.

'Up to you, Isla.'

Her lips actually ached from his ignoring them, and her body wanted to twitch from the lack of attention she craved. His hands were warm on her hips, his fingers just at the curve of her buttocks, and he moved not a muscle yet he stirred her deep on the inside. 'I thought you were the great seducer,' Isla said, willing her voice to be even, begging her heart to slow down.

'So it's my job to turn you on?' Alessi checked, staring into her eyes.

'Yes.'

'But I already have.'

Was it that simple? Isla thought. Because, yes, he already had.

'You will make the move, Isla.'

Was she here to be served her just deserts, was payback on his mind? She voiced just one of her many fears about this night. 'So you can blow me off this time?'

'God, no.' The need in his voice put paid to that fear and so did his words. 'I wanted you then and I want you now.'

Her eyes told Alessi she wanted him, too. 'So what do you have to say about that night?'

'I'm not going to apologise.'

He shrugged his shoulders but he didn't move and she thought she might die if their lips didn't meet, so she offered her haughty best.

'Sorry!'

'That's a poor excuse for an apology,' Alessi said. 'Say it with your mouth on mine.'

'Alessi...' Isla cringed. She had no idea what was happening, no idea what his game was. She wanted to put up her hand and take a time-out, to consult the rule book, phone a friend, but there was only one other player in this game and she could hardly consult him.

I've never done this before, Alessi, she wanted to reveal. *Apart from one kiss with you, I've never really been intimate or affectionate with a man before...*

Only that wasn't true.

Thirty seconds ago she had never been this intimate or affectionate but now she was pressing her lips to his mouth as if it was the most natural thing in the world. 'Sorry,' Isla breathed, feeling his lips stretch into a smile beneath hers as she joined in the game.

And she'd just been intimate again because her hands were running over his back as she whispered to his lips again.

'I can't hear you,' Alessi said, and her lips moved to his ear, to the lovely, soft lobe, such a contrast to the scratch of his jaw, and she was saying the same word again.

'Sorry.'

Sorry for being a bitch, sorry for shutting you out, sorry for a year of deprivation when it was so easy after all.

She was unbuttoning his shirt as her mouth moved to his neck. It really was that simple. He shrugged out of his shirt and she ran her hands over the lean chest, stroking his hardening nipples, and all she had to be, Isla realised, was herself, and she knew what she wanted.

It was Isla's fingers rather than Alessi's that undid the halter neck to her dress and the feel of skin, of his firm chest against her naked one, matched the moan that escaped from him, and then she removed her mouth from his neck and stood, taking in the feast going on in his eyes as he looked at her bare breasts.

'I've run out of sorries,' Isla said.

'I haven't.' Alessi's eyes lifted to hers. 'I'm sorry for every terrible thought I have had about you and I'm even sorry for the inappropriate ones—they didn't do you justice…'

His mouth came down on hers then, so hard that Isla thought she might taste blood. Almost a year of anger and pent-up frustration was unleashed from Alessi and for Isla it was electrifying and completely consuming to be so thoroughly kissed. His fierce tongue claimed her as her breasts were crushed to his chest. One of Alessi's hands was at the back of her head, the other on her bottom, yet it was Isla who was pushing in.

She resented the bottom half of her dress for coming between them. She loathed both his trousers and his belt. She wanted them gone, she wanted them both naked, she wanted her legs wrapped around him.

Alessi pulled back and her mouth chased him for more.

'Get on the bed,' he ordered, his words harsh but necessary or they'd be doing it up the wall.

'Where is it?'

He was as disorientated as she and it took a second for him to fathom the familiar route and it was hard getting there while being down each other's throats on the way.

They stripped at the bedroom door, with the same glee and abandon as if they were taking their clothes off to jump in a river on a hot summer's day. Isla's nerves left her at the door and they dived onto his bed together, want tumbling them over and over, only tearing their mouths from each other to drink in glimpses of the other's nakedness. He loved her large pink areolas and the blonde curls between her legs, and she in turn loved the darkness of his erection that nudged for attention even as his fingers slid inside her.

Isla simply forgot her own inexperience, forgot that she didn't know what to do, or shouldn't know what to do, for all that she *could* do was try and remember to breathe as his fingers deeply stroked her and his mouth noisily worked her breasts.

He touched her where, and in a way, she had never touched herself, and her body flared at the delicious invasion. Her spine seemed to turn to lava and she rocked to his hand.

'Come,' he ordered, and yet she had never done so. 'Come,' he said urgently, 'because then I'm going to take you...'

She looked down at his fingers sliding in and out of her yet she couldn't relax to his hand, no matter how she wanted to. 'Take me now...'

They were side on and facing each other, and Alessi required no second invitation. His leg nudged hers apart so they scissored his and his fingers moved from deep within and held his thick base and teased, stroking her clitoris, toying at her entrance, till her own hand was closed over his and urged him inside.

'Condom...' He went to reach for one, but that meant rolling, that meant leaving, and her hand stayed steady over his, for she could not bear to break the spell. He nudged in just a little way and her throat closed on itself as she glimpsed how much this was going to hurt. Pain was confirmed again with the second, deeper thrust.

Alessi felt her tension and misread it. Common sense paid a very brief visit and he reached for a condom. The pause as he slid it on was enough for Isla to catch her breath. She didn't like the pale pink of the sheath, she wanted the lovely darkness of before, the softness of his wet skin and the hard feel of him inside. It was that simple, but as he squeezed into her those wants were pale compared to the pleasurable hurt of being taken.

Alessi closed his eyes in pleasure at how tight she was, her moan, her sob, the bite of Isla's teeth on his shoulder spoke not of pain to him.

Or to her.

Yes, it hurt, yes, she wanted a second to regroup, but the salt of his skin in her mouth and the immeasurable force of him thrusting within was a small price to pay for no rest. There were no thoughts to be gathered; he was driving her towards something and Isla was the most willing passenger. She could feel her first orgasm building, each deep stroke of him taking her to the edge of what was surely inevitable, but then Alessi stilled.

'Don't stop,' Isla begged, but then she looked to the reason he had. The condom was shredded, rolled around his base, and decadent wishes came true, because she had loathed him pink and sheathed. She was absolutely on the edge of coming and the sight of him dark inside her simply topped her and it was Isla who took over, who continued the dance, and how could he not join her?

Both were watching, both dizzy with pleasure as Isla came. The first jolt of her body had Isla fight it, scared to let go, but trusting in him she did and with a small scream went with the pleasure. Alessi felt the pulses, the grip of Isla's tight space dragging him in, and he simply gave in and thrust into her, loving the sense of her unleashed. He felt a pull in his stomach and the rise of his balls and somehow, *somehow* there was that brief flash of common sense and he dragged his thick length from her, and both watched as he shot silver over her.

It was delicious to look down while too scary to look up and meet the other's eye.

It had been better than good.

CHAPTER TEN

ISLA WOKE TO the roaming of his hands.

There was a moment of bliss as instinct told her to roll towards him or just lie there and relish the slow exploration, to kiss him as she wanted to, and then she remembered the sheer recklessness of last night.

It was Alessi who addressed it.

'You owe Blake and Christine an apology,' Alessi said to her ear as he kissed it. 'It *is* possible to get too carried away.'

'It's fine,' Isla said, and somehow her voice sounded together. 'I've got it covered.'

He would assume, of course, that this good-time girl would have contraception all taken care of, especially as she was a midwife.

Isla closed her eyes on sudden tears.

What the hell would he say if he knew she'd been a virgin until last night, that she wasn't even on the Pill?

Isla was starting to panic, not that she would let him see.

'I have to go.' She rolled over and gave him a smile.

'Now?'

'Now.' Isla nodded.

'Hey…' His hand was on her shoulder as she sat up. 'There's no need to rush off.'

But there was.

She had to get home.

She had to think.

And so she climbed from the bed and headed out to the lounge, where her clothes lay strewn.

'I'll drive you,' Alessi said as she pulled on her dress.

The embarrassment of getting a taxi in last night's clothes was the only reason she agreed.

Alessi made do with last night's clothes also and the lack of conversation in the car had him rolling his eyes. 'I knew that you'd do this,' he said as he pulled up at a café.

'Do what?'

Alessi gave a mirthless laugh and got out and Isla sat there, watching him order coffee through the café window. Next door the shutters were going up on a pharmacy. Once home she could go and get the morning-after pill, Isla thought, and then closed her eyes because she knew that she wouldn't. She had nothing against others taking it, it just wasn't for her.

She sat there, telling herself she was overreacting, that she couldn't be pregnant, except her assurances had the same ring to her as her teenage mums' did.

She was twenty-eight!

Damn you, Alessi, Isla thought as he walked back to the car carrying coffee. *Damn you for making me lose my head.*

Not just last night but this morning, too, for she wanted more of him. She wanted that grim mouth to smile, she wanted his kiss and to be back in his bed, she wanted more of whatever it was they'd found.

'Here.' He handed her a coffee and Isla took a sip and screwed up her face.

'I don't take sugar.'

'How the hell would I know?' Alessi said as he started the engine. 'Because you don't communicate…'

Her shoulders moved as she let out a small involuntary laugh. 'Did you plan that?'

'I did.' He glanced over and gave her a smile. 'I actually know that you don't take sugar so I asked them to put in three.

'What's your address?' he asked, and after she had given it to him he resumed the conversation. 'Do you know how I know that you don't take sugar?'

Isla said nothing, just stared ahead as he answered his own question.

'Because I don't really like how I am around you, Isla. I don't like it that even though you run so very cold, I still find myself hanging out for the occasional heat. I notice things about you that I would prefer not to. Like you don't have sugar, like the day you told someone you were going to walk in your lunch break yet you never have. How you hold back on everyone and everything…'

'I don't.'

'You do.' Alessi glanced over as he drove her home. She was back to being unreadable, back to being cool and aloof and just everything that she hadn't been last night, and he wanted her back.

'We're going out this afternoon,' he said as they pulled up at her apartment.

'I've got plans.'

'Cancel them. I'll pick you up at one.'

'I might be out.'

'Then I'll be back at two.'

'Alessi...' Isla didn't know what to make of this. 'Last night—'

'I don't want to hear you regret it,' Alessi interrupted, 'or that it was something that shouldn't have happened or that it was just a one-off. Get it into your head that I'm going to date you, Isla, and that starts today. I'm certainly not waiting until Monday to find out if you're speaking to me or avoiding me.'

Isla let out a pale smile. 'It would have been the latter.'

'Which is why we are going out today. There is one thing we need to get straight though, Isla—I don't cheat, and I expect the same from you.' Her cheeks were on fire as he continued speaking. She knew he was referring to the night when she had practically offered to get off with him while Rupert and Amber had been back in the bar. 'I don't care what you got up to when you were with Rupert but if you are seeing me, then you are seeing only me. Do you get that?'

Isla nodded but her heart was heavy.

He really didn't know her at all.

'We have a companion,' Alessi said, when Isla opened her door at one to find him there, holding Niko in his arms. 'Allegra's husband, Steve, is working and she called and asked if I would mind having Niko for the afternoon as she needs a break. She rarely asks...'

'That's fine.' Isla smiled. 'Hi, there, Niko.'

'I thought we could go to the zoo,' Alessi said, but he must have seen her startle. 'You don't like the zoo?'

'I've never been,' Isla admitted. 'Actually, that's not strictly true, I've been to a couple of dinners there and a wedding once. I've just never...'

'*Been* to the zoo,' Alessi finished for her. 'Well, I have been many times. It's Niko's favorite place for me to take him.'

'I'd better get changed,' Isla said, because she'd put on a dress, assuming they would be going out for lunch. 'Jeans?'

'Shorts,' Alessi said. 'It will get hot walking around and, anyway, I like to see your legs.'

How could he manage to flirt while holding a three-year-old as well as offering to take her to the zoo, of all places?

It was hot and smelly and actually fun.

'Oh, my...' Isla fell in love with the orangutans, which was possibly to be expected, given her job, but the babies were so adorable.

'They are as hairy as some of my premmies,' Alessi said.

Isla glanced at him, hearing the genuine warmth in his voice.

'*Your* premmies?'

'Until they go home.' Alessi nodded.

'Wouldn't that take its toll?'

'Perhaps, but the night that my brother died it looked as if my parents might lose all three of us. There was a doctor there who stayed night after night and my parents always say that were it not for him, they could have gone home with no children.'

'That's your parents' memory, Alessi,' Isla said, ignoring the set of his jaw. It worried her, all the pressure that he put on himself. 'I'm sure there were a whole lot of others who played their part.'

'I don't need to be told to delegate.'

'Lucky you, then,' Isla said, ignoring the edge to Alessi's voice that told her this was out of bounds. 'I'm constantly being reminded to delegate by my team. Anyway, I just hope your phone's off, because I've never been to the zoo before and I might prove a terrible disappointment for Niko if you suddenly have to dash off.'

He gave a reluctant smile, which turned to a wry one an hour or so later when Jed rang through some results that Alessi was waiting for.

'Thanks for letting me know,' Alessi said. 'Yes, just continue with the regime.' As he ended the call Alessi looked over at Isla. 'I'll never turn my phone off.'

Isla just laughed. 'Neither will I.'

They just wandered, eating ice cream and taking it in turns to push Niko in his stroller. 'He gets tired,' Alessi explained. 'He's walking so much better now but on days like today it's better to bring the stroller along.'

'How bad was he when he was born?' Isla asked.

'Bad enough that we thought he might not make it,' he said. 'Allegra was very sick, too. It was a terrible time. My parents…' He was quiet for a moment. 'I think it brought a lot back for them.'

'About your brother?'

Alessi nodded but then tried to turn the conversation a little lighter. 'God, could you imagine the pressure if anything had happened to Allegra?'

'Pressure?'

'"Do your homework, Alessi, your brother would have loved the chance. When are you going to get married…?"' He rolled his eyes. '"Your brother would have loved that chance, too!"' He gave a wry smile. 'Thankfully Allegra and Steve have taken some of that heat off by marrying and having Niko. Don't get me wrong, I love my parents but they make it clear that I'm not doing all the things a good Greek son should.'

'Well, I don't do all the things that a good Delamere girl should.'

'Such as?' Alessi asked as they headed towards the elephants and he took Niko out of the stroller and put him onto his shoulders.

'Such as being a midwife. My parents thought I should study medicine, like my sister. It caused a lot of rows. Even when I got the position of head midwife my father suggested I'd be better off heading to medical school. Finally, though, he seems to get that it's not a hobby.'

'Don't you get on with them?'

'Oh, I do,' Isla said. 'We've had our differences. My midwifery for one, and that they were pretty absent when we were growing up. I get on much better with them now that I'm an adult. I can understand better why, now—their charity work is really important.'

'Family is more so.'

'I agree,' Isla said. 'I guess it's all about balance. My parents didn't have that, it was all or nothing for them.'

They stopped at the elephants. A calf had recently been born and there was quite a crowd gathered. 'Imagine delivering that,' Isla grinned.

'You love your job, don't you?' Alessi said, feeling more than a touch guilty at his assumption that her father had paved her way—clearly she'd had to fight to get where she was.

'I do.'

'Did you always want to be a midwife?'

'Not always,' Isla said, but didn't elaborate. She just watched as the little calf peeked out from between his mother's legs.

'I love the elephants,' Alessi said into the silence. 'I like the way they always remember.'

'I hate the way they always remember,' Isla said.

'Why?'

'Because some things are best forgotten.'

'Such as?' Alessi asked.

She turned and gave a weak smile but shook her head. She simply didn't know how to tell him or how to answer his questions about when she had decided to be a midwife. At what point did you hand over your heart, your past? At what point did you reveal others' secrets?

Isla didn't know.

'He's getting tired,' Alessi said as he lowered Niko from his shoulders. 'We'll take him to see his favourite thing and then get him home.'

'What is Niko's favourite thing?' Isla asked, glad for the change in subject.

It was the meerkats!

Niko hung over the edge of the barrier, shrieking with laughter every time they stood up and froze, calling out to ''Lessi' to watch.

'Look at that one,' Alessi said to Niko. 'He's on lookout while the others dig for food.'

Niko didn't care if he was on lookout; he just laughed and laughed till in the end so, too, were Isla and Alessi.

It was fun.

Just a fun day out and Isla hadn't had too many of those. She finally felt as if she was being herself, only it was a new self, someone she had never been—someone who was honest and open, except for the lies she had promised to keep.

At six, Alessi strapped an already fast asleep Niko into his car seat. 'Hopefully he will stay that way till tomorrow,' he said. 'I'll get him home and then we can go and get some dinner.'

'Won't it look odd if I'm with you?' Isla asked.

'Odd?' Alessi checked.

'For Allegra, seeing me out with you…'

'I'm not going to hide you around the corner and pretend that I've spent the day with Niko alone. Anyway, he's three, he's going to tell her that you were there.'

'I guess.' There was a flutter in her stomach as they pulled up at Allegra's house, but thankfully Alessi didn't put her through the torture of coming up to the door when Isla said that she'd prefer to wait for him in the car.

'I'll just carry him up the stairs and put him into bed,' Alessi said. 'I won't be long.'

Famous last words.

'Is that Isla in the car?' Allegra asked as she let him in.

'It is.'

'Alessi…' Allegra started, but didn't elaborate until

Niko was tucked up in bed and the bedroom door was closed behind him.

'What?' Alessi said. He'd heard the note of reprimand in his sister's voice when she'd seen who was in the car. 'It's no big deal.'

'Well, it is to me,' Allegra said. 'Can you try and not break up with *this one* before I have the baby. I don't want any bad feelings…'

'There won't be any bad feelings,' Alessi said. 'Isla would never involve you like that…' Then he halted, because he'd lied. It *was* starting to feel like a big deal. 'Anyway, I have no intention of breaking things up.'

Allegra gave a slightly disbelieving snort. 'The baby's still four weeks off, Alessi.'

'I know.'

Allegra paused at the bottom of the stairs and turned and looked at her brother, who she loved very much. 'Four weeks would be an all-time record,' Allegra said. 'Well, not an all-time…' Her voice trailed off. She didn't think the mention of Talia's name would be particularly welcome here. 'I like Isla.'

'I do, too.' Alessi admitted. 'Yes, perhaps it would be more sensible to wait till the baby is born but…' He gave a small shrug. 'I'd already waited for nearly a year.'

He had.

Alessi said goodbye to his sister and then headed back to the car. A part of him wanted to turn and retract what he'd said to his sister—push the genie back in the bottle—yet he did really like Isla.

He more than liked her, in fact.

It was a rather new feeling to have.

'Right.' Alessi climbed into the driver's seat. 'Do you want to go for dinner?'

'I do.' Isla smiled. 'I'm actually starving.'

'Name where you want to go, then,' Alessi said. 'I picked the zoo so it's your turn to choose.'

Isla thought for a moment. 'We could go to Geo's. I hear they've got a new menu.'

'Geo's?' Alessi frowned but then screwed up his nose. 'Maybe we could try somewhere else…'

'Why?' Isla pushed. 'You're Greek and I love Greek food and they do the best in Melbourne.'

'We'll never get a booking this time on a Sunday night.'

'I will,' Isla said.

'They have a dress code,' Alessi pointed out.

'Not for me…' She halted then. Geo's was one of the best Greek restaurants in Melbourne and it was booked out ages in advance, just not for the likes of Isla. She could feel the tension in the car and guessed it was thanks to her latest arrogant remark. God, she'd suggested a seriously expensive restaurant in the same way she'd asked for champagne the first night they'd met.

'Don't make me feel pretentious, Alessi.'

'I'm not.'

'Actually, you are.'

He could have driven off, Alessi realised, simply left it at that. Instead, he left the engine idling and told her the truth. 'Geo's is actually my parents' restaurant, Isla.' He watched as her eyes widened in surprise and then he surprised himself and let out the handbrake. 'Let's go there.'

'Alessi.' Isla let out a nervous laugh. 'I honestly

didn't know. I don't want to make things awkward for you.'

'Why would be it awkward?' he said, while determined not to make it so.

The restaurant was packed and heads turned as Alessi led her through. Isla was acutely aware that she was wearing shorts and runners, especially when a woman, who had to be his mother, came over and gave her son a kiss.

'This is Isla,' Alessi introduced them. 'She's a friend from work and we have just taken Niko to the zoo. Isla, this is my mother, Yolanda.'

'Come upstairs,' Yolanda said. 'Introduce Isla…'

'We're going to eat downstairs,' Alessi said firmly, and guided Isla to a table near the back. And as they took a seat he explained. 'If I take you upstairs then I'd have to marry you,' he teased.

'Downstairs it is, then.'

The food was amazing—even if Yolanda did tend to hover. Isla could hear laughter from upstairs. It was clear that Alessi had a huge extended family and a couple of them stopped by, greeting Isla warmly.

'Your family are close,' Isla said.

'Very,' Alessi agreed, and then told her a little about how the restaurant had started. 'We started getting more and more orders for catering. People would bring in their own dishes and ask my mother to make her moussaka in them so that they could pass them off as their own. Once we had finished school my parents were ready to take the gamble so the café was closed and Geo's opened. Upstairs is all for family. Downstairs is the main restaurant.'

'Do you come here a lot?'

'I try to drop in once a week,' Alessi said, 'maybe once a fortnight if things are busy at work.'

'And have you ever taken anyone upstairs?' Isla smiled, more than a little nosy where Alessi was concerned.

'One person.'

The smile was wiped from her face as she heard the serious note in his voice. 'You remember Talia from school?'

Isla nodded.

'We started going out when she first went to med school.'

'How long were you going out for?' Isla asked, and his response caught her by surprise.

'Two years.'

'Oh.' She'd always thought Alessi kept his relationships short-term. 'That's a long time.'

'Especially by Greek standards,' Alessi said, and took a breath. He never went into the past with women but he was starting to hope for more of a future with Isla, and for Alessi that meant being honest. 'We were about to get engaged. Neither my parents nor hers have ever forgiven me for calling it off.'

'You were young.' Isla tried to keep things light. 'Surely that's better if you weren't sure you were ready.'

'I was ready,' Alessi said, and watched as Isla's glass paused just a little before she placed it on the table. He was close to sharing, closer than he had ever been. He liked her take on things, he actually respected her directness and the slight detachment that came from Isla. She offered a rare perspective and he wanted more of that now. 'Apart from the reunion, do you keep in touch with Talia?' Alessi asked.

'A bit,' she said. 'Just social networks and things… Why?' She smiled. 'Do you still have a thing for her?'

'God, no,' Alessi said. It was the truth.

He looked at Isla—the fact that she and Talia were loosely in touch was enough of a reason not to tell her the truth about that time.

Or an *excuse* not to.

Isla would never break a confidence, he knew that.

Alessi knew then how serious he was about Isla because in more than a decade he had never once come close to telling another woman the truth behind that time.

But not here.

Not yet.

'How serious did you and Rupert get?' Alessi asked. 'Did you ever speak of marriage?'

'No.' Isla let out a short laugh. 'Rupert and I…'

Alessi watched as she suddenly took great interest in the dessert menu, which two minutes ago Isla had declined, and he was suddenly glad he hadn't revealed all.

Yes, he knew her a bit better but despite her apparent ease, Isla still revealed very little. 'Shall we go?' Alessi suggested, and Isla nodded.

'It seems strange not to have to wait for the bill.'

'We still have to account for our time.' Alessi smiled and rolled his eyes as his mother made her way over, insisting that they come upstairs for coffee, but Alessi declined.

'I have work at seven,' he said, determined not to

let his family push things, while determined not to hide. 'So does Isla.'

He drove her back to her apartment and they chatted along the way. 'Do you miss Isabel?' Alessi asked.

'I do,' Isla said, 'though it sounds as if she's having an amazing time in Cambridge...'

'How come she went?' Alessi asked. 'It was quite sudden.'

'It just came up,' Isla said, and gave him the same answer that she had to Sean. 'Who wouldn't kill for twelve months' secondment in England?'

'It had nothing to do with Sean?'

'Sean?'

'I just picked up on something.' Alessi glanced over. 'When he first started, I was down on MMU and Isabel was blushing and avoiding him as much as you would have avoided me tomorrow had I not dragged you out today...'

'I don't know what you're talking about.'

She did, Alessi was sure, but her trust was worth his patience and so he kissed her instead.

His kiss was more intimate than last night, Isla thought. It tasted not so much of passion but of promise and possibility. His mouth was more familiar and yet more intriguing because it pushed her further along a path she had never been on with a man.

Here they could end their amazing weekend.

Right now she could climb out of the car and go up to her apartment. Both of them could gather their thoughts, ready to resume normal service on Monday.

It was Isla who pulled back. 'I don't want anyone at work to know...'

'Of course,' Alessi said, and then guessed the reason they were still in his car, rather than her asking him up. 'Oh, yes, you share with Darcie.' He hesitated, wondering if asking her back to his for a second night was too much, too soon, yet it was Isla's boldness that took him by delighted surprise.

'She's on call tonight.'

It was new, it was delicious, it was a weekend that didn't have to end just yet as Isla invited him just a little bit further into her life.

CHAPTER ELEVEN

For a woman who had never dated, Isla got a crash course and the next two weeks were blissful. Even the hard parts, like attending Archie's funeral in the hospital chapel, were made better for being together.

'Thanks for everything you did, Isla,' Donna said as they said their farewells after the service. 'Especially with Jessica.'

'How is she doing?' Isla asked.

'She's upset, of course, but she really does know that none of this was her fault. She's so glad that they had that lovely evening together and that last day.' Donna turned to Alessi. 'Thank...' she attempted, then broke down, and Alessi gave her a cuddle.

'He was such a beautiful boy,' he said. 'I am so sorry that there wasn't more that could be done. You made the right choice, Donna. He got a whole day of being loved and cuddled by his mum and dad and big sister.'

Isla, who never cried, could feel tears at the backs of her eyes as Donna wept and nodded and then pulled away. 'I need to get back up to the unit for Elijah.'

'Go,' Alessi said. 'I will see you up there soon.'

He walked up towards Maternity with Isla. He'd

felt her standing rigid beside him during the service and had noted that not a tear had been shed by her.

'Awful, wasn't it?' Alessi said.

'Yep.'

'Does nothing move you to tears, Isla?'

She halted and turned to face him. 'Excuse me?'

'I'm just commenting...'

'What, because I don't break down and cry I'm not upset?'

'I never said that,' Alessi answered calmly. 'I was just asking if anything moves you to tears. Babies' funerals are very difficult.'

'I agree.'

'Why do you hold back?'

'What, because I don't cry...'

'You hold back in everything, Isla,' he said.

It wasn't a row, more an observation, and one Isla pondered as she set up that night for TMTB.

She was pleased to see that Ruby was back.

'Are we getting pizza tonight?' Ruby asked, and Isla nodded.

'We are. I've already ordered it so it should be here soon. How are you doing, Ruby?'

'I've got my scan tomorrow afternoon.'

'Is anyone coming with you?' Isla asked, and Ruby shook her head. 'Would you like me to come with you?'

'No, thanks.'

'Well, if you change your mind just ask them to page me.'

As everyone gathered there was one noticeable absence and Isla was delighted to tell the group the happy news. 'Alison had a little girl on Monday,' Isla said.

'The birth went really well and the baby is beautiful. I've got a photo on my phone that Alison asked me to show you.'

Her phone was passed around and Isla loved watching the smile on each of the young women's faces. It was always a nice time but it was also a little confronting for some of the group as they realised that some day soon it would be their baby being spoken about in the group. Clearly it was too much for Ruby because she quickly passed on the phone.

Isla was worried for the young girl and though Ruby hung around afterwards to take the last of the pizza, still she didn't want to speak with Isla and made her excuses and dashed off.

She needed someone she gelled with, Isla thought. Isla took no offence that that person might not be herself and the next day, when Ruby didn't page Isla to come for the ultrasound, Isla was actually trying to think who might be the best fit for Ruby when her pager went off.

'Isla, it's Darcie. I was wondering if you could come down to the antenatal clinic. I've got a patient, Ruby, and—'

'I know Ruby.' Isla smiled. 'Did she change her mind?'

'Sorry?'

'I offered to come with her for her ultrasound but she said no.'

'Well, she's asked for you now. Isla, there's an anomaly on the ultrasound. The baby has spina bifida. The poor kid has had the most terrible afternoon. Loads of tests and specialists. Heinz was speaking with her and she's got terribly upset...'

Isla groaned. As brilliant as Heinz, a paediatric neurologist, was, his people skills weren't the best. 'He broached termination and Ruby is beside herself.'

'I'll be there now. Who's the midwife?' Isla asked, wondering why she hadn't been told about this long ago. She knew Ruby's ultrasound had been scheduled for two.

'Lucas,' Darcie said, and then hesitated. 'I didn't call him in till just before that.'

'I don't know what's going on between the two of you,' Isla said swiftly, 'but sort it out. I don't care if you don't get on, I don't care if you're my flatmate. I care about my patients.'

She was furious as she walked down the corridor but took a calming breath as she stepped into the room. Lucas was sitting with a teary Ruby, who had clearly been through the wringer. She looked so young and vulnerable and she should have had an advocate with her, a friend, anyone, but instead she'd faced it all pretty much alone.

'It's okay, Ruby...' Isla said, but it was the wrong thing to say because an angry Ruby jumped to her feet.

'No, it isn't!' Ruby said. 'I've just been told that it isn't all right...'

'Ruby,' Isla said, 'I know it's so much to take in.' She just wanted to get her away from the clinic for a while, to talk to her without everyone hanging around. 'Why don't we go to the canteen?'

'I don't want to go the canteen with you, you stuck-up cow,' Ruby said. 'I just want...' She didn't finish but instead ran off. Isla went after her but she knew it was pointless.

'She just needs some time,' Darcie said when Isla saw her.

'I know,' Isla said, and looked at Darcie. 'I should have been told. Just because you and Lucas aren't talk-ing—'

'Hey!' Darcie broke in. 'Lucas did a CTG on a thirty-five-weeker at two and found no heartbeat. I'm going to deliver her tonight. He's been brilliant, he's been in with Mum and Dad all afternoon. Yes, we've had a row and we don't get on, but my not telling him about Ruby had nothing to do with that. We were swamped. I had no idea Heinz was going to talk to her, I just thought he was looking through the scans.'

'Isla—'

Isla turned as Lucas knocked on the door. 'Allegra Manos is here, she said you were to be paged when she arrived.'

'Thanks.'

'I'm sorry I didn't let you know about Ruby,' Lucas added. 'I was in with a mum—'

'Darcie explained.' Isla let out a tense breath. 'Sorry about that, Darcie.'

'Apology accepted.' Darcie smiled. 'It's just been one of those awful afternoons.'

Not that the other patients could know that, so both Isla and Darcie pushed out a smile and went in to see Allegra.

She looked fantastic and the baby seemed to be doing just fine.

'Everything,' Darcie said as she examined Allegra, 'is looking great. The baby is head down and a nice size and there's lots of fluid. How are the movements?'

'Lots of them,' Allegra said.

Darcie spoke at length with Allegra about a trial of labour and told her that they would part insert an epidural. 'It won't stop you from moving around but it means that if we do need to move to a Caesarean then everything will be set up, so we can move quickly if we have to and you can also stay awake.'

Darcie answered a few more of Allegra's questions. 'I'll be seeing you weekly from now on,' Darcie said as she stepped out.

'All looks good.' Isla smiled.

'Can you let Alessi know that for me? I know he'll be itching to find out. He's doing his best not to ring for updates.'

'I'll let him know,' Isla said, but when she paged him she got the head nurse in Neonatology, who said he was busy with an infant. 'Can I pass on a message?'

'It's fine,' Isla said. 'I'll try again later.'

Much later.

In fact, it was after eight when she made her way up to NICU and buzzed and was let in, and after washing her hands she was directed to Alessi, who was by little Elijah's cot. 'How is he?' she asked.

'Giving me far too many sleepless nights, but he's doing a bit better,' he said. He was putting an IV in Elijah's scalp and Isla stood quietly as Alessi concentrated. There was a little picture attached to his cot of him and Archie lying together on what must have been Archie's last day, and Isla tore her eyes from it as Alessi finished and peeled off his gloves. 'Thank you,' he said to the neonatal nurse who had assisted him. 'Is this a personal visit?' he asked as they walked from the cot.

'Sort of.' Isla nodded. 'I'm just here to tell you about Allegra. All went well—'

'We'll go into my office.'

Isla followed him in. 'Your office is very messy.'

'Because I'm never in it long enough to put anything away,' he said, and as a case in point his phone buzzed and he answered it. 'I'll be out in a few moments.' He then hung up the phone. 'How is Allegra?'

'Fantastic. It's all progressing well. The baby is head down and engaged and Darcie will be seeing her weekly from now on.'

'She still wants a trial of labour?'

'She does,' Isla replied. 'Darcie has gone through it all with her and Allegra will have an epidural placed just in case a Caesarean is needed.' She perched on the edge of his desk. 'What time are you finishing?' she asked, knowing that he should already be off now.

'I'm just waiting for some results to come in on Elijah.'

'I thought he was doing a bit better?'

'He is,' he said. 'I just want to check his labs.'

'Who's on call tonight?'

'Jed,' Alessi clipped.

'Can't Jed—'

'Isla, please don't,' Alessi warned, because this really was his tipping point. 'I work long hours. If it doesn't suit—'

'Oh, please.' She simply laughed in the face of his warning. 'I'm not some needy miss, worried that you're going to ruin dinner if you're late home.' She pulled him towards her and started to kiss his tired mouth. 'And I'm not trying to come between you and your premmies.' She locked her hands behind his neck and looked into the blackest, most beautiful eyes she had ever seen and was as honest as she had ever been. 'I don't care if you're here till five in the morning just as long as you need to be here, Alessi... I just happen to care about you. If you were one of my staff I'd have sent you home about three hours ago. In fact, I'd have told you to take tomorrow off, too.'

'I'm not one of your staff.'

'Lucky for you.'

Alessi looked at Isla. He loved how she'd bypassed his warning, how she'd admitted she cared, so he told her the truth.

'I can't send Donna and Tom home with no baby.'

'And you'll do everything to see that you don't,' Isla calmly assured him. 'But Elijah's going to be here for weeks, maybe months...' She could see the wrestle in his eyes. 'I'm not going to push it.' She gave him another quick kiss and jumped down from the desk. 'I'm heading home. Stop by if it's not too late.'

'Is Darcie on call tonight?'

'Nope.' Isla headed for the door. 'I doubt she'll drop dead with shock—half the hospital seems to have worked out that we're on.'

They *were* on.

Alessi knew that when at ten, instead of crashing in the on-call room, he was driving to Isla's. It had nothing to do with the promise of sex. He would probably be kicked out for snoring, he was so tired. It was balance, it was her, it was the calm of non-judgment and the freedom of choice along with cool reason.

'I'd just about given up,' Isla said, answering

the door in her dressing gown, her hair wrapped in a towel.

'Jed might call,' he warned her. 'I might need to go in.'

'That's fine,' she said. 'Do you want something to eat?'

'I had something earlier,' he said. 'I'd kill for a shower, though.'

He'd been to the apartment a few times but never while Darcie was there. She was tapping away on her computer while watching a movie and didn't seem remotely fazed to see him here.

'Help yourself,' Isla said, opening her bedroom door.

Alessi did.

To shampoo, to conditioner, to Isla's deodorant.

'You smell like me,' Isla said as he joined her in bed and then kissed him. 'You taste like me, too.'

Alessi really hadn't come here with sex on his mind and that became more apparent as their kiss deepened. 'I didn't bring anything...'

'Alessi.'

'Can we lose the condoms?' he asked. 'I don't care what tests, I'll do them, but...'

They were just so completely into each other that this conversation had only been a matter of time but Isla was grateful for the very small reprieve he had just given her.

'Yes...' She knew she should tell him there was no need for tests on her part and she would, Isla decided. She was moving closer and closer to opening up to him, just not now. Now she could feel his exhaustion, now it was so easy to be bold, to just move her lips from his mouth and kiss downwards, to hold him in her hands and feel him grow.

For Alessi it was heaven.

Her tentative lips did not alert him to her inexperience. Instead he just revelled in her slow explorations and the trail of her damp hair down his body.

Isla tasted him for the first time, loved the feel of his hand on her head and the gentle pressure that pushed her deeper. Selfish was his pleasure and that she revelled in. She could feel his occasional restraint, when he tried not to thrust.

Then there was the turn-on when he stopped trying and just gave in. The power, the feel, the taste, the rush of him coming had Isla come, too, at the intimate private pleasure, and then afterwards, feeling him relaxed and sated beside her, it was the closest she had ever felt to another person.

And Alessi felt it, too, for there in the dark, as pleasure receded, a deeper connection flowed in as she lay in his arms.

'I was wrong to accuse you of holding back when there are things that I haven't told you.'

Isla looked at him as he continued speaking.

'Talia was pregnant.' It was with Isla that he shared for the first time. 'When she told me I asked her to marry me and we decided to tell our parents about the pregnancy after the wedding.' He liked it that her face was still there, though her smile had gone, and he liked it that she didn't ask questions. 'We had a big dinner at the restaurant on the Saturday…'

He tried to explain better. 'In Greek families you

establish a connection before the man asks the woman's father, so even though we weren't officially engaged, it was a given that it was to come. On the Wednesday Talia missed lectures. I went over to check if all was okay and it was clear she was unwell. I thought she was losing the baby. I wanted her to go to hospital but she told me there was no need...' He watched Isla's slight frown. 'She told me then that she'd had an abortion that morning.'

'Without telling you?'

'Yep. She thought I would try to talk her out of it. She said that she wanted to have children one day but that she knew she couldn't study to be a doctor and be a teenage mum...' Alessi turned from Isla and looked back at the ceiling. 'I get that, I understand that. I get that it was her body...'

'It was your baby, though?'

Alessi nodded and he waited and hoped for Isla to share.

'Go to sleep,' Isla said, and Alessi smiled into the darkness.

If it took for ever he would find out what went on in that head, and then he smiled into the darkness again. 'Jed and I have swapped. I'm working this weekend.'

'But you're already on call twice next week,' Isla pointed out sleepily.

'I know,' Alessi said, 'but it will be worth it to have next weekend off. You know what next weekend is?' he checked. 'Valentine's Day. The anniversary of when we first met.'

'And?'

'I have plans for us.'

'Such as?'

'You'll find out,' he said. Yes, he'd had plans when he'd swapped the work arrangements with Jed—an intimate meal with Isla, perhaps a night in a gorgeous hotel, but right now those plans were getting bigger and he gave a wry laugh.

'Hopefully it will end better than the last one.'

CHAPTER TWELVE

IT WAS THE promise of the weekend and the fact that her period was due that had Isla knocking on Darcie's office door on the Monday morning.

'Hi, Darcie...'

'Hey, Isla.'

'I was wondering...' Isla started, but then she changed her mind. She would make an appointment with her GP, Isla decided, and turned to go. Except her period was due any time and for it to be safe she'd need to start the Pill on her first day. She also knew that she needed to have her blood pressure checked and things... So Isla took a breath. 'Have you got a moment?'

'Sure,' Darcie said. 'I've got precisely six.' She frowned when Isla didn't smile. 'I've got all the time you need, Isla. Is everything okay?'

'Oh, it's not a biggie,' Isla said. 'It won't take long. I was just wondering if you could write me a script for the Pill...'

'Sure,' Darcie said. 'Have a seat.'

Isla did, though again she was tempted to change her mind. 'What do you usually take?' Darcie asked, pulling out a blood-pressure cuff. When Isla didn't immediately answer, Darcie said, 'Sorry, Isla, but I'm not just going to give you a repeat without checking your blood pressure.'

Isla nodded. She knew that Darcie was thorough and was starting to realise what a stupid idea this had been as Darcie quickly checked it. 'All good.' Darcie nodded. 'So, what are you on?'

'I'm not,' Isla said.

'What type of contraception do you usually use?'

'Condoms,' Isla said, and then cleared her throat.

'Okay,' Darcie answered carefully. They both knew that condoms weren't the safest of choices.

'Look, sorry, Darcie, I should have gone to my GP. I just—'

'Isla, it's fine.' Darcie interrupted. 'I'm not just going to write out a script, though, if it's something that you haven't taken before.'

Isla nodded.

'Have you any history that I should know about?'

Isla shook her head.

'Blood clots, migraines…' She went through the list of contraindications.

'Nothing.'

'Good.' Darcie smiled. 'When did you last have a smear test?'

Isla sat there, her cheeks on fire.

'Sorry, I keep forgetting I'm in Australia,' Darcie said into the silence. 'When did you last have a Pap?'

Isla had never had a Pap because she'd never been sexually active.

'It's been…' Isla gave a tight shrug. 'It's been a while.'

'I'm not going to tell you off for leaving it too long,' Darcie said. 'Let's just get it over and done with. When is your period due?'

'Today or tomorrow.'

'Have you had any unprotected sex?'

'No.' Isla shook her head, but more to clear it. What the hell was she lying for? 'Once,' she amended. 'But he…' She let out a breath in embarrassment. God, no wonder the patients loathed all the questions. 'He withdrew.'

'Did you do it standing up?' Darcie grinned as she teased. They'd both heard it all before and knew that withdrawal was far from safe.

'I'm not pregnant,' Isla said. She knew that she wasn't—her breasts had that heavy feeling they always got when her period was near. Not that it put Darcie off.

'Fine, then you won't mind peeing in a jar to put my mind at ease. Then I'm going to do a Pap and give you a work-up and get all the boxes ticked so you can hopefully forget about things for another couple of years.'

'You don't have time.'

'I just made time.' Darcie smiled. She was a thorough doctor and refused to be rushed by anyone, especially her patients, and a little while later as she looked at the pregnancy card on the desk before her, a patient Isla suddenly was.

'Isla,' Darcie said, and Isla watched as she pushed the card over to her.

Isla stared at it for a long moment. There were possibly a thousand thoughts in her head but not a single

one of them did she show on her face. She just looked
up at Darcie.

'Can we leave the Pap for another time?' Isla said,
her voice completely clear, her expression unreadable.

'Of course, but, Isla—'

'Can we not discuss this, please?' Isla stood.
'Just…' She turned as she got to the door. 'You won't
tell anyone…'

'You don't have to ask me that, Isla,' Darcie said,
and Isla nodded. 'But if you want to talk any time,
you can.'

Isla muttered brief thanks and headed out to her
department, and for the first time ever she left early.

She lay on her bed and just stared at the ceiling and
all she felt was stupid, naïve and embarrassed at having got pregnant her *first* time.

It was all she could manage to feel as she lay there.

When the phone bleeped to indicate a text, she
knew it was from Alessi but she didn't even look at it.

She simply could not bear to think of telling him
or even attempt to fathom his reaction.

Far worse than his anger would be duty.

Isla lay there, recalling his words—how he'd done
the right thing by Talia, how he'd offered to marry her
as soon as he'd found out.

She didn't want that for either of them.

They'd been going out for a couple of weeks, which
surely meant, given his track record, that they had just
about run their course.

Isla tried to comfort herself, reminded herself that
the reason she'd been going on the Pill in the first
place was that Alessi himself had wanted to move
things forward, to lose the condoms.

On the proviso that she was on the Pill, though.

Isla felt a tear slide out and she screwed her eyes shut.

She heard the door open and Darcie come home and Isla wanted to call out to her, she wanted to sob, hell, she wanted to break down and cry.

But she didn't know how to, scared that if she let out a part of her fear then the rest would come gushing out.

Secrets she had sworn never to reveal.

CHAPTER THIRTEEN

ISLA DIDN'T HAVE to try too hard to avoid Alessi.

That night he was too wrecked to even drive home so he sent a text to Isla to say he was crashing at the hospital. About two seconds after hitting 'send' he did just that in the on-call room on the unit.

He dived back into work at eight the next day when he was on call again. He finally saw Isla on Tuesday but it wasn't a social visit—a newborn was rapidly deteriorating and all Alessi wanted from Isla was her cool efficiency, which he got.

In fact, Isla was doing her very best to keep calm.

Wrestling with her own news, trying to fathom that she herself would, in a matter of months, be a mum, she had been checking on a newborn when she found a baby looking dusky at her mother's breast. Isla moved the infant, hoping her breathing had just been obstructed temporarily but was silently alarmed by her colour and tone.

'I'm just going to take her to the nursery,' Isla said to Karina, the mother. 'She's looking a bit pale and the light is better there…' She would have loved to speak with the mother some more but the little girl was causing Isla too much concern and she moved swiftly through the unit, glad when she saw Emily there, who instantly saw Isla's concern.

'I'll page Alessi,' Emily said as Isla suctioned the infant and started to deliver oxygen.

Yes, Isla was calm and did everything right but there was this horrible new urgency there as Karina arrived in the nursery, tears streaming down her face.

'She was fine!' Karina was saying, and Isla could hear the fear, the love, the helplessness in her voice. 'Please, help her,' she begged as Alessi dashed in and took over.

'She's going to be fine…'

Alessi's calm voice caught even Isla by surprise. 'Just a little milk that's gone down the wrong way…' He was rubbing the baby's back and gently suctioning her, and thankfully she was pinking up.

He dealt with it all very calmly, even though there was some marked concern, which he explained in more detail a little while later after some tests had been done.

'As I said…' Alessi pulled up the X-ray on his computer and went through it with the mum. 'She has inhaled some milk and we're going to be looking for infection, which is why I'm going to have her moved to NICU to keep a closer eye on her for a few days…'

It had all been dealt with well yet it left Isla more shaken than it would usually, not that she showed it.

'Thanks for that.' Isla gave him a tight smile as his team went off to NICU with their latest recruit and she headed into her office, just wanting to be alone, but Alessi followed.

'Shouldn't you be with the baby?'

'She's fine,' Alessi said. 'Are you?'

'I just got a fright,' Isla admitted. 'I'd just popped in to chat with Karina…'

'It happens. I want to take a closer look at her palate when I'm up there. I think she might have a small cleft that's been missed.'

Isla just looked at him and tried to fathom that in a few months she'd be on this roller-coaster. 'I'll try and call you tonight,' Alessi said, and gave her a light kiss on her lips. Isla wanted to grab his shoulders and cling to him; she wanted some of his ease and strength to somehow transfer to her, but instead she stood there and watched him leave.

She knew she had to tell him.

Just not yet.

She wouldn't say anything until she could tell him without breaking down, till she'd somehow got her head around the fact that she'd soon be a first-time mother herself.

It was just all too much to take in, let alone share with Alessi, when she didn't know how he'd react.

Which meant that at nine on Friday evening, after a hellish week at work, as Alessi drove home he called Isla and got her cool voice when he needed warmth.

He got distance when he needed to be closer.

'Is it too late to come over?' he asked.

'Well, it is a bit,' she said. 'I'm pretty tired.'

'Sure.' Alessi forced down his irritation. He could sleep for a whole week yet he still wanted to see her. 'Isla, I was thinking about tomorrow…' He was just so glad the weekend was finally here.

He had it planned.

He was way past the flowers and dinner stage already.

'How about I pick you up around six—'

'I actually wanted to talk about that,' Isla broke in. 'I've just realised that I can't make it.'

'You can't make it?'

'I forgot when you said you'd swapped your shift that I already had plans for this weekend...'

'Such as?'

Such as trying to get my head around the fact that I'm pregnant, Isla wanted to scream. *Such as trying to tell you that I wasn't on the Pill. That you were my first...*

She was closer to tears than she wanted to be.

'Alessi...' She swallowed. 'I just can't make it.'

'Don't do this, Isla,' he warned. 'I'm coming now and you are going to talk to me.'

'There's nothing to talk about.'

'You know, you're right,' he said, his temper bubbling to the surface. 'Because it seems to me I'm the one who does the talking. I've told you so much these past weeks, Isla, and you've told me precisely nothing.'

'That's not true.'

'Bull!' Alessi shouted. 'I know little more about you than I did the night of the ball. You tell me nothing about how you feel or what you're thinking. Oh, sorry, I do know one thing that I didn't two weeks ago—you give good head.'

No, he could never know her, neither could he read her because instead of a shocked gasp or a swift attack he got the sound of dry laughter.

'You're right, you don't know me,' Isla said, because by her own silence he didn't and she'd surely left it too late to start opening up now.

* * *

'Game over, is it, Isla?' Alessi's voice was cool. 'At least have the guts to say it.'

'Game over,' Isla said, and hung up.

As Valentine's Days went, it was a pretty terrible one.

She woke to a text from Alessi, apologising, but telling her that she'd be getting flowers as he had been unable to cancel the flower order. And then there was a snarky addition: Believe me, Isla, I damn well tried!

Isla actually smiled wryly at his text.

She answered the door to her delivery of not one but two large bouquets.

One was from Alessi, saying that he couldn't wait for tonight.

The other was from Rupert, who must have forgotten to cancel his regular order from the florist.

'You have a very interesting life,' said Darcie, smiling.

Things had been just a touch awkward between them since Isla had found out she was pregnant but Darcie was nice enough not to push her to talk. Instead, she made Isla laugh as she swiped Rupert's bunch and said that she was going to pretend they were for her.

It was the only funny part of the day.

The only funny part of the week.

Isla's heart ached in a way that it never had before. She knew she had to tell Alessi, that somehow she had to face things—he would soon find out after all—but she was worried about his reaction. Of course she expected him to be upset. In her work Isla was more than used to that. She knew, though, that after the dust settled, when the initial shock of a pregnancy wore off, rapid decisions were often made.

She had never wanted their fragile relationship to be put under such early pressure and, worse, it was her own fault. But on Wednesday night, as she set up for TMTB, Isla knew her problems were comparatively small as a very pale face came around the door, followed by a slender body that housed a growing bump.

'Come in, Ruby.' Isla smiled and she forced another one when Alessi followed her in with an empty incubator he had bought down from NICU for his talk with the girls.

He ignored her.

'I'm sorry I called you a stuck-up cow!' Ruby said.

'It's fine, Ruby. I know that I can be a stuck-up cow at times!' She gave the young girl a little hug. 'It's so good to see you here. Do you want to get something to eat?'

Ruby nodded and made her way over to the table, which was groaning under the weight of cupcakes Emily had just *happened* to have made.

Emily was always going beyond the call of duty and it dawned on Isla that she would be the perfect midwife for Ruby. Isla decided that she would have a word about Ruby with her favourite midwife tomorrow, or whenever Emily was next on.

And then, as she looked at the faces of her TMTB group, some nervous, some excited, others ready, Isla felt the first glimpse of calmness that she'd had since Darcie had pushed the pregnancy card towards her and she had found out that she'd be a mother.

She looked at Ruby and saw the fear in her eyes but also the fire. She looked at Harriet, who was facing things bravely and passing around a picture of the ultrasound.

Yes, she was twenty-eight but Isla forgave herself then because teenage, twenty, thirty or forty—when it first happened and you found out you were going to be a mum, it was an overwhelming feeling indeed.

She didn't feel so overwhelmed now.

Scared, yes, nervous, of course, but there was excitement there, too, and as she glanced over at Alessi, who was pointedly ignoring her, Isla was grateful, too, that, no matter what his reaction was, this man was the father of her child.

'It's great to see so many of you.' Isla kicked things off. They did a small catch-up, finding out where everyone was at, but when it was Ruby's turn she said little and Isla moved things on because clearly Ruby wasn't willing to share her news yet.

'Most of you met Alessi four weeks ago,' Isla introduced their guest speaker. 'He's a neonatologist here at the Victoria. A couple of you already know that your babies will be going to NICU when they're born. Some of you might not be expecting your baby to end up there and so, if it does, it will come as a huge shock. That's why Alessi is here,' Isla explained. 'If your baby is on NICU then at least you'll have a familiar face and, as well as that, he's a wonderful doctor.'

She gave him a smile but again Alessi completely blanked her and instead he addressed the group.

'Thank you for having me along tonight,' he said. 'As Isla said, I am a neonatologist. Does everyone here know what that means?' When no one answered he asked another question. 'Does everyone know what NICU stands for?'

A couple of the newer girls shook their heads and Alessi did smile now, but it was a tight one and, Isla knew, aimed at her.

It said, *Ruby was right—you are a stuck-up cow!*

'Well, a neonatologist is a doctor who takes care of newborns. In my case, I care for newborns that need, or might need, extra support. NICU stands for Neonatal Intensive Care Unit, which basically means it is a place for babies who need a lot of support. The best place for a baby to be is where it is now...' As Alessi talked, Isla could see he already had the group eating out of his hand.

He was completely lovely with them.

'I'm very good at my job,' he said, 'but even with all the technology available, I'm still not as good as you are at keeping your baby oxygenated and nourished and its temperature stable...'

He opened up the incubator and turned on a few monitors and explained how they worked and what the staff were looking for, and really he did give an excellent talk.

'The nurses there are amazing,' Alessi said. 'When a baby is especially sick there is a nurse with them at all times, sometimes two. They don't get scared by the alarms, because they are very used to them. So although the alarms will make you feel anxious, don't think that the nursing staff are ignoring anything.'

Then his phone rang and Alessi rolled his eyes.

'That's my family ringing again and asking where I am,' he said, 'and that is one alarm that I *am* going to ignore!'

Isla smiled as he turned off his phone and gave the group his full attention.

He went through many things and then asked if anyone had questions, which they all did, even Ruby.

'What happens if a baby is disabled?' Ruby asked.

Isla had sat in on a meeting just that morning about her baby. There was talk of out-of-utero surgery, if a suitable doctor could be found, though Ruby didn't know about this yet.

She was in a very fragile place and Isla was very proud of her for asking questions.

'Many of the babies I look after will have disabilities,' Alessi said. 'When you say what happens…'

'Do you care as much about them?' Ruby asked. 'Or do you think the mother should have got rid of it? What happens if the baby is up for adoption?'

There was a long stretch of silence and Isla fought not to step in yet she glanced at Alessi and knew that she didn't have to. He was taking care with his answer as he looked at the hostile and very scared girl.

'The only thing I would think in that instance,' Alessi said, 'was that by the time the mother and baby get to be in my care, a lot of very difficult decisions have already been made and a lot of obstacles faced.'

He hesitated for a moment before continuing. 'A lot of my babies will leave the unit and require a lot of extra care just to do normal things. Many, too, leave healthy. My job, my goal, is to hand the baby to its carer, whoever that may be, in the best possible health. That is my goal every day when I go into work. You ask if I care as much. I care about every one of my patients. Some need more care than others and I see that they get it.'

She couldn't not tell him about the pregnancy. Isla had long known that but it was confirmed then.

She was keeping her baby and so the decisions that would be made for its care would involve Alessi also.

She looked at his wide, lovely smile as he even managed to get a small laugh from Ruby, and Isla imagined his expression when she told him they were bound for ever—that the cool and together 'I've got this covered' Isla hadn't even been on the Pill.

She deserved his reaction, she expected the row, and she'd prefer that than Alessi choosing to do the right thing, to marry her, stick together...

'Now, I'm going to have to leave.' Alessi broke into her introspection. 'I have some time for some questions but it is my parents' fortieth anniversary tonight and I am already in trouble for being late.'

He didn't rush them through the questions, though. Ruby had no more but she took a generous helping of sandwiches with her and left, while a couple of girls hung around to speak with Alessi. 'I'll return this,' Isla offered, unplugging the incubator, knowing that Alessi had other places he needed to be.

She wheeled the incubator back up to NICU and chatted with the nurses there for a while.

'How's Elijah?' Isla asked.

'Well, it's still early days,' the senior nurse said. 'He gave us all a terrible time last week but he seems to be holding his own at the moment. Donna will be coming in soon to bring in some breast milk. She generally comes in at this time if you want to hang around.'

'Not tonight,' Isla said.

Tonight she needed to get her head around her decision—somehow she would tell Alessi, but away from here, Isla thought as she walked back down to MMU.

'Oh!' As Isla pushed open the door, there was Alessi.

Alone.

'I thought you had to get to your parents'…'

'They can wait,' Alessi said. 'This can't. I want to know what happened, Isla. I want to know what's going on.'

Isla took a deep breath.

'Any time now, Isla,' he said. His phone was ringing and he saw that it was Allegra, no doubt demanding to know where he was.

'I'll be there as soon as I can!' Alessi had to keep himself from shouting and Isla screwed her eyes shut as he switched to Greek.

When he ended the call she met his eyes and it was time for the truth. 'I'm pregnant, Alessi.'

His reaction was nothing like she had expected. His face had already been pale, Isla realised, but it paled a little further and then he gave her a very small smile.

'Can you hold that thought?'

'Sorry?' Isla blinked.

'Allegra is at the party and doesn't want to make a fuss but she thinks she might be in labour.'

'Oh!'

'She sounds as if she's in labour.'

'Meaning?'

'One conversation, two contractions.'

'She needs to get here.'

'Try telling her that,' Alessi said, and handed her his phone. 'While *we* get *there*.'

CHAPTER FOURTEEN

IT WAS THE strangest car ride.

Isla's news hung between them while both were grateful for the pause.

Alessi wanted some time with his thoughts rather than say something he might later regret. *Is it mine?* was, for Alessi, the obvious question.

In turn, Isla was relieved that her secret was out and that the world was still turning.

'I think I've left it too late to get to hospital…' Allegra, from the echo Isla could hear, was in the bathroom.

'That's fine.' Isla's voice was calm. 'We're a couple of minutes away. I'm going to call for backup. Are you in the bathroom?'

'Yes.'

'Where's Steve?'

'Can I hang up on you and text him?' Allegra asked. 'I don't want the whole family piling in.'

'Give me his number,' Isla said. 'I'll text him from my phone, you just keep talking to me.'

'My waters just broke.'

'Okay,' Isla said. 'What colour is the fluid?' She heard Alessi let out a tense breath as it became obvious from the conversation that things were moving along rather rapidly.

'Clear.'

'Have a feel,' Isla instructed. 'There's no cord?'

'No. Isla, I want to push.'

'Try not push,' Isla said. 'We're at the traffic lights on the corner. Alessi's swearing because they're red.'

'I don't want my brother delivering me.'

'I know you don't want your brother to deliver you,' Isla said, and she caught a glimpse of Alessi's rigid profile. 'But luckily you've got me. I'm going to ring off and I'll see you in a moment.' She turned to Alessi. 'I'm jumping out when we get to the next lights.'

Their eyes met and there was so much unsaid. 'We're talking this out tonight, Isla,' Alessi said.

'I'm sorry, Alessi.' She told him the truth as the car moved the next five hundred meters. 'I wasn't on the Pill.' She felt his eyes on her briefly. 'I know I let you think I was... I meant to take care of it the next morning, get the morning-after pill, but I didn't...' Tears were threatening and she choked them down.

'Are you considering an abortion?' Alessi asked, and Isla shook her head.

'Then never apologise for your pregnancy again.'

She arrived at Geo's and walked in as calmly as she could, grateful she had been there before and that the staff let her straight upstairs as soon as she explained that Alessi was parking.

The speeches were going on as Isla made her way through the crowd and Alessi's father was speaking.

'Tonight I celebrate forty years with the love of my life. We have been together through good times and bad...' There was a long pause before he continued.

'We were blessed with three children, Geo, Alessandro and Allegra, tonight we sit in Geo's as a family, always.'

Alessi must have ditched the car because he was right behind her as she headed to the bathroom.

'Watch the door,' Isla said, and took a deep breath and stepped inside.

She'd delivered many women on the bathroom floor but she'd only deeply loved one of them.

Make that two, Isla thought as she stepped in and saw Allegra's red face and damp curls. Steve was there beside her and he blew out a breath of relief as Isla came over. 'Talk about timing,' Steve said.

'Perfect timing.' Isla smiled, dropping to her knees, knowing what to do.

'It's coming.'

Oh, it was.

'Get behind Allegra, Steve,' Isla said. 'Help pull her legs back.'

'Where's Alessi?' Steve asked.

'Gnawing on the door with his teeth.' Isla smiled.

'He must trust you,' Allegra said.

Alessi did.

But with no equipment, no help to hand, it tested Alessi on so many levels and it was a Herculean effort to stand outside.

Last time, with Niko, Allegra had nearly died.

It wasn't like last time, Alessi told himself.

Isla was there.

Isla was pregnant.

It was then that he properly acknowledged it. He looked at his parents, who were scanning the gathered crowd, waiting for their children to start speaking. A crowd was starting to gather where Alessi was playing doorman and a paramedic was climbing the stairs, wearing a crash helmet, which was possibly a giveaway.

'Yes,' Alessi said when his mother raced over. 'Allegra is having the baby.'

'Why aren't you in there?' Yolanda demanded.

'Isla's there. She'll call if she needs me.'

Alessi closed his eyes.

She just had called.

Private, deep, she had told him she was pregnant and he was eternally grateful for the drama of tonight, for not demanding to know if the baby was his, in some Neanderthal reaction.

Whatever the answer, he was there for her, too.

Alessi knew it.

Isla didn't.

'Is everything okay?' Steve asked, his eyes anxious.

'Everything,' Isla said, 'is perfect.'

Allegra pushed and when she couldn't push, she pushed some more and then let out a scream, not that anyone would hear outside, where there was music and chattering and laughter. And as Allegra rested her body against her husband, Isla demanded more from her.

'Again.'

'No.'

'One more, come on…'

'Do what Isla says.' Steve was both supportive and firm. Behind his wife, he held up her thighs and helped Allegra bring their child into the world.

Their baby was almost here—the head was out and with the next push it would be delivered. The door opened at that moment and Isla smiled as Aiden Harrison, a rapid-response paramedic who had arrived on motorbike, stepped quietly inside.

'Put your hands down, Allegra,' Isla said.

Allegra did and together she and Isla delivered the baby.

It was a gorgeous fat baby girl with big cheeks and chunky arms and legs, who cried on entering the world and was born with her eyes open. Allegra and Steve wept when they saw her, their strong, healthy baby, and so, too, did Isla.

Not a lot, but some tears did spill out, especially as Steve cut the cord.

'I think you've stopped the party.' Isla smiled through her tears because the noise outside had faded.

'Steve...' Allegra said. 'Maybe you could let them know that everything is okay?' She glanced up from her beautiful daughter. 'And let Alessi in, poor guy.'

His face was as white as chalk but he smiled when he stepped in and saw his niece.

It was so completely different from the last time.

Then, it had needed to be all sterile equipment and everyone avoiding meeting his eyes. Then it had been his sister and nephew on different intensive care units and the joy of childbirth completely missing.

Now smiling faces greeted him and the surroundings didn't matter.

A backup ambulance had arrived and as Allegra was transferred to a stretcher it was Alessi who held the baby.

There were repercussions to his job. He generally dealt with the babies that had run into complications, with the battlers to survive, but this little girl was feisty, dark, hungry, angry… Alessi looked into very dark navy eyes that in a matter of weeks would be as black as his.

She needed no help from him, just love, and this little lady had it.

So, too, did Isla.

He loved her—of that he was completely sure.

CHAPTER FIFTEEN

A PROCESSION OF cars followed the ambulance to the hospital and once there a celebration ensued.

Isla was more than used to the excitement within a Greek family when a baby was born but it was all multiplied tonight, because this little lady had been born on her grandparents' fortieth wedding anniversary. Isla was aware, too, of the exhaustion having so many people around might cause for a new mum, but Alessi sorted it and suggested that the party continue back at his place.

'Thank you so much, Isla,' Allegra said as Isla went to go. 'It might not have been the ideal location but it really was the best birth.'

'It was wonderful.' Isla smiled. 'You made it look very easy.'

'It has been the best wedding anniversary present ever.' Yolanda was ecstatic. Niko was asleep on her shoulder and would be staying with his *yaya* tonight, but first they headed back to Alessi's, stopping for champagne on the way.

The mood was elated as corks popped and Alessi watched as Isla took a glass and pretended to take a sip so as not to draw attention to the fact she wasn't drinking.

'Are you okay?' he asked.

'Of course.' Isla smiled.

'Isla?' Alessi checked, because he could see that she was struggling.

'I'm a bit tired,' Isla admitted, which was the understatement of the year. She was exhausted. The high of the birth was fading and the enormity of her revelation was starting to make itself known. They hadn't had a chance to discuss it and from the way things were going it would be a good while yet till they could.

'Go and lie down,' Alessi suggested.

'I can't just go to bed in the middle of a party. My father would have kittens if I—'

'He's not here, though. Isla, you can do no wrong today, you just safely delivered Allegra's baby. I know they are a bit over the top but they really are so grateful and relieved.'

'I think it's lovely how happy they are,' Isla said.

He led her to the bedroom and she walked in, glad to escape from all the noise. Alessi closed the blinds and Isla undressed down to her underwear and slipped into bed. He came and sat on the edge.

'Thank you for tonight,' he said.

'I really didn't have to do much. Your niece made her entrance herself,' Isla said. 'She's such a gorgeous baby.'

'It will be you soon,' Alessi said, and watched as her eyes filled with tears. He could only guess how overwhelming this all must be for her. 'How long have you known?' he asked, and then answered his own question. 'The Monday before Valentine's Day.'

'How do you know?'

'Your texts went from ten lines to two words,' Alessi said. 'Don't worry about all that now. Just get some rest.'

'You're not cross.'

'Cross?' Alessi checked. 'Did you expect me to be cross?'

'I didn't know what to expect.'

'I only get cross when you dump me for no good reason, Isla,' he said. 'Get some sleep. We'll talk later.'

There was a lot to talk about but when Alessi finally got to bed around two, he certainly wasn't about to wake her for The Talk. He had never intended to wake her at all, but Alessi hadn't forgotten how nice it was to have her in his bed and he had missed her so much.

Asleep, Isla wriggled towards the source of warmth. Her back was to him and, deprived of his touch for ten days now, her body knew who it wanted and her bottom nudged into his groin and sank into his caress as his arm came over her.

Alessi lay there. No, it would be completely inappropriate, he told himself, because there was that damn talk to have. Except his fingers didn't care about such matters and were stroking her through the silk of her bra and then burrowing in.

'Isla…' Alessi said, which wasn't much of a conversation. His mouth was on her shoulder, tasting her skin again and then moving up to her neck. The response in her had him harden further, the craning of her neck to meet his mouth, the consent, the want had a flare of possession rise in Alessi and there was no conversation to be had.

Isla was his.

His mouth suckled her neck and Isla bit down on her bottom lip as he deliciously bruised her. His hand was sliding down her panties and she wanted to turn but she didn't. She liked the arm holding her down and Alessi's precision as he took her from behind.

Of all his responses, of all the reactions she had anticipated, this hadn't been one of them. Alessi's hand was on her stomach, gently pressing her back into him, and Isla, who had never been taken like this, writhed in pleasure as his hand moved down and stroked her intimately.

'Alessi...' She said his name, the only thing now on her mind as he moved her towards orgasm.

And for Alessi, here in the darkness of his bedroom, yes, there were questions, but her body's response, their absolute connection meant the only truth that actually mattered was easily said. 'I love you.'

Isla stilled, but Alessi didn't. He thrust into her and didn't let her get her breath, neither did he allow the panic that suddenly built in her to settle. He just said it again, for their love was no accident.

She could feel him building to come, feel all the passion about to be unleashed, and it tipped Isla into raw honesty when she'd spent her whole life covering lies. 'I love you, too.'

Isla came before him and she loved how he held her down and didn't kiss her, or stifle her shout. He just let her be and drove her ever higher as he came deep inside her.

And still there was no need for The Talk because they had said what mattered.

Doubts belonged to the morning. There were none in his arms.

CHAPTER SIXTEEN

ALESSI WOKE BEFORE Isla and would have watched her sleeping had he not been so hungry.

Neither had had dinner, he remembered.

He wondered if she was as starving as he was.

If Isla was feeling sick in the mornings.

He just stared at her and wondered, which he'd been doing for more than a year, Alessi thought with a smile as he climbed from bed and went to the kitchen.

Coffee on, he started making breakfast and completely out of habit he checked his emails and then glanced at the news.

And then did a double take.

Yes, again she had him wondering.

'Morning, Isla…'

It was incredibly nice to be woken with coffee and breakfast and Alessi's smile, and she returned it but even as she stretched, doubts started piling in.

God, she'd told him she loved him.

Isla let out a breath.

Yes, he'd said he loved her but she was petrified of forcing his hand, thinking that Alessi might be simply making the best of a bad deal.

'This looks lovely,' she said, her hand shaking a

touch as she took the coffee from the tray, unable to meet his eyes.

'Is there something you need to tell me?' Alessi said.

'Isn't what I told you last night enough to be going on with?' Isla said. 'I know it's a shock. I know it's too soon...'

'It doesn't feel too soon,' he said. 'We're not teenagers, Isla.'

'I know, but even so...'

'It was a shock last night,' Alessi admitted, 'but it's a nice surprise now. How do you feel about it?'

'Nervous,' Isla admitted. 'I was terrified at first but now...' she looked at him '...it's starting to feel like a nice surprise, too, but I'm terrified of the pressure it might put on us.'

'Like marriage?'

Isla nodded.

'You don't want to get married?' Alessi asked. 'Isla, help me here, because the last woman I asked to marry me...' She could see him struggling. 'I don't want to put the same pressure on you. Looking back, I can see that we were far too young and not in love. You've heard the saying "Marry in haste, repent at leisure". I'm quite sure now that that would have been Talia and I.'

'I don't want it to be us.'

'It won't be,' Alessi assured her. 'Just so long as we are always honest with each other.'

'I feel like I've forced things...'

'Isla, I was going to ask you to marry me on Valentine's night. I had it all planned, right down to if you said yes, we were going to go the next day to the restaurant, upstairs this time, and tell my family...' He could see the disbelief in her eyes. He rolled his eyes and then climbed out of bed and went to a drawer, and Isla watched as he took out a small box.

'There.' He handed it to her. 'Do you believe me now?'

She looked up at him and then back to the ring.

It was white gold, with a pale sapphire. 'It matches your eyes, almost exactly,' Alessi said. 'I wanted a diamond but when I saw this...'

Again he asked a question. 'Is there something you need to tell me?'

'Such as?'

Alessi took a breath. 'Maybe there's something I need to tell you. I'm sorry if it comes as a shock. Your ex-boyfriend just came out. It's all over the news...' He saw the tears in her eyes and misread them. 'I'm sorry. Is this news to you?'

'I've always known.' Isla took a breath. 'There's never been anything sexual between us.'

'I don't understand.' Alessi frowned. 'Were you covering for him?'

'Yes,' Isla said, 'but he was covering for me, too.' It was the biggest confession of her life and far harder to admit than her pregnancy. 'I've never had a sexual relationship with anyone. Till you.'

'You're telling me that our night together was your first?' He shook his head, not so much in disbelief but that night he had felt her burn in his arms, the sex between them had been so good, so natural. 'You should have told me,' he said. 'You must have been so nervous...'

'No,' she refuted. 'I was always scared before, I wasn't that night.'

'Scared of what, Isla?'

'I don't really know,' she admitted. 'I thought I was scared of getting pregnant but I don't feel scared. Something happened when I was twelve...' She closed her eyes. 'I can't tell you.'

'I think you have to.'

'I can't tell you because it's not my secret to share, it didn't happen to me.'

'Whatever happened affected you, though,' Alessi said. 'What would you tell one of your patients?'

'To talk to someone.'

'So talk to me.'

'My sister.' Isla gulped in a breath as panic hit. 'Please, never say...'

'I would never do that.'

That much she knew.

'When I was twelve I heard her...' Isla let out a breath. 'She had a baby, I think it was about eighteen weeks...'

'You think?'

'I didn't know at the time,' Isla said. 'I delivered him. Isabel begged me not to say anything but I got our housekeeper, Evie. She took us to a hospital... It was all dealt with, our parents never found out...I promised never to tell.'

'You're not telling me about Isabel,' Alessi said. 'I don't need the details about her, I need to know what happened to you and what you went through.'

And so she told him, and Alessi watched as the supremely confident, always cool Isla simply collapsed in tears as she released the weight of her secret.

He held her as she spoke and then, as the tears subsided, Isla lay there and looked up at him and found out how it felt not to be alone.

'No more secrets,' Alessi said.

'I know.'

'You could have told me...' And then he stopped. 'I guess you had to trust me.'

'I should have told you that night,' Isla said, 'because I trusted you then, Alessi, or I wouldn't have slept with you...' She looked at the smile on his face and frowned. 'What's funny?'

'Not funny,' Alessi said. 'I guess that means that the baby's mine.'

'Of course—' Isla started, and then halted. Of course he would have had doubts, he would have been doing the frantic maths. Not once had it entered her head that he might wonder if the baby was his, but of course it must have been there for him. 'You loved me, even when you didn't know that the baby was yours...'

'Isla, I love you, full stop. We'd have worked it out, whoever the father was.'

He loved her. Isla accepted it then.

'Marry me?' Alessi said.

'Try and stop me.' Isla smiled. 'Can we not tell anyone about the baby yet, though? I want to keep it to ourselves for a little while.'

'And me,' Alessi said.

'We've only being going out for a few weeks...'

'Oh, no,' Alessi said, and took her in his arms. 'I've been crazy about you since the night I first met you and I was right that night...' He gave her a slightly wicked smile of triumph. 'You *did* want me.'

'I did,' Isla said, blushing at the memory. 'God, I've wasted so much time.'

'I wouldn't change a thing about us, Isla. You know there is another saying, Isla, *"Ki'taxa vathia' mes sta ma'tia sou ke i'da to me'llon mas".*'

'What does it mean?'

'It means I looked deep into your eyes and I saw our future. That was what happened on the night we first met and that is what is happening now. You are my future, Isla.'

'And you are mine.'

They had a past, they had the future and, Isla knew as Alessi kissed her, they were for ever together now.

* * * * *

A PROMISE...TO
A PROPOSAL?

KATE HARDY

To Gerard, Chris and Chloe – remembering
the best meal we've ever eaten!

CHAPTER ONE

'HERE?' RUBY ASKED.

'It's a sandy beach, we're below the high tide line, the tide's coming in right now and the wind's in the right direction—so I'd say it's just about perfect,' Ellis said.

Well, it would've been perfect if it hadn't been drizzling with rain. But today was what it was, and the weather didn't matter. Just as it hadn't mattered a year ago. The day that had blown a hole in all their lives.

She smiled. 'Tom always did say you were the practical one.'

And the one with itchy feet who could never stay in one place for long.

Except for the last eighteen months, which Ellis had spent in London solely because of Tom, his best friend since their first day at infant school. They'd gone to university together, and trained together in the same London hospital. When Tom had been diagnosed with leukaemia, that had been the one thing to bring Ellis back to England. He'd wanted to be there for his best friend and support him through to the end. Ellis had promised Tom in those last agonising months that he'd be there for Ruby, too, and support her through at least the first year after Tom's death.

Including today.

Which was why he was walking on the beach on a drizzly September day with Tom's parents and Ruby, on the first anniversary of Tom's death, to help them scatter some of Tom's ashes in his favourite place. A place that brought back so many happy childhood memories that it put a lump in Ellis's throat.

'Thanks for looking up all the information for us,' Ruby said. 'I wasn't sure if we had to get permission from someone first or even how you go about scattering ashes.'

'Hey, it's the least I could do. I loved Tom, too,' Ellis said. And when Ruby had first broached the subject about scattering Tom's ashes, he'd known exactly where Tom would've wanted it to be.

He spread a couple of waterproof blankets on the beach for the four of them to kneel on, and took four brightly coloured spades and buckets from a plastic bag.

It might be a dark day, the final goodbye, but Ellis wanted to remember the brightness. To remember Tom as he was before he was ill and to celebrate the close friendship they'd shared over the years.

'I remember you boys doing this when you were small,' Brenda said with a wobble in her voice as she dug into the sand and filled her bucket. 'You both loved the beach. It didn't matter if it was summer or winter— if we asked you what you wanted to do, you'd both beg to come here and make sandcastles.'

The lump in Ellis's throat meant he couldn't speak. He remembered. Days when life was simple. Days when his parents had been as carefree as Tom's. Though Tom's parents, he knew, wouldn't react in the same way as his parents had when it came to the death of their child. Brenda and Mike would talk about Tom with love and keep him alive in their hearts, rather than stonewalling everything.

Working in companionable silence, the four of them made a sandcastle. Just as they had when Tom and Ellis were small boys: only this time Tom's widow was taking Tom's place.

When they'd finished, Ellis produced a flag from his bag—one made from an ice-lolly stick and a photograph of Tom. It was one of his favourite memories: the day they'd opened their A level results together, whooped, and known they were both going to train as doctors in London. For Tom, it had been the next step towards a dream. For Ellis, it had been the next step towards escape from a home that had come to feel like a mausoleum.

'He was eighteen years old then,' Mike said softly as Ellis handed him the flag. 'With the whole world before him.'

How very little time Tom had actually had. Not even half a lifetime.

And how very much Ellis wished his best friend was still here. 'He was special,' Ellis said, his voice cracking.

'Yes. He was,' Mike said, and put the flag on the top turret.

Brenda and Ruby both gulped hard and squeezed each other's hand.

Ellis finished digging the moat round the outside of the castle; and then the four of them took turns scattering Tom's ashes in the moat and covering them over with sand. Ruby sprinkled rose petals on the top.

Then Ellis moved the blankets back a little way, set

up the two huge umbrellas he'd packed in the car when he'd seen the weather report, and uncorked a bottle of champagne.

'To Tom,' he said when he'd filled their glasses. 'And may our memories of him make the smiles outnumber the tears.' Even though right now it felt as if the tears were more than outweighing the smiles, Ellis was determined to celebrate his friend rather than be selfish about his loss.

Mike, Brenda and Ruby echoed the toast, even though their smiles were wobbly and Ellis could see their eyes were shiny with tears they tried to blink away.

Then the four of them sat and watched as the tide came in, slowly sweeping the sandcastle away with the ashes, and tumbling the rose petals and Tom's photograph in the waves.

Afterwards, Ellis drove Tom's parents home.

'Will you come in for something to eat?' Brenda asked on the doorstep.

'Thanks, but...' Ellis tailed off. Even being in this town made him feel stifled. He hated it here. What he really wanted to do was drive as fast as he could back to London. Away from the dark memories.

'Of course. You'll want to drop in to see your own mum while you're here,' Brenda said.

Ellis didn't have the heart to disillusion her, so he just smiled. Today of all days, he really couldn't face his parents. They'd be aware of what he'd just been doing, and they'd be thinking of Sally. And, as always, they'd retreat into coolness rather than talk to him or even give him a sympathetic hug. Even though Ellis understood why—when you'd lost someone you loved so very much, sometimes withdrawing from everyone seemed like the only way to keep your heart safe from further hurt—he still found it hard to deal with. He always felt as if he'd lost more than his beloved only sister, twenty years ago; he'd lost his parents, too. And although he'd remained reasonably close to his older brothers, his choice of career had put a distinct rift between them. Tom's parents had been Ellis's greatest support through his teen years, and he'd always be grateful to them for it. And for Tom's sake he'd look out for them now, the way they'd looked out for him.

Brenda hugged him. 'Thank you for being there for us.'

'Any time.' And he meant it. 'Just because Tom's…' He couldn't say the word. He just *couldn't*. 'Not here,' he said croakily, 'it doesn't mean you're not still part of my life, because you are. You know I think of you as my second set of parents. I always will.'

Tears glittered in Brenda's eyes. She patted his shoulder, clearly too moved to talk, and then hugged Ruby.

'I'll text you when we get back to London,' Ruby promised.

But she looked quizzically at Ellis when he drove straight out of the town and back towards London. 'I thought you were going to see your parents?'

'Not today.'

'Look, don't feel you have to get me back to London if you want to see them. I can always go back to Brenda and Mike's and wait until you're ready, or get the train back.'

That was the point. He didn't actually want to see his parents. Especially not today. Part of him lambasted himself for being selfish, but the realistic part of him knew it was necessary self-preservation. 'Another time,' he said.

'If you're sure.'

'Oh, I'm sure,' he said softly. 'My parents are… complicated.'

She reached over and squeezed his hand briefly. 'I know,' she said, equally softly.

In the months since Tom's death, Ellis had opened up a little to Ruby and told her about the tragedy that had taken the sunshine out of his world. How his older sister had taken a gap year before university, teaching in a remote school. Sally had fallen pregnant by accident and hadn't realised it at first; when she'd been so sick, everyone had assumed it was a virus. But by the time they'd realised she was suffering from hyperemesis gravidarum, a severe form of morning sickness, it was too late. She'd grown too weak, developed complications, gone into organ failure and never regained consciousness.

And Ellis's parents had never recovered from losing their only daughter. Their remaining three sons simply hadn't been enough to bring them back from the cold, emotionless life they'd led from that moment on.

Ellis and Ruby drove back in companionable silence, listening to Nick Drake. The kind of mellow, faintly melancholy stuff Ellis had enjoyed listening to with Tom. It went well with the rain and his mood.

Back in London, he parked in the street outside Ruby's house and saw her to the door.

'Thank you, for today, Ellis. I don't know what I would have done this last year without you,' she said.

'Hey, no problem—and you've helped me, too.' He hugged her. Bad move. Now he could smell her perfume, the sweet scent of violets. And she fitted perfectly in his arms.

She's your best friend's widow, he reminded himself silently. No, no and absolutely no. Don't even *think* about it. You do not make a move on this woman. Ever. Hands off.

'I'll see you at work tomorrow,' he said. 'Call me if you need me.'

'Thanks, Ellis.' She reached up and kissed his cheek.

For a moment, Ellis desperately wanted to twist his face to the side so the kiss landed on his mouth. For months now he'd wanted to kiss Ruby. But he held himself back. The feelings he'd developed towards her over the last year were completely inappropriate; plus he risked losing one of his closest friendships if he asked her out. He was pretty sure that Ruby saw him only as a friend, so wanting more was just *stupid*. Especially as he knew he wasn't a good bet when it came to relationships.

His normal job, working for a medical aid charity, meant that relationships were tricky. Either he had long-distance affairs where he hardly ever saw his girlfriend and the relationship ended by mutual agreement because his girlfriend just got fed up waiting for him; or they were short, sweet flings that ended when he moved on to another assignment. Except for his marriage to Natalia—he'd thought that would be the exception to the rule, that maybe he could have the best of both worlds after all. How wrong he'd been there. So nowadays he didn't do more than short, fun flings—where everyone knew the score before they started and nobody ended up disappointed.

When Ruby was finally ready to move on, Ellis knew

she'd want more than just a fling or a long-distance relationship. More than he could offer her. Asking for more
than friendship would just ruin a relationship that had
become really important to him over the last eighteen
months. And to have her solely as his friend was way
better than not having her in his life at all, wasn't it?
So he'd just have to keep himself in check.

'I'd better go,' he mumbled, and left before he did
something really reckless and stupid. Like kissing her.

And he brooded all the way home. His current job as
an obstetrician at the London Victoria was only temporary, covering another registrar's maternity leave, and
his contract was due to end in a couple of months' time
when Billie was due to return. He'd already agreed to do
a month's assignment for the medical aid charity, helping to set up a new medical centre in Zimbabwe, when
his temporary contract at the London Victoria ended.
Going to work abroad again would mean he'd be out of
temptation's way and he wouldn't hurt Ruby.

Then again, Ellis had promised Tom that he'd look
after Ruby. Until he knew that she was ready to move
on and had found someone else to share her life—someone who was good enough for her and would treat her
as she deserved—how could he desert her?

It was a tricky line to walk.

So he'd just have to bury his feelings, the way he normally did, and everything would be just fine.

Ruby watched Ellis drive away, feeling guilty. For a
moment she'd been tempted to kiss him on the lips instead of on the cheek.

How could she possibly want to kiss another man?
And especially how could she have thoughts like that

on the first anniversary of her husband's death? How mean-spirited and selfish and plain *wrong* was that?

She closed the door with a grimace of self-disgust.

Plus she knew that Tom had asked Ellis to look out for her. Letting Ellis know that she was starting to see him as more than a friend might make everything go wrong between them. He'd always been such a perfect gentleman towards her. Trying to push their friendship in another direction might mean that she lost him—and she didn't want that to happen. She liked having Ellis in her life. Liked it a lot.

Though she had a nasty feeling that she was going to lose him anyway. Ellis had always had itchy feet, according to Tom, and she knew that Ellis wanted to go back to the medical aid charity. The place where he'd always felt he'd belonged.

Losing Tom had ripped Ruby's heart to shreds. Over the last year, she'd gradually put the pieces back together, and it would be very stupid to let herself fall for someone who'd made it very clear that he didn't do permanent. Someone who didn't want the same things she wanted. Someone she knew she'd lose to his job. Yes, he would come back to England from time to time to see her—but she'd be lonely in London, waiting for him. Yet, if she went with him, she'd end up feeling horribly homesick and missing her family. Neither option was right for her. Which meant that Ellis really wasn't the right man for her, much as she was attracted to him, and she needed to think with her head rather than her heart.

Now they'd scattered Tom's ashes and she was back in London again, Ruby didn't quite know what to do with herself. She wished she'd asked Ellis to go somewhere for dinner with her or something; right now, she felt so *lonely*.

She mooched around for the best part of an hour, not able to settle to reading or doing crosswords. Even cleaning the bathroom until it sparkled didn't make her feel as if she'd achieved anything; she was in limbo.

Then the doorbell rang.

Her heart leapt. Had Ellis come back?

No, of course not. How stupid of her to think it.

She opened the door to see her best friend, Tina, bearing what looked suspiciously like a box of home-made cake.

'With today being what it is, I thought you could do with some company tonight,' Tina said, 'and this.' She lifted the box. 'Lemon cake.'

Ruby's favourite. And Ruby knew without a doubt Tina had made it especially for her. It was probably still warm.

'There isn't anyone in the world I'd rather see right now,' Ruby said, meaning it. Not even Ellis. Because with her best friend Ruby knew she wouldn't have that edge of guilt and faint shame that she seemed to feel around Ellis nowadays, outside work. 'Thank you. Thank you so much.' She hugged her best friend, hard.

Tina hung her coat in the hallway and made herself at home in the kitchen, putting the kettle on and getting the teapot out of the cupboard, the way she and Ruby had done hundreds of times over the years in each other's kitchens. 'So how did it go this afternoon?'

'Really well. It didn't matter that it was raining. Ellis had brought a couple of huge umbrellas and waterproof blankets for us to sit on.' Ruby smiled. 'We made a sandcastle and put the ashes in the moat, covered it with rose petals, toasted Tom with champagne and let the sea wash the sandcastle and the ashes away together.'

'It sounds perfect—well, as perfect as something like that could be.' Tina finished making the tea, put the lemon cake on the plate and cut them both a slice, then handed Ruby a steaming mug. 'To Tom,' she said, lifting her mug and clinking it against Ruby's. 'I'll miss him horribly. But I'll always be glad I knew him, because he was just the nicest guy in the world.'

'Yeah.' Ruby took a sip of her tea to take the lump out of her throat.

'Hey. It's OK to cry,' Tina said softly.

'No. I want to remember him with smiles, not tears,' Ruby insisted. 'He wouldn't have wanted anyone to be miserable.'

'But?'

Ruby and Tina had clicked immediately when they'd met on the first day of their nursing training at the age of eighteen, and they'd been friends for long enough to have a pretty good idea what each other wasn't saying.

'I feel a bit guilty, that's all.' Ruby wasn't quite ready to admit her feelings for Ellis, but she also knew that Tina was the best person she could float ideas past. Someone who'd be honest with her.

'Why on earth do you feel guilty?' Tina looked puzzled.

'Because tomorrow it'll be a year and a day—the last traditional day of mourning—and over those last months Tom said to me quite a few times that he didn't want me to be alone and grieving for him. He said he wanted me to live a happy life with someone who loves me as much as he did.'

'Now you're putting a lump in my throat.' Tina

hugged her. 'Though he's right—you're still young. In fact, at twenty-nine you're practically a baby.'

Ruby laughed. There were all of six months between them, with Ruby being one of the youngest in their academic year and Tina one of the oldest. 'Thirty's not exactly old, Tina.'

'No.' Tina looked at her. 'Rubes, are you saying you want to date again?'

'I love Tom—I always will—but I think I'm ready to move on. Scattering his ashes today felt a lot like closure,' Ruby said. 'But is everyone going to think I'm heartless and I should wait a lot longer before even thinking about moving on?'

'No. Some people will probably mutter about it being too soon,' Tina said, 'but remember that you can't please all of the people all of the time, so don't let that get to you. It's none of their business. You're the only one who can really say when you're ready.'

'I guess.' Ruby bit her lip. 'I just...' She shook her head and sighed. 'Sorry.'

'As you said, Tom wanted you to be happy and he wanted you to find someone else. You have his blessing, and you don't need anyone else's.'

Even if I fell for his best friend?

But Ruby couldn't quite bring herself to ask that. She'd barely admitted it to herself and she still needed time to get used to the idea.

'You know, we've got a new registrar in Neurology. He's a nice guy. Single. New to London. Maybe...' Tina let the suggestion hang in the air.

'Maybe,' Ruby said.

'Don't make a decision now. Just think about it,' Tina

said gently. 'In the meantime, I think we need a feel-good film and more cake.'

'Brilliant idea. Let's do it,' Ruby said, and ushered her best friend into the living room.

But she found it hard to concentrate on the film, because she couldn't stop thinking about Ellis. Ellis, with his haunted grey eyes. Ellis, who had itchy feet but had stayed in one place for the longest time since his training, specifically to be there for her.

Her husband's best friend.

What if...?

CHAPTER TWO

RUBY EXAMINED MRS HARRIS GENTLY.

'So is everything OK?' Mrs Harris asked anxiously.

'I'm happy with how you're doing,' Ruby said, 'but we do have a tiny complication, in that your little one is quite happy being bottom-down rather than top-down. So I just want a quick chat with the doctor to talk through your options for the birth.'

Mrs Harris bit her lip. 'So the baby's in the wrong position?'

'Bottom-first rather than head-first—it's called being a breech baby,' Ruby explained. 'It's a really common position in early pregnancy, but the baby usually turns by itself into the head-first position before birth. Your baby hasn't turned yet, that's all.'

'Does it mean there's something wrong with the baby?' Mrs Harris asked.

'No. It happens with about three in a hundred babies, and there are all kinds of reasons for it, some of them being plain baby awkwardness because they want to do things their way rather than follow their mum's birth plan,' Ruby reassured her. 'I'll just go and get Dr Webster, and then we can talk it through with him.' She squeezed Mrs Harris's hand. 'Try not to worry. There

are a few things we can do to persuade the baby to turn.'
She smiled, and went to find Ellis in his office.

Her heart skipped a beat when she saw him. Ellis
was wearing a charcoal grey suit, a white shirt and an
understated tie rather than green Theatre scrubs, and he
looked utterly gorgeous. He wouldn't have looked out
of place on the pages of a glossy magazine as a model
for an upmarket perfume house.

And she needed to stop herself thinking like this.
Ellis was her friend and her colleague. Asking for more
was just greedy.

She tapped on the open door and leaned against the
jamb. 'Hey, Ellis. Can I borrow you for a second?'

He looked up and smiled at her, and her heart skipped
another beat.

'Sure. Problem?' he asked.

'Complication,' she said. 'I have a first-time mum
who's thirty-seven weeks. Her baby's quite happily settled in the breech position. I know her birth plan is
firmly centred round a natural birth with no intervention.' And she also knew that a lot of doctors would
take one look at Mrs Harris's situation and immediately
insist on a caesarean section. Given Ellis's experience
outside the hospital, Ruby really hoped that he'd take
a different tack and give Mrs Harris a chance to have
the birth she really wanted. 'So I wondered if you'd
mind coming and chatting through her options for the
birth,' she finished.

'Of course I will. You did warn her that babies never
respect their mum's birth plans, didn't you?'

She smiled back. 'I always do.'

'So what are you thinking?'

'We'll start with an ECV to see if we can get the baby

to turn,' Ruby said. 'But, if it doesn't work, I'm hoping that I can talk one of the obstetricians—' she gave him a pointed look so he'd know she meant him '—into agreeing to a trial of labour for a vaginal breech delivery.'

'I think we've only had a couple on the ward since I've been here, and I wasn't on duty at the time,' Ellis said. 'Are the doctors here not supportive of vaginal breech births?'

'Theo's wonderful,' Ruby said. Theo Petrakis, the director of the maternity ward at the London Victoria, believed in supporting his midwives and keeping intervention to a minimum. 'But, as you say, it's not that common—and I need someone who's had a reasonable amount of experience in delivering breech babies.'

'Which is why you're talking to me?'

She gave him her sweetest smile. 'Got it in one.'

'She's a first-time mum, so we have no guarantee that her pelvis is big enough to cope.' Ellis looked thoughtful. 'OK. If ECV doesn't work then—on condition the baby's not too big or small, the baby's head isn't tilted back and I'm happy that the mum's pelvis is going to cope—I'll support you and you can call me in, even if I'm not on duty when she goes into labour. But in return I need a favour from you.'

Ruby's heart skipped yet another beat. What was he going to ask for?

A kiss?

She shook herself mentally. How ridiculous. She really had to stop fantasising about Ellis. This was totally inappropriate. They were at work, and she needed to keep her professionalism to the forefront. 'Sure. What do you want?'

'I'd like you to talk your mum into letting a couple

of the junior staff observe their first ever breech birth. One midwife, one doctor.'

'Great minds think alike. I was going to ask you if there was anyone you wanted to come and observe.' And she really liked the fact that he'd thought of the midwifery team, too, not just the obstetricians. She smiled. 'I want to reassure Mrs Harris that we'll try our best to help give her the birth experience she really wants, but I'll make it clear that if the baby's in distress at any point then we might need to give her a section, so she needs to be prepared for that to happen.'

'Which is again where I'd come in,' Ellis said.

'Just flutter those disgustingly long eyelashes at her. Actually, on second thoughts, perhaps you'd better not,' she said. 'You already look more like a movie star than a doctor.'

'Very funny, Rubes,' Ellis said, but he didn't look the slightest bit offended.

Which was another reason why she should put this whole thing out of her head. If she made an approach to Ellis and he turned her down...Even though she knew he'd be kind about it, it would still put a strain on their friendship. On their working relationship. And Ruby didn't want to take the risk of wrecking either of them.

Maybe it was just loneliness making her feel this way, and she should take Tina up on her offer of setting her up with the new registrar on the Neurology ward.

'Penny for them?' Ellis asked.

No way was she going to tell Ellis what she was thinking about. 'Just my first-time mum,' she said with a smile. It was true; it just wasn't the *whole* truth.

Back in the examination room, she introduced Ellis. 'Mrs Harris, this is Dr Ellis Webster, one of our registrars. Ellis, this is Mrs Harris. She's a first-time mum, the baby's thirty-seven weeks, and the baby's quite happy in the breech position.'

'Nice to meet you, Mrs Harris.' Ellis shook her hand and smiled at her. 'Ruby tells me that you'd like as natural a birth as possible.'

'I definitely don't want an epidural. I want to manage with gas and air,' Mrs Harris said. 'And I really didn't want to have a section.' She bit her lip. 'But, because the baby's lying the wrong way, does that mean I have to have a section?'

'It's a possibility,' Ellis said, 'but it might be possible for you to have a vaginal delivery. With the baby being breech, it means that the head—which is the biggest part of the baby—is the last bit to be delivered, so it's a little bit more complicated. May I examine you?'

At her nod, he examined her gently.

'As Ruby said, your baby's definitely bottom-down. But we can try to persuade the baby to move. There's a procedure called an ECV, which stands for external cephalic version. Ruby here's very experienced.'

'What happens is that I'll press down on your abdomen and encourage the baby to turn a somersault—a bit like him doing a forward roll inside your stomach,' Ruby explained.

'And it always works?' Mrs Harris asked.

'It works about for about fifty per cent of babies,' Ellis said. 'And if it doesn't work today, then we can always try again tomorrow. Though I should warn you that even if the baby does turn, sometimes the baby then decides to roll back again.'

'So if you do this ECV thing, what about the baby?'

Mrs Harris asked. 'Will he be OK? It's not going to hurt him?'

'He'll be fine,' Ruby reassured her. 'Plus we'll monitor him before, during and after the ECV to keep an eye on him. There is a tiny risk that you might start having contractions, and also the baby's heart rate might go up a bit—usually it settles again pretty quickly, but I do want you to be aware that sometimes the baby's heart rate doesn't settle again, and in that case you'll need to have a section.'

'But it's a tiny risk?' Mrs Harris checked.

'Tiny,' Ruby confirmed.

'All right, then.' Mrs Harris paused. 'Will it hurt me?'

'It can be a bit uncomfortable, yes,' Ruby said. 'But, if it hurts, all you have to do is tell us and we'll stop immediately.'

Mrs Harris looked worried. 'But if it doesn't work, does that mean I'll have to have a section?'

'The baby's a good weight. He's not too big or too small,' Ellis said. 'Though I would want to check that his neck isn't tilted back before I agree to try a vaginal delivery. If the baby's head is tilted back, then I'm afraid you will need a caesarean section, because that'll be the safest thing for the baby.'

'Is there anything else I can do to help the baby turn, or make sure he stays the right way round if you do the ECV? Can I sit or lie in a certain way?' Mrs Harris asked.

Ruby shook her head. 'I'm afraid it won't make any difference.'

'So why hasn't he turned round the right way? Why is he bottom-down instead of head-down?'

'There are lots of reasons,' Ellis said. 'Sometimes

it's down to the position of your placenta. As I said earlier, the biggest part of the baby is the head, so the baby
tends to fidget round and make sure he's in the most
comfortable position, which means his head will be
in the biggest space—in your lower uterus, so he'll be
head-down. But if you have a low-lying placenta, then
the biggest space is in your upper uterus, so the baby
will be bottom-down.' He smiled. 'Sometimes it's just
plain old chance. Babies have a habit of doing things
their way, and I know a lot of mums who haven't ended
up having the birth they'd set their heart on. So all I'd
say is please try not to be disappointed if we can't follow your birth plan to the letter.'

'We'll do our best to make it work for you,' Ruby
said, 'but Dr Webster's right—at the end of the day,
babies can be very stubborn and they'll do things their
way.'

'I think this one's going to be like his dad,' Mrs Harris said ruefully. 'Can Ian be here when you try and
make the baby turn round?'

'Of course,' Ruby reassured her. 'We can try this
afternoon, just after lunch. Will that give him enough
time to get here?'

Mrs Harris nodded. 'I'll call him. Thank you. Both
of you.'

'I'll see you later this afternoon, Mrs Harris,' Ellis
said with a smile.

The rest of Ruby's clinic ran on time. Just as she broke
for lunch, she saw Ellis coming out of the staff kitchen.
'Got time for lunch?' he asked.

'That would be nice,' she said.

They headed down to the canteen, chatting companionably. At the counter, Ellis as usual chose the vegetarian option.

'Any excuse to stuff your face with pasta and garlic bread. You're such a carb junkie,' Ruby teased.

'Protein's important, but I've worked in areas where people are so poor and the cost of raising—' He broke off. 'You're teasing me, aren't you?'

'It's very easy to tease you, Ellis—you're so serious,' she said with a smile. 'Look, I know why you're vegetarian and I admire your principles.'

'But you don't share them,' he finished.

She shook her head. 'I'm sorry, but vegetarian bacon is never going to be as good as the real thing for me.'

He laughed. 'You're such a hedonist. Anyway, Rubes, you can talk about being a carb junkie. I've seen you and Tina with cake. It lasts for about three seconds when you two are around.'

'Busted,' Ruby said with a grin.

'Are you OK about doing the ECV this afternoon?' he asked.

'It's fine,' Ruby said. 'I'd really like to bring Coral, our new trainee midwife, in to observe, if Mrs Harris doesn't mind—and if you don't mind.'

'Of course not. You know I agree with you; it's always a good idea to give students as broad an experience as possible.'

'That's one of the things I like about you—you're so practical and sensible. Thanks,' she said.

Practical and sensible. Not how he'd been when he'd married Natalia, Ellis thought wryly. He'd lost his head and they'd both paid the price.

Though Ruby had said that was *one* of the things she

liked about him. He couldn't help wondering: what else did she like about him?

He shook himself. This really wasn't appropriate. Ruby Fisher was his friend. His best friend's girl—well, widow, but that was a technicality. Time to back off. 'I try to be practical,' he said lightly.

'Ellis, I, um, wanted to run something by you,' she said.

She looked worried, and Ellis frowned. 'What's wrong?'

'Not *wrong,* exactly...but today's a year and a day since Tom died.'

Yeah. He knew. He'd spent the anniversary with her on a Suffolk beach yesterday.

'And a year and a day is supposed to be the traditional length of time for mourning.'

He went cold. Where was she going with this?

'I'm never going to forget Tom,' Ruby said, 'but he always told me that he didn't want me to spend the rest of my life mourning for him, and he wanted me to move on.'

Wait—*what*?

Was she saying that she wanted to date again? That she'd met someone? Who? Where? How? Ellis couldn't quite process this.

'And Tina's going to set me up on a blind date with her new colleague in Neurology,' she finished.

Ruby was really going on a date? With someone else? But—but...

'Ellis? You haven't said anything.' She looked even more worried. 'Do you think it's too soon?'

'I...' He blew out a breath. This was a minefield. If he said the wrong thing now, he'd hurt her—and that was the last thing he wanted to do. 'I think,' he said slowly, 'that you're the best one to judge that. Only you know when you're ready.'

But the idea of seeing her with another man made him feel sick.

It was different when she'd been married to Tom. Ellis would never, ever have done anything to destroy his best friend's marriage. But now Ruby was widowed. And Ellis hated the idea of her going out with someone else.

If she really was ready to date again, maybe he could ask her out himself.

But, if she said no, then how could they go back to their old easy friendship, once they knew they didn't feel the same about each other?

He didn't want to risk losing her.

So he was just going to have to suck it up and deal with it. Even if it felt as if someone had just filleted him.

Typical Ellis. Sensible and measured. *I think you're the best one to judge that.*

Which told Ruby without a doubt that he wasn't interested in her. Otherwise that would've been his cue to suggest that she dated him, wouldn't it?

So it was just as well she hadn't suggested anything to him. It would've put an irreparable strain on their friendship, and she valued him too much to risk losing him.

'I guess you're right,' she said. 'I just didn't want people to think that I was the Merry Widow, not caring about Tom. And I feel guilty about wanting to date again.' She felt even more guilty about the fact that she was attracted to Ellis, particularly as he'd just made it clear it wasn't reciprocated.

'You're always going to love him,' Ellis said. 'But at the end of the day life still goes on. And Tom didn't want you to be lonely. He wanted you to be happy. What anyone else thinks is simply their opinion. They have the right to think whatever they like, but they don't have the right to shove it down your throat. You do what makes you happy, Rubes.'

Yeah.

Though sometimes she wondered if she'd ever find that kind of happiness again. If she was being greedy and expecting too much. Some people didn't even have that kind of happiness once in their lives, so what right did she have to expect to find it twice?

Ellis reached over to squeeze her hand, and her skin tingled all the way up her arm.

'Be happy, Ruby. You've got my full support. And if anyone says otherwise, send them to see me and I'll put them straight.'

He sounded as if he were her big brother.

And she'd just have to learn to see him as a kind of sibling instead of the man she wanted to start dating.

After lunch, Ruby called the Harrises in from the waiting area.

'I was wondering—would you mind if Coral, my trainee midwife, came in and observed the procedure?' she asked.

'No, that's fine, love,' Mrs Harris said. 'I'll do whatever you want if you can get this baby to do that forward roll.'

'I'll do my best. Thank you.' She smiled at Mrs Harris.

'I'm going to check how the baby's doing, first, on the ultrasound. If I'm happy with that, I'll give you some drugs to relax your womb—it won't hurt you or the baby, but it'll mean your baby has a bit more room to do that forward roll.'

'All right. Is that nice doctor going to be here?'

'Dr Webster? Yes. He's just making a quick phone call, and then he'll be right here. And I'll go and collect Coral so I can introduce her to you.' Ruby smiled at her. 'Lie back and bare your tummy for me. Though I'm afraid my gel's a little bit colder than it is in the ultrasound suite.'

'I don't mind,' Mrs Harris said, smiling back.

Once Ruby had established that everything was fine, she moved the screen so that the Harrises could see the baby. 'There he is—looking very comfy right now.'

'Hopefully he won't be stubborn and he'll move,' Mrs Harris said wryly.

'I'll give you those drugs now.' Ruby administered them swiftly. 'Make yourself comfortable, and I'll be right back,' she said.

When she returned, Ellis was already there. Ruby introduced the Harrises to Coral.

'So what we're going to do today is an external cephalic version—ECV, for short. The idea is to move the baby's bottom away from his mum's pelvis,' Ruby explained. 'I've already given Mrs Harris some drugs to help relax her womb, and we've seen the baby on the ultrasound. What I'm going to do now, Mrs Harris, is to push firmly on your abdomen to encourage the baby to do a kind of forward roll. It'll take maybe a minute to a minute and a half. As I said earlier, it might be a little bit uncomfortable but it shouldn't hurt. If it does hurt, I need you to tell me straight away and I'll stop.'

'All right.' Mrs Harris looked nervous, and Ruby noticed that she was holding her husband's hand really tightly.

'You might even see him do a forward roll in your tummy, so keep an eye on my hands,' she said with a smile.

Coral came quietly to the side so she could see and, gently but firmly, Ruby performed the manoeuvre, trying to ease the baby into a transverse position before he moved into the head-down position.

But the baby stubbornly refused to move.

After two minutes, Ruby stopped.

'Is something wrong?' Mr Harris asked anxiously.

'No—just that this baby really doesn't want to move today,' Ruby said.

'The longer the procedure takes, the less likely it is to work,' Ellis explained. 'But try not to worry. We can always try again tomorrow.'

They checked the baby again with the ultrasound. 'He's doing just fine,' Ellis reassured the Harrises. He glanced at the notes. 'Actually, his heart rate is pretty much as it was before Ruby started the ECV, so I'm happy for you to go home now, or you can stay in the waiting room until you're ready.'

'If we try again tomorrow and it still doesn't work, that means I'm going to have to have a section, doesn't it?' Mrs Harris asked.

'Not necessarily,' Ruby reassured her. 'Remember what we said this morning. We can still try for a vaginal delivery if the ECV doesn't work next time. We'll just need a bit of patience.'

'If it helps, I've delivered one or two breech babies in the middle of a field before now,' Ellis added.

'In the middle of a *field*?' Mr Harris looked surprised.

'I worked for a medical aid charity for a few years,' Ellis said. 'So I've delivered babies after natural disasters where there isn't even any running water in the area.'

Mrs Harris bit her lip. 'And here I am, moaning about it all, when I know I'm going to have a comfortable bed and all the medical equipment anyone needs! That's terrible. I feel...' She grimaced. 'Well, guilty, now.'

'You really don't need to. This is all new to you, and it's perfectly natural that you're concerned,' Ellis said. 'Actually, I'd be more concerned if you *weren't* worried.'

'I think she should have a section,' Ian Harris said. 'I looked up breech births on the Internet, and they said it's likely that the baby's head will get trapped or the baby will be brain-damaged.'

'The Internet,' Ellis said gently, 'is full of scary stories. It's the same with magazines—they're going to tell you all about the unusual cases and the dramatic stuff, because it's the drama that sells copies. They won't tell you that most women have a perfectly safe, normal delivery. As Ruby says, you just need a bit of patience with a vaginal breech birth. I believe in being hands off and letting the mum set the pace, and I only intervene if there's a problem.'

'So I won't have to have an episiotomy?' Mrs Harris asked.

'Hopefully not. We'll see how it goes,' Ellis said. 'Though I will say that if your labour isn't progressing after an hour, then I'll recommend a section. In my experience, when labour doesn't progress, it means there's a complication and you need help.'

'All right,' Mrs Harris said.

Ruby could see that Mrs Harris was biting back the tears, and sat down on the bed beside her to hold her other hand. 'We'll do our best for you, I promise,' she said softly. 'We're on your side. All we're saying is that if it doesn't work out quite the way you want it to, then please don't blame yourself. You've given it your best shot and that's more than good enough.'

'OK.' But Mrs Harris still looked close to tears.

Ruby hugged her. 'Hang on in there,' she said. 'It's going to be fine.'

CHAPTER THREE

Mrs Harris came in with her husband the next day for another attempt at the ECV. 'I've been feeling a bit off, all day,' she said. 'I woke up in the middle of the night with a bit of a tummy-ache. Obviously I must've eaten something that didn't agree with me last night.'

Or maybe, Ruby thought, it was something else causing that tummy-ache. She had a funny feeling about this—and her funny feelings were usually right.

'Come and lie down, and I'll examine you before we try the ECV again,' she said.

Mrs Harris had just settled back against the bed when she grimaced. 'Sorry. That was another twinge.'

Ruby examined her gently. 'Has anyone mentioned Braxton-Hicks to you?'

'The practice contractions, you mean?'

'They're the ones,' Ruby said.

'Yes—but I don't think I've had any.' Mrs Harris's eyes widened. 'Hang on—is that what the twinges mean? I'm having a practice contraction?'

'Given that you're three centimetres dilated,' Ruby said, 'then, actually, I think this is the real thing.'

'But I'm only thirty-seven weeks! It's too soon for the

baby to be born.' Mrs Harris bit her lip. 'Do you think it was that ECV thing yesterday that's caused this?'

'Possibly. Or it could be that your baby's just decided that his birthday's going to be today,' Ruby said with a smile. 'Don't worry about him being thirty-seven weeks. Not that many babies are born on their official due date—some are a couple of weeks before, and some are ten days or so late. By this stage your baby's lungs are definitely mature enough to cope with being born.'

'So will I have to have a section?'

'Hopefully not,' Ruby said cheerfully. 'I'm just going to get someone to call Dr Webster for me. And I need to give you a scan to see exactly how the baby's lying.'

'Cold gel again?' Mrs Harris asked ruefully.

'I'm afraid so,' Ruby said.

She came out of the cubicle and asked one of the auxiliary staff to find Ellis for her, then went back to see the Harrises and do the scan. She turned the screen so that the Harrises could see it. 'And here we can see one baby getting ready to be born. His head's tucked forward, just as I'd want it to be, and he's in what we call the frank breech position—that's the least complicated one, with his legs straight up in front of him.'

'So I can try for a normal birth?' Mrs Harris asked.

Ellis arrived in time to hear the question. 'I examined you yesterday and I'm happy that your pelvis is big enough to cope with having the baby. He's not too small, so there's a lower risk of having problems with the cord; and he's not too big, so he's not going to get stuck. I'm happy with the position he's in, with his head nicely tucked forward—so, yes, we can do this.' He smiled. 'As I said yesterday, I believe in keeping things natural as far as possible, so I'm not immediately going to say you'll have to have an episiotomy and forceps to help you deliver. It might end up that way, but we'll do our best to help you have the birth you want. Though I do want to remind you that if your labour doesn't progress, any delays mean that the baby's likely to be in distress and you'll need to have a section. No heroics, OK?'

'Agreed,' Ian Harris said firmly.

'Agreed,' Mrs Harris said, though she didn't sound quite so sure.

Ellis smiled at Ruby. 'Dilation?'

'Three centimetres.'

'OK. It's going to be a while yet before your baby arrives, so I'd suggest walking about a bit—the gravity will help him move down,' Ellis said.

'Would you mind very much if Coral—the trainee midwife you met yesterday—and one of the junior doctors came in to observe?' Ruby asked.

'No, that's fine,' Mrs Harris said. She squeezed her husband's hand. 'We're going to have our baby today, Ian. I can't believe it.'

It was a couple more hours before Mrs Harris was ready to start delivering the baby. Coral, the trainee midwife, and Lance, the new first-year doctor, came in to observe and Ruby introduced them both to the Harrises.

'Being on your elbows and knees will be the most comfortable position for you, as well as being the most effective position for delivering the baby, because you can move about a bit,' Ruby said. 'And resting on your elbows rather than your hands will protect your wrists.'

'Unless you really want an epidural, I'd recommend having either gas and air or pethidine as pain relief,' Ellis added, 'because an epidural will slow everything down.'

'I don't want a section,' Mrs Harris said, 'so I'll manage with gas and air.'

'Good on you,' Ellis said.

'The main thing to remember about a breech birth,' Ruby explained to Coral and Lance, 'is that you keep your hands off and be patient—you don't want the mum clenching her muscles if you touch her.'

'You intervene only if it's clear that the baby needs help,' Ellis said. 'Which is why we're using a foetal monitor to keep an eye on his heart rate.'

Ruby encouraged Mrs Harris to breathe through the contractions.

'I can see the baby now,' she said at last. 'When you have the next contraction, I want you to give a nice big push for me.'

The baby's buttocks arrived first, and then with the next contraction and the next push the back and shoulders were visible.

Ruby glanced at Ellis. As always when she delivered a baby with him, she noticed that he was almost misty-eyed. Ruby was, too; the moment a new life came into the world was so very special, and it was such a privilege to share it.

And Ellis was a particularly good doctor to work with; he was supportive, he listened to both the mum and the midwifery team, and he didn't try to rush any of the mums straight to Theatre at the first sign of a complication.

At the next push, the baby's legs came down.

'Well done,' Ruby said. 'You're doing just great. His legs are down, now. Keep breathing for me.'

The baby's shoulders and arms came out next, and

then Ruby glanced again at Ellis. At his nod, she moved into position, ready to catch the baby.

'Almost here. Next contraction, give me the biggest push you can. Scream if you need to. Shout. Whatever you want to do, that's fine. Just push,' she said.

And finally, the baby's head emerged.

'The baby's not crying,' Mr Harris said, looking panicky.

And the baby was blue. At a first glance, Ruby would give him an Apgar score of four—very low.

'It's fine,' Ellis reassured Mr Harris. 'I know right now this looks very scary, but this is totally normal for a breech birth. Do you want to cut the umbilical cord, and then we can get this little one warmed up a bit and ready for a cuddle?'

Thankfully it was enough to distract Mr Harris; Ruby swiftly clamped the cord and Ellis gave the scissors to Mr Harris to cut the cord while Ruby wrapped the baby in a warm towel.

Ruby then took the baby over to the warming tray for warm air to be blown on him.

'Do you want me to sort out the baby while you deliver the placenta?' Ellis asked.

She smiled at him. 'Yes, please.'

By the time she'd delivered the placenta, she was relieved to hear plenty of crying coming from Baby Harris, and she heard Ellis say, 'I'm pleased to say your little boy's pinked up very nicely indeed. He's got an Apgar score of nine.'

Ruby knew that last bit was aimed for her, and she felt the strain between her shoulders disappear. Everything was fine. And, better still, Ellis also hadn't mentioned anything about hip dysplasia, which could sometimes be a problem with breech babies.

Finally, Baby Harris was in his mum's arms, skin to skin, and took all of three sucks for his first feed before falling asleep.

Ruby examined Mrs Harris. 'I'm pleased to say that you don't need any stitches,' she said. 'You did absolutely brilliantly. Congratulations to both of you.'

'We could never have done it without you,' Mrs Harris said. 'I was so scared we'd have to just do what the doctor said.'

Ruby smiled. 'They're all pretty good here, actually.' She lowered her voice to a stage whisper. 'Though Ellis Webster is a bit special. But don't tell him I said that, or his head will swell so much that he won't be able to walk through the door for a week.'

Mrs Harris laughed.

'Let's get you settled down in the ward,' Ruby said, 'and you can get to know your baby.' She stroked the baby's cheek. 'He's beautiful.'

'Do you have children?' Mrs Harris asked.

'No.' She and Tom had thought very seriously about it, but then Tom had been diagnosed with leukaemia and it had never been the right time to discuss it again after that. 'Maybe one day,' she said wistfully.

And how odd that a picture flashed into her head. Of herself, tired yet glowing with happiness and holding a baby. And of Ellis sitting next to her, holding her hand and stroking the baby's head.

Ridiculous. And totally inappropriate.

Ellis was her friend, and *only* her friend. And she had a date lined up on Saturday night with a completely different man, the new registrar on her best friend's ward. She really shouldn't be thinking about that kind of thing.

Ellis didn't see Ruby over the weekend. He wanted to call her, but he knew she was going on a date with a colleague of Tina's. So he needed to back off. To give her a chance to get to know the guy and enjoy dating again.

Even though what he really wanted to do was to scoop her over his shoulder and carry her off to his lair.

Ridiculous. He knew that Ruby saw him only as a friend. So he was going to have to ignore this stupid antsy feeling. She deserved to feel happy again. It was just a pity it meant she'd find that happiness with another man rather than with him.

So on Monday lunchtime, he summoned his brightest smile when he saw her. 'Want to go grab a sandwich?'

'That'd be nice.'

He waited until they'd sat down in the canteen before he asked, 'So how was your date?'

'Fine.'

Her smile was a little too bright. 'But?' he asked.

She wrinkled her nose. 'He was a nice guy, but I don't think he was ready to date again yet.'

Was that Ruby's way of saying that she'd just discovered she wasn't ready to date again yet, too?

He battened down the hopes as she continued, 'I don't think he's quite over his divorce yet.'

'Ah. Baggage.'

She gave him a rueful smile. 'I guess we all have baggage when we get to this age.'

'Mmm.'

'Look at you,' she said softly.

Oh, no. He really didn't want to discuss that. He didn't like talking about his feelings. And he definitely didn't want to talk about his baggage. Ruby knew he was divorced, but he hadn't told her the whole messy story.

'Tom always said you'd never settle because you were trying to save people, to make up for the way they couldn't save your sister.'

'I guess that's part of it,' he said. 'Though I always wanted to be a doctor, even when Sally was still alive.' After Sally's death, he'd vowed to work abroad rather than stay in an English hospital, and it had caused a rift with his brothers; they couldn't understand why he risked himself the way he did, and they'd told him they didn't want to lose him the way they'd lost Sally. But, however much he'd tried to talk them round, he hadn't been able to make them see that he wanted to save all the other potential Sallys, and to do that it meant working abroad. 'And it's not why I became an obstetrician, either. I always planned to work in emergency medicine, like Tom. But then I did a rotation on the maternity ward and I fell in love with it—that special moment where you witness the miracle of a brand new life.'

'That's why I became a midwife, too,' she said softly. 'It never, ever gets old.'

'And it's even better in a world where things are sticky and you really feel that you need a miracle to happen and make things better. That first little cry...' Every time, it made him misty-eyed and glad to be alive, all at the same time.

'You still have itchy feet, don't you?' she asked. 'I know you're going back to the medical aid charity in a couple of months.'

'It's been arranged for a really long time,' Ellis said. And he did want to go back. The trouble was, he also wanted to stay in London. But he wasn't sure if he could—not if Ruby started dating someone else and it got serious. He'd promised Tom that he'd be there for Ruby, and he'd keep his promise; but he wasn't sure that his promise could stretch to watching her date another man and being happy about it. 'Anyway, we weren't talking about me,' he said, trying very hard to wriggle out of the subject. 'We were talking about your date.'

'I guess it was a case of nice guy, wrong time,' she said with a shrug.

'Would he be the right guy at a different time?' It was a bit like prodding a bruise, but Ellis wanted to know.

'Probably not,' she said. 'There wasn't that spark between us. Whereas the first time I saw Tom...'

'Yeah. I know.' He reached across and squeezed her hand briefly.

Mistake. Because every nerve-end in his own hand tingled at the contact.

He knew about sparks, all right. Ruby most definitely made him feel that spark. His feelings for anyone he'd dated before just paled by comparison—including his ex-wife. But Ruby was vulnerable, she was still missing Tom, and she was still probably not quite ready to move on. Adding his job to the mix...In his book, it all made her very firmly off limits.

'Hey. If you're not busy with a date at the weekend, maybe we could do something together,' he said lightly. 'There's that new action film.'

'You want me to go and see a guy-flick with you?' She laughed. 'Ellis, much as I love you...'

As a friend, he reminded himself sharply.

'....action flicks really aren't my favourites.'

'Hey, this one has a plot,' he protested.

'As if,' she scoffed, still laughing. 'All right, if you're so desperate to see it, I'll go with you. But it's on the understanding that I want ice cream *and* popcorn.'

'Deal,' he said. It wasn't a *date* date. But it would be enough. Because he didn't have the right to ask for more.

CHAPTER FOUR

It was a busy week on the ward. Ruby's favourite day of the week was spent delivering twins in a birthing pool; the water birth was calm and peaceful, and it was a good experience for Coral, as well as being exactly what the mum wanted.

Saturday afternoon turned out to be dull and rainy, so she went to the cinema with Ellis to see the action flick. As promised, he bought her popcorn and ice cream; although the film wasn't really her cup of tea, she still enjoyed his company.

After going to a tiny bistro for pasta and a bottle of red wine, Ellis saw her home.

'Want to come in for some coffee?' she asked.

'I'd love to. Thanks.' He smiled at her.

When they were both sprawled comfortably on the sofa with a mug of coffee, Ruby said, 'Tina says I shouldn't give up on the dates just yet.'

'She's planning to set you up on a blind date with another of her colleagues?' Ellis asked.

'No. She suggested I try one of those online match-making sites.' She looked at him and raised an eyebrow. 'What, you don't approve?'

'It's not like going on a blind date with someone

who's a friend of a friend, which means you sort of know them already, or at least know that they're OK. With a dating site, you're planning to meet a total stranger,' Ellis said. 'And people don't always tell the truth on those things. They can put a photograph up that's years out of date and claim to like a lot of interesting things, just to get someone to pick them for a date.'

'Maybe the odd person would do that—odd in *both* senses of the word—but most people don't do that sort of thing. Don't be such a cynic. And think about it, Ellis. Once you're our age, most of your friends are in a relationship and so are most of their friends, which means you know hardly anyone else who's single. Apart from through friends or work, how else are you going to meet someone?'

'I guess you have a point,' he said.

She paused. 'Actually, you know, you could try it.'

'What?'

'Putting your profile on a dating site.'

'Why?' He looked at her in bewilderment.

'Because you haven't dated at all in the last year or so.'

'Yes, I have,' he protested.

'Here and there. Nothing serious.'

No. Because he didn't do serious relationships. Not since his divorce. He preferred to keep things light and uncomplicated, and he'd concentrated on his career rather than his love life. Not to mention the fact that he'd been fighting off inappropriate feelings towards Ruby for months. 'I've been busy,' he prevaricated.

'Ellis, you really don't have to put your life on hold for me,' she said gently.

He froze at her words. Did she *know*?

'I know Tom asked you to look after me, but that shouldn't be at the expense of your own happiness.'

He relaxed again. Clearly she was just thinking of his promise to Tom, and she didn't have a clue how he felt about her. Which was just as well. Because he didn't know how she felt about him—or if she could ever come to see him as anything more than her late husband's best friend. 'I'm fine as I am,' he said.

'But don't you get lonely, Ellis?'

'From time to time I do,' he admitted. 'But I have good friends and a job I love. That's enough for me.' And if he kept telling himself that, eventually he'd end up believing it.

At work on Tuesday morning, Ellis had a written request from the court. Something he really wasn't expecting. And something he really wanted to talk to Ruby about.

He went in search of her. 'Got a minute?' he asked. 'There's something I want to run by you.'

'Sorry, I've got wall to wall appointments this morning,' she said. 'And I'm running late. Can I come and grab you at lunchtime?'

'Sure—there's no immediate rush.'

Except at lunchtime Ellis had been called away to help at a difficult birth, and when he was on a break in the afternoon Ruby was in the middle of delivering a baby.

In the end he ended up meeting her after work for a drink.

'So what did you want to run by me?' she asked.

'I had a written request for information this morning,' he said. 'From the court.'

'The court?' She blinked. 'That sounds ominous.'

He shook his head. 'Nothing that should worry anyone in the department—it isn't a negligence case or anything. It's to do with a baby you and I delivered about a year ago—little Baby Edwards. Sadly, his parents have split up, and Billy Edwards wanted a paternity test.'

She grimaced. 'That's sad—and even sadder still because it's probably not that unusual nowadays.'

'This case is definitely unusual,' he said. 'That's why the court wrote to me. The results came back and showed that Billy Edwards is the baby's father.'

Ruby looked puzzled. 'So if he's the father, which proves the paternity, why did the court write to you?'

'Because it turns out that Grace Edwards isn't the baby's mother.'

Her frown deepened. 'How come? Was she an IVF mum with a donated egg?'

'No. I looked up the paperwork today. Conception and pregnancy were all without any complications or intervention. Grace Edwards only had a section because the baby was getting distressed.'

'So if her former husband was definitely the father and the egg was hers, then surely Grace has to be the baby's mother? I mean, that's basic biology, Ellis.'

'You'd think so—but the genetic tests say not. And DNA doesn't lie.'

'Maybe there was an error in the tests?' she suggested.

He shook his head. 'They did a second set of DNA tests, just to make sure there wasn't some kind of error in the first set. The results show exactly the same thing: Baby Edwards is genetically related to Billy, but not to Grace.'

She blinked. 'This is surreal. How is that even possible, Ellis?'

'That,' he said dryly, 'is why the court's written to me. I'm going to discuss it with Theo Petrakis, but I wanted to talk to you first, to see if you remembered anything unusual about the birth.'

'No. I mean, I'd probably have to reread the paperwork to refresh my memory, because I can't remember every detail of every single baby I've ever delivered over the years.' She frowned. 'But I guess all midwives would remember births that have any out-of-the-ordinary features. I don't remember this one being an unusual case.'

'I'm going to have a chat with one of the genetic counsellors, too. Just to see if I'm missing something,' Ellis said. 'Because there definitely feels as if there's a piece of the puzzle missing. I just can't work out what.'

'Well, if you want a wing-woman, come and grab me,' she said.

Any time, he thought, but stopped himself before he said something stupid. 'Thanks.'

The following weekend, Ellis and Ruby were sitting on the balcony of his flat overlooking the park, enjoying the unseasonably mild evening and a bottle of wine.

'Tina was nagging me again this morning about signing up for the dating website,' Ruby said. She wrinkled her nose. 'Though I don't think I'll ever meet anyone who matches up to Tom.'

'Of course you won't, but it's still relatively early days,' Ellis said.

'So it's too soon to date again?'

'Only you can answer that,' he said. And even though he wanted to tell her to look right under her nose, he was going to do the supportive thing. The *right* thing. 'We could always make a list of what you're looking for from your perfect man.'

'You'd help me do that?'

'I guess Tina would probably be better at that than I would,' he said.

'But you could give me feedback from a male point of view—which my best friend, being female, can't,' she pointed out.

'OK. Let's do it the old-fashioned way—pen and paper, first.' He went into the living room and fetched a notebook and pen. 'What do you want to do first?'

'My profile, I guess. How do I describe myself?' she asked.

The most beautiful woman in the world. Not that he was going to say that out loud. But with that elfin crop and those huge blue eyes, she reminded him of Audrey Hepburn. Though there was nothing fragile and Holly Golightlyish about Ruby. She was strong. Brave. Gorgeous.

He looked at her. 'Pretty, petite midwife?'

She groaned. 'No, because then I'll get all sleazy stuff about men wanting naughty nurses in super-short uniforms. I don't want to have to deal with that.'

'How about pretty, petite professional?' he suggested.

'And that's three Ps in a row—it looks wrong.'

He laughed. 'Make that four and add "picky".'

She laughed back. 'I guess.'

'I know. Pretty, petite medical professional seeks...' He paused. 'So what are you looking for, Ruby?'

'Someone taller than me,' she said.

'That's not exactly difficult, given that you're all of five foot two,' he teased.

She cuffed him. 'All right, we'll skip height. And, actually, looks aren't really that important.'

'So you don't want a guy who looks like a movie star?'

'Well, no woman with red blood in her veins is going to turn down a man who looks like Brad Pitt,' she said. 'But, seriously, it's personality that's more important.'

'Good sense of humour?'

'But not someone who does constant wisecracks— that'd drive me mad. And I don't like people who make someone else the butt of their humour all the time; I think that's mean-spirited.'

'Serious, then.'

'But with a nice smile and a sense of fun.'

'As I said, picky. Serious male with a nice smile and sense of fun.' He paused. 'Do you think you should add "professional" in there, too?'

'Could do.'

He wrote it down. 'What else?'

'Not a sports fiend. I don't want to spend my week-ends freezing cold at the side of a football pitch. Some-one who likes films, a wide range of music and long walks.'

'OK. And what are you looking for? Friendship? Romance?'

'Both,' she said. 'I want to be friends as well as lovers.'

Yeah. *So did he.*

'Friendship leading to potential romance,' he said.

'You sound as if you've done this before. Or read a lot of personal ads.'

He smiled. 'I can assure you, I've never dated any-one through a personal ad. It's usually someone I've met through work.'

'But you haven't dated that much since I've known you.'

Partly because he didn't do serious relationships; and partly because he hadn't met anyone who made him feel even the slightest way that Ruby made him feel. It wasn't fair to date someone when you knew you couldn't give the relationship a real chance. When your heart was held elsewhere. 'I've been busy,' he said blandly.

'Maybe now's your chance to try it. We'll do your profile, next,' she said.

'Hey—I'm not planning to join a dating site,' he protested.

'Fair's fair,' she said. 'If I'm doing this, so are you. Hand over the pen and paper.'

He gave in.

'So. TDH doctor.'

'TDH?'

'Tall, dark and handsome.' She rolled her eyes. 'Come off it, Ellis. Even you must know that one.'

'Along with GSOH,' he deadpanned. 'What everyone says in their profile.'

'You're serious and deep,' she said.

He grimaced. 'Which makes me sound boring.'

'No, you do have a sense of fun—it's just that sometimes you need teasing out of your shell. Serious and deep,' she repeated, 'with principles.'

'And now I sound like a character from a Victorian novel. The one who doesn't get the girl because he's stuffy.'

'You're not stuffy, Ellis.' She grinned. 'Principles and dimples.'

'Dimples?' He looked at her, mystified.

'When you smile. You do know I've heard some of

the mums on the ward sigh over you? As well as all the female staff?'

'No, they don't.' He groaned. 'OK. We need to stop this, right now.'

She shook her head. 'Uh-uh. We're doing this. What are you looking for, Ellis?'

He could lie.

Or he could take a risk and tell her the truth.

'Someone bright and sparkly, to make my dimples come out,' he said softly.

'That's better,' she said. 'Vegetarian?'

'No, not necessarily,' he said. 'I'm looking for someone who enjoys food, films and walking by the sea.'

'For friendship leading to potential romance?'

'That sounds about right. So what do we have?' He shifted so they could both see the notepad, and flicked back to the page he'd written on.

'Pretty, petite medical professional seeks serious professional male with a nice smile and sense of fun, who likes films, music and long walks, for friendship leading to potential romance,' he read aloud.

She took the notebook from him and turned over to the next page.

'TDH doctor, serious and deep—with principles—seeks bright, sparkly female to make his dimples come out. Looking for foodie film-buff who enjoys seaside strolls, for friendship leading to potential romance.'

He groaned again. 'I hate that bit about the dimples. It sounds really pathetic.'

'Tough. It's staying. Your dimples are cute.' She flicked back to her list. 'You know, Ellis, this list could be describing you.'

His heart skipped a beat.

Was this the chance he'd been looking for? Was she telling him in her quiet, understated way, that she'd consider dating him?

'And my list,' he said softly, 'could be describing you.'

They looked at each other, and it felt as if the air was humming.

Should he make a move?

If he did and she reacted the wrong way, he could always blame the wine tomorrow morning, apologise profusely, and rescue their friendship.

And if he made a move and she reacted the right way...

'Maybe,' he said, 'neither of us needs to put an ad on the dating site.'

She didn't pull away or look horrified at the idea.

So he leaned forward and gave in to what he'd wanted to do for a year or more. He touched his mouth very lightly to hers.

CHAPTER FIVE

RUBY'S MOUTH TINGLED as Ellis's lips brushed hers very lightly. Warm. Sweet. Exploring rather than demanding. Gentle. Every kiss, every touch, made her want more.

She'd dreamed of this moment, but the reality was something else. Full of delight—and full of terror. Delight, because now she knew that the attraction she felt towards Ellis was mutual; but terror, because if this all went wrong she knew she'd lose him from her life, and she didn't have the strength to cope with losing anyone else right now.

When he broke the kiss and drew back, his eyes were dark. With worry, guilt or both? she wondered. Because she couldn't tell a thing from his expression. And she was racked with panic.

'Sorry. I shouldn't have done that. I…' He broke off with a grimace.

'No.' She reached across and took his hand. 'Ellis. You and I…we're friends.'

'Yes. Of course.'

'I like being with you,' she said carefully.

'Uh-huh.'

Now he sounded as if he'd gone into polite and neutral mode. So did he think this was a mistake? Or was he worried that she thought it was a mistake? Maybe she needed to take the risk and be totally honest with him.

'You tick every box on my list. But if I date you...' She took a deep breath. 'It scares me, Ellis. You don't tend to date women very often, and when you do the relationship doesn't last for very long. And you're going back to the medical aid charity in a couple of months.'

'For a month's assignment, yes,' he confirmed. 'As you know, I'm helping to set up a new medical centre in Zimbabwe.'

'But isn't that...' She looked at him wide-eyed. There was so much unrest in the country. It was a huge risk.

As if he guessed what she was thinking, he said quietly, 'It's an area that's fairly remote and really in need of help. Especially obstetrics. There are so few medics, and so many fatalities that could easily be prevented.'

Which she knew was a huge draw for him. Even though he'd said he hadn't become an obstetrician for his sister's sake, she knew that he wanted to make a difference, the way someone should've made a difference for her. Of course he needed to be there.

But was he going just to set it up? Or would he stay for a few months after that?

'And what happens after your month's assignment?' she asked.

'I don't actually have an answer for that right now,' he admitted.

Ruby said nothing, but Ellis could see the worry in her eyes. She was clearly thinking that if he dated her, she was going to end up being hurt when he left.

Hurting her was the last thing he'd ever want to do. And even though right now he really wanted to kiss her again—kiss her until they both forgot the world outside—he knew he had to do the decent thing. The unselfish thing.

'OK. Let's forget all about this and stick to being just friends,' he said.

'Yes. No.' She shook her head. 'I don't know. I wasn't expecting this.'

'I'm sorry.'

'I'm not. And I am. And…' She grimaced. 'I'm not making any sense at all, am I?'

'No, you're not,' he agreed, and she noticed the slightest glint of humour in his eyes. Though she knew he was laughing with her rather than at her.

Time for another burst of honesty, perhaps, she thought. 'I wanted you to kiss me just now,' she told him.

His face was completely inscrutable now, and she had no idea whether she was fixing a problem or making things even more of a mess.

'But, at the same time, it scares me. I can't afford to lose you from my life, Ellis. And your relationships never last for very long. You said yourself that you've never settled for anyone, not even your ex-wife—and you're going away again soon and you don't really know if you're coming back.'

'I haven't settled down because I've never met anyone who really made me want to settle down, not in the long term,' he said.

She hadn't pushed him about the details of his marriage, though he'd made it very clear when they'd talked in the past that he wasn't still in love with his ex. But when he said he'd never met anyone who made him want to settle, did that also include her? Ruby wondered.

Or could she be the one who could make him feel differently about settling down?

'Plus you're Tom's best friend,' she said. 'And I feel guilty.'

'Did you feel guilty about dating Tina's colleague?' he asked.

'No,' she admitted.

'So what's the difference between dating him and dating me?'

'Because I know you.' Because Ellis *mattered*—though she didn't quite want to admit that. And because the world needed people like Ellis, people who were prepared to be selfless and make a difference. Asking him to stay would be so selfish of her.

'You could,' he said, 'pretend that you don't know me. Pretend that I'd just answered your ad.'

She was still holding his hand; he rubbed his thumb gently against her palm. 'Ruby. You said you wanted to date again. But at the same time it scares you, right?'

'Right,' she admitted.

'Because you're worried it will go wrong?'

If he'd asked her the question about anyone else, she would've said no. But where Ellis was concerned, she worried that it would go wrong. That she'd lose him back to the medical aid charity—that his month's assignment would turn into two, then six, then a year... That he'd quietly vanish from her life, just as quietly as he'd walked in and become her rock when Tom was diagnosed with leukaemia. Leaving her lonely again. And feeling guilty for feeling lonely, because she knew what he did was important, and in the scheme of things her loneliness was the proverbial hill of beans.

'I don't know,' she said, feeling more confused than she had in a long time.

'What shift are you on, on Friday?' he asked.

'Early.'

'Then why don't we give it a try on Friday evening?' he suggested.

'Have an actual date, you mean?'

'Uh-huh.'

She took a deep breath. 'Doing what exactly?'

'Dinner, maybe. Dancing. Whatever you'd like to do.'

Would there be more kissing? Her body flooded with heat at the idea.

'Ruby?' he asked softly.

Could she be brave and take the risk—date the man she'd started to think of as more than just a friend? And could she squash the guilt she felt about dating again? She swallowed hard. 'Provided we go Dutch, OK.'

'No. If I ask someone out to dinner, that means I'm paying,' he said firmly. 'And there aren't any strings attached, if that's what you're worrying about. Dinner is just dinner. End of.'

'Then do I get to pay next time? To keep it fair?'

He frowned. 'I'm more than happy to pay for your dinner, Ruby. I'm not expecting you to…' He blew out a breath. 'Well. That's not how I operate.'

She knew what he wasn't saying. He wasn't expecting her to sleep with him in exchange for her dinner. The problem was…she did want to sleep with him. And that made her feel even more awkward and guilty. What was wrong with her? Was it just that it had been a while since she'd been physically sated? Was this some crazy hormonal thing? Or was it more than that? The whole thing left her feeling like a confused mess. 'I guess.'

'So will you have dinner with me on Friday, Ruby?' he asked softly.

'I...'

'We'll take it light and easy. We dress up a bit, eat nice food, drink lovely wine, then maybe go dancing if you'd like to.'

It sounded so good. Everything she wanted. But did she want more from this relationship than he did? And why was she so drawn to Ellis anyway—when she knew he loved his job working abroad, always on the move, and she wanted something different? If she looked at it sensibly, Ellis was the last person she should date. He didn't want the same things out of life that she did. He'd been brilliant, a total rock since he'd come back to London for Tom, but she knew he couldn't put his life on hold for ever. That wouldn't be fair. And their real lifestyles weren't compatible, with him moving on all the time and her staying in the same place.

To cover her confusion and her worries, she asked, 'Can you even dance?'

'That's for me to know,' he said, 'and you to find out. Provided you wear high heels and lipstick.' He brought her hand up to his mouth and kissed the back of her fingers, looking her straight in the eyes as he did so. And it sent desire licking all the way down her spine. How had she never noticed before just how hot Ellis was?

'Friday,' he said. 'I'll pick you up at seven. And I'll see you at work tomorrow.'

Dating Ellis.

The very idea put Ruby into a flat spin.

And she couldn't get those kisses out of her head.

The way his mouth had felt against her skin…Her whole body tingled at the memory.

She still couldn't quite believe that she'd agreed to this. And, worse still, that she'd actually told him she was attracted to him and he ticked all the boxes on her wish list for a partner.

He should have run a mile. Especially given that he didn't date much and his relationships never lasted long. And, given that he was planning to leave England again in a couple of months and he wasn't totally sure that he was coming back, he shouldn't be interested in her. He should've brushed everything aside.

But he hadn't.

He'd actually asked her out.

And he'd said that she fitted his wish list, too.

This could be perfect. Happiness she'd never expected to find again—and with a man Tom would most definitely approve of, because he'd loved Ellis like a brother.

Yet it could also be the worst mistake she'd ever made. How awkward would it make things at work if things went wrong between them? He wasn't just her friend, he was one of the colleagues she liked working with most.

And what would happen when he left? Could they make a go of a long-distance relationship, or could they find some sort of compromise? Or would it end up being a total mess?

She was going to have to be very, very careful.

In the middle of a busy morning on the ward, Ellis got a call from one of the ultrasonographers. 'Ellis, can I have a second opinion?'

'Sure. What's the problem?'

'I'm not happy with the baby I'm scanning right now. I think the baby's showing signs of anaemia—the blood flow's a bit too quick for my liking.'

Ellis knew that meant the baby's blood was likely to be thinner, with fewer red blood cells—and that might mean the need for surgical intervention to correct the anaemia. 'How old is the baby, and who's the mum's midwife?' he asked.

'The baby's twenty-six weeks, and the midwife's Ruby.'

The best person he could've hoped for. She always developed a real rapport with her mums. Ellis loved working with her—which was probably the best reason for him not to date her and risk that working relationship. He pushed the thought away. 'OK. I'm coming now, and I'll see if I can get Ruby to come with me.'

She was in the middle of a consultation, but agreed to come along as soon as she was done.

The ultrasonographer introduced him quickly to Mrs Perkins. 'Dr Webster's just come along to give me a second opinion,' she explained.

As soon as Ellis looked at the screen, he agreed with her assessment: the baby's blood flow was definitely too quick.

'Is something wrong with my baby?' Mrs Perkins asked, looking worried.

'At the moment it's just a precaution, so try not to worry,' he said. 'It might be that the baby's a little bit anaemic, but we can to do something to sort that out. Do you mind if I look at your notes?'

As soon as Ellis saw Mrs Perkins's blood group, he had a pretty good idea of what the problem was. 'Your blood group's rhesus negative,' he said. 'And I can see here that you've been having anti-D injections.'

She nodded. 'They're not the nicest things in the world, but it's worth it to keep the baby safe.'

Clearly it had been explained to her that if the baby's blood group was rhesus positive, her body would develop antibodies that would cross the placenta and attack the baby's red blood cells, causing anaemia. Injections of anti-D would stop her body developing antibodies.

Except, by the look of it, the anti-D hadn't worked. So there was a little more to this than met the eye.

'And your husband's blood group is rhesus positive?' he asked.

She nodded. 'That's why they said I had to have the anti-D, because the baby's blood was likely to be rhesus positive as well.'

At that point, Ruby came in. 'Hello, Helen.' She smiled at Mrs Perkins and squeezed her hand. 'How are you doing?'

'I'm fine, but they think my baby's anaemic.' Mrs Perkins bit her lip. 'And I had all the anti-D injections. I didn't miss a single one.'

'I know.'

'There is one circumstance where the anti-D doesn't work,' Ellis said quietly, coming to sit on her other side. 'I apologise in advance if this brings back any bad memories, and I know your notes say that this is your first baby, but have you ever been pregnant before?'

'I don't think so,' Mrs Perkins said.

'It might be possible,' Ruby said gently, 'that you didn't realise you were pregnant—that maybe your period was a bit late and you put it down to stress, and then your period was heavier than normal.'

'I...' Mrs Perkins shook her head, and a tear trickled down her cheek. 'This is so stupid. I can't remember.'

'It could have been a long time ago,' Ellis said. 'But it's really common for women to be pregnant, not re-alise it, and lose the baby before they have any idea they might be pregnant. If that happened to you, it's very possible that your body was already sensitised to the antibodies, so the anti-D wouldn't work for you.'

'So it's my fault the baby's anaemic?'

'Not at all,' he reassured her, squeezing her hand. 'You did everything by the book. It's just one of these things. But I would like to do some more tests, Mrs Perkins. I'd like to take a blood sample from the baby.'

'How does that work?' she asked.

'I take a tiny, tiny sample from the baby with a nee-dle—it's not so nice for you, because it means putting a needle through your abdomen into your womb,' he said. 'The same way an amniocentesis is done.'

She shook her head. 'It doesn't matter about me. I just want the baby to be all right.'

'I promise you, we're going to keep a close eye on you so you don't have to worry,' Ruby said.

'We can do the sample right here, right now—or we can wait for someone to come and be with you, if you'd rather,' Ellis said.

'I want Joe,' Mrs Perkins said. 'My husband. He was supposed to be here for the scan, but there was an emergency at work and he got called in.' Another tear trickled down her cheek. 'Or am I putting the baby at risk by waiting?'

Ruby put an arm round her shoulders and hugged

her, and Ellis handed her a tissue. 'No, you're not. It's absolutely fine to wait until your husband can be here before we do the blood test,' he reassured her.

'What happens if the baby's anaemic?'

'I don't want to frighten you, but severe anaemia can cause the baby's heart to fail, or even mean that you have a stillbirth,' he said gently. 'But we can tell how much of a problem the anaemia is from that blood sample, and if necessary we can give the baby a blood transfusion.'

Mrs Perkins looked shocked. 'You mean I'll have the baby today? But I'm only twenty-six weeks! That's...' She shook her head. 'Surely I can't have the baby now?'

'No, you won't be having the baby today. I mean we can do a transfusion through a needle while the baby's still in your womb,' Ellis explained gently. 'We'll do it under a local anaesthetic so you won't feel it, but it does mean you'll need to stay in overnight, and we'll need to do this every couple of weeks until the baby's born. But the transfusions will stop the anaemia.'

'I'll call Joe for you, shall I?' Ruby asked.

Mrs Perkins nodded. 'But if the baby's anaemic, how come I didn't feel any different? And I've made sure I've eaten plenty of leafy green veg, and I eat lean red meat twice a week.'

'It's honestly not anything you've done,' Ellis reassured her. 'And that diet sounds about perfect for you and the baby. Try not to worry. And I'll see you a bit later this afternoon, OK?'

The baby's blood sample showed a worrying level of anaemia, so Ellis and Ruby went to see Mr and Mrs Perkins.

'Is our baby all right?' Mrs Perkins asked.

'The sample says the baby's anaemic, but as I explained earlier, a blood transfusion will fix that,' Ellis said.

'So the baby gets a transfusion while still inside Helen?' Mr Perkins asked. 'Isn't that dangerous?'

'It's invasive, yes, and you're right that the procedure gives a very small risk of miscarriage or early labour,' Ruby said.

'What if the baby doesn't have the transfusion?' Mr Perkins asked.

'Then the anaemia will get worse and it could cause other problems.'

'Such as?' Mr Perkins asked.

'The baby might develop heart problems. And I'm sorry to say that, in the worst case scenario, the baby could be stillborn.'

Mr Perkins went white.

'My advice is that, although it's an invasive treatment, the baby needs the blood transfusion, and the advantages outweigh the risks,' Ellis said gently.

'If we say yes, how does it work?' Mrs Perkins asked.

'We'll give you a local anaesthetic to numb the area so you won't feel it,' Ellis said. 'And we'll give you a sedative to relax you, plus a sedative to the baby to make sure that the baby doesn't move during the procedure.'

'That means you won't feel the baby moving for a little while afterwards,' Ruby said, 'but that's perfectly normal and the sedative will wear off for both of you within a couple of hours.'

'We'll do an ultrasound scan to show us where the baby is,' Ellis continued, 'and then we'll give the baby a few millilitres of blood through a needle in the um-bilical cord—that means the blood's absorbed better.'

'And it's a one-off?' Mrs Perkins asked.

'We'll give you weekly scans from now on,' Ellis said, 'to see how the baby's doing—but it's quite likely that the baby will need a transfusion every two to four weeks until birth.'

Mr Perkins looked at them, wide-eyed. 'Whose blood does the baby get?'

'It's donated blood, fully screened—type O rhesus positive,' Ellis said.

'I'm O positive. Can I give the blood?' Mr Perkins asked.

'I'll check with the haematologist, and you'll need to have some tests before they can say yes, but if it's OK with the haem team then it's more than fine by me,' Ellis said. 'From now on you'll be under my care and Ruby's, so you'll always see us when you come to the hospital—and if you ever have any worries at any time, I want you to ring us or come and see us, OK? Because that's what we're here for—to look after you and to reassure you if you're concerned about anything, no matter how small it might seem.'

'OK. We'll do it.' Mrs Perkins bit her lip. 'When does the first one happen?'

'Today,' Ellis said. 'And I'd like you to stay in over-night, just so we can keep an eye on you.'

'I agree,' Mr Perkins said. 'If anything happens, Helen, you'll be in the right place.'

'But the chances of anything happening are really, really small,' Ellis reassured them. 'Is there anyone you need to call?'

'No—but can I stay with Helen while it's being done?' Mr Perkins asked.

'Of course you can,' Ruby said.

To Ellis's relief, the haematology tests meant that Mr Perkins was able to donate the blood. The procedure only took a couple of minutes, and he and Ruby talked the Perkinses through every single step, making sure they could see the baby on the screen and pointing out the baby's heart beating to reassure them that the sedative wasn't a problem.

'As Ruby said earlier, it takes up to three hours for the sedative to wear off,' Ellis reminded them afterwards. 'Don't worry if you don't feel the baby moving for a little while. I'm going to prescribe antibiotics to make sure you don't get any infection. But if you feel hot or any kind of pain, or there's any redness or bleeding around the area where I injected you, tell the nursing staff straight away, OK? And I'll be in to see you later.'

'Now that's something you couldn't have done in the middle of a field or an earthquake,' Ruby said to Ellis softly when Helen Perkins had gone up to the ward to settle in. 'And you loved every second of it, didn't you?'

'Cutting edge stuff, you mean? Yes, I did,' he admitted. 'What I like most is being able to make a real difference.'

And now he'd seen that he could make a real difference working in a London hospital just as easily as he could working for a medical aid charity, Ruby hoped that would mean he was more likely to come back to London after his assignment.

'Are you still OK for Friday?' he asked.

She nodded. 'I'm still OK.'

'Good.'

To her shock, he leaned over and kissed her swiftly on the mouth.

'Ellis!' she said.

'Just checking,' he said softly. 'See you later. I want to go and make sure that Helen Perkins has settled in OK.'

And she'd just bet he'd ring in later that evening when he was off duty, just to make sure. It was the kind of man he was. A good man, one who cared deeply.

But the idea of actually dating him still thrilled her and terrified her in equal measures. It could be oh, so good between them. But what if his month's assignment made him realise how much he loved moving on? What if his itchy feet came back? Would he expect her to go with him? She didn't want to leave the London Victoria; she loved her job here. Yet she also knew that Ellis loved his freedom. So one of them would have to make a sacrifice. She didn't want Ellis to have regrets or feel trapped because of her; that wasn't fair. If he came back after his assignment, it had to be because he wanted to be with her, not because he felt any obligation towards her or to Tom. Ruby didn't want Ellis to give up everything for her sake, and she had a feeling that Ellis wouldn't want to make her give up everything for his sake, either.

So maybe she should call off the date. Push the attraction to one side and be sensible. Find someone else—someone who was quite happy to stay in London.

The problem was, the attraction between them was growing stronger by the day. Especially since she'd discovered that it was mutual and that Ellis didn't think of her as just a friend.

Maybe, then, she should just stop thinking. Let it happen. And hope that it was going to work out.

CHAPTER SIX

RUBY WAS GLAD of a super-busy day on Friday so she didn't have time to think about her date with Ellis that evening.

When she got home after her shift, she spent ages working out what to wear.

He'd said high heels and lipstick. Which meant dressing up. She tried on every dress in her wardrobe, and in the end she opted for her favourite little black dress, teamed with high heels.

She'd just finished doing her make-up when the doorbell went. She glanced at her watch. Dead on seven. So it wasn't a neighbour or an unexpected delivery; it was Ellis.

A shiver ran down her spine. She felt ridiculously nervous. There was no reason for it: this was Tom's best friend, a man she'd known for eighteen months and who'd been there for her at her darkest hour. A man she knew she could rely on. So she shouldn't be in the slightest bit edgy about seeing him.

Yet tonight was different—their first date—and it felt as if butterflies were doing a stampede in her stomach.

She opened the door. He looked breathtakingly

handsome in a dark suit, crisp white shirt and silk tie. His smile was slightly shy as he handed her a bouquet of pink roses.

'I thought red ones might be a bit over the top,' he said.

She smiled back at him. 'Thank you, Ellis. They're beautiful. I'll just put them in water. Come in.'

'You look lovely.'

Was it her imagination or did he sound as nervous as she felt?

He bent his head to kiss her cheek, and somehow they ended up clashing heads.

He gave her a rueful look. 'Sorry. I didn't mean to hurt you. I, um...' His voice faded, as if he didn't have a clue what to say to her.

'It's fine,' she reassured him. More than fine, because it told her that he was just as nervous about this as she was.

As she found a vase and put the flowers in water, he leaned against the kitchen worktop. 'I've booked dinner at a place not too far from here. It's a nice evening, so would you like to walk or shall I call a taxi?' Then he glanced at her shoes. 'Ah. Scratch that. I'll call a taxi.'

'Well, you did tell me to wear high heels,' she reminded him with a smile. 'But no, you're right. It's a nice evening, so we can walk. Let me grab a pair of flatter shoes, and I'll change into these ones again when we get there.'

On the way to the restaurant, his hand bumped against hers a couple of times. When she didn't pull away, the next time he caught her fingers in his, and held her hand the rest of the way to the restaurant. It was the lightest, sweetest contact: and it sent a tingle all the way through her.

Though it also put her head in a spin and she didn't have a clue what to say to Ellis. On a normal night, she would have chatted away to him about everything under the sun; but tonight she had to resort to talking about work. 'I hope Helen Perkins is getting on OK.'

'I'm sure she is. It's worrying for parents, though, when something like that happens.' He grimaced. 'I have a feeling this might be one of the rare cases when I suggest an early section, for the baby's sake.'

'I'll back you,' she said. 'Better to be slightly disappointed at not sticking to your birth plan, than to be... Well.' They both knew what the worst-case scenario was in cases of foetal anaemia. The kind of birth that broke her heart because it felt as if all the light in the world had just gone out, and there was nothing you could do to make the loss easier on the parents.

'Yeah,' he said heavily.

When they got to the restaurant, Ruby changed her shoes and handed her bag and coat in at the cloakroom. But, on the way to their table, she tripped. To her horror, she heard a snap and when her foot wobbled she had to grab Ellis's arm to stop herself falling flat on her face. Clearly she'd just broken the heel of her shoe.

'It's just as well we walked so I have another pair of shoes with me,' she said wryly. 'I'll go back to the cloakroom and get them.'

'I'm sorry,' he said.

'It's not your fault. It's me being clumsy. I'm sorry. Don't wait for me. I'll join you at our table.' She slipped off her shoes and walked barefoot back to the cloakroom. So much for dressing up. And those heels had been her favourite pair, glamorous black patent leather which actually managed to be comfortable as well as pretty.

She tried her best to push the disappointment aside and joined Ellis in the restaurant.

Once they'd ordered their food and a bottle of New Zealand Sauvignon Blanc, it was Ellis's turn to be clumsy. He leaned over to top up her glass of wine, and ended up knocking it all over the table. The tablecloth was soaked, and some of the wine landed in her lap.

'Oh, no.' He looked horrified. 'I'm so sorry.'

'It's OK. It'll soon dry off. Anyway, it's white wine so it'll come out in the wash. It's not as if you spilled red wine over a cream lacy dress or something.' She smiled at him. 'I think that makes us one-all in the clumsy stakes tonight.'

'I guess so,' he said wryly, 'but I *am* sorry, Rubes. This was meant to be a nice evening out.'

And so far it had pretty much been a disaster. Anything that could've gone wrong had actually gone wrong. 'It doesn't matter,' she reassured him.

The waiter changed the tablecloth for them and reset the table, but he didn't look pleased about the extra work or try to make conversation with them as he sorted out the table. And then it seemed an endless wait for their meal to arrive; Ruby noticed that people who'd been seated after them had already been served with their food—which was odd, because she and Ellis had both ordered something simple, not something that would take a huge amount of preparation or a long time to cook.

Ellis was clearly thinking the same thing, because he said, 'I wonder if they've forgotten us?'

Though they couldn't ask because there wasn't a waiter to be seen in the dining room.

'I'll go and find someone,' he said. 'Back in a tick.'

He came back looking apologetic. 'It seems our order slipped off the pile. They're sorting us out now.'

'Never mind,' she said brightly.

And when the food finally came, Ruby didn't have the heart to tell Ellis that her chicken was tough and her vegetables were soggy. Though, from the way he picked at his food, she was pretty sure that the meal he'd chosen was just as badly cooked.

'Would you like a dessert and coffee?' he asked politely.

'Thank you, but I think I'll pass,' she said.

'Me, too,' he said. 'I'll get the bill.'

The bill took an excruciatingly long time to come, but eventually Ellis managed to pay for their meal.

This had to be the worst date ever.

So much for sharing a nice dinner out and then going dancing. The food had been awful, the service had been worse, and as Ruby had broken the heel on her shoe he didn't want to suggest dancing and make her feel awkward.

And he didn't have a clue what to say to her as he walked her home. Which was crazy, because he'd always been able to talk to Ruby.

Maybe this was a sign, he thought, that they shouldn't do this. The last thing he wanted to do was to end up hurting her when things went wrong between them, the way his marriage had imploded. She deserved better than that.

'Would you like to come in for coffee?' she asked when they reached her front door.

On a normal evening he would've said yes and spent time chatting to her. Tonight, he just wanted to go home before something else happened to increase the strain between them. 'No, I'd better let you get on,' he said.

'Well, thanks for this evening,' she said with a bright, bright smile.

Ellis knew she was being polite, because it had been truly awful. Even the dates of his teens hadn't been this bad. 'Pleasure,' he said, even though it hadn't been.

He didn't kiss her goodbye, not even on the cheek; he just gave her an awkward smile, waited until she'd let herself in, and left.

And he was still feeling bad by the time he'd walked home. In the end, he gave in and texted her. *I'm so sorry about tonight. It was a total disaster.*

His phone beeped almost immediately with a reply. *Not your fault.*

Wasn't it? The problem with her shoe wasn't his fault—but the restaurant most definitely was. He should've checked the online reviews first, because they would've highlighted that the food was awful and so was the service.

His phone beeped again. *If you were as nervous as I was, I think it all went wrong because we both tried too hard.*

Nervous?

Yeah. He'd been nervous, all right. Worried that he was going to mess everything up. Clearly she'd felt the same. And he'd barely managed a proper conversation with her. They'd ended up talking shop. How pathetic was that? He knew he could talk to Ruby about anything under the sun. They didn't need to rely on awkward conversations about work.

Time to put it right. He picked up the phone and called her.

'Hey, Ellis.'

'Hey, yourself. You're right, Rubes. I was nervous, too. Which is stupid, because we've known each other for so long.'

'I guess.'

'If we'd just gone out together as we normally do—' as friends, though he didn't say it '—we would have laughed it all off. But you're right. Because it was a date, we had all these expectations of what it ought to be like, and I guess we made it difficult for ourselves.'

'Uh-huh.' Her voice was expressionless.

'Maybe,' he said, 'we could try again. But this time we should keep it simple and take the pressure off.'

'What do you have in mind?'

Pretty much what they'd talked about when they'd made those ridiculous lists for that dating site. 'I'm working a late shift tomorrow, but I thought we could have a walk somewhere nice on Sunday morning, if you're off duty—and also depending on the weather, because it's not going to be much fun if it's bucketing down with rain. And then we can find somewhere to grab lunch.'

'That sounds great,' she said. 'What time?'

'Meet you at yours at ten? Oh, and no high heels.'

She laughed. 'Definitely not, if we're going for a walk. OK. See you then.'

Ellis felt a lot better by the time he rang off. And better still when Sunday dawned bright and sunny—a perfect late September morning, with a blue sky and the sun burnishing the bronze, reds and golds of the autumn leaves.

He rang her doorbell and waited for her to answer.

This time when he kissed her cheek, there was no clash of heads, no awkwardness. It felt *right*. He could smell the soft floral scent she wore and his mouth tingled where it touched her skin.

She'd looked gorgeous in high heels and a little black dress on Friday night, but she looked just as gorgeous this morning in faded jeans, a blue silky long-sleeved top that brought out the colour of her eyes, and flat walking shoes. A pocket Venus, Ellis thought, all curves that he wanted to gather closer—but he'd try and take it easy today.

They caught the Tube through to Kew, where Ruby insisted on paying for their tickets to the gardens. 'You bought dinner on Friday, so I'm paying. No arguments.'

'Only on condition that you let me buy you lunch,' he said.

'That's a deal,' she said with a smile.

He enjoyed waking through the gardens with her to the Arboretum, where they explored the treetop walkway. His hand brushed against hers several times and then her fingers curled round his; the light contact made him feel all warm inside. This felt so much more natural than their posh date on Friday night. Maybe, just maybe, they could get this thing to work.

They stopped in one of the cafés for a lunch of hot soup, artisan bread and cheese. It was much simpler than Friday's food, but came with much better service; this time, he relaxed with her and could enjoy her company instead of worrying what would go wrong next.

They wandered through the glasshouses together, hand in hand, then headed back outside to crunch through the fallen leaves. Ellis found a conker fresh out of its shell beneath the chestnut tree and presented it to Ruby with a smile. 'It's the same colour as your hair.'

'Thank you. That's very poetic, Ellis.' She smiled back at him and put the conker safely in her pocket.

That smile undid him. He couldn't resist pulling her into his arms and dipping his head to kiss her. He brushed his lips lightly against hers, once, twice; then she caught his lower lip gently between hers.

Odd how a single kiss could put his head into such a spin.

He wrapped his arms more tightly round her, and her arms were wrapped round his neck, holding him just as tightly. His eyes closed as she let him deepen the kiss, and it felt as if the late afternoon sunshine was filling his soul.

When he broke the kiss, her pupils were huge and there was a slash of colour across her cheekbones. He wanted to tell her how beautiful she looked, but the words felt flat and not enough, so he stole a last kiss and hoped she'd guess what was in his head.

Finally, when the light started to fade, they headed back on the Tube to her flat.

'I'm not ready for today to end just yet,' Ruby said on her doorstep. 'Will you stay for dinner?'

'I'd like that. I can be your sous-chef, if you want.' He knew his way around Ruby's kitchen; he'd cooked quite a few meals there towards the end of Tom's illness, to give Ruby a break and make sure that both she and Tom had something nutritious to eat to keep their strength up.

'That sounds good to me.' She rummaged through the cupboards, found a bottle of white wine and held it so he could see the label. 'I know it's not chilled, but is this OK?'

'More than OK,' he said with a smile. 'And this time I'll try not to knock my glass over.' Funny, it was easy to laugh about their disastrous date now. At the time, he'd been mortified and felt as gauche as a teenager, but he had a feeling that this was going to become a favourite story for both of them in years to come: the night of the Worst Date Ever.

'Is risotto OK with you?' she asked.

'More than OK—I love risotto,' he said.

She poured them both a glass of wine, and Ellis chopped the vegetables while she made the base for the risotto. Working with her in the kitchen felt as natural as working together at the hospital. As if this was meant to be...

They ate at the kitchen table, and it was perfect. The right food, the right company, the right ambience. Especially as Ruby produced posh ice cream for pudding, and even posher shortbread to go with it.

'Today's been really lovely,' she said when they'd finished eating and done the washing up.

'I've enjoyed it, too. I'd better let you get on, though.' He'd taken up the whole of her day already. Any more would be greedy.

'I'm not actually doing a lot—all I plan to do is curl up on the sofa and watch that dance competition show on the television,' she said. 'You're very welcome to stay and join me, if you don't have anything better to do.'

How could he resist?

Especially when they ended up sitting with her on his lap and his arms wrapped round her.

'So which is your favourite kind of dancing, ball-room or Latin?' he asked.

'Ballroom, I think. I love it when the woman is dressed like a princess and they dance a dreamy waltz.' She laughed and sang a snatch of 'Moon River'.

'I didn't know you could sing,' he said, surprised.

'Not that well,' she said. 'I've got a limited vocal range. Tom says—*said*,' she corrected herself, 'that I only manage that one because Audrey Hepburn's vocal range was tiny, too, and "Moon River" was written especially for her to be able to sing it.'

'You remind me a bit of Audrey Hepburn,' Ellis said, tipping his head to one side. 'All pixie haircut and huge eyes. Well, except obviously your eyes are blue.'

Ruby looked pleased. 'She's one of my favourite actresses. I love her films—and Grace Kelly's.'

Ones with happy endings? That was something he couldn't guarantee for her. Not wanting to break the mood, he said nothing and just kept holding her.

The next dance was a waltz—but this time not the dreamy, princessy sort that Ruby had said she liked. It was a dark, edgy and sensual...

'That's amazing choreography.' Ruby fanned herself. 'Oh, to able to dance with someone like that.'

The temptation was too much for him. 'Dance with me?' he asked.

'Now?' She blinked. 'Hang on. Are you telling me that you can dance like *that*?'

'I worked on an assignment for the medical aid charity with an Argentinean doctor,' he said, 'and she taught us all how to tango. And that dance on the TV just now was much more like a tango than a waltz.'

'Ellis, you always manage to surprise me.' She gave

him a slow, sensual smile that made him catch his breath. 'I'd love to.'

'Go and put some high heels on,' he said, 'and I'll push the furniture back a bit to give us some space.'

'I can't believe you're going to tango with me in my living room.' She was all pink and flustered and absolutely adorable, and Ellis ached to kiss her.

By the time she'd come back, wearing high-heeled shoes, he'd moved the furniture to give them more of a dance floor and connected his iPod to the Internet, to find the music the couple on the television had just danced to. He muted the sound of the television, but he left the picture on.

'Ready?' he asked. At her nod, he said, 'Just follow my lead.'

The music was sexy and intense, like the dance itself, and her eyes were so dark they were practically navy.

Ellis loved every second of having her in his arms, leaning close and making her sway with him in the corners.

At the very end, he bent her backwards over his arm. Her throat was bared to him, and he couldn't resist kissing his way along the arch of her throat.

'That,' he said huskily, 'was what Friday was supposed to be.'

He could see the pulse beating at her throat; the dance had clearly affected her just as much as it had affected him.

'Ellis, I...just, wow,' she said, her voice deeper than usual and slightly breathy. 'I had no idea you could do that.'

'We had someone on the team who could play the

guitar really well. He used to play while Sofia taught the rest of us to dance,' he said.

'It never occurred to me that you'd have time off, time to have fun together. I thought when you worked with a medical aid charity, it was intense and full on.'

'It was, but we still managed to find some good times—even in the middle of a disaster zone,' he said. 'And that helped us get through the rougher times at work. The days when our skills just weren't enough.'

'I can understand that,' she said. 'Ellis, can I be greedy and ask if we can do it again?'

He'd really have to resist the urge to carry her off to her bed afterwards. But he'd find the strength, if it meant pleasing her.

He put the music on again, and exaggerated the moves of the dance so their bodies were closer still, this time. Though he resisted kissing her at the end. There was only so much his self-control could take, and kissing her again would definitely make it snap.

'That,' she said softly, 'was amazing. Thank you.' She smiled. 'You're a bit of a dark horse, Ellis Webster.'

'Maybe. Let's watch the rest of the show,' he said, and settled her back on his lap on the sofa.

When the show finished, he kissed her lightly. 'And now I really do have to go. I'm on early shift tomorrow.'

'Thank you for today, Ellis. I really enjoyed it.' She kissed him back. 'Can we, um, do this again?'

'Date or dance?'

'Both,' she said.

He smiled. 'Let's sort out our off-duty tomorrow. And maybe we should make another list, this time of places we want to go.'

'Top of mine would be Hampton Court Maze,' she

said promptly. 'I've never, ever been there. Considering how long I've lived in London, that's atrocious.'

'Then we'll do that, the next day we both have off,' Ellis said.

'Provided it isn't raining,' she said with a grin. 'I have a feeling that the maze won't be as much fun if we get drenched through.'

'Agreed.' He kissed her again. 'Sleep well. And I'll see you at work tomorrow.'

CHAPTER SEVEN

RUBY LAY CURLED on the sofa with a midwifery journal, not really concentrating on the articles because she was still thinking about Ellis.

She'd had no idea that he could even dance, let alone dance well. He'd really made her pulse speed up when he'd twirled her round and bent her back over his arm like that. And when he'd kissed her throat…She shivered at the memory. Ellis Webster was the first man since Tom who'd made her feel that thrill of attraction, and it threw her.

She turned the page, scanned the headline of the article and did a double-take.

By a strange coincidence, this article might just have a bearing on the court case Ellis was dealing with. She read through the whole thing more carefully and decided that yes, it was definitely relevant and Ellis needed to see this. She went in search of the sticky notes she kept in her kitchen drawer, so she could mark the first page of the article for ease of reference.

The next morning, Ruby caught Ellis during his break. 'Do you have a moment?' she asked.

'Sure. What's the problem?'

'It's a solution, I hope,' she said. 'You know the DNA

tests said that Grace Edwards wasn't the genetic mother of her own baby?'

'Yes.'

'Did you have a word with Theo or the genetics team about it?'

'I haven't managed to get hold of the genetics team, yet,' he said, 'but I did talk to Theo, and he's scratching his head about it as much as I am. Why?'

'Because I might just have a theory. I was reading a midwifery journal last night and there was a case study from America that reminded me of Grace Edwards's situation. I brought it in with me so you could read it. Hang on a sec and I'll get it from my locker.' She fetched the journal and handed it to him. 'I've marked the first page of the article with a sticky note at the top. I might be misreading things, but it also might be that Grace Edwards has the same biological quirk as the woman in the case study—that she's a chimera, so she has two sets of DNA in her body instead of the usual single set.'

Ellis skimmed swiftly through it and raised his eyebrows. 'You know, I think you could be right, Rubes. So maybe Grace started life as a twin, with two separate eggs fertilised by two different sperm. Then, at some point very early in the pregnancy, the eggs fused together and Grace absorbed her twin.'

'So Grace has two sets of DNA and she's also her own twin.'

'Yup.' Ellis blew out a breath. 'Which is pretty mind-blowing.'

'According to that article, having two sets of DNA means that your skin might not have the same DNA as say your heart or your lungs,' Ruby said.

'So it's possible that the cells in Grace's ovaries

originally belonged to her twin and not to her. And in that case it means that her twin is the biological mum of the baby,' Ellis said thoughtfully.

Ruby nodded. 'And that might be why Grace's DNA isn't showing as being the same as that of her baby. It was awful for the poor American mum in the article. She had to have someone appointed by the court to be there at the birth of her next child to witness that she gave birth to the baby. And then, when they did the genetic tests, there was no genetic link between the mum and the baby—even though the court witness was able to say that she definitely gave birth to the baby. Then they did some more tests on cells from different organs in the mum's body, and discovered a match for their DNA.'

'In the case of a chimera, you can't predict which cells will have which twin's DNA. So, as you said earlier, you could have a case where someone has skin and blood cells from one twin and organ cells from another,' Ellis said thoughtfully. 'And the only way to find out is to test several different sorts of cells for DNA to see if they match. Rubes, you're a genius.'

'Hardly,' she said. 'I just happened to see a case study in a journal.'

'But you made the connection,' he pointed out. 'At least now I can give the court a professional opinion, and Theo will back me up so we can suggest they do further DNA tests. Can I borrow this journal for a while?'

'Of course you can.' She smiled at him. 'I'll let you get on.'

'Just a sec. When are you next off duty?'

'Thursday.'

'Me, too. How about going to Hampton Court, if it's not bucketing down with rain?'

'Sounds good to me,' she said.

'It's a date,' he said softly, and Ruby felt warm all over.

Wednesday was a stickier day. As soon as Ruby spoke to the woman who'd come in to the antenatal walk-in clinic, she knew this was a case she really didn't want Ellis to deal with—it was something that would bring back difficult memories for him.

'I just can't keep anything down,' Mrs Bywater said. 'I've read all the books and I've done everything they say I should do about morning sickness. I don't cook anything, I have cold foods rather than hot foods and I stick to super-boring bland things that don't smell.' She grimaced. 'But the problem is, *everything* smells. My mum said I ought to come in and see you because this isn't normal and I've been like this for a month. It's not morning sickness—it's morning, afternoon and night, and I'm losing weight when I'm meant to be putting it on.'

'I think you have something called hyperemesis gravidarum. It's a severe form of morning sickness which affects about one in a hundred women,' Ruby explained. 'It can run in the family. Do you know if your mum ever had it, or do you have a sister who's had it?'

'Just a brother,' Mrs Bywater said. 'I don't think Mum was sick like this when she was pregnant, but I do know she had postnatal depression.' She gave Ruby a wry smile. 'I guess I've got that to look forward to as well.'

'Not necessarily, though we will keep an eye on you

and make sure you get plenty of support.' Ruby poured her patient a glass of cold water. 'Sip this slowly,' she said. 'From the urine sample you gave me, I think you're quite dehydrated and I want to admit you to the ward— we'll need to take blood samples and give you some fluid through a needle into your veins.'

'And then I'll stop being sick?' Mrs Bywater asked.

'You're twelve weeks at the moment,' Ruby said, looking at her notes. 'I hate to tell you this, but often hyperemesis lasts until twenty weeks, and some people find that it lasts a bit longer than that.'

'No.' Mrs Bywater gave a sharp intake of breath. 'I don't think I can cope with that. I just feel so *ill* all the time. And for it to go on for months and months…' She shuddered.

'There are some things you can do,' Ruby said. 'Keep a log of what you eat and when you're ill, so you can see if there's a pattern about timing or types of food that you find difficult. Eating little and often is better than having big meals, and when you do manage to eat something you need to sit upright for a while afterwards, to reduce the likelihood of getting gastric reflux.'

'And don't clean my teeth straight after eating, take lots of small sips of cold water or suck on an ice cube, and try and get as much fresh air as possible,' Mrs Bywater said.

Ruby smiled at her. 'You've definitely been reading up. That's all really good advice. I'm going to admit you, at least for today and maybe tomorrow as well, and we'll give you some fluids to hydrate you and re-plenish your electrolyte levels. And then you can get some proper rest.'

She'd hoped to catch one of the other obstetricians

when she went up to the ward, but Ellis would have to be the first one she saw.

'I think,' she said carefully, 'maybe you're not the right doctor for this particular mum and I need one of the others instead.'

'Why?' he asked.

She lowered her voice. 'Because this particular mum has hyperemesis.'

Hyperemesis gravidarum. The condition that hadn't been treated properly and had led to his sister's death. 'No. Actually, I'm *exactly* the right person to treat her,' Ellis said firmly. Because then he could make quite sure that what had happened to Sally wouldn't happen to this particular mum.

'Ellis, are you sure you want to do this?' Ruby rested her hand on his arm.

He nodded. 'I know you mean well, and thank you for thinking about me. But I need to do this.'

'If you're sure.' She still wasn't sure about this. At all. Surely treating a patient with this condition would rip open old scars?

'I'm very sure,' he said softly.

And she knew he would be totally professional—he always was. Just at what cost to his heart? Pushing away her misgivings, Ruby took him over to the side room and introduced him to Mrs Bywater. 'Dr Webster's very experienced,' she said, 'and he'll be able to help you.'

'Thank you. I...Excuse me!' Mrs Bywater clapped a hand over her mouth, clearly just about to be sick.

Ruby swiftly handed her a kidney bowl. 'Here. It's fine.'

When Mrs Bywater had finished being sick, Ruby

took the bowl away, first making sure there was a clean one to hand if she needed it.

'Poor you,' Ellis said sympathetically. 'Have a sip of water to make your mouth feel a bit better.'

'Nurse Fisher said I might be like this until twenty weeks—or even later,' Mrs Bywater said miserably.

'Unfortunately she's right, but there are a number of things we can do to help,' he said gently. 'Firstly we need to give you some fluids to hydrate you and re-plenish your electrolyte levels. I'm going to use some-thing called Ringer's solution, because it gives you the extra levels of calcium and potassium. Before we start, though, we're going to check the levels of minerals in your blood so we can make sure we balance everything out for you.'

If the doctor who'd treated Sally had thought to do that before hydrating her, and given her thiamine, she wouldn't have ended up developing the complication of Wernicke's encephalopathy...

Ellis pushed the thought away and concentrated on his patient. 'And you need some rest,' he said. 'I'm guessing that you're not sleeping so well.'

'I'm even sick in the night,' she said. 'And my ribs hurt from being sick all the time. I was even spitting up blood this morning—that's what scared me into com-ing to the walk-in clinic.'

'Being sick puts a bit of strain in the small blood ves-sels of your throat,' Ellis said, 'and it causes them to rupture, so that's why you've seen blood. But it's hon-estly nothing to worry about.' He took the blood sample swiftly. 'We can also give you some medication to help with the sickness.'

Mrs Bywater looked anxious. 'But doesn't that cause problems for baby if I take medication?'

'Anti-sickness drugs did cause developmental issues in babies years and years ago—in the years before you were born,' he said, 'but I'm glad to be able to reassure you that the modern drugs don't affect the baby at all. And the medication will make you feel a lot better— it'll help you to function normally again.'

'All I want to do is feel normal again,' Mrs Bywater said feelingly. 'I don't think I'm ever going to have another baby if pregnancy's always going to make me feel like this!'

'I'm afraid that women who have hyperemesis are more likely to have it in future pregnancies,' he said. 'It just means you'll need to plan ahead to make sure you get the right support and help next time.'

She shook her head. 'There's definitely not going to be a next time. I can't cope with this for a second time.'

'Ruby will finish booking you in,' he said, 'and then as soon as your blood results are back I'll know what to put in the drip. And I promise you, in the next few hours you're going to feel an awful lot better.'

'Thank you,' she said. 'You've been so kind.'

'That's what I'm here for,' he said. 'And if you're worried about anything at all, no matter how little or silly you think the question might be, just ask me or Ruby. Or you can ask any of the team on the ward, because they're all really nice. And we'll make sure you're feeling better as soon as possible.'

Once the blood results were back, Ellis checked the additions to the Ringer's solution with Ruby. 'Given that she's dehydrated, I think we need to warm the area with compresses before we put a needle in, and warm the first litre of fluid so it doesn't come as a shock to her.'

'Good idea,' Ruby said.

He went over to Mrs Bywater and explained what they were going to do.

'Why do you have to put a warm compress on my hand?' she asked.

'It makes your veins dilate a little bit so it's easier for me to put the needle in,' Ruby explained, doing precisely that. 'And it's easier for you, too.'

'Thank you,' Mrs Bywater said.

'That's what we're here for,' Ellis said with a smile. 'I'm going to get you rehydrated, then we'll give you some anti-sickness medication and you can get some well-earned rest.'

After her shift, Ruby headed for Ellis's office where she could see him catching up with paperwork. She rapped lightly on the door. 'Hey.'

He looked up. 'Hey, yourself.'

'I'm taking you for ice cream,' she said.

'Why?'

'Because ice cream always makes things better.'

'I'm fine,' he said.

She put her hands on her hips and stared at him. She knew he wasn't fine. His grey eyes had gone all haunted, and she had a pretty good idea why. Just as she'd suspected, Mrs Bywater's case had brought back all the bad memories for him. He'd helped the patient, but at what cost to himself?

Ellis had been there for her in her darkest days; and she wanted to be there for him, on one of his own dark days.

'OK. You're right,' he admitted at last. 'Give me twenty minutes to finish the paperwork?'

'Fifteen. And no more than that.' She didn't want to give him time to brood. Time to hurt.

He followed her instructions to the letter and they went to a café just round the corner. Ruby bought them both a sundae.

'Was how I felt that obvious?' Ellis asked.

'No, not at all. You were totally professional. I only worked it out because I have privileged information,' she said.

'I guess.' Ellis ate his ice cream in silence, and Ruby let him because she knew it was pointless pushing him until he was ready to talk.

Finally he put his spoon into the cone. 'They thought Sally just had some kind of bug,' he said. 'There had been a virus doing the rounds making people throw up, and she'd had something like it a month or so before. Nobody even considered Sally might be pregnant. She was on the Pill. She took it properly and she wasn't careless; she didn't miss a dose.'

But being sick meant that the medication was less effective, Ruby knew. Maybe Sally hadn't realised that she needed to use extra protection for the next fortnight to make sure she didn't accidentally fall pregnant.

'I don't think anyone out there realised that what she was suffering from was an extreme form of morning sickness.' A muscle twitched in his cheek. 'Unless you've read up on it or you work in the area, you wouldn't know that hyperemesis can start as early as four weeks of pregnancy—maybe even before you realise that you're pregnant. So I get why everyone assumed it was just a bug again.' He blew out a breath.

'They called the medic to see her. He knew she'd been vomiting a lot, so he assumed that she needed rehydrating and gave her IV fluids.' He paused. 'Without checking her thiamine levels first.'

Ruby had a nasty feeling she knew what was coming next, because prolonged vomiting depleted the body's thiamine levels. Rehydration with a solution containing dextrose would deplete the thiamine levels even further, leading to more problems. 'And she developed Wernicke's encephalopathy?' she asked.

He nodded. 'She had visual disturbances and an unsteady gait, and she was disoriented. The classic triad symptoms, in hindsight—but everyone assumed it was just the virus making her throw up all the time that had knocked her for six and made her wobbly on her feet.' He dragged in a breath. 'She ended up with DIC.'

Ruby knew that disseminated intravascular coagulation was where the blood didn't clot properly, and if it wasn't treated the patient could go into shock or even organ failure.

'She went into organ failure,' Ellis continued softly. 'She collapsed and she never regained consciousness.'

'You do know that's not going to happen to *your* patient, don't you?' she asked.

He nodded. 'I've never had any patients out in the field with it, so I haven't lost anyone there.'

She reached out and held his hand. 'So basically when you're working for the aid charity, you're trying to stop what happened to your sister happening to anyone else.'

'That or any other condition.' He paused. 'I guess I know I can't save everyone.'

'Nobody can, no matter how good a medic they are.

Sometimes you just can't save someone, because the circumstances mean that nobody could save them. All you can do is your best, and that has to be good enough because you can't humanly do any more,' Ruby said softly.

'I know.'

Intellectually, maybe, but she could tell he didn't feel it in his heart. 'Obviously I didn't know your sister, but I bet she's looking down on you right now, and I bet she's so proud of the man you've become.'

'I hope so.' He squeezed her hand. 'I didn't mean to go all brooding on you, Rubes. Sorry.'

'Don't apologise. It must be hard when you come across the same condition that took your sister. That's why I didn't want you to see Mrs Bywater.'

'I know, but I'm glad I did—because I feel I've made a difference.'

'Even though it's ripped the top off your scars?' she asked.

He nodded. 'It's harder knowing that if Sally had been given the right treatment she would've survived— but I guess that's true of a lot of my patients. I know I can make a difference. And that's one of the reasons why I love doing what I do. I can stop other families falling apart the way mine has.'

'Tom said your parents closed off afterwards.'

He sighed. 'Now I'm older, I can understand why. They're protecting themselves from more hurt.'

'It must've been hard on you and your brothers, though. Especially as you were so young.'

'They were sixteen and fourteen, and I was twelve.' He lifted a shoulder in a half-shrug. 'We got by. We had each other.'

'I'm glad you're close to them.'

He wrinkled his nose. 'I was. But we fell out a bit after I graduated. They were pretty upset about me working abroad, and they still haven't really got used to it, even after all these years. They think I'm putting myself in danger.'

'That's because you *are* putting yourself in danger— whether you're working in a war zone or in an area hit by flood, earthquake or whatever,' she pointed out.

'I'm still here.' He shrugged it off. 'Anyway, Tom's parents have been like second parents to me. They were brilliant when it all happened.'

'I'm glad—and I'm glad they still have you.'

'And they have you,' he said softly. 'And now, can we please change the subject, Rubes?'

'Sure.' Though Ruby couldn't stop thinking about it for the rest of the evening. The way he'd talked, it sounded as if he wanted to be back at the medical aid charity and he might not want to come back after his assignment. So she'd better be sure not to lose her heart to him completely...

Thursday turned out to be a perfect autumn day, with blue skies and a crispness to the air. Ellis and Ruby caught the train down to Hampton Court.

'What a gorgeous building,' she said as they got their first view of the house.

'Shall we walk round the gardens first, in case the weather changes?'

'Good idea—and I really want to see the maze,' she said.

Funny, as a child, she'd been faintly bored when her parents took her to stately homes, always more keen on spending time in the adventure playground than looking at the plants. Now, she loved strolling through the gardens, enjoying the skill of the designer in highlighting colours and shapes. The autumn colours in the old tilting yard were particularly gorgeous, and she loved the formality of the Privy Gardens with its geometric designs and its statues, and seeing the fountains and the swans on the lake. Walking hand in hand with Ellis, Ruby felt a burst of happiness that had been missing from her life for a long while. And she intended to enjoy every second of it.

'So this is the oldest hedge maze in the world,' she said as she read the information board at the entrance to the maze.

'Apparently it takes twenty minutes to get to the centre.' Ellis smiled at her. 'Are you ready for this?'

'I'm ready,' she said, smiling back.

They took several wrong turns among the yew hedges, and Ellis kissed her in every dead end. Although it took rather longer than twenty minutes to reach the centre, Ruby didn't care; today was all about having fun and enjoying the moment.

'I love all the sound effects they've put in to the maze,' she said. 'When you think you can hear children laughing, or the swish of skirts—it's almost like hearing the ghosts of the past, little glimpses in time of what it might have been like here.'

Ellis looked at her. 'I can just imagine you in Tudor dress. With your colouring, I think you'd have looked fabulous in a rich blue velvet. Like your eyes.'

She stole a kiss. 'Very poetic, Dr Webster. And I can see you in a cloak and a velvet hat. A royal purple one.'

He started to sing 'I'm Henry the Eighth, I am', and she groaned.

'I think I might be creating a monster, here.'

He just laughed. 'Let's go and have a look round the house.'

When they got to the house itself, they discovered that you could actually borrow a red velvet cape.

'I think we ought to do this,' Ruby said with a smile.

'Absolutely,' he agreed.

The rich red velvet suited his colouring, and she could imagine him as a courtier in Tudor times. As tall, as strong and as handsome as the young King Henry VIII himself.

She loved the chapel with its rich blue and gold ceiling, and the tapestried hall where Shakespeare's men had once played. But the bit that really caught her attention was the chocolate kitchen.

'Funny, I always associate Henry VIII with Hampton Court. I never really think about the later kings and queens who lived here,' she said. 'But having a special chocolate kitchen—why on earth would they keep it separate from the other kitchens?'

'This was built for William and Mary,' the guide told them. 'Chocolate was a very expensive drink back then, so it was reserved for the aristocracy. The chocolate maker was one of the highest ranking servants in the palace. He had his own bedroom, which was huge luxury back then, plus he was one of the few people who was actually allowed to serve the king in his private apartments.'

'So was the chocolate they drank very different to what we have today?' Ruby asked.

'They made it all by hand. They roasted the cocoa beans on the fireplace over there—' the guide indicated the area '—and then the kitchen boy took off the shells. They put the cocoa nibs on a heated stone slab and crushed them into a paste with a stone roller, then put the paste into moulds to set into a cake.' He showed them the little cakes of chocolate in cases of waxed paper.

'Was that for eating?' Ellis asked.

'No, bar chocolate wasn't invented until almost Victorian times. The chocolate back then was just for drinking,' the guide explained. 'They'd mix one of these chocolate cakes with water, wine or milk in a pan, then add sugar and spices—the most popular ones were vanilla or chilli. And the king would have hot chocolate for breakfast along with some sweetmeats.' He smiled at them. 'Actually, the palace kitchens have already made the sweetmeats, and we're going to have a demonstration and make drinking chocolate the old-fashioned way for visitors to taste, if you'd like to come back and see us this afternoon. The demonstrations are on the hour, every hour.'

'That sounds great. Thank you,' Ruby said with a smile.

'That's the sort of thing I can imagine you and Tina doing,' Ellis said when they'd moved on to let the guide talk to other visitors. 'Having hot chocolate and sweetmeats for breakfast.'

Ruby laughed. 'I'll have you know that cake for breakfast is one of life's great pleasures.'

'I was right, you are a hedonist,' Ellis teased.

'You bet.' She smiled back at him. 'Life's for living, Ellis.'

'Yes. It is.' His hand tightened round hers.

They continued looking round the house, and went back to the kitchens later in the afternoon for the choc-

olate demonstration. Ruby preferred the vanilla chocolate, but Ellis preferred the chilli.

'A bit like the Spanish explorers who discovered
chocolate,' she said. 'I can see you as one of them. A
Conquistador.'

And that was where Ellis really fitted: not in the city,
but in a wilder place. So it would be wise not to lose
her heart to him, because one day his itchy feet would
take him back to where he belonged. He'd teased her
about being a hedonist; but she'd never been able to
see the attraction of having a holiday in a tent, sleeping on the ground and without running water. In some
respects, they were total opposites and this was never
going to work out.

But for now, she was going to live in the moment and
just enjoy this thing blossoming between them.

On Sunday afternoon, Ruby went shopping with her
best friend. Tina was going to be godmother to her sister's baby and needed a suitable outfit, and Ruby had
promised to go help her find something.

'It's a shame it didn't work out with Roger,' Tina
said, referring to her new colleague.

'He's a nice guy,' Ruby said. 'But I'm not sure he's
ready for dating again yet. I don't think he's over his
divorce, poor man.'

'So what about you? Did you sign up with that online dating agency?'

'Not yet.'

Tina gave her a narrow look. 'Is there something
you're not telling me?'

Yes, Ruby thought, but it was too early to talk about
it. There was definite attraction between her and Ellis,

but would he ever be ready to settle down? She said with a smile, 'Why don't you try this dress on? I think it'll really suit your colouring.'

'You're trying to distract me. So there *is* something,' Tina said. 'OK. You can spill the beans now, or I'll interrogate you over coffee and you can spill the beans then.'

'That's not exactly a choice, Tina.'

'I'm your best friend, Rubes. Who else are you going to tell?'

'True. All right. I'm seeing someone,' Ruby admitted, 'but it's early days.'

'Who?'

'We both want to keep it quiet,' Ruby warned.

Tina flapped a dismissive hand. 'You know perfectly well I'm not going to tell anyone. Who is it, Rubes?'

'Ellis.'

'Ellis? You mean Ellis Webster?' Tina looked surprised.

'What's wrong with Ellis?' Ruby bit her lip. 'Is it because he's Tom's best friend, so it's not appropriate?' It was something that had worried her—how people would react to their relationship.

'No, it's not that.'

'Why, then?'

'It's because Tom always said that Ellis would never settle down—and he's been back in England for a year and a half or so,' Tina said. 'And isn't he planning to go back to the medical aid charity?'

'He's booked to go out with them for a month in a few weeks' time, yes. But that doesn't mean he'll stay out there. If Billie decides to take a career break, then Theo might offer Ellis the job,' Ruby said.

'And is Ellis ready to settle down in England?'

That was something Ruby wasn't sure about. And, if not, would Ellis feel trapped by her? 'I don't know,' she admitted.

'That's what worries me,' Tina said gently, giving her a hug. 'That he still has itchy feet, and you'll lose him to his job and end up hurt.'

'Or we might both decide we're best off just being friends.'

'Maybe.' Tina paused. 'What do you really want, Ruby?'

'To keep seeing Ellis, and for him to settle here. I've felt like this about him for a while,' Ruby admitted. 'I was going to sign up for that dating agency, but I asked him to give me a male point of view on my list of what I wanted in a date. It turned out that he ticked every single one of the boxes.' She paused. 'And I teased him into doing the same—and I ticked all his boxes, too. So we, um, thought we'd give it a try.'

'Then I hope, for both your sakes, that it works out,' Tina said, giving her another hug. 'As long as he makes you happy. But if he ever hurts you…'

'He won't. Not intentionally,' Ruby said.

'Just don't fall for him too hard,' Tina said softly. 'He's a nice guy, but he has itchy feet—and you don't.'

'As I said, it's early days,' Ruby said lightly. 'Now, are you going to try on this dress?'

Tina let her off the hook and went to try on the dress. But it left Ruby wondering. Was Tina right? Should she start backing off from Ellis? Was she hoping for too much? Or was it just way too early even to be thinking about the future and she should just enjoy the moment?

CHAPTER EIGHT

LATER IN THE WEEK, Helen Perkins was scheduled for another intra-uterine blood transfusion for the baby. Ellis made sure that she was booked in with him, and Ruby made sure that she was there to support Helen and Joe.

Ruby had heard nightmare stories from other nursing colleagues about arrogant doctors with non-existent people skills who never listened to the patients because they always thought they knew best, and seemed to forget that they were dealing with people rather than a textbook case. But, apart from the fact that Theo wouldn't let anyone like that work on his ward, since Ruby had been working with Ellis she'd found that he was a natural with patients.

She liked the way he chatted to the Perkinses, and explained what he was doing at each step and answered every question they had without making them feel stupid. And she really liked the way he stayed for a little while after the procedure rather than rushing off to his next patient, making sure that Helen and Joe weren't worried about anything. Dr Ellis Webster was definitely a good man. And she couldn't quite get her head round the fact that they were actually dating. They were still keeping their relationship to themselves, but Ruby was beginning to believe that she'd been granted a second chance at happiness, with a man who could make her as happy as Tom had.

'Next time you come in for the baby's transfusion,' Ellis said to Helen Perkins, 'you'll probably be the one to tell me what happens next.'

'An overnight stay in the ward, and I have to tell you straight away if I have any pain or fever. And I mustn't worry if I can't feel the baby moving for the next couple of hours, because the sedative takes a little time to wear off,' she said with a smile.

He smiled back. 'I stand corrected—I think you're already my star pupil.' He moved the screen so the Perkinses could see the baby's heart beating and be reassured that all was well. 'One snoozing baby,' he said. 'So everything's just as we expected.'

'Thank you, Dr Webster.' Joe Perkins shook his hand. 'We really appreciate this.'

'I know, but it's my job and I don't want any of my new parents to worry,' Ellis told him. 'I'd much rather you asked me a gazillion questions than went away worrying.'

What if I asked you questions? Ruby thought. Would you answer them as honestly as you answer your patients? Or would it scare you away? But she kept her counsel and accompanied the Perkinses up to the ward.

The following Monday morning, Theo called Ellis into his office.

'Billie wants to come back part-time in a month and a half, as a job share,' he said. 'I'm currently arguing budgets with the suits. At the moment, they're saying no, but I'm looking at my figures again to prove that we need another full-time obstetrician on the team and I'm pretty sure I can make a solid case. I know you're going back to the medical aid charity for a month's assignment, but I'm hoping you're planning to come back afterwards and I'd like to interview you for the job.' He smiled. 'It's a formality, really, simply because I have to advertise the position, but I want to offer you the job. Bottom line, Ellis, you're a good fit in the team. You've got the right attitude towards our patients, you've got much wider experience than anyone else at your level, and you're really good at teaching the younger staff and giving them confidence. I'd like you here for good.'

'Thank you,' Ellis said, inclining his head in acknowledgement of the compliments. 'But right now I don't actually know what I'll be doing in a month's time, and it wouldn't be fair to leave you hanging on.' Would the lure of his former job make him want to stay on for another month? Or would he come back to London to be with Ruby? Would it all work out between them? It was still too early to tell—and he didn't want to make the same mistake he'd made with Natalia, rushing into the relationship only to discover that they wanted different things. Yes, he'd known Ruby for an awful lot longer—but until a couple of weeks ago their relationship had been strictly platonic.

Was Ruby the one who'd make him want to settle?

And what if he let her down, the way he felt he'd let Natalia down?

'Think about it,' Theo said. 'Don't say yes or no right now. Think about what you really want.'

'Thank you.'

'For what it's worth, I think you and Ruby are good together.'

Ellis stared at his boss in shock. Theo *knew*?

The question must have been written all over his face, because Theo said softly, 'She hasn't said anything to me, and nobody's gossiping about you. Don't worry, you're not the hot topic on the hospital grapevine.'

'So how on earth do you…?' Ellis was still too flabbergasted to frame the question properly.

Theo smiled. 'Because I've been there myself, when I started dating Maddie. And I definitely needed a good shaking at one point. Just make sure that doesn't happen to you.' His smile faded. 'And if you do decide to accept the job offer and stay here, remember that nothing, but *nothing*, disrupts my team here.'

'Agreed,' Ellis said. 'Patients are always my priority at work. And I'm professional enough to keep my private life very separate from my job.'

'Good.' Theo shook his hand again. 'We'll leave it open for now, but come and see me when you're ready to make a decision. I want you to say yes to the interview, if nothing else. But when I offer you the job—because I really can't see that any other candidate will be better than you—I also want you to be absolutely sure about it, OK?'

'OK.'

Ellis caught Ruby on her break. 'Are you busy after work?'

'Nothing I can't move. Why?'

'I could do with bouncing some ideas off someone.'

'I'm your woman,' she said immediately.

Yes, I rather think you are, he thought. But does that

scare you as much as it scares me? 'Let's do it over dinner. Is tapas OK with you?'

'Tapas would be lovely.' She smiled at him. 'See you
after our shift, then.'

After work, Ruby and Ellis went to a small Spanish
bar in the middle of London. She settled back in her
seat. 'This place is very nice. I haven't been here before,' she said.

'I looked it up online first, and it has good reviews.'
He spread his hands. 'Let's just say I learned from that
particular mistake.'

'The Date of Disastrous Proportions. Me, too.' She
smiled back at him. 'This is a fabulous menu, Ellis.
Shall we order a pile of dishes to share?'

'You're welcome to order meat if you want to,' he
said. 'You don't have to go vegetarian for my sake.'

'I'm absolutely fine with veggie food. Though I must
admit the Serrano ham croquettes do look nice,' she
said wistfully, 'if you don't mind me ordering them?'

'No, that's fine.'

They ordered a mixture of dishes—*patatas bravas*,
Manchego cheese and quince paste, Manzanilla olives,
tomatoes, bread, a bowl of garlicky wilted spinach, the
Serrano ham croquettes that had caught Ruby's eye, and
a traditional Spanish omelette, together with a bottle
of good Rioja.

Ruby had a feeling that Ellis was brooding about
something. And it would be better to face it sooner
rather than later. 'So what did you want to talk about?'
she asked.

'Theo asked me to see him today.' He grimaced.

'Maybe I should shut up now, before I break a confidence.'

'You know I won't say anything to anyone,' Ruby said. 'And it's pretty obvious why Theo would want to talk to you, given that you're Billie's locum and her maternity leave ends soon. So I assume she's coming back?'

'Part-time,' Ellis confirmed.

She bit her lip. 'So where does that leave you?'

'Full-time until she's back. Then I'm doing my month's assignment with the charity.' He paused. 'Theo's looking to recruit another full-time registrar and he wants me to apply for the interview. He says it's a formality but he has to advertise the job externally as well.'

'I get that.' But this was a crunch moment, Ruby thought. Would Ellis apply for the job at the London Victoria, or would he look for a post in a different London hospital—or would he want to stay with the medical aid charity?

Ruby wanted him to stay—but she wanted him to stay because *he* wanted to stay. She didn't want him to feel trapped.

Face it, she told herself. Be brave. Ask him straight out. 'I know you came back to London for Tom's sake, and you've stayed here since he died because he asked you to keep an eye out for me—but what do you really want, Ellis?'

Everything.

Though Ellis was pretty sure he couldn't have Ruby in his life and go back to the medical aid charity. He knew she loved her job here and she was happy in London, so he couldn't ask her to leave it all behind and go travelling the world with him, never staying more than a few weeks in one place.

He really did miss the travelling and the camaraderie of the medical aid charity team, even though he liked his colleagues at the London Victoria very much. There was that extra edge when he worked abroad, where every second was vital.

An old pop song flickered through his head, asking him if he should stay or if he should go.

It was going to be a hard choice. Either way, he was going to have to make a sacrifice. Stay here in London and be with Ruby and miss his old life; or go back to his old life abroad and miss Ruby.

'This thing between us,' he said. 'It's very new.'

'Uh-huh.'

Her face was absolutely expressionless. He had no idea what she was thinking, though he had a feeling that she was trying not to put any pressure on him. Which made him feel horrendously selfish, because Ruby was clearly trying to put him first. He was trying to do the same for her. Were they working at cross-purposes, here? Or could they both have everything they wanted?

The only way to find out was to ask.

'The medical aid charity isn't just for doctors, you know,' he said. 'They recruit nurses, too. Midwives.' He paused. 'If I went back permanently, would you consider going out with me and working for them?'

Her expression changed, then, to one of total surprise. She clearly hadn't expected that to be an option.

Was that a good or a bad thing?

Panicking, he said, 'Ruby, you don't have to answer straight away. I pretty much sprung that on you.'

'Uh-huh.'

And he was all at sea again, not being able to guess how she felt. Though he could see that she looked wary. And he knew it was a huge decision, not one she could make quickly or lightly. 'Take your time,' he said. 'Just think about it in the back of your head, and we'll talk about it again when you're ready.'

'OK.'

He changed the topic of conversation to something light, and when their food arrived they were able to distract themselves with that. Especially when Ruby ordered churros with a cinnamon-spiced chocolate sauce for them to share, and he had to stop himself leaning over and kissing a tiny smear of chocolate from the corner of her mouth.

'I know the coffee here is probably going to be as excellent as the food,' he said, 'but would you like to have coffee back at my place?'

'Good idea,' she said. 'It'll be easier to talk.'

In other words, discussing something in private.

Adrenalin trickled down his spine. Did that mean she'd made a decision about what he'd asked her? Would she go with him, or would she stay?

He paid the bill and they caught the Tube back to his flat. He made them both a coffee and brought out a packet of buttery biscuit curls.

'Now these are nice,' she said with a smile. 'I'm impressed, Dr Webster.'

'Good.' But even the sugar rush couldn't distract him. He needed to know. Now. 'Have you had enough time to think about what I said?' he asked softly.

'Yes.' She took a deep breath. 'I know it's a really worthy thing to do, and I feel horribly selfish about saying this, but working for a medical aid charity really isn't for me, Ellis. I love my job here and I want to stay relatively near to my family and Tom's. Manchester's only a couple of hours away from London on the train, and so is Suffolk. If I work abroad, I won't get to see any of them very often. I might not even be working in a place where I can get a phone signal to talk to them.'

And he knew that Ruby was emotionally close to her family and Tom's. Of course she wouldn't want to be physically far away from them. It was unfair of him to ask her to change that for his sake.

She reached over to squeeze his hand. 'But I also care enough about you to let you go, if you want to go back. I'm never going to hold you back or trap you.'

But it meant he had a choice to make. Go back to working abroad without Ruby: or stay in London and be with Ruby. He couldn't have both.

'What if I apply for the job in our department, come back to London after my assignment and—provided that Theo offers it to me, because he might find a better candidate—I accept the job?' he asked softly. 'Do we take our relationship to the next stage?'

'Is that what you want?'

'To take our relationship to the next stage?' His fingers tightened round hers. 'Yes.'

'But?'

Typical Ruby, picking up what he wasn't saying. 'But the last time I got married, it all went so wrong. And it kind of scares me. If I give up my job abroad, stay here and try to make a go of it with you, and it all goes wrong...' He blew out a breath. 'I don't want to hurt you.'

'I don't want to hurt you, either,' she said. 'So what happened? Why did you split up? I mean—don't get me wrong, I'm not prying, but maybe if you look at what happened you can learn from your mistakes or something?'

'Maybe.' He sighed. 'I met Natalia when we were both working at the medical aid charity. It was one of those *coup de foudre* moments—you know, you meet someone for the very first time and you feel as if you've been struck by lightning. You just click instantly.'

She nodded.

'We were both assigned to a team helping a community after bad flooding. We had a mad affair. And then one day she was caught in a flash flood. Luckily they managed to rescue her. But she could've drowned. She was the first person I've ever been scared of losing—and I guess I acted on that fear instead of thinking it through and letting myself calm down and be logical about things.' He gave her a rueful smile. 'You always say I'm practical and sensible. I wasn't, then. I asked her to marry me, even though we'd barely known each other for a month, and she said yes. And, two weeks later, the paperwork was all sorted and we got married.' He grimaced. 'In a rush. And that's why Tom wasn't my best man. There wasn't enough time to tell him I was getting married and get him a flight out there.' He looked away. 'And I still feel guilty about that. It was supposed to be one of the most special days of my life—the kind of day I'd want my best friend to be part of, too.'

'Just as you were Tom's best man,' she said softly. 'And you flew back to England for three days, so you'd be at our wedding.'

'The year before I got married. Yeah. Which should've told me that I was doing the wrong thing when I married Natalia. I should've talked to Tom about it and at least waited so he could come and be my best man.' He sighed. 'It was a whirlwind romance and we both lost our heads a bit. We didn't really know each other well enough, and we should've waited a while and got to know each other an awful lot better.' He gave her a rueful smile. 'I assumed Natalia loved the job as much as I did and she'd be happy to keep travelling with me, working in a different country every few weeks and seeing the world and knowing we were making a difference. But she wanted something else.'

'Something you didn't?'

He nodded. 'She assumed that getting married meant I wanted to go back to one of our home countries and settle down. Probably a capital city. Moscow or London—she didn't mind which.'

'But you obviously didn't want to settle.'

'No.'

'And you didn't talk any of this through before you got married?'

She sounded surprised—shocked, even. And she had a point. They hadn't thought it through or talked it through. 'I was twenty-five and I still had an awful lot of growing up to do. I guess, so did she. We ended it reasonably amicably, or as amicably as you can end any marriage,' he added. 'We both realised that we shouldn't have got married in the first place; we should have left our relationship as a mad affair and waited for the right person. We lost touch after the divorce, so I have no idea if she found her Mr Right—but I hope she did. I'd like to think she's happy now.'

'Fair enough.'

Ruby's voice was even, but Ellis noticed that she'd gently wriggled her fingers out of his grasp. Did that mean she'd changed her mind about him—that she felt his track record meant that he wouldn't be a good bet for her?

'So do you know what you want out of life now?' she asked. 'Do you still want to go back to the medical aid charity?'

'Yes, I do, because I love my job,' he admitted. 'But part of me wants to stay with you.' Even though the two things were mutually exclusive. Job or Ruby. That was the choice.

'I've already lost someone I loved deeply,' she said. 'I'm not sure I'm ready to take that risk again. I don't want to lose you to your job. So maybe you and I should go back to being just good friends.'

'Is that what you want?' he asked.

'Yes and no,' she said. 'I want to be with you, Ellis. But I also know you need to follow your heart and I'd never stop you doing that. If you decide to stay here in London when you still have itchy feet, then at some point in the future you're going to feel trapped and you'll start to resent me for holding you back. The whole thing's going to end up—' she grimaced '—and please don't think I'm being bitchy, because I'm just trying to be realistic here. I worry that things between us are going to end up like your marriage did. They'll go wrong, because we want different things from life and we haven't talked it through properly. We haven't given each other enough time.'

'I married Natalia in a rush because I was scared of losing her, and I ended up hurting her because it turned out that we didn't want the same things. I've grown up a lot since then,' Ellis said. 'But I admit that over the past few years I've kept my relationships just for fun, so we all know the score and nobody gets hurt.'

'I can understand that,' she said.

'Since I've met you, it's been different,' he said. 'I know Tom loved you deeply, and you loved him. And while Tom was alive I would never, ever have made a move on you. But somewhere over the last eighteen months my feelings towards you changed. I don't think of you as just a friend, Rubes.'

'So what are you saying, Ellis?'

He took a deep breath. Crunch time. 'I want to be with you.'

'We've known each other for a long time, but it's still very early days with us dating. Supposing we find out we really don't want the same things?' she asked.

'Then we'll talk about it and find a way to compromise. Isn't that what a grown-up relationship's meant to be about?'

'I guess so.' She looked at him. 'And that's what you want? A grown-up relationship? With me?'

'I do,' he said softly. 'Right now, I can't promise you that everything's going to work out. That it's all going to be perfect and plain sailing.'

'Nobody can ever promise that,' Ruby said. 'Because life happens and changes things.'

'But what I can promise,' he said, 'is that I'll always try to be honest with you.'

'That's all I can ask for,' she said. 'And it's enough for me.'

'So, you and me.' He took her hand again, and drew it up to his mouth. 'I can't quite believe this is happening.'

'Me, neither.'

'Ruby.' He leaned towards her and touched his lips

to hers. For a moment she remained tense, and then she gave a small sigh and relaxed into his arms.

This was what he wanted.

Ruby, soft and warm and in his arms. Kissing him until they were both dizzy.

He deepened the kiss, and the next thing he knew he was lying on the sofa, with Ruby sprawled on top of him. His hands had slid underneath the hem of her top and were splayed against her back.

'Sorry. I'm taking this a bit too fast,' he said softly, restoring order to her clothes and then sitting up again, moving her so that she was sitting on his lap with his arms wrapped round her.

'Sorry.' She stroked his face. 'And here we are. Apologising to each other and being super-polite.'

'I've wanted you for a long time,' he said. 'But, as you said, this is still early days. I'm happy to wait until you're ready for the next step.'

'Thank you. Because I want this, too—but...'

'I know. It's scary.' He dropped a kiss on her forehead. 'Can I be honest with you? I really don't want our first time together to be in London. I want it to be somewhere else, where neither of us has any memories.'

'Is it going to be a problem? The past, I mean?'

'No.' He was definite about that. 'I'm not trying to compete with Tom, and I know you're not comparing me to him because we're very different men. And I loved Tom dearly—as much as if he was one of my brothers. But I want something that's just going to be for us,' he said. 'I assume you've already been to Paris and Rome with Tom?'

She nodded. 'They're my two favourite cities,' she

said. 'And Tom and I visited a lot of Italy over the years. Florence, Venice, Sorrento, Verona, the Lakes.'

'Not Italy, then. Or Paris. But somewhere just as magical.'

'How about you?' she asked. 'Where's the most magical place you've ever been?'

'The Australian Outback,' he said without hesitation. 'Uluru—Ayers Rock is amazing, Rubes. It glows red at dawn, and purple and blue at sunset. I've never seen anything like it. And the stars are stunning, because there's no artificial light source. You just look up and see the Milky Way and the Magellanic clouds stretching across the sky. It's one of the most incredible sights I've ever seen.'

'Were you there for long?'

'A few days. I wasn't working—I just took the opportunity to get on a plane and spend a couple of weeks travelling round Australia. I was privileged to go on a tour round Uluru with one of the Anangu people. He showed me the springs, caves and rock paintings, and he told me about the Aboriginal dreamtime stories of the area. And we talked about medicine—did you know they use the sap of the centralian bloodwood as a disinfectant and an inhalant for coughs and colds?'

She smiled. 'I should've guessed you'd end up talking about that sort of thing. You're all about the wild and untameable, aren't you?'

'Only in part. I'm guessing that you prefer cities?'

'Ones with pretty buildings, lots of history and good food. I'm not so fussed about shopping,' she said.

'Maybe we could go somewhere together,' he said. 'Just the two of us.'

Her eyes widened. 'And then we take the next step?'

'Not necessarily. No expectations—the same as going out for dinner with you didn't mean that I expected you to go to bed with me. We just spend a bit of time together and take life as it comes. We'll have separate rooms so there's no pressure. If it happens, then fantastic; if it doesn't, then we'll wait until we're both ready.'

'No pressure,' she repeated.

'Is your passport current?'

'Yes.' She stroked his face. 'Are you thinking of soon?'

'Yup. When's your next off-duty where you have three days off in a row?'

'I'll need to check on my phone. Then maybe we can synchronise it.'

'Sure.' He kissed her lightly. 'And we'll see what happens.'

A few days away together, in a place that had no memories for either of them. A place where they'd make new memories. Where maybe they'd make love for the first time.

Part of Ruby was thrilled. She loved the idea of spending time with Ellis, sharing a new city with him, discovering little cafés and art galleries.

Part of her felt guilty. It still wasn't *that* long since Tom's death. Was this too soon?

And part of her wondered if this was the beginning of the end of her relationship with Ellis. She'd seen the wonder in his face when he'd been talking about the Australian Outback, the longing in his eyes when he'd mentioned the medical aid charity. Would the odd few days in Europe really be enough to keep his itchy feet happy? Or would the lure of his job be too much for him, once he went back for that planned month's assignment?

CHAPTER NINE

TRAVELLING AGAIN. EVEN though it wasn't quite the same—he was going simply to have fun, rather than working to make a difference in the world—the idea of seeing another part of the world filled Ellis with joy. Especially because he was going to share it with Ruby. Somewhere new for both of them.

During his lunch break, he went to the travel agent's to pick up some brochures for city breaks, then left Ruby a text.

Have pile of brochures. Want to come and plan our trip after work?

Sorry, can't. On lates until Friday, then I'm going to Manchester for the day to see my family, was her reply.

He damped down the disappointment.

Sure. Let me know when you're free and we'll do it then.

You could come to Manchester with me, if you like?

As her official date?

He wasn't sure he was ready to go public with their

relationship, yet, let alone go to meet her family as her date. Not until they were both sure about where this was going. He knew how he felt about Ruby, but he also knew that he didn't have a good track record. Until he could be absolutely sure that this was going to work out and he wasn't going to hurt her, the way he'd hurt Natalia, he didn't want to make things too official.

Ellis had met Ruby's family at the wedding and at Tom's funeral, and Tom himself had always spoken highly of his in-laws. But meeting them as Tom's best friend was a very different kettle of fish from meeting them as Ruby's partner.

Sorry, working Friday, he typed back. Maybe next time you go?

Ellis and Ruby were both free on Sunday, and spent the afternoon poring over the travel brochures.

'An ice hotel—that sounds really romantic,' Ruby said. 'And we might get to see the Northern Lights. I'd love that.' Her smile faded. 'That was on Tom's bucket list, too. Except we didn't have the time.'

He hugged her. 'I know. Maybe we'll do that another time,' he said softly. 'This is only a short break, and there's no guarantee we'll actually see the lights.'

'Plus the short daylight hours mean we won't have time to explore any of the cities,' she agreed. 'OK. How about Barcelona?'

'Apparently the Sagrada Familia is amazing. So that's a possibility.' He paused. 'Or maybe Vienna.'

'Sachertorte and Mozart,' she said promptly. 'And it'll be late October when we go, so the Austrian Christmas markets might have started, too. That'd be nice.'

'Or,' he said, 'what about the city of a thousand spires?'

'Where's that?'

'Prague. In the Czech Republic. Next door to Austria.'

She grinned. 'That's where you really want to go, isn't it?'

Yes. He'd seen the pictures in the brochures and known immediately that he wanted to visit the city. But how did she know? 'What makes you say that?' he asked carefully.

'The way your eyes lit up when you said it. Like they did when you talked about the stars in the Australian Outback.'

'Busted,' he admitted. 'I, um, sort of made a list. In my head. Nothing formal, and I wouldn't have made a proper list without you.'

She laughed. 'I didn't think you'd be able to wait.'

He hadn't. The itch to travel, and to plan a trip, had been too strong. He *missed* travelling, seeing new places and meeting new people and learning new things.

She glanced through the brochure. 'All those bridges across the river—Prague's very pretty. It reminds me a bit of Florence, or maybe Paris.'

'And at this time of year there might be a chance of a sprinkle of snow. It could be really romantic.'

'Sold. Let's do it,' she said.

'Great. The hotels all seem to be gorgeous art deco buildings.'

'That's lovely. And, by the way, we're going halves on this trip,' she reminded him.

He sighed. 'We've already had this conversation. You know, about accepting gracefully when it's made clear that there are no strings? I just want to spoil you a bit, Rubes.'

'Buying me dinner isn't the same as taking me away for a three-day break, Ellis.'

'I wouldn't offer if I couldn't afford it,' he said softly.

'We're going halves.' She folded her arms.

'How about I pay for the hotel and flights, and you pay for dinner?' he suggested.

'And entrance fees to wherever we go,' she added.

If it made her feel more comfortable, then he'd agree. 'OK.'

'Good.'

Though her arms were still folded and there was a little pleat in her brow—something he'd noticed when she was unhappy about something. 'I'll try and find us somewhere central,' he said. 'And remember I said I'll book separate rooms, so there are no expectations and there's no pressure. We're just going away and enjoying ourselves, exploring somewhere new to both of us.'

To his relief, the frown faded. 'Thank you, Ellis,' she said softly. 'I appreciate it.'

'I know.' He kissed her lightly. 'And we need a guide book.'

She laughed, and he frowned. 'What's so funny?'

'Given that you're such a seasoned traveller, I expected you to—well, just go with the flow.'

'No. When I get the chance to explore somewhere new, I read up about the place in advance so I can plan what I want to see and make the most of my time there.' He smiled. 'I don't do it quite down to the microsecond, but some places are closed on certain days and it'd be a shame to miss out on them because we hadn't bothered to check up beforehand.'

'OK. I'll pick up a guide book tomorrow lunchtime,'

she said. 'I haven't been away for quite a while, so this is really exciting.'

'What I'm most looking forward to,' he said, 'is spending time with you, chilling out and discovering things together.'

'Sounds good to me. So I take it I need to pack walking shoes and comfortable clothes?'

'And maybe a posh dress, in case we decide to have dinner somewhere fancy.'

She laughed. 'Promise you're not going to spill wine all over me?'

He laughed back, knowing she was referring to their disastrous 'first date'. 'I'll try not to.'

Ellis called for Ruby the day of their departure; then they took the train to the airport and queued up at the flight desk to process their baggage.

'So whereabouts is our hotel?' she asked.

'We're just off Wenceslaus Square,' he said, 'so we're about a ten-minute walk from the Old Town Square, and maybe another five minutes from there to the river.'

'That sounds perfect. Thank you.' She stood on tiptoe and kissed him, and it made him feel warm all the way through.

Once they were through customs and passport control in Prague, they saw a taxi driver waiting by the barriers holding a board with the name 'Webster' written on it in capitals,

'I booked the taxi transfer in advance, to save us having to queue,' he explained.

'Which is why your name's on the board.' She smiled. 'I thought that sort of thing only happened in films.'

'Me, too.' He took her hand. 'But it's fun.'

The taxi driver didn't speak English. 'Thanks to working with doctors of all nationalities with the medical aid charity, I've got a smattering of a lot of languages,' Ellis said. 'Though I don't know much Czech beyond please, thank you, hello, goodbye and ordering a couple of beers.'

'Just as well we have a phrase book, then,' Ruby said, taking it from her bag.

The airport was in the middle of the countryside, and they enjoyed the autumnal views on the way to the city. Prague itself was beautiful, with lots of white four- and five-storey buildings with orange roofs. Everywhere they looked, they could see domes, mosaics and lots of windows.

'This is gorgeous. It reminds me a bit of Paris,' Ruby said.

'Me, too—but look.' He gestured to the skyline; there were lots of turrets and towers with spires, all very gothic and very pretty.

'I can see why they call it the city of a thousand spires. There must be a dozen on that tower over there alone.' She smiled at him. 'I'm so looking forward to this, Ellis.'

His fingers tightened round hers. 'So am I,' he said softly.

The taxi drew up outside their hotel. Ellis helped Ruby out of the back of the cab, then tipped the driver. A doorman wearing a top hat took their luggage, and they checked in at the front desk. The hotel reception was gorgeous, all marble and art deco glass; there was a table in the centre containing huge vases with stunning arrangements of lilies and peonies.

'This is amazing,' she said once they'd got their card

keys for their rooms and were heading up in the lift. 'But, Ellis, this must have cost a fortune. It has to be the swishest hotel in Prague.'

'No, the swishest hotel is overlooking the river, actually. I did ask, but sadly their presidential suite is currently booked by a film star,' he said, and laughed. 'Plus it was ever so slightly out of my budget. This isn't.'

'I wasn't expecting this to be so—well...' She gestured round them. 'It's gorgeous, but I feel bad that you've spent so much money on me.'

'Remember what I said about being gracious. I want to do something nice for you, so let me have the pleasure of making you smile.'

'I guess.' She bit her lip. 'Sorry. Now I'm being an ungrateful brat. I didn't mean it like that.'

'I know. But there really are no strings attached. This is just a couple of days for us to explore somewhere new and have some fun,' he said. 'No timetables and no schedules—though I admit I've reserved us a table here tomorrow night, because they have a band playing and I thought it might be fun to dance together after dinner.'

'That sounds lovely.'

'Let's unpack,' he said, 'and then we can go exploring. How long do you need?'

'Ten minutes,' she said.

'Great.' He smiled at her. 'See you out here in ten.'

The room was amazingly swanky. The bed was incredibly wide and very comfortable, and the bathroom was all gleaming marble and thick fluffy towels. It didn't take Ruby long to unpack, and she was ready to meet Ellis in the ten minutes she'd promised.

'I feel thoroughly spoiled,' Ruby said when she

walked through her door to find him waiting in the corridor.

'Good. That was the idea.'

His grey eyes were sparkling with what she guessed was happiness; the same feeling that was bubbling through her.

He smiled and took her hand. 'Let's go and see the sights.'

The city was beautiful and Ruby really enjoyed walking through the Old Town. There were lots of gorgeous art deco buildings with yellow, pink or white walls, a dome on the roof and huge arched windows.

A crowd of people was waiting outside one particular building.

'That's the astronomical clock,' Ellis said when he'd consulted his guide book. 'It's the oldest working astronomical clock in the world, and it shows the movement of the sun and moon through the zodiac.'

'It's so pretty with all those swirling greens and blues and golds.' She glanced at her watch. 'Does something happen on the hour?'

'Apparently the figures move. Shall we wait and see?'

On the hour, the figure of Death struck the bell, to the cheers of the waiting tourists.

'It's amazing that it's six hundred years old and still working,' she said. 'I'm so glad we came here.'

They walked from the old town square down to the Vltava river, then found a small café overlooking the wide, fast-flowing river where they could grab a sandwich and coffee for lunch.

'Would you like to go on a river trip?' Ellis asked.

'That's a great idea. I hardly ever got to go on a boat

as Tom used to get horribly seasick. Even with travel sickness pills, he couldn't handle a gentle cruise down the Thames.'

'I remember,' Ellis said. 'There was a school trip in the South of France where we were supposed to go out in a glass-bottomed boat and see all these amazing fish, except when we got out of the harbour the water was a bit choppy. I didn't get to see any of the fish either, because I was too busy trying to find extra sick bags for him—the crew hadn't brought enough and suggested that people shared bags, and that made Tom throw up even more!'

'Poor Tom. It must have been awful for him—and not that nice for everyone round him, either.' She smiled at him. 'I'm so glad we can talk about him, Ellis. That it's not going to make things awkward between us.'

'We both loved him,' Ellis said simply, 'so it's an extra bond between us. Of course it's not going to be awkward. And I'd never cut him out of my life and refuse to talk about him.' He knew she was well aware of what he hadn't said: the way his parents were about Sally. 'I want to remember the good times and smile about them. Just as I do about Sally.' And how he wished he could fix it for his parents, so they'd still have some of the joy left in their lives. He slid his arm round Ruby's shoulders and gave her a hug.

He held her hand all the way on the river trip. And his fingers tightened round hers when they passed the lover's bridge festooned with padlocks. 'It seems to be a tradition in a lot of European cities now,' she said, 'to put a padlock on a bridge with your initials on it.'

'Which is a bit more environmentally friendly than carving it into a tree trunk,' Ellis said.

Once they were back on dry land, they walked over the Charles Bridge, admiring the statues and the views of the other bridges across the Vltava. 'I can hardly believe this bridge is nearly seven hundred years old,' she said. 'I loved the story the guide on the boat told us about mixing the mortar with eggs to make it stronger. I wonder if that really happened?'

'Who knows? As you say, it was a good story.'

They wandered hand in hand through the streets. Ruby hadn't felt this relaxed in a long time, and she was really enjoying exploring the city with Ellis, stopping whenever something caught their eye to consult the guide book for more information.

They found a small, romantic restaurant serving local dishes, and the waiter smiled in approval when Ellis spoke Czech to order two beers.

'What do you recommend that's typically Czech?' she asked the waiter.

'*Svíčková na smetaně*,' he said, which turned out to be dumplings and beef in creamy sauce with cranberry compote and sweetened whipped cream.

The vegetarian option was *smažený sýr*—a thick slice of cheese, breadcrumbed and fried, served with potato salad.

'It all looks amazing but not so good for our arteries,' she said when the waiter had gone again.

'I'm pretty sure we'll walk it off tomorrow,' he said with a smile. 'I thought we could go and explore the castle.'

'Sounds great,' she said.

The food was excellent; the dumpling was larger than Ruby expected, made into a large roll and sliced. She liked the tartness of the cranberry as it cut through the richness of the cream. 'I definitely need to join you in walking this off tomorrow,' she said with a smile.

Once they'd shared a pudding—a potato dumpling stuffed with plums, steamed, and served with melted butter and a sprinkle of sugar—they walked back to the hotel, enjoying the way the city was lit up at night.

'This was a brilliant idea,' she said. 'Thank you, Ellis.'

'My pleasure.' He slid his arm round her shoulder, and she slid hers round his waist, enjoying his nearness.

Back at the hotel, they ordered hot chocolate at the bar; then finally they headed to their rooms.

Was this when it was going to happen? Ruby wondered, her pulse hammering.

Ellis kissed her goodnight at the door, his mouth warm and sweet and coaxing.

But then he pulled back. 'Goodnight, Ruby. Sleep well.'

Clearly he wasn't expecting her to invite him in to her room—and he hadn't invited her to his, either. So he'd meant it when he'd said there were no strings, no expectations. Odd how that made her stomach give a little swoop of disappointment.

But maybe he was right. Rushing into anything could be a mistake. And he'd admitted to making a huge mistake, rushing in to marriage in the past. He must feel just as wary as she did.

'You, too,' she said brightly, and let herself into her room.

Once she'd showered and cleaned her teeth, she changed into her pyjamas and climbed into bed. She lay there awake, thinking of Ellis. Wandering round such a romantic city with him, hand in hand; the way he'd kissed her at unexpected moments; and the warmth and sweetness of his arms round her.

What would happen if she picked up the phone and dialled his extension?

She thought about it to the point where she actually picked up the phone and dialled the first digit of his room number. But then she replaced the receiver, not wanting to get this wrong and make things awkward between them.

Tomorrow was another day.

Maybe tomorrow.

Ellis lay awake, thinking of Ruby. Outside her door, she'd looked so vulnerable for a moment that he'd wanted to hold her and not let her go. Yet at the same time he hadn't wanted her to feel pressured. He'd booked separate rooms on purpose, to make it clear that he was happy to wait until she was ready to take their relationship to the next step.

What if he called her now?

What if he asked her to come to his room—just to cuddle up and go to sleep together?

But that would be unfair. He didn't want her to feel obliged, just because he'd paid for the trip. Plus it was still early days between them.

He'd wait until she was ready, just as he'd promised himself. He'd keep cool, calm and collected.

But, oh, he wished…

CHAPTER TEN

RUBY HAD BREAKFAST with Ellis the next morning in
the hotel restaurant: a mushroom and cheese omelette
cooked by the chef, toast, fruit with yoghurt, and freshly
squeezed orange juice followed by a cappuccino.

'This is the perfect start to the day,' she said with a
smile. 'And it's nice not to be grabbing a granola bar
and a banana and eating them on the way to work.'

'So you like being waited on?' Ellis asked.

She laughed. 'No. I'm just enjoying being spoiled.
Weren't those your orders?'

'Absolutely.' He smiled back.

It was another crisp, bright autumn day: perfect for
exploring. They bought tickets from a kiosk; using a
mixture of guidebook Czech and sign language, they
found out where the tram stop was and took a tram to
the castle. There was a jolt when the tram turned one
corner and she stumbled, not quite sure where to grab
on to as there weren't overhead bars or straps like there
were on the Tube in London. Ellis caught her before
she fell.

'Thank you.'

'No worries.'

It felt natural then to wrap her arms round his waist

and stay where she was until they reached the tram stop for the castle.

They had a beautiful view from the hill.

'According to the guide book, this is the largest castle in the world,' he told her.

Ruby could believe it; there seemed to be courtyard after courtyard, and the walls seemed to stretch out for ever.

They went into the oldest section of the castle and walked up a set of wide, shallow brick stairs. 'I have to say, I was expecting narrow stone spiral stairs,' she said, 'like the ones you get in a lot of English castles.'

He consulted the guide book and raised an eyebrow. 'That's because these weren't for people.'

'Not for people? Who were they for, then?' she asked, puzzled.

His eyes sparkled. 'Would you believe, horses?'

'No way!'

'They used to joust in the Vladislav hall, so the knights would ride up these stairs,' he said. 'Honestly. I'm not teasing.'

When they walked into the hall, she realised that he was telling the truth. It was a massive room, very long, with vaulted ceilings, the most enormous windows and huge wrought iron chandeliers. 'I can imagine it. There's enough room for the knights to joust and people to watch them.'

Afterwards, they strolled through the palace gardens, enjoying the amazing view of the city from the castle walls.

'The cathedral reminds me very much of Notre Dame, with the twin towers and the rose window,' she said as they went into yet another courtyard and discovered the cathedral of St Vitus. Inside, she loved the soaring vaulted ceilings and the Mucha window.

'And there's a bell tower… I know they don't have a grotesque gallery here like they do at Notre Dame, but I still think we have to climb it,' Ellis said.

'Agreed,' she said with a smile.

'You look all pink and adorable,' he said when they got to the top.

'You mean, I'm not as fit as I like to think I am,' she said wryly. 'Especially as you're not even glowing, let alone hot and sweaty like I am!'

'Nope, you're all pink and adorable,' he repeated, and kissed her.

They stood looking out at the views, with Ellis standing behind Ruby, his arms wrapped round her and holding her close. Funny how being with Ellis made her feel like a teenager again.

Almost as if he'd picked up on her thoughts, he asked, 'Can I take a selfie?'

'Sure, as long as you send it to me as well.'

He stooped to press his cheek against hers and took a picture of them both smiling. 'Me and my girl,' he said softly, 'and there's the spire to prove we're right at the top of the cathedral.'

Me and my girl. It sent a thrill all the way through her.

They enjoyed wandering through the rest of the castle, visiting the tiny houses in Golden Lane. Ruby was fascinated by the herbalist's house, with its narrow wooden shelves full of stone jars and bottles, with bunches of herbs hanging up to dry from the rafters. 'This is what we would have worked with, all these years ago,' she said.

'In some of the places where I've worked, it's more than we'd have now,' he said. 'Even hot water can be a luxury.'

Ruby wondered again, would Ellis stay with the medical aid charity? Was visiting a place like this enough to stop his itchy feet returning, or was it making things worse? She didn't like to ask him outright—it felt like an ungrateful question, especially as he'd gone to the trouble to make this break special for her—but she remembered Tina's warning. She'd be a fool to let herself fall for someone who didn't want to stay around.

When they'd finished looking round the castle, they grabbed a *trdelník* from one of the fast-food stands just outside the castle gates. The rolled dough was made into a spiral, grilled on a stick and sprinkled with sugar and cinnamon. 'This is gorgeous,' she said after the first taste. 'It's like a cross between the crêpes in Paris and the doughnuts you'd have at the seaside in England.'

They walked through the cobbled streets of the Lesser Quarter into Petrin Park. 'We have to see the Observation Tower while we're here,' Ellis said. 'It's a copy of the Eiffel Tower but about a quarter of the size—though, because it's on a hill, it's actually higher than the Eiffel Tower and the views are meant to be amazing.'

The day had turned windy and when they got to the top of the tower Ruby was a bit taken aback to discover that it actually swayed in the wind. As if Ellis realised what was making her nervous, he wrapped his arms round her again, making her feel safe. 'The guide book was right. The views are amazing,' she said, 'and I think that golden roof is the theatre we passed when we were on the river.'

'And the Dancing House,' he said, pointing out the modern building that looked just like a couple doing the waltz on the other side of the river. 'Maybe we can have a closer look at that tomorrow.'

'Sounds good to me.'

Hand in hand, they walked back to the hotel.

'Our table will be ready in an hour and a half,' he said in the corridor outside their doors. 'Unless that's not giving you enough time to get ready, we could go to the bar for a drink first?' he suggested.

She smiled. 'You know I'm not one of these women who needs hours and hours to do her hair and make-up. A drink at the bar sounds good. Shall I knock on your door when I'm ready?'

'That'd be perfect,' he said with a smile, and kissed her. 'I've really enjoyed today. I'm glad I shared it with you.'

'Me, too—even though that tower was a bit scary when it started swaying,' she said.

Ruby showered, did her hair, changed into the new little black dress she'd bought especially for Prague, and did her make-up. And she felt ridiculously nervous as she knocked on his door.

Ellis was wearing a formal dinner suit and bow tie. She was used to him wearing a suit at work, but this took it to another level. 'You look amazing,' she said, feeling her eyes widen.

'So do you.' He drew her into his arms. 'Right now I really want to kiss you, but I guess I shouldn't smudge your lipstick.'

'You can kiss me later,' she said.

'I hope that's a promise.'

'It is—and I always keep my promises,' she said.

They had a glass of wine in the bar, and then it was time to go into the restaurant. Ruby glanced at the menu and gasped. 'Ellis, it's Michelin-starred.'

'I know, and it counts as part of the hotel bill.'

'It most certainly does not. Our deal was that I'm paying for dinner.'

'You can buy me lunch tomorrow,' he said. 'I'm paying, and you're not allowed to argue. Remember, graciousness.'

She rolled her eyes. 'Thank you. But you really didn't have to.'

Once their waiter had poured the champagne, he brought them both an *amuse-bouche* of ravioli filled with mushrooms and truffles, served with foamed butter.

'This is to die for,' Ruby said.

Ellis smiled. 'What was that in the ad you wrote for me about finding a foodie as a partner?'

She laughed. 'Absolutely.'

The starter was a soft buffalo mozzarella served with rocket and tomatoes and balsamic, light and quivery and beautifully presented. Ellis had beetroot ravioli filled with ricotta and thyme and served with more of the foamed butter, while Ruby had grilled sea bass with Mediterranean vegetables. But the best bit for her was the pudding—crème brûlée, her favourite, and the waiter actually brought a blow-torch to the table along with the dessert. 'There's a tiny drop of brandy on the top so the sugar will be flambéed,' he explained, then set fire to the sugar so it would melt into a hard crust.

'This has to be the best meal I've ever eaten in my entire life,' Ruby sighed when they'd finished.

'From a foodie like you, that's quite a compliment,' Ellis said.

After dinner, as Ellis had promised, there was dancing. A woman with a smoky voice was singing soft jazz, accompanied by a piano, double-bass, and guitar. The lighting was soft and, together with the music, made the room feel very intimate. Ellis swayed with her, holding her close, and Ruby felt as if she could dance all night.

She closed her eyes and gave herself up to the music and his nearness. Right at that moment, she could believe that the two of them were the only ones in the room. And Ellis was an excellent dancer; he led her round the floor so she didn't have to worry about putting a foot wrong.

Finally the singer said goodnight and the band left the stage.

'Do you want to go to back to the bar?' Ellis asked.

'No, I think I've had quite enough alcohol for tonight,' she said. What she really wanted was to ask him to come back to her room with her, but she didn't quite have the nerve to say so; shyness kept the words inside.

'I'll see you back to your room,' he said.

The lift was all mirrors inside, and their reflections stretched out to infinity.

'I could kiss you to infinity right now.' His voice was low and husky, and the words sent a thrill right through her.

'Do it,' she whispered back.

He gave her the sexiest smile she'd ever seen, dipped his head and brushed his mouth against hers. Every nerve-end tingled; she wrapped her arms round him and kissed him back until she couldn't think straight.

There was a soft ding and the lift doors opened.

He broke the kiss, looking dazed.

Somehow they managed to walk out of the lift and down the corridor to their rooms.

He paused outside her door. 'I guess this is good-night,' he said softly.

She could do the sensible thing and say goodnight.

Or she could give in to the demands flooding her body and ask him to stay.

For a heartbeat she was torn between the two. She knew that making love with Ellis would change things between them again, and supposing it changed things the wrong way?

But she'd never been a coward. If things between them went wrong in the future, then they went wrong. Right here, right now, she knew what she wanted. Ellis.

'What if I don't want it to be goodnight?' she asked, her voice equally soft.

'Are you saying...?'

'Stay with me, Ellis.'

'Are you sure about that?'

'Very sure.' She took her card key from her evening bag, slipped it into the lock and opened her door.

Then he scooped her up in his arms and carried her into the room. He nudged the door closed behind them, then set her back on her feet, keeping her body close to his so she was left in no doubt about how much he wanted her.

The curtains were already closed, and there was just the low light of the bedside lamp.

'It feels as if we should have candlelight,' he said.

'This is the next best thing,' she said. 'It'd probably set the fire alarms off if we had candles in here anyway.'

'You're so practical. It's one of the things I love about you.'

'Thank you.' She inclined her head in acknowledgement of the compliment.

'Something else I love,' he said, 'is your mouth.' He traced the curve of her lower lip with the tip of his finger. 'It's a perfect cupid's bow.'

She opened her mouth and drew the tip of his finger inside, then sucked hard.

He gasped and his eyes darkened. 'Ruby, you drive me crazy. I want you so much. I've wanted you for so long.'

'I want you, too.' She reached up and undid his bow tie.

He smiled at her. 'Oh, so this is the way we're doing it, is it?' He spun her round, unzipped her dress, then kissed a path all the way from the nape of her neck to the base of her spine, sliding the dress down her body as he did so.

She stepped out of the dress and turned to face him. 'My turn.' She started undoing the buttons of his shirt. Her fingers were a little clumsy, but it didn't matter; the heat in his expression encouraged her to keep going. He shrugged off his jacket, and she untucked his shirt from his trousers so she could finish undoing it and slide the soft cotton off his shoulders.

'Perfect,' she said, running her fingers over his pecs. 'I've always thought you could be a model for any of the posh perfume houses.' She let her fingers slide down to his abdomen. 'And a perfect six pack.'

'Careful—my ego might explode.'

She laughed. 'You're not an egotist, Ellis.'

'Good.' He drew her closer and kissed her again, his

mouth warm and sweet and very sure. Then he broke
the kiss and held her gaze. 'Right now, I want to kiss
you all over.'

'Sounds good to me.' Her knees felt like jelly; she
hadn't felt this nervous or this turned on in a long while.

'I'm glad. And, just so you know, I intend to take
my time.'

The huskiness in his voice made the heat running
through her gear up another notch.

He kissed from the corner of her mouth down to
the curve of her jaw. Instinctively, she tipped her head
back and he kissed his way down the side of her neck,
teasing and inciting. She was aware of the pulse beating madly in her throat, and then his mouth skimmed
it, skimmed it again, and nibbled and teased until she
thought she was going to burst into flames with desire.

Then he straightened up again and traced the lacy
edge of her bra with his fingertip, taking his own sweet
time. Just as he'd promised.

'Do you have any idea how much I want you?' she
whispered.

'I hope it's as much as I want you,' he said.

She smiled, and let him slide the straps of her bra
down her arms. At work he was a total professional;
nothing ever fazed him and his hands were steady and
sure. Yet right now his hands were shaking and his
breathing was shallow. Clearly he was as affected as
much as she was by this thing between them.

He undid her bra strap and let the garment drift to
the floor. 'You're so beautiful,' he said. 'And I want you
so much I can't think straight.'

'Me, too,' she said, and lifted a hand to stroke his face.
He pressed a kiss into her palm, drew his hands down

her sides and then stroked upwards again so he could cup her breasts. His thumbs grazed her nipples and made her shiver.

She slid her hands into his hair; it felt soft and silky beneath her fingertips. Then she kissed him, pressing against him.

He pulled her closer and kissed her back.

Ruby wasn't sure who removed the rest of whose clothing, but the next thing she knew Ellis was carrying her to the wide, wide bed and had pushed the coverlet aside. He laid her down on the sheets; then she felt the mattress dip with his weight as he joined her.

'Ruby, you're so beautiful—everything I dreamed of and more.'

His fingers were feather-light as he touched her, making her skin feel hotter. He followed his hands with his mouth, and she arched against the bed.

'Now, Ellis,' she said. 'Please, now.'

She felt the bed dip again as he stood up and opened her eyes in shock. Had he changed his mind?

Then she realised that he was taking his wallet from his jacket, removing a foil package.

'Protection,' he said. 'And, just so you know, I wasn't making assumptions. Just being prepared.'

'Practical and sensible.'

'Which isn't,' he said as he joined her back on the bed, 'the same as boring.'

No, she didn't think this was going to be boring in the slightest.

She reached for him and kissed him hard.

This time, it felt safe to let the desire ignite. Her head fell back as he kissed his way down her body, exploring the hollows of her collar-bones and the valley between her breasts, stroking the soft undersides and making her sigh with pleasure.

She slid her fingers into his hair as he teased her nipples with the tip of his tongue. Then he drew the hard peak into his mouth and sucked.

'More,' she whispered, and he kissed his way downwards over her abdomen. She shivered. She wanted this so much; she couldn't remember the last time she'd wanted someone so desperately.

He shifted to kneel between her thighs. She felt him lift her foot and kiss the hollow of her ankle. As he worked his way slowly north, she felt as if her bones were dissolving; she was so ready for him.

She felt the slow stroke of one finger along her sex, and it made her whimper with need. And then he bent to replace his finger with his mouth. As his tongue flicked across her clitoris she completely lost it; her climax hit her like a wall.

Ruby was still almost hyperventilating as she finally opened her eyes.

Ellis held her close. 'Well. That was interesting.'

'Ellis...' Her brain felt scrambled and she couldn't even string two words together.

He just smiled. 'It's good to know that I can turn the smartest woman I know into mush.' His smile grew tinged with wickedness. 'But I haven't finished yet.'

'Better be a promise,' she mumbled.

'Oh, it is.' He kissed her again, touched her and stroked her until she was back at fever point, and then she heard the tear of the foil packet and the snap of the condom as he moved to protect her.

And then, finally, he eased inside her.

Incredibly, she felt her climax rising again.

And this time, when the wall hit her and she cried out, she heard his answering cry and felt his body surge against hers.

Afterwards, he said softly, 'I need to deal with the condom.'

'Sure.'

When he came back from the bathroom, he climbed back into bed beside her and drew her into his arms.

'Ellis, I…'

He pressed a finger lightly against her lips. 'Don't speak. Tonight, let's just be.'

And it had been so long since she'd slept in someone's arms. So long since she'd felt warm and safe and cherished.

She reached over to switch out the light, and cuddled into him. And finally she fell asleep in his arms.

Ellis lay awake for a while longer, just holding Ruby.

What had just happened between them had been a total revelation—a connection he'd never experienced with anyone else, even Natalia.

It gave him hope for the future. Maybe, just maybe, this thing between them would work out.

But, at the same time, it brought back all the panic. He'd thought that he loved Natalia, and that she'd felt the same about him. They'd been good together. Yet his marriage hadn't lasted—they'd discovered within weeks that they'd made a huge mistake because they wanted totally different things out of life.

What did Ruby want out of life? Another marriage like the one she'd had with Tom, perhaps, settled and close to both their families? He didn't know if he could offer her that. Would he be enough for her? Would he be able to suppress his wanderlust for her? Had he just made another huge mistake with the potential to hurt someone he cared about?

He smiled wryly. So much for telling her, 'Tonight, let's just be.' Instead of enjoying this moment, relaxing in the warmth and sweetness, he was full of doubts.

Maybe he should take his own advice, just for tonight, and live in the moment. Just be. Tomorrow there would be time for reflection. Tonight, he'd just enjoy holding her asleep in his arms.

CHAPTER ELEVEN

THE NEXT MORNING Ruby woke, feeling warm and comfortable. A surge of embarrassment heated her skin as she remembered last night, and then a flood of guilt washed away the embarrassment.

She felt a kiss against her shoulder. 'Ruby. Chill out,' Ellis said softly.

'How long have you been awake?' she asked, turning to face him.

'Long enough.' He stroked her face. 'What's the matter?'

She took a deep breath. 'You and me. Last night.'

'Problem?' His voice was neutral and his face was expressionless, so she didn't have a clue how he was feeling. Did he regret this? Did he think they should go back to being friends? Did he feel as mixed-up about this whole situation as she did?

'Yes. No.' She closed her eyes. 'I don't regret what we did. But I do feel guilty about it.'

'Why?' he asked gently. 'Ruby, we're both single. We have feelings for each other, and we simply acted on those feelings last night.'

'You're the first since Tom,' she whispered. 'The only one apart from Tom.'

'Which makes me feel incredibly honoured,' he said softly.

She opened her eyes then and looked at him. 'Honoured?'

'Honoured,' he repeated, 'that you chose me. Ruby, there's no need to feel guilty. You're not betraying Tom.'

'It feels like it,' she said.

He shook his head. 'Tom loved you enough to want you to be happy after he died. And you're not trying to push his memory out of your life. It's OK to move on. We've been dating for a few weeks and we've known each other for an awful lot longer than that.'

'I guess I'm being ridiculous.'

'No. You're human. You can't turn your feelings on and off just like that—neither of us can.'

'Are you saying that you feel guilty, too?'

'Technically, you're my best friend's girl,' he said. 'So, yes, in a way I do feel guilty. But I would never, ever have done anything to jeopardise your marriage if Tom had still been alive. Tom's been gone for more than a year now. I know we both still miss him and we always will, but we have to face up to the fact that he's gone. And I think he'd be pleased if we could find happiness together.' He gave her a rueful smile. 'Though I have to admit, he'd probably give me a huge lecture about commitment and making sure I don't hurt you.'

'Right now we can't promise each other for ever,' Ruby said.

'Which is fine,' Ellis reassured her. 'We can promise each other for now. Enjoy the moment.'

'While it lasts?'

'Which might be for longer than both of us think. If we're lucky.'

'I need to stop brooding,' she said wryly.

'And I need coffee,' he said. 'How long will it take you to shower?'

The glint in his eyes prompted her to say, 'That depends on whether I'm showering alone.'

He grinned. 'I like your thinking, Rubes. In fact...'

They were almost too late for breakfast. And Ellis didn't look quite as pristine as he normally did when he emerged from his room with his luggage, ready to go in the hotel's store-room until their taxi arrived to take them back to the airport.

'So, our last day in Prague,' he said when they'd checked out and had the receipts for their luggage. 'Where would you like to go?'

'You're the one with the guide book. Where do you suggest?'

'I'd like to take a closer look at the Dancing House,' he said. 'And there's this café where Einstein used to hang out.'

She laughed. 'And you want to follow in his footsteps?'

'Just for coffee. I think I'll pass on developing theories of relativity.' He laughed back.

They went to see the Dancing House, and Ellis persuaded another tourist to take a photograph on his phone of himself and Ruby in front of the building in the same dance pose. They walked along the river bank, hand in hand, enjoying the autumn sunshine, then found the café on Ellis's wish list. It was all chandeliers and gorgeous Viennese-style cake and coffee; and there were chess sets out on various tables with a note telling patrons to enjoy a game if they wished.

'Fancy a game?' Ellis asked.

Ruby shook her head. 'Sorry, I've never played.'

'I could teach you.'

'Thanks, but I don't think chess is for me.' She raised an eyebrow. 'Something else I didn't know about you, Ellis.'

'Me? I'm an open book,' he said lightly.

The bright morning sunshine had given way to threatening clouds by the time they'd finished their cake and coffee, so they spent the rest of the day in art galleries and museums, before collecting their luggage and meeting their taxi to the airport.

Prague would always have a special place in her heart, Ruby thought. The place where she and Ellis had first made love.

But, once they were back in England—what then? Would they stay close like this? Or would the world get in the way?

And there were other considerations, too. They weren't the only ones to think about.

She pushed it to the back of her head and chatted easily with Ellis all the way back to England.

Though he'd clearly been thinking about it too; when he saw her to her front door, he asked softly, 'So where do we go from here?'

'I don't know,' she said. 'What do you want?'

'Are you ready to go public?'

She wrinkled her nose. 'Don't take this the wrong way, but can I talk to Tom's parents about it first?'

'I think that would be kind,' he said, 'and I agree with you. If they're not comfortable with the situation, then we need to keep it to ourselves a little longer, until they've had time to get used to the idea.'

'Thank you. For understanding,' she said.

'Any time.' He kissed her lightly. 'I guess I'll see you at work tomorrow.'

'Yes. And thank you for Prague. It was special.'

'It was,' he agreed. And for a moment she could swear that she saw sadness in his eyes.

'You're twenty-two weeks, according to your scan, Mrs Falcon,' Ellis said gently.

'I really can't get my head round this.' Anita Falcon shook her head. 'I'm forty-five years old. I'm a professional. I've got a fifteen-year-old. How could I possibly not realise I was pregnant again, until last week?' She shook her head. 'I've seen the newspaper stories about women who don't have a clue they're pregnant until they actually have the baby. I always thought that was crazy—I mean, if you're pregnant you get morning sickness, your periods stop, you have a definite bump and you can feel the baby moving. How can you not *know*? I just…' She shook her head, and a tear trickled down her face. 'Ten years ago, I would've been thrilled. It'd be a dream come true, being able to give Max a little brother or sister. But how can I possibly cope with a baby now, when I have my parents living with me, and my dad has dementia, and my son is going to be doing his exams next June? Not to mention Nick—my husband—might be made redundant next month, so we can't afford for me to give up my job, even if it's only for a few months. And it's so late now that even if I could face the idea of a termination, it's not going to be possible. It's my own stupid fault for not having a clue.' She covered her face with her hands, and Ruby could see her shoulders heaving with sobs.

She sat down next to Anita and put her arm round

her. 'Hey. Don't beat yourself up. There are plenty of reasons why a woman might not realise she's pregnant. From what you've just told me, you're under quite a bit of stress right now.'

Anita rubbed the tears away from her eyes with the back of her hand. 'It's been hard to get the right help for Dad. Dealing with the authorities is like banging your head against a brick wall. We all want him to keep his independence as much as possible, and I wanted to take the strain off Mum—that's why they moved in with us.'

'It's difficult, sharing a home with your parents again after years of not living with them,' Ellis said. 'And it's doubly hard if they're not in the best of health. You're worrying about them, and you're worrying about your son as well—and your husband's job.'

'I thought it was just stress mucking my system up,' Anita said. 'I haven't had a period for four months—but my periods were a bit all over the place before that, so I just assumed I was heading for the menopause. The same as having to get up at night for a wee; I thought it was my age. I went and had a chat with the local pharmacist, and she said she was the same age as me and it was probably nothing to worry about, but do a pregnancy test just to put my mind at rest.'

'Good idea,' Ellis said.

She dragged in a breath. 'Back when I was pregnant with Max, you just had a blue line on the test stick and you had to guess whether it was a dark enough blue to be a positive result. Nowadays, the tests have a screen that tells you how pregnant you are—and the one I did definitely said "not pregnant". So I thought it was OK, that I was right about my system being all over the place with menopause and stress.'

'Sometimes you can get a false negative result on a test,' Ruby said. 'Though you're right. A lot of women hit the perimenopause at your age and your periods go all over the place.'

'I haven't had any morning sickness,' Anita said, 'and I was terrible when I had Max. Even tin cans used to smell and make me feel queasy. Right from the second week to the twelfth, when I was pregnant with him, I had to run to the bathroom if someone came into work wearing really strong aftershave or hairspray. This time, there was nothing. Not the slightest bit.'

'Your body doesn't always react the same way in pregnancy. Some women have horrendous morning sickness with one baby and nothing at all with another. How about your weight?' Ellis asked. 'Has that changed much?'

'I've put on about ten pounds.' Anita grimaced. 'Though I put that down to middle-age spread. And stress. I haven't exactly been eating brilliantly—when the going gets tough, the tough get chocolate, right?'

'Right,' Ruby said. 'Some women don't put on that much weight during pregnancy. If they're doing a lot of exercise—say they're training for a marathon—or they're overweight to start with, the pregnancy might not show for quite a while.'

'Plus, if you have a uterus that tips back the other way—as one in five women do—you wouldn't have noticed a bump anyway for at least the first twelve weeks,' Ellis said.

Anita stared at them, the tiniest bit of hope on her face. 'So I wasn't just being stupid, not realising I was pregnant?'

'You weren't being stupid at all,' Ruby reassured

her. 'And there's a fifteen-year gap between your pregnancies, so your body won't remember what it feels like to have a baby moving around inside. Plus you've been worried sick about quite a lot of things, and you haven't been looking out for the signs of being pregnant. So that'd be why you missed that little fluttering of the baby moving.'

'I did have terrible heartburn last week. I never had that when I was pregnant with Max. I thought it was just a combination of stress and comfort eating, and I knew I ought to be doing something about my weight but I just couldn't face it, not with everything else going on. Chocolate is the only thing that's kept me sane. I couldn't believe it when my GP said he thought I might be pregnant.' Anita bit her lip. 'And I've been eating all the wrong things—soft cheese, lightly cooked eggs, wine. I haven't taken any folic acid, I've been eating rubbish instead of really nutritious food, and...' She broke off, clearly fighting back the tears.

'And you're panicking that you've harmed the baby,' Ellis said. 'But what I saw on the scan was a baby who's the right size for dates, has ten fingers and toes, and has a steadily beating heart. I didn't see anything that would worry me, as an obstetrician. Plus you still have another eighteen weeks or so to eat green leafy vegetables until they're coming out of your ears.'

'You bet I will.' Anita gave him a wobbly smile. 'So I'm not the only woman who's ever done that?'

'Far from it,' Ellis said with a smile. 'And it will take a bit of getting used to. Do you have other family who can support you?'

'An older brother,' Anita said. 'But he sticks his head in the sand about Mum and Dad, so he won't do anything to help me with them. He's always got an excuse not to visit us. And it's not even as if he lives over the other side of the country.'

Guilt prickled the back of Ellis's neck. Over the years he'd had plenty of excuses not to visit his parents. Mainly because he worked so far away.

'Families aren't always easy,' he said feelingly. 'How about your husband's family?'

'Let's just say how much my mother-in-law will enjoy telling people that I'm supposed to be so clever, but I was too stupid to know I was pregnant and too stupid to know how to use contraception,' Anita said wryly. 'But I do have the best friend in the universe. She'll be there for me. And I think, once Max and Nick get over the shock, they'll be there for me, too.'

Ruby squeezed her hand. 'That's great. And you've also got us. Anything you're worried about between your appointments, come and talk to us. We have a walk-in clinic here in the department as well as the regular appointments.'

'Thank you.' Anita took a deep breath. 'I'm sorry I've been so wet. Crying and all that. That just isn't me.'

'Hormones,' Ruby said sagely. 'Plus you have a lot on your plate. In your shoes, I'd be just the same.'

'Really?'

'Really.' Ruby patted her shoulder. 'Right. Let's finish doing your checks, and we'll make another appointment for you in two weeks' time—we want to keep a closer eye on you simply because you're an older mum, not because there's anything to panic about. But if you're worried about anything in the meantime, come and see us.'

'You've been so kind about this. Both of you. I mean,

you have to see this stupid, ditzy woman who doesn't even know she's pregnant until she's over halfway through...'

'Don't put yourself down,' Ellis said. 'Actually,' he added, 'studies show that about one in about five hundred women don't realise they're pregnant until they're twenty weeks gone, so you're not stupid at all.'

'Thank you. Both of you.' She took a deep breath. 'This baby wasn't planned, but it's never going to feel unwanted.'

Later that evening, Ellis and Ruby were curled up together on his sofa.

'That poor woman who came to see us this afternoon,' she said. 'She's got a huge amount to deal with.'

'A late baby's tough for anyone, but she's caring for her parents as well, and she's supporting her son through his GCSEs and worrying about her husband's job. It's hardly surprising she was too stressed to notice the signs of pregnancy,' Ellis said.

'If I was in her situation,' Ruby said, 'I'd have to leave London and go back to Manchester. I couldn't leave my parents to struggle, and I wouldn't want to uproot them from everything that's familiar and make them move to London with me. I'm an only child, so there's nobody else to pick up the slack or share it with me.'

'If it happened to my parents, they'd be difficult about it,' Ellis said. 'I think they'd hide how much they were struggling and they'd stonewall the three of us if we asked any questions.' He sighed. 'I worry about them. So do my brothers. But we can't force them to be close to us or accept more help than they're prepared to take.'

'And I guess when you're working hundreds and hundreds of miles away, rushed off your feet and with a million different things to think about, it helps fill in the gaps so you don't have as much space to worry,' she said softly.

'You mean, I use my job to escape? There's a lot of truth in that,' he said ruefully. 'And I feel a bit ashamed of myself for that. I thought about that when Anita was telling us how her brother makes excuses not to visit. I guess I do, too.'

'Ellis, you're human,' she said, stroking his face. 'We all have our limitations. And you can't save everyone or fix things for everyone.'

'I know.' He kissed her lightly. 'Some things can't be fixed. And you have to put up with the fact that you're doing everything you can, even if it doesn't feel anywhere near enough.'

'I wish I had a magic wand,' she said.

'Me, too. But thank you for making me feel better about it.'

'I haven't done anything.'

'You have. I can talk to you and know you're not judging me. That makes a huge difference.'

'Oh, Ellis.' Her eyes sparkled with tears.

'Hey. Let's change the subject now and talk about something nice.'

'Brenda and Mike are coming up to London, next weekend.' Ruby paused. 'I think it's time to tell them about us.'

'With me by your side,' he said. 'I love Tom's parents. Even if you and I weren't together, I would've probably asked if I could drop in just to say hello to them.' He stroked her face. 'But now you and I are together, of course I want to be there and help you tell them.' He stole a kiss. 'And I'm also hoping that I can persuade you to stay here with me tonight.'

'I don't have anything with me.'

'I have a spare toothbrush, practically all the toiletries you'll need except face cream—and taking one night off isn't going to give you immediate wrinkles—and I can always put your clothes through the washing machine now so they'll be clean and dry in the morning. Your uniform's kept at work, you don't have a dog or cat to go back and feed, and I do a seriously mean scrambled egg on toast. Oh, and freshly squeezed orange juice—and I mean freshly squeezed by me, not poured from a bottle.'

She laughed. 'Very persuasive, Dr Webster. I have no arguments against any of that. I'd love to stay.'

'Good.' He kissed her again. Another step towards the relationship he thought they were both looking for. Another reason to stay in London. At the same time, though, it scared him. He knew Ruby so much better than he'd known Natalie. They were compatible in every way. And yet the doubts were still there. He'd failed at his last marriage—his last serious relationship. Would he fail at this one, too?

CHAPTER TWELVE

'I FEEL RIDICULOUSLY NERVOUS,' Ruby said on the Sunday morning.

'It'll be fine. Don't worry,' Ellis reassured her.

'I guess.' But she couldn't help feeling antsy. She wanted to be with Ellis—but she also didn't want to lose Brenda and Mike. Once they knew she was dating again, would they reject her?

The doorbell rang; Ruby opened the door and Brenda and Mike greeted her with a hug and flowers.

'Oh, Ellis, you're here too—how lovely to see you as well.' Brenda hugged him and Mike shook his hand warmly.

'Can I get you some coffee?' Ruby asked.

'That'd be wonderful,' Brenda said.

'I'll make the coffee,' Ellis offered.

'And I'll put these lovely flowers in water,' Ruby said with a smile.

'When are we going to tell them?' Ruby whispered in the kitchen.

'I vote for sooner rather than later,' Ellis whispered back.

'OK. I'll be brave,' she said.

Once they were all sitting down in the living room

with coffee and posh cookies that Ruby had bought from the deli round the corner, she said, 'There was something I wanted to talk to you about.'

'Of course, love,' Mike said.

Ruby took a deep breath. 'Please don't think I'll ever forget Tom or push him out of my life, but—'

'—you've met someone,' Brenda cut in gently.

Ruby stared at her, surprised. Was it that obvious? 'Um, yes,' she said awkwardly.

'Love, it's been more than a year since he died and you're still young. I'm quite sure Tom didn't want you to spend the rest of your life on your own, missing him,' Brenda said.

'So you don't mind if I see someone?' Ruby asked.

'As long as he treats you right,' Mike said. 'If he isn't good to you, then I'll have a problem with it.'

'That won't be a problem,' Ellis said. 'Remember, Tom asked me to take care of her.'

'Have you met Ruby's young man, then?' Brenda asked.

Ellis coughed. 'Let's just say you've known him for quite a few years, too.'

They both stared at him, and he saw the second that the penny dropped. The surprise in their faces was swiftly chased away by relief.

'But,' he said, 'we didn't want to go public until we knew you were OK with it.'

'We're OK with it,' Brenda said softly. 'More than OK.'

Mike smiled. 'I wish we'd brought champagne now.'

'Actually, I did, hoping that I wasn't tempting fate,' Ellis said. 'Though if you hadn't been OK with Ruby seeing me, then I would've suggested using it to toast our Tom. Shall I go and open it?'

'Absolutely yes,' Brenda said. 'And we wish you both every happiness, we really do.'

Later that evening, Ellis and Ruby lay together on her sofa.

'I'm so glad they were OK about us,' she said.

'Me, too. So are you ready to go public tomorrow?' he asked.

'I think so.' She looked awkward. 'I probably ought to confess that I told Tina, a while back.'

Her best friend. Would she approve? 'And was she OK about it?' Ellis asked, careful to keep his voice neutral.

'Actually, she brought up your itchy feet.' She sighed. 'And she told me not to fall for you too hard or too fast.'

'My feet aren't itchy,' Ellis said, 'but it looks as if I'm going to need to convince you of that—and a few other people, too.'

She stroked his face. 'It's not that I doubt you. But you're used to moving about all the time.'

'I've stayed in London for well over a year and a half now,' he pointed out.

'Don't you miss it, working abroad and seeing different places all the time?' she asked.

'Yes. But I'm pretty sure I'd miss you more,' he said softly.

The news gradually spread round the hospital. Ruby was surprised and pleased that everyone seemed to wish them both well, especially when they made it clear that the personal relationship would make absolutely no difference to their professional relationship.

The next morning, Ellis came over to the midwives' station to show Ruby a letter from Grace Edwards. 'You know you thought she might be a chimera? She had more DNA tests, and they showed that you were right. The court case has been settled now, and she says the relationship with her ex is starting to become more amicable for the child's sake.'

'That's good. I'm so glad it's working out better for her now.'

Ellis stole a kiss. 'Not just for her. Everything's working out. I never would've believed I could be so happy.'

'Me, too.' She kissed him back.

'Tsk, you two, you're supposed to set a good example to your juniors,' Coral, the trainee midwife, teased as she passed them.

Ellis just laughed. 'We are.'

Over the next few weeks, time seemed to go at the speed of light. Ellis and Ruby spent every possible minute together. But finally it was his last official day at the maternity unit. That evening, all the staff from the unit who weren't on duty went out for a pizza to say goodbye to him, and presented him with a special care package for his trip to Zimbabwe—including socks, chocolate and soap, which made him laugh—and a card signed by every single person on the team.

'We want you back, Ellis,' Theo said. 'No pressure, of course, but we want you back. And I'm expecting the answer to a certain question the second you get back on English soil.'

In other words, whether he'd accept the job offer. Ellis smiled. 'OK. Message received and understood.'

'And we want regular texts to know how you're getting on,' Iris, the senior midwife, chipped in.

'Actually, I'm not going to be able to be in touch with anyone while I'm away,' Ellis said. 'This clinic I'm going to in Zimbabwe is so remote that there isn't any Internet access, and there's no mobile phone coverage.'

Ruby swallowed hard. He'd already told her this, so she was prepared for it, but it was still hard to get her head round it.

'So I guess sending us the odd postcard won't be possible either?' She tried for levity.

'By the time I'd found someone to take a letter to the nearest big town with a mail system and buy a stamp for it—well, I'd probably be back here before the postcard reached you, even if I sent it on my first day.'

It finally hit home. No phone, no texts, no emails, and not even a letter. A whole month without contact. She trusted Ellis—she knew he wasn't the kind to cheat—but how did people cope with the loneliness of long-distance relationships like this, when they couldn't even contact each other for weeks at a time? Was this the way her future was going to be?

She changed the subject and teased Ellis along with the rest of the team, but when they went back to his flat afterwards he held her close.

'Rubes, I know it's going to be hard, not being able to talk to each other for a whole month,' he said. 'But if there's an emergency, you know you can call John at the medical aid charity and he'll get someone to radio a message through to me,' said. 'And, if you really want me to, I can pull out of the assignment.'

He'd really do that for her?

She could see the sincerity in his eyes. Yes, he'd give it up for her.

But she couldn't ask him to do that. Especially on the day before he was meant to be going. She shook her head. 'You promised you'd go. I'm not going to make you break a promise.' She just wished there could be another way.

Though the only other way she could think of was for her to go with him. Which would mean letting down everyone at the ward, and deserting her family, Brenda and Mike. She couldn't do that, either.

And giving Ellis an ultimatum wasn't fair; it would tear him apart. She knew he was a man of integrity. He was going back to do the job he loved—maybe for the last assignment. Or maybe not. For his sake she needed to be brave about this. To make him feel that it was okay for him to go—even though watching him leave would hurt like hell. 'Go get 'em, tiger.' She gave him a wobbly smile.

That night, they made love for what might be the last time, and the sweetness was almost unbearable. Ruby just hoped that Ellis wasn't aware of the tears trickling silently down her face as she lay awake in his arms afterwards, pretending to sleep.

The next day, Ruby went to see Ellis off at the airport.

She looked at the kitbag slung over his shoulder as they left his flat. 'I can't believe that's all the luggage you're taking with you for a whole month.'

'I learned to travel light.' He smiled at her. 'Ruby, I *am* coming back, you know.'

'I know.' His assignment was for a month. Of course

he was coming back. But would it be for good, or would it be to tell her that he'd rediscovered how much he loved his job and he needed to go back to it?

'Ruby, I lo—'

She pressed the tip of her finger against his mouth. She had a feeling she knew what he was going to say—and she didn't want to hear it. Not right at this moment. 'Wait until you're back,' she said softly. Until he'd been away from her and had had time to think about it. Until he really knew what he wanted to do—whether he needed to go back to working abroad, or whether he wanted to come back to London to stay. If he could still say it in a month's time, then she'd know that he really meant it.

They travelled to Heathrow on the train in silence, and had a last cup of coffee together while they waited for his flight to be called.

And then the flight to Harare was announced over the tannoy system.

'I guess this is me,' he said. He held her tightly. 'I'll see you in a month. And I'll be counting the days. I'll think of you every single day.'

'Me, too.' She wasn't going to cry. She wasn't going to let him go on that plane feeling guilty and miserable because of her. 'You go and you make that difference to the world. I'm proud of you.' And she was proud of him. Just… she didn't want him to go. 'I'll keep an eye on your flat for you and make sure you've got fresh bread and milk indoors when you get back.' She dragged in a breath. 'And I'll see you in a month's time.'

'I'll ring you as soon as I can switch my phone on and get a signal.' His grey eyes were tortured. 'Ruby. I wish I wasn't going.'

'If you don't go, you'll regret it for the rest of your life. So go. Do what you're brilliant at. Help set up that clinic and make life better for people.' *Go with her love,* though she wasn't going to say that and put pressure on him. 'Have a safe journey,' she said. Though she wouldn't even know if he did arrive safely. She could check the airport website to see if he'd landed; and then she'd just have to trust that everything went well after that. That any unrest in the country wouldn't affect the clinic. That he wouldn't catch some awful virus. *That he'd come back.*

A whole month without him.

And it stretched out as if there was never going to be an end.

'Ruby.' His voice sounded as clogged as her throat felt.

He kissed her hard. 'I'll be back soon,' he said.

'I know.' Even though she didn't know whether it would be just to say goodbye, or to tell her that he wanted to be with her.

She waited in the airport until his flight had taken off, even though she knew he wouldn't be able to make her out through the window. She just needed to be there until he'd finally gone.

And just why was the sun shining so brightly on the train home? Why wasn't it miserable and raining, the way it felt in her heart?

The following day, Ruby went to see one of their new mums, whose baby had been born at thirty-six weeks and now, at three days old, the baby had a distinct yellow tone to her eyes and skin. For a moment, Ruby wished Ellis was there, because he was so good at explaining things like this to new parents. Then she pulled herself together. Ellis wasn't there; this was her job, and she was just going to have to deal with it.

'Basically the baby has a bit too much bilirubin in her body—that's why her skin and her eyes have that yellow tinge,' she explained.

'What's bilirubin?' Mrs Patterson asked.

'It's a yellow substance the body makes when red blood cells—the ones that move oxygen round the body—break down. Usually the liver removes the bilirubin from the blood—actually, your liver did the job for her while she was still in the womb. Three out of five babies have a bit of jaundice—that's why we do that heel-prick test on the first day, to check her blood. She's quite jaundiced, and Coral tells me that you've had a bit of a problem feeding her.'

'So is it my fault?'

'Not at all,' Ruby reassured her. 'The jaundice explains why she's not feeding well.'

'So will she have to have medication to treat it?'

'Believe it or not, the treatment's a bit of sunshine—but at this time of year there isn't much sunshine around, so what we're going to do is fibre-optic phototherapy,' Ruby said. 'Which is a fancy way of saying we're going to lie her on a blanket which shines a special light onto her back. Her skin will absorb the light and it makes oxygen bind to the bilirubin, helping it dissolve so her liver can break it down.'

Mrs Patterson looked surprised. 'That's all? You just lay her on a special blanket?'

'And we keep checking the levels of bilirubin in her blood until they start dropping. It does mean she's going to lose a bit more water from her body than usual, so we might have to give her some fluid in a drip to keep her hydrated—but basically that's it, and you can be with her the whole time. You can still feed her as normal and change her nappies,' Ruby explained. 'She'll be much better in a day or two.'

'And then she's going to be all right?'

'She's going to be just fine,' Ruby confirmed.

It was true for the baby; and if she kept telling herself often enough that everything was going to be fine, then it would be true for her and Ellis, too.

Ellis was really glad that the pace in Zimbabwe turned out to be punishing. Being so busy that he didn't have time to think about how much he missed Ruby was a blessing—as was being so tired that he fell asleep almost as soon as his head touched the pillow at night. And although he was friendly with the other medics on the team, he didn't socialise as much as he would have done in the old days. Instead, he spent every evening writing to Ruby, in a notebook he'd bought especially for the purpose. He wouldn't be able to send her a postcard or a letter every day, but he would at least be able to give her the book when he returned. So she'd know that he'd meant what he'd said—that he'd thought about her every single day when he was away.

On his last day, he had a radio call from John, the assignment handler at the medical aid charity. 'Ellis, I know it's a lot to ask, but could you stay a bit longer? A couple of weeks?'

Two years ago, he would've said yes without even having to think about it. Extending an assignment was something he'd done quite a few times.

Now, it was different. He'd spent a whole month

missing Ruby and it was like a physical ache. He loved what he did, but the job wasn't enough for him any more. Not without Ruby.

Because he loved her.

Bone-deep *loved* her.

And he needed to be back with her.

'I'm sorry,' Ellis said. 'But no. Don't get me wrong—I love this job, but I've met someone. In London. And now I need to go home. For good.' He was shocked to feel the lump in his throat: London *was* home. Because Ruby was there.

As long as she hadn't changed her mind about them while he'd been away.

'Fair enough,' John said. 'It sounds as if we've been lucky to have you back for the last month.'

'I promised I'd do this assignment,' Ellis said, 'and I wouldn't break my promise.' Even though he'd been tempted to. He'd done the right thing.

'We'll miss you,' John said. 'And if you ever change your mind—even if it's just for a few days—we'd have you back any time.'

'You'll be the first to know,' Ellis said.

CHAPTER THIRTEEN

ELLIS HAD DELIBERATELY given Ruby the wrong date for his return; he'd told her that he'd be back the day after his real return date, knowing from experience how likely it was that his journey home would be disrupted. In the past he'd worried his brothers by turning up later than they expected, and he didn't want Ruby to be anxious about whether something had happened to him when he wasn't in a position to get in touch with her.

The journey home seemed to take for ever—from the journey by jeep from the camp through to the airport in Harare, and then the flight itself. With two layovers, it took the best part of a whole day to fly back to England. And every minute felt like a lifetime.

As soon as Ellis was through passport control at Heathrow, he got his phone out of his pocket. But somehow he managed to fumble it, and it dropped to the floor. When he picked it up, he groaned. 'You've got to be *kidding* me! How am I going to ring Ruby now?'

'Got a problem, mate?' a voice said beside him.

Ellis turned to face his fellow passenger and ruefully showed him the cracked screen. 'I've managed to baby this thing for a whole month while I've been setting up a clinic in an incredibly remote area, but as soon as I'm back here I drop it just once and…' He shook his head. 'What an idiot.'

'Here, use mine.' The man handed Ellis his phone.

'Are you sure?' At the other man's nod, Ellis smiled. 'Thank you very much. I'll keep it quick and I'll pay you for the call.'

'It's fine, mate. I know how I'd feel if I'd been away and couldn't ring my missus to tell her I'd landed safely.'

'Yeah. I told her I'd be back tomorrow because I didn't want her worrying if I was held up. And I just can't wait any longer to talk to her.' He opened the screen to dial Ruby's number, and stopped. 'Oh, no. I don't believe this. I can't actually remember her mobile number. How stupid am I?'

The other man gave him a rueful smile. 'That's where these things fall down, isn't it? We rely on them to remember everything for us, and when they don't work we're stuck.'

'Very true,' Ellis said, equally ruefully. Plus, after more than twenty-four hours spent travelling, he could barely think straight. All he wanted was to go home and see Ruby.

He handed the phone back to the other man. 'Thank you anyway. I appreciate the offer.'

'I hope you manage to get hold of her.'

'I'll find a way,' Ellis said.

Once he'd walked through customs to the airport shopping complex, he found the nearest shop that sold mobile phones. 'How long does it take to fix one of these?' he asked, showing the assistant his cracked screen.

'At least until tomorrow, I'm afraid,' the assistant told him.

Not what he needed to hear. Time for Plan B. 'Okay, how long would it take to migrate all my data across to a new phone?'

'The guy who does that sort of thing won't be in for another couple of hours, and he might already have stuff to do, so I can't say.'

A couple of hours and then unlimited waiting? No chance. Ellis knew he could be back in the centre of London, actually *with* Ruby, in the time it'd take to sort out his phone so he could call her. 'Thanks, but I'll manage. Can I just buy a cheap pay-as-you-go phone to tide me over until I can get this one fixed?'

'Sure.'

Armed with a working phone, Ellis managed to get the hospital switchboard number from the Internet, and two seconds later he was patched through to the maternity ward.

'Hey, Iris. Don't say a word—it's Ellis. Is Ruby there?'

'Yes, she is. I thought you weren't due back until tomorrow?'

'My journey home was a bit smoother than I expected,' Ellis explained. 'What shift is she on?'

'Early.'

'Excellent. Can you keep her there, please? And don't tell her that you've spoken to me. I want to surprise her.'

He knew he was taking a risk. He'd missed Ruby like hell. Hopefully she'd missed him just as much—but on the other hand she might have had time to think about the situation and decided that she couldn't cope with his lifestyle. He knew she didn't want to join him in working abroad; and he knew she was scared that he'd feel trapped if she asked him to stay in London. But, while he'd been away, he'd come to his own decision. One that he hoped would work for her, too.

'I'll do my best,' Iris said.

'Thank you. I'll be there as soon as I can.'

The good thing about travelling light meant that it wasn't too much of a drag to carry his kitbag around. He caught the fast train back to central London, and then the tube across the city to the London Victoria. He paused only to buy the biggest bunch of flowers that the hospital shop could offer, then headed up to the maternity ward.

Iris was at the reception desk. 'Welcome home. Perfect timing—she's in the staff kitchen, and I'm pretty sure she's on her own,' she whispered with a wink.

'Thanks.' Ellis blew her a kiss and went straight to the staff kitchen.

Ruby was leaning against the counter, sipping a mug of coffee; she almost dropped it when she saw him. 'Ellis! I thought you weren't back until tomorrow!'

'Sometimes the flights get delayed—and I didn't want you having to hang around the airport for hours waiting for me, worrying that something terrible had happened. That's why I told you I'd be back tomorrow instead of today.' He placed the flowers on the counter, dropped his kitbag, swept her into his arms and swung her around. 'I've missed you so, so much,' he whispered and kissed her hard.

She matched him kiss for kiss, and her arms were wrapped as tightly round him as his were round her.

When he finally managed to break the kiss, he noticed that her skin was reddened. 'Oh God, I'm so sorry. The beard. I should have shaved first—and had a shower.' He grimaced. 'Sorry. I'm not exactly fragrant.'

She laughed. 'Don't worry. The main thing is that you're here. How long did it take you to get here?'

'Six hours in the jeep from the clinic to Harare, a bit of a wait there, nearly twenty hours from there to Heathrow in between layovers, and then way too long to get back to the middle of London.' He dragged in a breath. 'I was going to call you from Heathrow, but I dropped my phone. Would you believe, it was fine all through Zimbabwe, yet I managed to break it practically the second I was back in England?' He rolled his eyes. 'The guy next to me was really kind and lent me his phone—and then I couldn't remember your number. How stupid is that?'

She stroked his face. 'If it makes you feel any better, I don't think I can remember your mobile phone number, either—I rely on my phone to remember it for me.'

He moved his head so he could drop a kiss in her palm. 'I missed you so much. I know you stopped me saying it at the airport when you waved me off, and I know why, but I need to say it now. I love you, Ruby. I love you so much. And I want to stay here in London with you.'

'Ellis, you've been away for a month. You've been travelling for what, a day and a half, you probably haven't had much sleep, and this is a conversation I think we need to have when you're properly awake.'

Her voice was gentle, but fear trickled through him. Had he totally misread the situation? Had she changed her mind about their relationship while he'd been away?

She fished in the pockets of her trousers and brought out her door keys. 'Your flat is probably freezing cold, and you won't have any food in the fridge—I was going to sort all that out this evening, because I was expecting you back tomorrow and I thought I'd have time to do it tonight. I'll get my spare key from Tina. So why don't you just go back to my place, have a shower and get some sleep, and I'll see you when I get back after my shift? Help yourself to whatever you want from the fridge.'

'Thank you.' He put her keys carefully into his pocket. 'I wrote to you every day while I was away.' He opened his kitbag and took out the small notebook he'd carried everywhere with him. 'I thought it would be easier to write everything in here than carry around loads of bits of paper that I'd probably end up losing.' He handed her the notebook. 'It could be a bit of lunchtime reading for you.'

She went pink. 'You wrote to me every day?'

'Every single day,' he confirmed. 'It was the only way I had to be close to you when I was thousands of miles away.'

'I missed you so much.' Her voice sounded rusty. 'Ellis, I love you too.'

Everything in his world settled and felt right again. They felt the same way about each other—so somehow they would be able to work things out.

He wrapped his arms around her again and held her close. 'You're right, I need some sleep,' he said softly. 'But when I wake up, you'll be home with me. And then we can talk.' He kissed her lightly, then took the notebook back from her, went to the last page he'd written and carefully removed it.

'What are you doing?' she asked.

'When you read this particular page, I want to be with you,' he said. Then he remembered the flowers. He scooped them up from the counter and handed them to her. 'For you. I know they're not the best, but I just wanted to...' Right now, he was too tired to string words together.

'They're lovely, Ellis. You've been travelling for hours and hours and hours, and yet you still made the time to bring me flowers.' She kissed him again. 'Go home. Sleep. I'll see you soon.' She hugged him one last time. 'Welcome back. And I'm so, so pleased to see you.'

Her smile warmed him all the way back to her flat.

Ellis just about managed to shower and shave, though he couldn't quite face making himself anything to eat. He cleaned his teeth, then dragged himself into the spare bedroom—where he'd slept so many times before during Tom's final illness—and fell into oblivion almost the second that his head hit the pillow.

Ruby was glad that she hadn't arranged to have lunch with anyone. Right at that moment, she wanted to be on her own to read Ellis's letters to her. With the notebook stowed safely in her handbag, she went to the hospital canteen to buy a sandwich and some coffee, then found a table in a quiet corner and settled down to read.

The letters read almost like a diary. Ellis told her all about setting up the clinic, what the rest of the team was like, and told her about some of the patients he'd treated. Yet it wasn't just a practical day by day account of his life out there—he also wrote down his feelings. How much he missed her while he was away, how he'd always loved being able to make a difference to the world through his work and yet it just didn't feel right any more being away from London. How he'd looked up at the stars at night and thought of her, then realised they weren't even going to see the same stars because they weren't in the same hemisphere, and it made him feel lonely.

There was a huge lump in her throat. So his feelings for her hadn't changed. He really had missed her while he'd been away—and it looked as if there was a real chance that they had a future together.

Right at that moment, Ruby just wanted to be home with Ellis. Though she still had a whole afternoon until her shift was over. She was kept busy with clinics, but even so the time seemed to drag.

And then finally she was able to go off duty and go home. When she let herself into the flat, everything was silent. She walked quietly through to her bedroom, but Ellis wasn't sleeping in her bed. Clearly he was still being sensitive to her feelings and not sleeping where his best friend had once lain.

Even more quietly, Ruby opened the door to the spare room. Ellis was fast asleep, and she could see the tiredness and strain still etched on his face. Although part of her wanted to wake him up, she knew that it wouldn't be fair; he needed some rest to recover from all that travelling. She could see his kitbag on the floor, so there was at least one thing she could do for him; without waking him, she picked it up and quietly closed the door behind her.

The next thing Ellis knew, there were faint sounds coming from the flat. Clearly Ruby was at home, bustling about and yet trying her hardest not to wake him. Wishing he'd thought to call back at his flat first to get some clean clothes, he climbed out of bed, wearing only his boxer shorts, and bent down to where he'd left his kitbag.

Except there was an empty space where he was expecting to see it.

Had he left it in the bathroom, too tired to carry it in here? But it wasn't there, either.

Ruby must have heard him walking about because she called, 'Hey, Ellis?'

'Hey, yourself,' he said, following the sound of her voice and finding her in the kitchen. 'Sorry, I can't quite remember where I left my clothes.'

She smiled. 'In your kitbag, and at the moment they're most of the way through the washing cycle.'

'So basically I'm wearing the only clothes I have that are dry?' he asked.

'I thought you'd sleep a bit longer and they'd be ready by the time you woke up.' She looked guilty. 'Obviously I've been really noisy. Sorry I didn't mean to wake you.'

'You didn't wake me.' He wrapped her in his arms. 'Ruby, I'm so glad to be home.'

As the words left his mouth, he realised how much he meant it. London *was* home. He hadn't felt like that about a place for a very long time—since before Sally died, really—and it felt strange. Strange, but good.

'I'm glad to have you home,' she said. 'You must be starving.'

'I think I'm still too tired to be hungry,' he admitted. 'Right now, I just want to be with you. Though I could do with a cup of tea.' He glanced down at himself. 'And I'm really not respectable enough to be standing in your kitchen.'

'I gave all Tom's clothes to the charity shop,' she said, 'so I can't offer you anything of his to wear, and I don't think my dressing gown would fit you.'

He laughed. 'And I'm not sure pink's my colour anyway.'

'The best I can do is a towel, if you're cold.'

'I'm not cold. Just…' He paused. 'Maybe a little un-derdressed.'

'The view's quite nice from where I'm standing.' she said, and he loved the way colour stole into her face.

'The view's very nice from where I'm standing, too,' he said, and kissed her lingeringly.

Between them, they managed to make two mugs of tea, then sat down at her kitchen table.

'Did you read the notebook?' he asked.

She nodded. 'Every single page—except the one you took out.'

'Which I put in my…' A nasty thought hit him. 'Rubes, did you empty my pockets before you put my jeans in the washing machine?'

She went white. 'No.'

'Ah.'

'Are you saying I put your last letter to me through the wash?' She clapped a hand to her mouth. 'Oh, no. I can't have done.' Tears glistened in her eyes. 'Now I'll never know what you said.'

'I remember every word I wrote,' he said softly. 'I wanted to be there when you read them, but maybe it's better this way—with me telling you. I missed you out in Zimbabwe, Ruby. There was this big hole in my life, and my job just wasn't enough any more. On my very last day, John put a radio call through to the clinic, and he asked me if I'd stay on for a couple more weeks. Two years ago, I would've said yes without even hesitat-ing. But this time I said no. Because I wanted to come home, Ruby. I wanted to come home to you. I wanted to be with you.'

He slid out of his chair and on to one knee in front of her. 'This isn't where I planned to do this. I was planning to find somewhere romantic—maybe somewhere by the sea, or maybe in one of the glasshouses at Kew with some exotic flowers in the background.' He gave her a wry smile. 'And I was going to be properly dressed. But as I was sitting on the plane, I knew exactly what I was going to say to you, and now I realise that it doesn't matter where I say it or what I'm wearing—and I don't want to wait any more. I love you, Ruby. I want to be with you. I don't want to go back to my old life, working abroad, because it just isn't enough for me any more. I've found the one person who makes me want to settle down—you. And I want to make a family with you, here in London. You're the love of my life. Will you marry me?'

She paused for so long that he thought she was going to say no.

And then, very shakily, she said, 'Yes.'

That was when Ellis realised that he'd actually been holding his breath.

He dragged in a lungful of air, then got to his feet, pulled her out of her chair and wrapped his arms round her. 'Thank God. I thought you were going to say no. I was so scared you might have changed your mind about us while I was away.'

A tear trickled down her cheek. 'Ellis, I missed you so much. And I was so scared that you wouldn't want to come back.'

'No. I missed you more with every passing day. And it's never been like that for me before. I couldn't wait to come home.' He stroked her face. 'And now I'm home for good.'

'Ellis, you don't have to give up your old life completely,' she said. 'I don't want you to have any regrets in the future. Maybe if you went out for, I don't know, a couple of weeks every six months, then you could still do the stuff you love and feel that you're making a difference to the world.'

'Though you've taught me that I can make a difference right here—like I did with Helen Perkins and the intra-uterine transfusion,' he said. He paused. 'You're right, I will miss it sometimes—I've spent most of my career working abroad. But what you've suggested could work.'

'But?' She spoke the word that was echoing through his head.

'I'd still hate leaving you behind. I know I asked you before and you said no, but if I was only going out for a really short assignment once in a while, would you consider going with me?'

'If it's only for a really short assignment, then yes, I could cope with that,' she said.

'Good. I love you.' He kissed her. 'And once my clothes are dry, we'll go and tell the world our news.'

She kissed him back. 'That'll be a while yet. So I think maybe we have time to go and have a private celebration, first.'

'That's one of the things I love about you,' he said with a grin. 'You're full of great ideas...'

EPILOGUE

Two years later

ELLIS SAT ON the edge of the bed in the maternity department of the London Victoria, with his arm round Ruby and his finger being clutched very hard by their tiny, red-faced son.

'Life doesn't get any better than this, Mrs Webster,' he said softly. 'And I love you both very, very much.'

'We love you, too,' Ruby said. 'Don't we, Tom?'

In answer, the baby simply yawned, and they both laughed.

'I'm glad you got back in time for his birth,' she said.

'I nearly didn't. First babies are meant to be late, not two weeks early. Especially when their father is working in the middle of nowhere, several hundred miles away, for just one short week, thinking that he probably had a month until the baby arrived.' He rolled his eyes. 'Talk about timing. I think this one's going to be stubborn as anything.'

'Just like his dad,' she teased.

'Getting to the airport, opening my phone and seeing the text from you that you'd gone into labour…I nearly passed out,' he said.

She grinned. 'Tsk. And all the babies you've delivered, Dr Webster.'

'It's very different when it's *your* wife and *your* baby,' he said, and bent to drop a kiss on the baby's forehead. 'Luckily the woman in front of me in the queue for passport control asked me if I was all right— and when I told her my news, she told me to go in front of her. And so did everyone else in the queue, passing it forward. They all made way for me so I didn't have to wait so long to get to you. The kindness of strangers is truly amazing.'

'It certainly is,' she agreed. 'Though you've done your share of giving and kindness, too. Think of it as what goes around, comes around.'

'I guess.' He smiled. 'I love you, Rubes. And our baby. I can hardly believe we made someone so beautiful and so perfect.' He met her gaze. 'How many times have we heard new parents say that and smiled? But it's true. And I can't wait to take you both home.' Home, to the terraced house with a garden they'd bought together just after they'd got married. 'And for all the grandparents to come and see him—because this baby's going to have three sets. Your parents, my parents, and Tom's— because they're practically my parents too and there's no way I'll let them feel left out.'

Ruby smiled at him. 'That's another thing I love about you. You've turned into a real family man.'

'With a little help from you. You've done a lot to thaw my parents out.' He smiled back at her. 'You've changed my life, Ruby. I never thought I could ever be this happy and settled.'

'And I never thought I'd find this kind of happiness

a second time,' she said softly. 'It felt greedy, expecting too much.'

'No—as you said, what goes around, comes around,
and you're one of life's givers. If I make you and baby
Tom as happy as you both make me—well, that's all
I want.' He kissed her. 'I think everyone on the ward
is dying to visit you, so I'm going to let them all come
and make a fuss of you while I have a shower and get
rid of all the travel dust.'

'And the stubble. Looks sexy, but...' She pulled a
face. 'Ouch.'

He laughed. 'Yeah. You say that every time. I love
you. And Tom. And I'm so proud of you both.'

She laughed back. 'We're proud of you, too. Go and
get rid of the travel stuff. And then you can take us
home.'

He smiled. 'Your wish, my love, is my command.'
Home.

And he really was home. For good.

* * * * *